P9-AON-680

.All You Have to Do Is Call

TITLES BY KERRI MAHER

The Kennedy Debutante
The Girl in White Gloves
The Paris Bookseller
All You Have to Do Is Call

All You Have to Do Is Call

KERRI MAHER

Berkley
New York

BERKLEY
An imprint of Penguin Random House LLC
penguinrandomhouse.com

Copyright © 2023 by Kerri Maher

BERKLEY and the BERKLEY & B colophon are registered trademarks of
Penguin Random House LLC.

Library of Congress Cataloging-in-Publication Data

Names: Maher, Kerri, author.
Title: All you have to do is call / Kerri Maher.
Description: New York : Berkley, [2023]
Identifiers: LCCN 2023010244 (print) | LCCN 2023010245 (ebook) |
ISBN 9780593102213 (hardcover) | ISBN 9780593102237 (ebook)
Subjects: LCSH: Abortion Counseling Service—Fiction. |
Abortion services—Illinois—Chicago—Fiction. |
Abortion—Illinois—Chicago—Fiction. | Women—Social
networks—Illinois—Chicago—Fiction. | Women—Social
conditions—Illinois—Chicago—Fiction. | Nineteen seventies—Fiction. |
Chicago (Ill.)—Fiction.
Classification: LCC PS3613.A349295 A79 2023 (print) |
LCC PS3613.A349295 (ebook) |
DDC 813/.6—dc23/eng/20230531
LC record available at https://lccn.loc.gov/2023010244
LC ebook record available at https://lccn.loc.gov/2023010245

Printed in the United States of America
1st Printing

For Kevan and Kate, dynamic agent-and-editor duo, who did everything they could to make sure this story became a book. You have both taught me so much about women supporting women, and I feel immeasurably lucky to have you in my corner.

The best protection any woman can have . . . is courage.

—Elizabeth Cady Stanton

All You Have to Do Is Call

Spring 1969

VERONICA

The last thing Veronica saw before the blindfold went on was how blue Siobhan's eyes were. Blue and translucent, like the water she'd swum in with Doug on their honeymoon. Incredibly, they also gleamed. *Thank you for being here with me,* her friend's eyes said.

The volume on her surroundings—twittering birds, passing cars, a distant siren through the cracked windows of the Oldsmobile—turned up to an almost deafening blast as the efficient woman with the Italian accent who wore a brown wool skirt tied one bandana, then another, over Veronica's eyes, tugging the material down so that it almost occluded her nostrils, obliterating any possibility of pin-the-tail-on-the-donkey cheating in that sliver of light and sight on either side of the ridge of her nose.

Then she heard the brisk knotting of fabric as Siobhan was blindfolded; her friend's hand tightened around hers, and she felt a sudden dampness in their mingled palms and fingers. Veronica pulsed Siobhan's hand. *I'm here.*

"*Va bene,*" the Italian woman said, sliding herself out of the back of the sedan, the wool of her skirt producing an obscene noise against the leather of the seat. Then, after a series of thuds and creaks and

3

clicks, Veronica felt the engine of the car rumble and vibrate beneath her, and Siobhan's hand became a fist inside hers.

"*Siamo pronte*," said the woman as the car began to move, pinning Veronica's body to the back of the seat.

She wondered how Siobhan was feeling and if she was thinking about shouting, *Stop the car!* and changing her mind. The abortion itself was enough to be scared of, enough to make anyone get cold feet. But add to that the illegality and the unknowns—will the doctor be as gentle and thorough as their friend had promised, nothing like the equally thorough but thoroughly shitty doc their other friend had gone to who'd told her to keep her legs crossed next time; how much bleeding; how much pain; how much how much how much—and Veronica could completely understand why a woman, even one who'd already walked through as much fire as Siobhan, would stop the car.

But Siobhan said nothing.

She'd been single-minded and determined for two weeks, ever since she had secured this appointment, but feelings could change, especially in a situation like this, now that it had ceased to be a concept and was really and truly happening. Even Veronica had begun to feel nauseous, and she wondered if she was somehow taking on some of Siobhan's overflow. She hoped so. If she could siphon off all Siobhan's fear, she would; she'd carry it for her so that her friend could just be a shell for the next few hours. At least she was allowed to go with Siobhan; this doctor was the only one of the three choices who allowed someone to accompany the woman to the appointment.

For crying out loud, doing this alone is unthinkable.

The ride was shockingly short. They couldn't have gotten much farther than the northern edge of Hyde Park, or the other side of the University of Chicago campus, or maybe the end of the Midway Plaisance, where seventy-six years ago women in corsets and bustles had strolled through the White City, ridden the very first Ferris wheel, and watched a belly dancer called Little Egypt gyrate in a mortifyingly named routine called the hootchy-kootchy.

Veronica felt the car loop into a parking place, and when their chauffeur opened the door, she scooted off the smooth leather seat, feeling Siobhan follow her out the same door. She emerged into air that felt shady, cool, and damp. It smelled damp, too, like a basement, tinged faintly with rotting banana. A covered parking lot? She couldn't hear any other cars; all traffic and street noise was far in the distance.

The Italian woman took Veronica's hand in her dry, efficient one, and tugged her away from the car. Veronica pulled Siobhan along with her, their shared nausea ramping up with each unsure step in the dark.

Soon they were in an elevator, the doors closing on them. Veronica's ears popped with the change in pressure. She tried to swallow, but her throat was so dry, the trickle of saliva burned.

Up, up, up they went, driving Veronica's feet, legs, stomach, into the floor. Veronica held tight to Siobhan's hand and pulsed a few times. Siobhan pulsed back.

Ding!

Her feet hit carpet the moment they stepped out of the elevator. She felt it squish under her huaraches, heard it let out a nearly inaudible *sht* with each step. Soon the Italian woman stopped, dropped Veronica's hand, gripped her at her waist, then turned her slightly but roughly; she did the same to Siobhan, or so Veronica assumed because she felt her friend twist, though she didn't loosen her hold on her hand.

"Sit," the woman commanded, though it sounded almost musical in her Italian accent.

Veronica pulsed Siobhan's hand, then gently let go in order to squat and feel behind her. Lo and behold, there was a smooth wooden chair. She eased herself down, then felt to the side of her, and there was Siobhan's leg. Their hands found each other again, and this time, Siobhan took Veronica's one in her two.

"Are you okay?" Veronica whispered.

"No. But I will be." Siobhan's voice was clear and steady. Amazing.

"I'll be here. I'm so proud of you."

They sat in silence for a few minutes, and Veronica thought she heard some sort of quiet motor and a faint bubbling noise. A fish tank? She tried to picture exotic blue and orange fish swimming lazily through seaweed and water, hiding in some coral.

Then there was the unmistakable flush of a toilet, and some running water. *One, two, three, four, five, six, seven, eight, nine . . .* At least whoever it was had washed their hands. A door opened and closed. More soft footsteps.

"The doctor is ready," said the Italian woman.

Veronica's hand was suddenly free, suddenly cool, unbinding itself from her friend's clasp.

"I'll be right here," Veronica said, and Siobhan did not respond.

As soon as a door closed, separating her from her friend, there were a few minutes of muffled noises, indistinct words and creaks and shuffles, and then there was only the fish tank.

Veronica waited.

She tried leaning her head back to see if there was a wall to rest it on, but no. Her head felt suddenly like an anvil on her neck. She supposed she could move her blindfold a smidge and look around, but she didn't dare, as if to do so would jinx the whole thing. Much to her own disappointment, her default gear had always been rule following. Growing up, her best friend, Patty, had been the one to suggest taking the L into Chicago instead of seeing a movie, or filling flasks with her father's whiskey to take to football games. How ironic, considering what a square life Patty had settled into with Matt and their three kids, while Veronica had flitted from protest to protest, all of which had put her in a position to secure this very illegal abortion for Siobhan, whom she'd known for just a few years.

Veronica traced her decision to start breaking rules back to the day she heard Dr. Martin Luther King Jr. speak on the radio about the complacency of good people. But there had been no cause to embrace in the tidy suburb of Park Forest where she'd grown up, with those regular rows of grass and garages. She chafed at their sameness and longed for the color and irregularity of her aunt Martha's life in Hyde Park. Aunt Martha, her mother's spinster sister, had taught high school chemistry for two decades before getting promoted to an administrative position, and took her only niece to museums and outdoor jazz concerts and every restaurant with foreign food in the city. Veronica especially loved going to the Ethiopian restaurant where they tore off pieces of a deliciously soft, sour bread and used it to scoop up bites of spicy foods that exploded in her mouth like delicious bombs, detonating a latent curiosity inside her.

What was she doing, though, thinking about *food* at a time like this? When Siobhan was, presumably, lying on her back and trying not to cry or scream or vomit, while . . . she didn't even know what. How was an abortion performed, anyway? She had a very rudimentary knowledge of a dilation and curettage, based on the descriptions given by women in her consciousness-raising groups: there was a speculum, of course, and a chemical loosening of the cervix, then scraping and cramping. Very often there was too much poking and prodding, and always there was the sense of being horribly, emphatically alone. Occasionally there was a request for extra payment. A tip. Because being "that kind of girl" meant you knew how to please a man.

Veronica had heard that this doctor, the one helping her friend right now, wasn't like that. But one could never be too sure with a "back-alley abortion," even if in point of fact she was sitting in a building with an elevator, in a room with a fish tank.

Blindfolded, so that she could never find these people or this place again.

I swear to God, if I hear Siobhan cry or yell, I'll take this damn thing off and kick my way through the door.

Veronica felt her heart speed up with the possibility of it. Her breath shortened.

Before her thoughts had a chance to spin more out of control, she heard a door open, and in seconds, the Italian woman was sitting Siobhan next to Veronica again.

"Are you okay?" *Jesus, is that the best I can do?*

"I'm okay." There was that clarity in her friend's voice again.

"Sit here a little while, so we can monitor the bleeding," said the woman.

"Thank you," said Siobhan, sounding genuinely grateful.

An antsy minute passed, then Siobhan asked, "Remind me when you and Doug and Kate head to the lake?"

Summer. Surreally, she and Siobhan spent the time talking about their summer plans. Well, Veronica's summer plans. Siobhan's plan was to teach as much summer school as she could to help pay for her divorce from Gabe, whom she'd left ten days before, three days after securing this appointment. "My brother and parents are helping me," she'd told Veronica, "which I hate because I need to be done with depending on other people. That was what got me into this mess in the first place. I thought Gabe was going to take care of me. But his kind of care isn't worth it."

Siobhan was the opposite of a woman who knew how to please a man, and Veronica felt proud to call her a friend.

"Time to check your pad," the Italian woman said, then pulled Siobhan away again.

Veronica heard more doors and water and flushing, then the woman was tugging her out of the chair, saying, "She's fine. Time to go. Make sure she takes the antibiotics."

They let themselves be led out the way they'd come in: elevator, parking lot, car, ride. When the woman stopped the car and said, "You can take off the scarves," and they did, Veronica was momentarily blinded by the searing midday light. It hurt, and she shut her eyes tightly, then fluttered them open with her hand in front of her face to lessen the intensity.

Later that afternoon, while her daughter, Kate, played with Siobhan's daughter, Charlie, in the weedy little garden off the back of the dilapidated greystone house that was in need of repairs she and Doug had promised to do "someday, when we have enough money," Veronica brought Siobhan a tall glass of iced tea and a slice of yogurt cake. They sat together on folding beach chairs, watching the girls make mud pies, getting gloriously filthy in their T-shirts and shorts, arms and legs sprouting out of their clothes in limbs that were longer and leaner than Veronica had expected this spring, all that delicious toddler chub gone.

"How are you feeling?"

"Pretty good."

"You want to stay here tonight, in case you feel bad later?"

"Maybe. Let's see how I feel in a few hours."

Seconds of silence ticked by, then Siobhan said, "I am so relieved."

Veronica wanted to say, *Let's not count our chickens until you're a week out and we're sure there's no infection,* since she'd heard that could happen—*did* happen, way too often, though the plastic baggie of pills they'd been given was reassuring. Instead, she said, "I'm so glad."

"In fact, I feel like I can do anything. Like Gabe doesn't scare me anymore."

"That must feel amazing."

What would it feel like to have the greatest weight on your heart lifted? Hers wasn't Doug, not like Siobhan's was Gabe. She wasn't sure what hers was, not really, but she'd been lugging it around for years.

She'd be twenty-nine in a few months. Maybe it was time she figured it out.

A week went by, and Siobhan got stronger. She told the women in their consciousness-raising group about her experience, and everyone marveled, congratulated, clapped, and nodded.

Then, ten days later, Veronica's phone rang. Jenny from the group needed the phone number for the doctor Siobhan had gone to.

A few days after that, a stranger named Blaire called Siobhan.

With increasing frequency, Veronica and Siobhan found themselves accompanying women, or sending them, to the Italian woman and her unseen doctor. Once, that doctor hadn't been available and so Veronica had given out the name of another doctor, and he turned out to be one of the bad ones, who'd lectured the woman about God and sin and hell, and told her she didn't need tetracycline, which only landed her in the ER with a fever three days later, where the nurses hooked her up to an IV full of antibiotics and told her not to be so careless next time. And even though most of them were what could only be called "good abortions," every time the blindfold went on and a woman was rendered powerless, Veronica found herself thinking, *There has to be a better way.*

Fall 1971

1

PATTY

"This looks delicious!" Patty exclaimed as she took the fragrant Bundt cake from Veronica, who was wearing one of her hippie skirts, which swayed in time with her cascade of honey-hued hair and the musical stack of bangles on her arm. For years, her dearest, oldest friend had smelled like lavender and sounded like a wind chime, while Patty herself favored tailored yet flippy and flirty skirts and dresses, outfits she admired from the windows of Marshall Field's or the pages of *Cosmopolitan*, a magazine she tried to hide from her nine-going-on-thirteen-year-old daughter, Karen.

"It felt like a gingerbread kind of day," said Veronica, and her friend's familiar smile was such a relief after the day she'd had.

It had started well enough. The morning had been cold and blue-sky crisp, and she and the kids had sung along to "I'll Be There" when it played on the radio as they drove to St. Thomas the Apostle. Then the four of them—Patty, Karen, Junie, and Tad—had crunched over the last of the fallen leaves from the car into the cathedral for Sunday mass. Matt had skipped today. He was doing that more and more recently, always using work as an excuse not to go to church, or the PTA cocktail party, or Karen's ballet mini-recitals. Patty was getting worried; he'd never checked out like this before, and she was constantly stopping herself from wondering, as she had during mass, what might be keeping him.

Once church was over, the many hours of the day had been a forced march of chores. It was impossible to overstate the relief Patty felt on welcoming Vee and Doug and Kate into her home; tears of relief needled her eyes. It had been *so long* since she'd seen Vee. Too long. More than a month, which was unusual for them.

Thankfully, Matt was also happy to see them, and the kids were always glad to add Kate to the mix. As the little ones ran off, Matt said to Doug, "Beer?"

"I need one after that game this afternoon," said Doug.

The Bears to the rescue. Patty was glad Matt could relax into some guy time, but . . . she missed him. There were no two ways about it.

Alone in the kitchen, Veronica said to Patty, "Are you okay?"

"Is it that obvious?" *Only to such an old friend, I hope.*

Patty didn't think they'd be friends now if she and Vee hadn't forged such a strong bond in that anemic seventh grade production of *Macbeth*, where the two of them had stolen the show from Rachel Livingston and Ben Milliken, cackling over their lobster pot of dry ice and scaring the bejeezus out of everybody when they chanted "Double, double, toil and trouble / fire burn and caldron bubble." Eighteen years later, Veronica and Doug lived in the rapidly changing neighborhood of Hyde Park, and Patty and Matt in the more traditional enclave of Kenwood—geographic choices that said nearly everything about them. If she and Vee had simply met at a mixer for Lab School parents, where Kate and Junie had been nursery school classmates, they would have eyed each other with suspicion. *Too patchouli,* Patty would have thought. *Too uptight,* Veronica no doubt would have thought. But there was something fierce in the friendship they had grown as young women dabbling in the small freedoms and transgressions to be shared at soda fountains and football games in what they both perceived to be the suspicious sameness of the then-shiny-and-new suburb of Park Forest, where their fathers had swept their wives and children into the postwar dream of peace and prosperity.

Patty had almost lost Vee once in the very early sixties, when her friend's increasingly radical views—she'd tried to become a Freedom Rider, for Pete's sake!—made it hard to find anything to talk about at dinner parties. But then Vee got pregnant with Kate at the same time Patty found herself pregnant with Junie, her second, and Vee had needed help: the advice, comfort, and solidarity only one young mother can give another, which reminded them both of what they'd shared as teenagers. Patty would always think of their serendipitously timed two girls as rescuing her friendship with Vee. Dear, dear Junie and Kate.

Now, seven years after those girls' births, Veronica knew exactly where to find the cake knife and dessert plates in Patty's kitchen even if a new distance had begun to settle in between them.

Veronica cut a slice of the cake, put it on a plate, and pushed it toward Patty. "You know what Aunt Martha always says. Life's short. Eat dessert first."

"I wouldn't dream of flouting Aunt Martha's advice," Patty said, picturing Veronica's flamboyant kimono-wearing maiden aunt who'd been a fixture at every event of their growing up together—plays, recitals, graduations, weddings, showers—to which she'd brought what seemed like an impossibly chic urban glamour, like perfume from her city apartment. Patty often wondered what it would have been like to be her, a teacher who'd never married and who traveled as far away as Egypt on vacations. Aunt Martha's life in Chicago was in no small way part of the reason both of them had wound up living in the city rather than in one of the fancier suburbs to which their own parents had gravitated as Park Forest became, in Patty's late mother's words, "too different."

"Didn't she just get back from Sweden?" Patty asked.

"A few months ago. Now she's in India. I'm so jealous."

"I don't think I could stomach all the poverty," Patty said, feeling vaguely ashamed of herself, as she tended to when she confessed something like this to Vee. And yet she felt compelled to be honest with her oldest friend; with anyone else, she'd keep her mouth shut.

"It would be hard to see." Veronica nodded. "But necessary. And there's so much more to the country than that."

"I suppose. Well, anyway. I am not surprised at all that Aunt Martha is making the best of her retirement." Patty pulled the plate with Veronica's cake on it toward her and took a bite. It was perfection, like everything that had ever come out of her friend's oven. Patty shoveled bite after spicy, crumbly bite into her mouth. "This is so good."

Veronica smiled. "Hey, have you . . . Have you heard from Eliza at all?"

Patty shook her head. "The last I heard was that postcard from Toronto, like three or four months ago?" On the back of a rectangular card with a bright red Canadian maple leaf on the front, Patty's sister had written:

> Hi, Sis,
>> The band's playing almost every night. Want to come for a show?
>
> —E

And that was it. Even if she'd wanted to attend a show, there was no way to contact her sister to find out where to go. Patty sighed the same sigh she'd been sighing ever since Eliza had left the letter with their father three years ago saying:

> I'm not missing. I'm on the road with Christopher, and you don't have to look for me. I'll be in touch.

She'd graduated from high school six weeks before. Patty knew she'd only stuck around that long to get her usual check of $250 on her eighteenth birthday.

"Although . . ." Patty trailed off. She didn't want to sound paranoid. "Yeeeeessss?"

"Well," she admitted, "I have been getting some hang-up calls lately, and I keep wondering if they are Eliza. I've gotten three so far. I pick up the phone, say hello, and there's a short silence, then a dial tone."

"It's definitely not one of Karen's friends prank calling?"

Patty laughed. "God, no. Those are so obvious. 'Is your refrigerator running? Then you better go catch it!'" Patty faked a kid voice.

Veronica laughed and then shrugged. "Well, if it is Eliza, I hope she speaks up soon. Has your dad heard anything?"

Patty shook her head. "No. And we had lunch last week, like we always do on the first Wednesday of the month, when Linda's getting her monthly massage and facial." Patty huffed. "I don't get it. I mean, I love a good facial, but Mom . . . She was nothing like that."

"I remember. If she couldn't create it herself, she didn't do it. Remember that summer you made all those soaps?"

Patty recalled the mint and peony scents that had mingled with the other waxy, burning aromas of soapmaking that summer. She and her mom—and kindergarten Eliza, too, now that she thought of it— had laughed so hard, then cried, and ruined so many ingredients, but in the end, they had a stack of fragrant, jewel-toned bars of soap to show for their labors. God, she missed her mother. And losing Eliza so soon after her mother's death had only enlarged the hole in Patty's heart. She hoped so much it was Eliza calling, that there could be another chance for them.

"And how are *your* parents?" Patty asked.

"June and Ward Cleaver in the Everglades? Oh, the usual. I don't call after five, though these days it's getting closer to four, so I don't have to hear Mom slur her words or repeat the same conversation from the day before. And I can't call before lunch, or Dad will be on the golf course."

"Well, that's at least a few-hours-long window," Patty joked.

"So," said Veronica in her resolutely subject-changing tone, "weren't you going to tell me why you look so stressed out today?"

Patty took another fortifying bite of cake, then said, "I don't know where to start. Junie had to go to the bathroom during the homily, and she took forever, and when we got back, Karen and Tad were practically in a full-out brawl in the pew. I was mortified." Another bite.

"Then I spent the afternoon trying to convince Karen and Junie to finish their homework and clean their rooms, and to keep Tad entertained without making another enormous mess. And . . ." She lowered her voice. "Matt's been in a mood all day. He got into it with one of his partners last week about something to do with the office space or taxes or . . . oh, I don't know, I can't keep track. He spent the entire day raking leaves and listening to football, so he wasn't helpful at all. Why he doesn't hire someone to rake the damn leaves, I'll never understand."

Veronica gave Patty an all-too-familiar smile: it was sympathetic, but a little patronizing, too.

"What? What's with the smile?"

"There's no smile, Patty."

"Oh, yes, there is. It's the same one you used to put on back in college when I moaned about my grades and you knew full well I spent more time at Alpha Phi than I did studying. Until you finally just told me I couldn't get by on charm anymore and actually had to crack open a book."

Veronica laughed. "Okay, okay. But truly, I don't think there's a simple solution here. This is your husband we're talking about, not your midterms."

Though Patty craved another slice, she reminded herself of the way her jeans had fit the day before, and pushed the empty plate aside. "I mean, I get it, it's stressful to be a cardiologist, but . . . Doug must get like this sometimes, right?"

"Rarely. Sometimes he stays at work until after I'm asleep, but he always leaves it at the office."

Sometimes Patty didn't know what to make of them. Veronica *never* complained about Doug, her shaggy but handsome former-piano-prodigy now rising-star-lawyer husband. With her other friends, woes of and about the husbands were prime topics of conversation. Was Veronica really that content, or was she hiding something? "Enough about me," Patty said emphatically. "What have you been up to lately? I feel like I haven't seen you in ages."

"Weeeellll," Veronica drawled. Patty could practically see the gears grinding in her friend's head. "I'm pregnant."

Patty clapped her hands together, squealed, and went to hug her. "I'm so happy for you!"

Veronica smiled and hugged Patty back. "Thanks. Please don't say anything to Doug, though. I mean, he knows. But we're not ready to talk about it with everyone yet."

"I understand," Patty said. Her poor friend. What a nightmare her miscarriage two years ago had been—and in the fifth month, too. Veronica, usually so full of life, had barely left her house for three months. Patty had done much of her laundry and cooking through the worst of it. "Of course you want to make sure everything's okay. How are you feeling so far?"

"Pretty good. I'm seeing a doctor and a midwife this time, to cover all my bases. The midwife is great. Very focused on staying healthy and tuning in to my body."

"Whatever makes you feel good. And I'm glad you're seeing a midwife."

Veronica cocked an eyebrow. "Really?"

"Don't look so surprised. Matt might be a doctor, but I think women—and midwives are all women, right?—know a lot more about childbirth than men. Even the doctors."

"You sure I can't entice you to join the Union?"

Patty rolled her eyes at the mention of her friend's radical feminist club. The women of the Chicago Women's Liberation Union *didn't shave their legs*, and she'd heard they were even proponents of abortion. Patty was all for birth control, despite what some of her more conservative friends at St. Thomas thought. For heaven's sake, preventing a pregnancy was certainly better than the alternative. "I draw the line at the Junior League."

They laughed together, an acknowledgment that they could have a sense of humor about where their similar views ended. Fizzy as this moment of shared confidence made her, Patty couldn't shake the sense that there was something else Veronica wasn't telling her about why she'd been so busy lately.

Still, Veronica's surprise news changed the whole mood of the night. In between snippets of conversation and serving and clearing dinner, Patty imagined fun games for a baby shower. She'd have to reach out to Veronica's friend Siobhan to see if she wanted to throw it together with her, which she wished she didn't have to do, because Siobhan was such an enigma. She was a painter whose pictures Patty found hard to decipher, and she was divorced from that lovely man Gabe, Charlie's father. *Why are they divorced?* Patty often wondered. Why put your kid through the ringer like that unless it was absolutely necessary? It didn't appear to have been necessary; Siobhan herself had once said, "No one cheated." And Veronica had refused to tell Patty what had happened, which really annoyed her; they used to love sharing other friends' secrets while holding each other's tight. But now Veronica apparently felt that Siobhan's secrets were worth keeping.

Maybe their mutual friend's baby would be a reason for Patty and Siobhan to get to know each other better. Patty liked to think she was open to surprises.

That night, when all the dishes were done, Veronica and Doug and Kate had gone, and their own kids were finally asleep, Patty climbed into bed next to Matt and snuggled close to him. He was reading *National Geographic* but didn't look away to see that she was wearing a silk nightie. She'd made sure she smelled like toothpaste and a fresh, faint spray of Chanel No. 19 behind her knees.

She slid her hand down his chest, over one of the faded Northwestern T-shirts he always wore to bed along with soft blue boxer shorts. "Hey there, handsome," she said in his ear as her hand came to rest suggestively at the hem of his shirt.

He set down his magazine and peered at her over the wire rims of his reading glasses. She loved those glasses. He looked so *doctorly* in them. And with the gray that was starting to appear at his temples— *oh, Lord*. After all these years, she still wanted him; she knew he'd become a little self-conscious about his receding hairline and the way his daily runs no longer seemed to keep him as slim as they once had. "I feel like I'm turning into my dad," he'd grumbled recently. She'd kissed him on the cheek and tried to make light of it, saying, "I like that you're not exactly the same as you were. It's almost like sleeping with a different man." He'd raised a dubious eyebrow in reply.

Now he put his hand on hers and squeezed, then gave her a half smile of regret. "I'm too distracted tonight. I'm sorry. You know how Sundays are."

For years, Sunday had been an excuse to hide from the kids and release some of the pressure building about the upcoming week. Moving her hand a few inches down and hoping to produce a response, she breathed in his ear, "I know exactly how Sundays can be."

He leaned over and kissed her on the forehead. "I wish I could, but not tonight," he said.

Dragging her hand reluctantly away, she turned from him and picked up the novel that had been sitting on her bedside table for weeks. She couldn't focus on it. The persistent arousal was at war with anger and disappointment, and it felt like something between her stomach and ribs was going to explode.

This wasn't the first time this had happened.

When had they last made love, anyway? Four months ago? Five? She'd tried everything she could think of—adult dinners after the kids were in bed, lingering touches on his back, gently stroking his arm while they watched Johnny Carson, kissing his neck, cheek, lips, for no reason other than to remind him that she was there, that she wanted him.

Why didn't Matt want her?

It couldn't be because she was losing her looks, because she was both vain and ruthless enough to accurately compare herself to other women. She was petite and compact, and her breasts—which had done their job nursing three children, thank you very much!—still looked good in a bra (and she'd invested in a number of quite alluring ones with the thought of making love to Matt on top while she kept them on). Her skin was smooth and unlined, and it darkened to an even toast color in the summer. She'd recently had her hair cut so that it flipped at the bottom like that of Mary Tyler Moore—whom, she was often told, she looked a lot like. He used to love messing her hairstyles up, his fingers laced into her locks and tugging on them. Like he used to love her shift dresses and the boots she sometimes paired with them. Good Lord, the first time she'd worn an outfit like that, he'd pulled her by the arm into his office, shut the door, pushed the dress up, and taken her on his desk. She ached just remembering how much he'd wanted her.

What had happened to them? And what could she do to change the course they were on?

2

MARGARET

Kshhkshekkksh went the paper lining as Margaret leaned back on the narrow table, feeling the cold of the metal surface through the thread-bare cotton gown she was wearing, her knees bent up and her feet in hard, shiny contraptions called stirrups that bore no resemblance to the soft leather loops astride the horses she'd ridden in her youth through the wilderness of southern Maine. She was hundreds of miles, a time zone, and a lifetime away from that landscape now.

"Can you move a little farther down?" asked Dr. Metzler in a gentle tone of voice, almost apologetically. He was a grandfatherly type with a full plume of white hair and a trim salt-and-pepper mustache. Margaret wondered how long he'd been the University of Chicago gynecologist. The only gynecologist. Margaret had waited two long weeks for this appointment, as they made no exceptions for faculty. And since she was new faculty and didn't know anyone well enough in Chicago yet, this was the only place she could think of to get this exam and hopefully a prescription for the pill. Back at UC Berkeley, the university doctors didn't even ask if you were married before writing the script, and she hoped and assumed this campus doctor would be just as liberal.

Scooting herself down so that her legs bent tighter and her toes curled from the effort, Margaret stopped when she felt the edge of the table against her rear end.

"Very good," said the doctor, already looking under the tent of her gown at what there was to see between her legs—a tender, dark place she'd never even seen herself, and had felt squirmy with embarrassment the three other times anyone else had looked at her there: her pediatrician when she turned eighteen, to "make sure everything is in order"; the gynecologist in grad school; and Aaron. She wondered what Dr. Metzler saw. Or smelled—though she'd taken pains to shower as close to this appointment time as possible. She assumed he could tell she wasn't a virgin.

Without warning, he inserted the speculum, and when she gasped and shivered with surprise, he said, "Just relax."

She tried to breathe deeply and think about something else—anything except her upcoming date with Gabe Johnson, which was the real reason she was here on this damn table. She thought instead about the pretty handmade plates and bowls she'd seen at the little boutique in Old Town; maybe they weren't so out of her price range if she only bought four of each size. Or perhaps two.

The doctor widened the speculum and Margaret tried not to clench, but it was hard; it was such a cold, unnatural sensation. And frankly, it hurt. Not only did it feel like her vagina was holding up the instrument's weight, a Jell-O salad trying to keep a chef's knife upright, but it felt like the speculum was pinching her all the way up in there.

She breathed and pictured those plates and heard her mother tell her, "Why buy dishes when you'll get them all for free when you get married?"

Married.

Here she was, twenty-eight years old, getting on the pill so she could have sex with Gabe Johnson. Her mother would be horrified. But even her mother would agree that the last thing she needed was to get pregnant her first year as a tenure-track professor; she'd just disagree with her method of not getting pregnant.

"Just another minute," Dr. Metzler said as something poked at the very base of her vagina—her cervix, she guessed.

Ouch.

She couldn't help clenching that time.

"It would be easier for me if you could relax," the doctor said.

It would be easier for me if you would hurry the fuck up. "I'm sorry," she replied.

Do I have enough time to get to Old Town between now and tonight? She needed a reward for this. And her date started at seven, down here in Hyde Park, which was a good forty-five minutes on the L, at least. She wasn't sure; she was still learning her way around the city.

"All done, at last," Dr. Metzler said as, mercifully, he narrowed the speculum and finally—finally—pulled it out.

Margaret hurried to sit up straight, feeling herself close back up, her vagina warm and comfortable between her own two legs.

The doctor made a few purposeful movements with glass slides and long cotton swabs on the counter in the corner of the room, then turned to her and said, "You look perfectly healthy, but whenever a girl like you comes to see me, I think it's wise to run all the tests we can. Mustn't have syphilis running rampant on campus."

"I don't have syphilis."

"It's common not to know you have it. And of course there's also gonorrhea and chlamydia."

"It's fine if you want to run those tests," said Margaret, though her heart was beating resentfully in her chest. "What I really came for was a prescription for the pill."

He shook his head. "I'm sorry, that is strictly off-limits for under-graduates."

"I'm an English professor. I got my PhD from UC Berkeley last year." *So you can call me Doctor, Doctor.*

His eyes widened as he looked at her as if for the first time. She knew she didn't look *that* young. Had he really bothered looking at her before this moment, her degree would not be capturing his attention like a convertible Porsche in a grocery store parking lot.

He cleared his throat. "Are you married? Engaged? We do things differently in Chicago than they do out west."

She couldn't believe this appointment was unfolding this way. "Would you prefer I send my history professor boyfriend in here to ask for it himself?" *Like I had to have my dad cosign on my credit card? And my lease?*

"That won't be necessary," he said, taking the ballpoint pen out of the breast pocket of his white coat, clicking it open, and dashing off the script. He handed it to her with a brief, disapproving glance. "If I were you, I'd wear a wedding band when you take it to the pharmacy," he said, then quickly let himself out.

She looked down at the dark blue Movado watch her father had given her when she graduated from Cornell six years ago, and thought, *Yes. I have just enough time to go get those plates.*

"I think maybe we ordered too much," said Margaret, looking at the five dishes glistening under the red lantern lights of the restaurant, sending up pungent, garlicky steam under their noses.

"Yeah, our eyes were bigger than our stomachs, but I like a challenge." Gabe slid a set of wooden chopsticks out of their paper sleeve, broke them apart, then used them to pluck a piece of eggplant from the hot pot and pop it in his mouth. "Mm-mmm. Excellent."

It was hard to believe she was sitting across a table from Gabe Johnson at all, and on a third date, no less. Three years ago when they'd first met, she was a grad student and he a visiting professor, and a date would have been impossible because he'd been married. To

Siobhan Johnson, a painter. The professor and the painter. If she hadn't wanted to sleep with Gabe so badly, she'd have wanted to *be* them.

She released her own chopsticks, took a bite of the kung pao chicken, and made her own murmur of pleasure, eyes closed. When she opened them again, Gabe was smiling at her.

"What?" she asked, feeling her cheeks flush at the intensity of his expression.

"I'm still amazed and happy you wound up here, that's all."

So am I. "Well, Chicago does seem to be my kind of town." She smirked at her own corny joke.

"It won't let you down," he replied, and they both laughed as the Sinatra tune struck up in her mind.

"I mean . . . how can you not love the city that invented deep-dish pizza? It was all I ate for a week after I arrived. And the way the city glitters at night is just . . ."

"I know," he agreed. "I grew up in Ann Arbor, but my parents would take us into Chicago a few times a year to go to the Art Institute and Marshall Field's, and I used to beg to stay in a hotel room as high as possible, just so I could look out the window at bedtime."

"It *sparkles*."

He nodded, smiling.

"More than New York, even. I had no idea till I got here. And you can go to the beach, right here in the city! That just feels . . . crazy. Even in Los Angeles, the beach is more separated from the city part of the city, you know?" Margaret recalled the sticky, sore-limbed days of unpacking her office and apartment just six weeks ago, and how she'd cool off by wading into Lake Michigan, skyscrapers at her back. There was such a marvelous cognitive dissonance to it.

Gabe nodded, chuckling. "I interviewed at USC once upon a time. L.A. has nothing on Chicago."

"And yet it also has a small-town feel, doesn't it? I love that Ernie at Medici knows I like my coffee light but not sweet, and Sophia at the Co-Op tells me which apples are crunchiest."

"Light but not sweet, eh? I'm taking notes." He tapped his temple with his index finger.

"I look forward to quizzing you," she said, and the look they shared over their meal might have set their table aflame.

They continued talking and eating, conversation roving easily over other Chicago landmarks, then to their students and the classes they were teaching that semester.

"I'm surprised your office hours are as empty as mine," she said, responding to his complaint about student apathy.

"Because coming to discuss Reconstruction with your middle-aged professor is so enticing?"

She laughed. "Well, when I was an undergrad, I used to dream up excuses to go to my favorite professors' office hours. Especially the ones I thought were cute."

A sly grin emerged as he finished chewing a spicy string bean. "Oh? I bet every one of those professors was flattered."

"I doubt that. I was awkward and unformed back then."

"That's hard to picture."

"I take that as a compliment. But no, I was still a scared little turtle when I started graduate school. It took the Free Speech protests to make me come out of my shell."

"Oh, yes, Mario Savio on his car in the quad, decrying the regents. Did you join in?"

"Sort of. I believed in what the students were saying, but my real battle was in convincing my parents that the unrest was no reason for me to return to Maine." Her mother's panicked voice—*What will happen to you there? Come home where it's safe*—was still shrill in Margaret's mind. "My mother is . . . 'Old-fashioned' is an understatement. She's taken exactly three airplane flights in her life: two legs round-trip to Yellowstone for her honeymoon, and a third one-way to the Grand Canyon. She had such a panic attack on that plane that she took three days of trains all the way back home. And this is in spite of the fact"—*or maybe because of the fact*—"that my dad flies planes for a living." He and her ski instructor brother, who'd come to check out Squaw Valley, had been the only members of her family to visit Margaret the whole six years she'd lived in California.

Gabe shook his head. "Parents, right? I think my own would be more likely to visit me if I was farther away, somewhere more exotic than the city they've visited their whole lives. Now that they're retired, they're rarely home."

"Are they anywhere exciting now?"

"Golfing in Argentina."

"Wow. That's ambitious. I'd love to go to South America. I read a collection of Borges stories a few years ago and loved them."

Gabe shrugged. "I've had so much going on these past few years, I haven't had time to think about travel. Anyway, I'm sure Charlie would rather go to Disneyland."

"I've heard Disneyland is surprisingly fun. I'd love to go."

"Argentina and Disney. You are full of contradictions, Dr. Jones."

"Better that than boring."

Gabe gently knocked his knee against hers under the table. "Much better," he agreed, and Margaret felt desire tighten between her legs.

"I seem to remember that back in Berkeley you had a boyfriend?" he asked.

"Yeah," she tried to say as casually as she could. "Aaron. We broke up a while ago." Oh, Aaron. He'd been so promising when they met. Cool, even. He rode a motorcycle and played drums in a band. After a hot and heavy first year together, his father died suddenly, and he withdrew into a cloud of pot that even her slinkiest lingerie couldn't cut through. He wouldn't even argue with her about anything. She broke up with him at the end of a second sexless, monosyllabic year together that coincided with Gabe's semester as a visiting professor at Berkeley.

"Anyone else since then?"

One one-night stand. Two relationships that lasted fewer than three months each. She'd given up on relationships for a while and instead focused on finishing her dissertation, then on publishing as much as she could and applying for tenure-track positions. It made her wonder if perhaps love was antithetical to meaningful work.

"Nope," she replied.

"Lucky me," he said.

"I'm as surprised as anyone to be sitting here together," she ventured. "Back when we met the first time, you and your wife sounded like a dream couple."

His expression darkened fast and starkly. "I thought so, too."

"I'm sorry, I didn't mean . . ."

"No." He held up his hand. "It's not your fault. Please, don't apologize."

"You don't have to talk about anything you don't want to. I'm sorry I pried."

"No, I'd be curious, too, in your shoes. She . . . She hurt me very deeply. She hurt *our daughter* deeply."

His face was stony with controlled anger. What had Siobhan done to him? To their child?

"I'm so sorry," she said.

"You have nothing to be sorry for." Then, with a purposeful shake of his head, he returned to the lighter tone of earlier in the evening. "Those are subjects for another time. I want to hear more about your book proposal."

She'd never dated a man with whom she could talk about work *and* movies, or the reading she did for pleasure and the reading she did for work. He was actually interested in the book she was writing about George Eliot, the Brontës, Alcott, and other lesser-known women

writers of the nineteenth century. Even though he was a history professor, he obviously loved the literature of his period—mid-nineteenth-
century America—which overlapped with hers.

The night three years ago came to her mind so clearly: Sitting in
the audience of Faculty Club at Berkeley, where she'd been a third-
year graduate student and Gabe a visiting professor from Chicago,
she'd watched him at the podium in his pressed white shirt and brown
cords, wearing black-rimmed glasses to read passages about freedom
and the American experiment by Henry David Thoreau and Frederick Douglass. It was intoxicating. His voice was low and dense, and his
hair was wavy and just long enough to graze his ears. And that beard—
how could a beard be sexy? And he was so *smart* about the ways in
which the Transcendentalists planted deep in the ground the seeds
that would grow slowly, so slowly, into the civil disobedience of the
mid-twentieth century. It was such similar thinking to what she was
grappling with in her dissertation about the ways in which "romantic"
fiction of the period troubled conventional notions of womanhood in
precisely the ways that would inspire a later generation of women to
agitate for suffrage.

"I can't eat another bite." He leaned back in his chair and put his
hands behind his head in a languid, satisfied pose. His body was lean
and long, and he still had that beard.

Jesus.

Setting down her chopsticks, she realized that not only had they
demolished most of the food in front of them, but they'd never bothered using their own plates.

"It's not even ten," she said. "Want to come back to my place for a
drink?"

3

VERONICA

Camouflage time, she thought to herself as she stripped off the soft, comfortable skirt and turtleneck she'd worn all day at the Service and got into the shower to begin transforming herself into a presentable mother and wife for the Lab School's big annual fundraiser that night. She wanted to hate these things, with their small talk and hand-wringing about kids' reading levels, as if there weren't boys dying in Vietnam, Black people who couldn't vote or get a decent education, and women who couldn't get child care because of the Comprehensive Child Development Act that Tricky Dick had vetoed even though *both* the House and Senate had passed it. But she didn't hate them. She was part of the charade; there was too much of her mother, too much of Park Forest and *I Love Lucy* and Fourth of July fireworks and Jo March and Scout Finch in her to have gone totally counterculture. By the time people were turning on, tuning in, and dropping out, she was hosting bake sales for the nursery school. These days, she could talk about the influences of Eric Carle and Barbie with the best of them. At least the debates about Barbie weren't so milquetoast.

Very often she wished she could be more like Patty, safe and content in her Kenwood fortress and undivided in her attention to family.

Her whole life, though, something had attracted Veronica to crusade. As a child, she read book after book about the suffragists, imagining herself carrying banners and marching in long white skirts. Then as a teenager, she devoured news articles about the marches and boy-cotts in the southern states, where men and women walked and sat in solidarity for equal rights. She wrote history papers about Margaret Sanger and Elizabeth Cady Stanton, and took classes in college about rebellions from India to Russia. All of that had been theoretical, though, until Jane—or the Service, as it was known internally—when she'd finally picked up a sword and begun to fight for something she be-lieved in. Equality, autonomy, and freedom for women.

As the hot water from the shower scalded her shoulders and back, Veronica picked up a little brush and scrubbed her nails, which always seemed to have grime from the day beneath the white tips, her one concession to her mother's refrain, "pretty nails, pretty girl," because she could never find the time for varnish or a manicure. She managed to tear a cuticle and open up a fissure that bloomed crimson. *Of course. No good grooming goes unpunished*, she thought with frustra-tion at how out of practice she was at these little rituals and how necessary they were for nights like these.

With a towel wrapped around her hair and a Band-Aid on her finger, Veronica pulled on stockings, then a long black dress she hoped would fit over her thickening middle. Now that she was finishing her first trimester, she was starting to look pregnant when she was naked at least; a small but unmistakable lump had taken up residence below her navel, and the tender breasts and gassy intestines had begun to subside.

Not that she was complaining. Every day she had normal and healthy, if sloshy and uncomfortable, symptoms was another day she was still pregnant. She wouldn't truly feel like she was in the clear until well after the fifth month, though, given what had happened last time. All that blood, and the rough, painful D&C to make sure her womb was clean and wouldn't get infected. If only she and Siobhan had known how to do the procedure then, Veronica never would have gone to the OB; when the miscarriage was finished, she'd have gone to Siobhan or one of the other Service members who knew how to perform a gentle and effective dilation and curettage.

But of course, without that experience, she might not have become so determined to take up the curette herself, and the Service might not have become what it now was. *There has to be a better way*—how many times had she said that to herself before she realized that no one else was coming to help? It was up to her to offer that better way.

Thank God for Empire waists, she thought as she examined herself in the mirror, hair still incongruously tied in a white towel as her body towered in a column of swishy chiffon. She pulled off the towel, and her long hair tumbled over her shoulders. The soft flesh of her larger-than-usual breasts spilled fetchingly out of the dress. *Not bad for a thirty-one-year-old pregnant lady.*

"Mommy, you look so pretty!" Kate bounced into the room and flopped on her parents' big bed wearing the black cat pajamas she'd gotten for Halloween and Veronica had to wash every other day because Kate refused to wear anything else to bed.

"Thanks, Bugaloo. Hey, we match. Come here."

Kate slid off the bed and stood in front of her mom, and in the mirror they looked like echoes of each other with their wavy hair, pale faces, and freckled noses atop their black-clad forms. Kate hugged her mom. "When's Betsy gonna get here?"

"Soon." *Thank goodness for their favorite babysitter.*

Doug swept in next. He'd showered before Veronica and looked very dapper in his black suit. "You look good enough to eat," he growled at Veronica, kissing her on the cheek and sending a shiver straight through her. "But we're going to be late if we don't hurry."

Veronica did the best she could with her underused hair dryer and makeup, and fastened the pearls her parents had given her for her wedding around her neck. She left her sleeve of bangles on the dresser but hung her favorite peacock feather earrings from her lobes, then Betsy arrived with a whole puppet show in a box, and Veronica and Doug made their escape in a cab that took them to the enormous home of Cheryl and George Murray, the Lab School's biggest boosters and the reason Kate attended private school instead of the perfectly good public schools Veronica had taught in before she became a mother. Where to educate their daughter had been the first real fight of their marriage, with Doug advocating for the progressive school "where Kate will learn through art and theater instead of drills and tests."

"But we live here in Hyde Park, which is a glorious rainbow, and the students at the Lab School don't look like her neighborhood. They look like Patty's neighborhood."

"She'll still have her neighborhood friends. I'm worried about the schools, Vee. You've said yourself they're disorganized and hurting for funds. I want Kate to have the best."

It didn't help that George Murray had been Doug's favorite law school professor, the one who'd inspired him to start his career as a public defender, irony of ironies: Doug went to bat for people who couldn't afford representation while sending his own kid to an elite private school far away from the children of those very people; and now, after paying his dues as a defender, Doug had recently made the move to work with George in his prestigious practice on a variety of high-profile criminal cases that sometimes made their way to the federal and appellate courts.

Her mother had loved the idea of the selective school, of course, and Veronica had been outnumbered in family discussions about where to educate Kate. Fortunately, the place was run and populated by a pretty liberal set of people; Veronica could count on one hand the number of parents she'd met who thought getting involved in Vietnam had been a good idea, though what had happened at the

Democratic National Convention in '68 was more divisive. Even if they didn't put their children where their mouths were, they put their money there, often enough—it was hard to keep up with the number of food and clothing and toy drives. Despite all that broad-mindedness, though, there was no way Veronica could let on that she was the leader of Jane, the city's underground women's lib organization that provided safe, clean, illegal abortions to any woman who needed one. And Kate had not stayed friends with the neighborhood kids; her whole friend group was in the homogeneous school. Ironically, Veronica was too busy with Jane to remedy that, much to her embarrassed consternation.

In the vast marble foyer of the Murrays' home, their coats were whisked away by Black men wearing white gloves, and she and Doug were handed flutes of champagne. They were quickly accosted by Patty and Matt, which suited Veronica fine. She wished Siobhan could be here, since Charlie also went to the Lab School, but she didn't want to get a sitter, and, as she put it, "I don't have any money to spend on a dress or anything they're going to auction off, so why bother?" Her ex, Gabe, and her parents paid the tuition for Charlie, which was reduced anyway because Gabe was faculty at the university. Gabe never came to functions like this, which was a good thing, because Veronica couldn't trust herself to be civil to him, especially after a drink or two. Two at the most tonight, for her midwife had counseled her not to drink at all during this pregnancy except on special occasions.

Veronica fell into a groove. With a band playing mellow swing music, and cocktails and canapés always in hand, it was easy to forget where they were. They seemed suspended in time, occasionally dancing, constantly laughing, and animatedly talking about their children and upcoming holiday plans. At one point, she noticed the Band-Aid on her finger, and hastily tore it off and stashed it in her little purse. Thankfully, the cut wasn't still bleeding.

She even found herself having fun until she emerged from the opulent brass-and-coral bathroom and glimpsed someone familiar in a black-and-white uniform carrying a shiny silver platter with salmon mousse on crackers. Veronica was horrified that she couldn't remember her name, not that it would have been her real name anyway. She just recalled that the server had been her second-to-last D&C on Wednesday. She appeared healthy and energetic, though, which was a good sign. The Service followed up on the phone with every woman who came to them, but only half of them ever picked up, so it was hard to know how everyone was doing.

Has she seen me? Should I say hi? Her two worlds had collided, and Veronica was paralyzed. It seemed rude not to acknowledge the woman. But would it draw undue attention to her? To Veronica herself? The pull Veronica felt toward the woman was strong, though; she wanted to know how she was faring three days later, if there was still bleeding, if she felt . . . *freer.* Which was the whole point of the Service—to *liberate* women by helping them take control of their own bodies.

Oh, fuck it. I can be cool. No one else has to know what we're talking about.

She marched over to the woman and said, "Those look delicious. May I have one?"

The woman's head jerked up at the sound of Veronica's voice, and her mouth dropped open for a second when she saw Veronica's face. She handed Veronica a napkin and cracker, and said, "Hello, ma'am."

Ma'am is my mother. "Please." Veronica smiled warmly. "Call me Veronica. I don't want to draw attention to you, but I wanted to see if you're doing okay?"

Nodding and swiveling her eyes around the room, she replied, "Fine, fine. No problems at all."

This was clearly a lie, but there was no way to find out what kind of lie it was. Was everything not fine in her uterus? Her home? Her relationship? Anyway, she wasn't going to tell Veronica, especially not when the woman who'd performed her abortion was wearing a dress that made her look like an extra in a Bond film. Or maybe more to the point, a latter-day Scarlett O'Hara.

"Well, if you need anything at all, you have our number."

"Yes, ma'am."

"It was nice to see you." Veronica tried to telepathically communicate all the care and courage she could at this woman, whom she didn't know at all and yet knew as intimately as two women could know each other.

For the rest of the night, Veronica assiduously avoided meeting the woman's eyes, and was thankful that everyone at the party was too drunk to have noticed the moment she'd shared with her. Despite that cover, though, Veronica felt edgy all night, flinching when Doug touched her shoulder and feeling less and less inclined toward conversation. When Crissy Belkin's husband, Max, started mouthing off that *Nixon better get us the hell out of Laos* during dinner, Veronica all but put her hands over her ears. Long ago, when her mother started mixing her first cocktail at three thirty instead of five and her father came home at seven half in the bag, Veronica had developed the skill of being able to tune out the people in front of her, of catching just enough words to be able to reply intelligently, but not to truly engage. It was a handy talent when you had to lead a double life, which meant keeping your truest self under wraps at all times.

"Did you have fun?" Doug asked in the cab on the way home.

"Oh, as much as I ever do," she said, leaning against him. It was late and she was exhausted after a day at the Service, then the party, and she wanted to draw some strength and solace from his sturdy form.

"Well, I appreciate your putting on a good face." He planted a kiss on her cheek. "By the way, who was the woman you were talking to? One of the servers?"

Veronica sat up straight. "She came to the Service earlier this week. Did anyone else notice? I tried to be discreet."

Doug yawned. "Oh, you were, as always." He put a hand on the rounded part of her belly. "Have you given any more thought to taking some time off? I worry more now, with this one on the way."

Absolutely not. But she tried to sound as sympathetic as she could. "You know we're short-staffed. We're trying to train new people, and in fact I'm meeting someone new this week, but it's hard when we can barely keep up with demand."

"I just . . . don't want anything to happen, you know?"

Another miscarriage. An arrest. They were real concerns. She couldn't blame him. But she needed the Service to feel whole—without it, she'd feel like only part of herself. Doug understood this; at least, he had before this pregnancy. Now, every time he brought the topic up, it felt like she'd entered some sort of time warp that took them back to 1950, where he was the Husband and she was the Wife.

"I know," she said, squeezing his hand with hers. "I'll be careful."

"You know I support your work at the Service, right? I think it's important, what you're doing. And brave. But we've wanted this child a long time, and you—*we*—had such an awful experience last time, and . . . This might be selfish," he said, "but I'd like to think you'd prioritize the baby over Jane."

"But there's no choice to make right now, is there? The pregnancy is going fine. And you know I'd go crazy trying to be Patty. Working is good for me, and what's good for me is good for the baby."

"Alright," he said, giving her hand a squeeze before he let it go.

She sighed. Things had been so much simpler when she'd had Kate. Then, she'd been a teacher, and much as she enjoyed teaching, she wasn't passionate about it like she was passionate about Jane. Jane was her other child in a way, but it was more hers than Kate or this new child could ever be, because it made her feel more independent, more herself, than mothering did. And when she'd had the miscarriage, Jane was still only a referral service, and hadn't yet begun to absorb so much of her time, so she refused to see the link between working and miscarrying. Why couldn't Doug just accept that and trust her?

What was harder to explain to him, because he was a man and would never have to live the same kind of divided life that she would—that she *did* live, even now—was that she wanted to soak up as much independence as she could before this baby arrived. Mothering required constant merging and compromising—with Doug and with the children themselves. Newborns especially required total self-effacement. And nothing in society was set up to help women regain independence once they became mothers; to the contrary, everything was set up to keep them dependent. Now that she had work she actually loved, she felt an urgency to do as much of it as possible while she was able.

Leaning over in the cab, she kissed him on the cheek, then rested her head on his shoulder. "Something tells me this one is going to be fine," she said.

After a moment's hesitation, he put his hand on her knee, which was always a sure sign they were in something together. She breathed deeply with relief, but she knew the conversation was not over.

PATTY

"Hello?"

"Hello, this is Patty Buford. May I please speak to Siobhan?"

"Hi, Patty, this is Siobhan."

She sounded friendly enough. Not exactly over the moon to hear from her, but what could Patty really expect? She pictured the other woman holding the phone and wearing her uniform of paint-stained bell-bottoms and fisherman's knit sweater, her tightly coiled mane of wiry auburn hair held back in a low ponytail. Even in such uninspired clothes, Siobhan was a beauty who resembled the softly seductive subjects of Impressionist portraits, though her own art hardly resembled those paintings. Patty found Siobhan's paintings frustrating beyond belief, though she could understand why they appealed to Veronica— well, the new Veronica. Not the one Patty had grown up with.

Patty remembered the day her old friend had breathlessly taken her to a gallery in Old Town to show her "these amazing paintings by a new friend of mine, Siobhan Johnson," as the stack of bangles Veronica had recently started wearing jingled their approving excitement on her arm. Patty had looked at the paintings, and at her friend's absorption in them, and realized that Veronica belonged more to the world of those paintings than she did to the world they'd grown up in. The bracelets; the flowy, ankle-length skirts she now favored; the remarkable length of her hair.

On enormous canvases, Siobhan had plastered together collages of magazine advertisements for beauty products, with actual literal plaster, dotting the surface with tubes of lipstick and eyeliner, and compacts with blush and foundation; she'd then used black paint to outline grossly oversized women over the crusty surface. Patty understood full well that Siobhan was making *feminist art*, and though Patty considered herself a feminist—she believed that women should be able to work outside the home if they chose to, like her own mother had once, and that they should make the same money as men for equivalent work—she didn't understand why some women's libbers had to depart so extremely from the world of long-standing feminine arts like makeup or pretty curtains or nicely prepared meals. What was so wrong with lipstick? The fact that Veronica did get dressed up on occasion, like for the Lab School fundraiser the other night, made it all the more puzzling. Contradictions abounded. That day in the art gallery was almost as painful to Patty as the day Eliza had taken off, leaving only the note saying not to look for her. Though neither of those days held a candle to the day her mother finally succumbed to uterine cancer.

Mustn't think about that now. But the memories were there, clamoring at the door in her mind.

Applying her most cheerful tone, Patty tried to make some benign chitchat with Siobhan about their daughters Junie and Charlie, who were in the same grade as Veronica's Kate, but it fizzled quickly.

"So," Patty said, "you know the good news about Veronica?" She had checked to make sure Siobhan did know before making this call, but she had to break the ice somehow.

"Yes, I'm so excited for her and Doug."

"Me, too. And, well, I thought it would be fun to throw her a little baby shower, so of course I wondered if you might want to do that with me?" She tried to sound as enthusiastic as she could.

Siobhan didn't answer right away. "That's a lovely idea, but . . . I think we might want to wait."

"To make sure everything progresses according to plan, you mean?"

"Exactly."

"Well, of course. We wouldn't throw the party until the last trimester anyway, until we know all is well."

Another pause. Patty wrapped the phone cord impatiently around her index finger, unwound, then wound again.

At last Siobhan said, "I think it's possible we should wait until after the baby arrives."

"After? Why?"

"What if she winds up on bed rest? What if she miscarries again? Or worse, what if the baby doesn't survive?"

Survive? That's awfully morbid. "If we get to month seven, I'm sure we'll be home free."

"You'd be surprised."

"Goodness, I know those sorts of things used to happen with some frequency. But this is almost 1972. We're in a city with world-class hospitals." *It's one thing for a woman with grown children like my mother to die of cancer, and quite another for a baby or her mother to be harmed in childbirth.*

The next pause was almost unbearable. Patty was just about to open her mouth when Siobhan said, "Listen, I want to celebrate this baby as much as you do, and I'd be very happy to throw a shower with you. I just want to be careful of the timing. You know, it's the Jewish tradition to wait to celebrate the baby after the birth."

"Are you Jewish?"

"No, no, I just think their caution is to be admired."

"Of course," Patty said, feeling like a popped helium balloon.

43

"Um . . . How about we see how the next few months go, then talk again? Maybe feel Veronica out a bit on having a party? She'll be so *tired* after the baby arrives. She won't be in a mood to celebrate."

"Oh, I think she might be."

Do you need to sound so smug?

"Well, we'll see," said Patty. Then, glancing around her kitchen for a reason to get off the phone, her eyes fell on the oven—which was off—and she said, "Oh, goodness, I forgot I had some banana bread baking. Please excuse me. We'll catch up more soon?"

"Sounds good."

"Buh-bye."

"Bye, Patty."

Click.

That woman!

She'd known Vee for eighteen years, and Siobhan had known her for—what? Four? Maybe five? With Technicolor brilliance, Patty could still recall the afternoons she and Veronica had come home from high school and lazed on Veronica's double bed, which had seemed so grown-up compared to her own pink canopy twin at the house that was consumed with little-kid junk. She loved Eliza, but at fifteen, Patty could have done without the sticky books, wet stuffed animals, and painful-to-step-on doll accessories that her decade-younger sister left strewn around the place. After a year of complaining about her own clothes and perfumes and books and special things going missing while she was at school, Patty convinced her parents to let her put a lock on her door, but she was most emphatically not allowed to use it once she got home, and so all Eliza did was bug her all afternoon.

Veronica's place was an oasis with her laissez-faire mother, who was almost always sipping a juicy, sparkling cocktail and reading a big, fat novel, or playing some sort of card game with friends who also sipped beautiful cocktails. In Veronica's room they could do what they liked: listen to Elvis and Ella records, chew gum, plot how to get cigarettes before the football game, decide which clothes were worth spending their allowance on, and discuss who was going out with whom, and if they had kissed someone or done more. Eventually their conversations advanced to sharing whom they were kissing and exploring what "more" actually meant. Patty laughed now to recall how agonizing the difference between over and under the shirt had seemed back then.

It wasn't until years later that Patty realized Veronica had wished her own mother had been more like Patty's. She recalled listening impatiently and jealously as her mother and her best friend stood at the kitchen counter, talking about things Patty had no real interest in.

"I can't believe the boycott's lasted five months already," Veronica said as she plucked an oatmeal cookie off a plate. Eliza was mercifully napping, for once. *Boycott?* It took Patty a few seconds to realize her friend was talking about the bus boycott in Montgomery, Alabama, hundreds—thousands?—of miles away. The South seemed like a foreign country to her then, as exotic as Vietnam seemed these days.

"I'm so proud of them," her mother said. "Because of their blisters and fortitude, things might finally start to change in this country."

Veronica glanced out the window at the rows of white or brick houses with verdant square lawns, bicycles and tricycles on every driveway. "Will places like this ever change, though?"

"Eventually," Patty's mother said. "Ironically, it might take longer up here. The North likes to think it's more enlightened, but we're just fooling ourselves."

Veronica nodded her agreement. "I hope they win," she said, and Patty knew enough to know her friend was rooting for Dr. Martin Luther King Jr. and the other Negroes protesting against segregation. She was on their side, too, of course. But Patty would have much preferred discussing Grace Kelly's wedding dress, or whether the new

Alfred Hitchcock movie, *The Man Who Knew Too Much*, would be any good, and she hated that her own lack of engagement with current events meant that she was excluded from this conversation.

Likely sensing that very feeling in her daughter, Mom took a cookie for herself and said, "I have a long list of things to do before Eliza wakes up from her nap, so I'll let you two girls get to whatever you need to do."

"Thank you, Mrs. Callahan," said Veronica.

Patty let out a long, loud breath, shoving aside the next unwelcome memory that arose of her mother's last days, about a year after the hysterectomy that revealed the cancer had spread to other organs. By then, her once-vibrant mother spent most of the day in bed. Patty had made so many batches of her mom's favorite cookies and brought them to her, only to have her take a nibble, then throw it up. Her father had been so deep in his grief, he'd barely been able to get in the shower once a day, so it had fallen to Patty to take care of him and her teenage sister. Cleaning, cooking, laundry. Whatever they needed to keep the household running.

Who had been there for her through those dark days? Veronica. With phone calls and surprise visits and casseroles and cups of tea served while she collected, then washed, the laundry scattered all over the house, Veronica had made sure Patty got through the worst of it.

She'd be damned if she was going to let Siobhan Johnson get in the way of that kind of history.

Patty strode purposefully down the nursery school hallway of the Lab School, which smelled strongly of crayons, Ritz crackers, and wool mittens toasting on the radiator, thinking, *I can't even imagine doing all this again.* Tad had only one more year, and then he, her youngest, would at last be off to kindergarten. She loved her children more than anything, and loved being their mother, but the idea of doing the baby and toddler stage again—diapers and wet sheets and jars of pureed food, applications to school and midday pickups, struggles with naps and standoffs over broccoli—made her stomach churn. She couldn't believe Vee was up for it again.

When she reached Tad's classroom, which contained a colorful explosion of paper and letters and books and blocks, Patty couldn't help but smile. These rooms were so full of life and creativity and purpose. She tried as hard as she could to duplicate it in the playroom of her house, but the kids didn't mind her like they minded their teachers, and so the place was always a messy disaster instead of a welcoming enclave of possibilities. Even so, sometimes she'd find a picture one of them had painted, or a collage pasted together from magazine clippings, and she'd realize they were using all the materials, using their minds, thinking and pretending, and all the cleaning up she did in there would feel worthwhile.

When Tad caught sight of her at the door to his classroom, he ran to her with an enormous smile and flung his arms around her legs, the last of her children to still make such public displays of love. The hit of it was better than wine, and she would miss it when he got too big, like Junie and Karen. "Mommy! Can I do swings with James?"

Patty's eyes found those of Crissy, James's mother, who also had an older child, Benjamin, in Junie's grade. Crissy nodded her assent, and Patty said, "Swings it is!"

Tad whooped off with his friend.

Outside on the playground, Patty and Crissy stood, bouncing to keep warm, with other mothers and children who wanted to savor the last of the fall weather before temperatures drove them inside until March—or even, God help them, April. After comparing new recipes they might try for Thanksgiving, Crissy said, "Have you heard about Gabe Johnson?"

"Why am I the last to know everything today?" Patty couldn't help but whine, thinking of Siobhan Johnson's know-it-all tone on the phone earlier. Then she realized it might make her feel better to have a bit of gossip on the woman's ex-husband. "Spill it."

"Sam and Jan Wilder saw him with a younger woman at Hoe Toy the other night. Jan said it was obviously a date."

"How much younger?"

"She said it was hard to tell. Maybe her midtwenties?"

Gabe was probably in his mid or late thirties. That wasn't so scandalous. Patty felt a bit disappointed by this gossip. "Well, good for him," she said.

Crissy cocked a surprised eyebrow.

"What?"

"I thought you were friends with Siobhan."

Patty snorted. "Hardly. I'm friends with Veronica. I don't understand Siobhan, or her divorce. I mean, why? Why put your kid through that? Gabe seems lovely."

"I'm sure Veronica knows."

"Probably, but she's the soul of silence when it comes to Siobhan."

"Like any good friend would be, though more's the pity for us," Crissy said.

Patty nodded, feeling jealous once again.

The two women watched their boys run themselves ragged a little longer, and Patty let this news about Siobhan's ex settle. She wished it didn't make her feel just the tiniest bit better that the woman's former husband was dating before she was.

When Patty finally got home that afternoon, barely able to unlock her door as she balanced two paper bags of groceries, her purse dangling from the crook of her arm, the phone was ringing. Her heart jump-started as it always did when she heard the cheerful sound resonating in stereo from several phones around the house. "Hang on, hang on, hang on," she said as she rushed toward the kitchen, as if the caller could hear her.

After dumping the bags on the counter, she reached to pick up the receiver and said, "Hello? Patty Buford here."

There was a half second of silence, and then a dial tone.

Damn it.

Eliza?

With each hang-up, Patty became more and more sure this was her sister. Despite being separated by a decade, they were connected by blood and tragedy.

She hung up, then picked the receiver back up and dialed her father, holding the plastic between her ear and shoulder so she could put away groceries while she spoke.

"Hello?"

"Hi, Linda, it's Patty. Is Dad there?"

"Oh, hellllooooo, Patty. How aaaare you?"

Patty rolled her eyes as she hefted a gallon of milk into the fridge. "I'm great. How are you?"

"Well, I'm a tad under the weather, you know, but I'm sure I'll be fine."

I am not taking that bait. "I hope you feel better soon. Is Dad there?"

"Of course. Hold, please." *As if she was his secretary or something,* Patty couldn't help but think with derision. *Mom never sounded like that.*

"Hello there, kiddo, what's up?" *Dad. Thank God.*

"Hi, Dad, I'm good. The kids are good. I'm looking forward to our lunch next week. But hey, I just got a weird hang-up phone call, and I wondered . . . have you gotten a similar kind of call lately?"

"Not that I know of. Why?"

"Could you ask Linda?"

"Sure. Give me a sec."

Patty heard muffled voices on the other end.

"Nothing here. Want to give me a clue?"

"I don't know . . . I just thought maybe it was Eliza."

Her father was silent. They rarely talked about her sister, and any-time she was mentioned, it was at Patty's instigation.

"Nope, no hang-ups here, honey," he said, chipper as ever.

Patty gripped the kitchen counter. This conversation was going no further. As usual. "Okay. I'll see you next week."

"Next week it is!"

They hung up. She wanted so much to believe the caller was Eliza. She missed her. Patty felt a surge of pride remembering her sister pulling into the lead during a freestyle swim race, and how they'd gone with their parents to celebrate with big ice cream cones on a cold February afternoon because ice cream was Eliza's favorite treat. She remembered curling up on the couch together Sunday mornings, under the same blanket, and watching whatever old movie was on television, putting off whatever homework each of them needed to complete and sharing cookies and Kleenex when Cary Grant and Deborah Kerr met on the roof of the Empire State Building, or Audrey Hepburn finally went back to being a princess after her adventures in Rome. Patty had tried so hard to recapture that togetherness with her sister after their mother died, but nothing she offered was accepted.

No matter how many times she'd gone to confession and said Hail Marys and begged for forgiveness for failing her, the guilt she felt over Eliza's leaving still sometimes stabbed her like a sharpened blade. Father Miller, Veronica, Matt—they'd all reassured her that she'd done the best she could for her troubled little sister after their mother's death. When their father couldn't cope, Patty and Matt had taken Eliza in, and they'd tried so hard to give her a home. But with three kids under five, and Tad a wailing newborn with colic, Patty had been out of her league. At that point, her home had barely been a stable place for her own growing family, let alone a teenager who—in retrospect—needed much more than three meals a day and a curfew. But Patty hadn't known how to provide that elusive *more*.

But I should have, shouldn't I?

You were suffering your own loss, she heard a chorus of reassuring voices answer her. *You did the best you could.*

Did I?

And now the guilt was magnified by loneliness, with Matt so distant recently, and Veronica busy and pregnant again. Patty might not want another child, but she was the littlest bit jealous of the closeness this pregnancy would no doubt give Veronica with Doug and Kate; children had made her and Matt closer. She wanted so much to feel closer to the people she loved, including her sister.

Patty jumped every time the phone rang for the rest of the afternoon and evening, rushing to pick it up before the second ring, but every call was normal, boring.

Fruitless.

Sisterless.

5

MARGARET

Monday was the first meeting of the Women's Faculty Collective, a new group that strove "to promote women in places of importance throughout the university." Not only did she like the sound of the group, Margaret was getting desperate for some local friends, and she had to find something other than work to keep her mind from straying back to Gabe Johnson over and over again. Not that it wasn't fun to keep their time together on constant replay. Their first night together after the Chinese food had been nothing short of spectacular. And he'd come to her place the next day, too, bottle of red in hand. They'd made love before and after eating the steaks she cooked.

When she arrived in the conference room two floors under the English department, there were two young women about her own age studiously reorganizing their leather satchels to avoid talking to anyone, and then there were three older women, pearl and skirt-suit wearers, the kind who always seemed to have their lipstick perfectly applied and their brassy, colored hair cut short and coiffed away from their faces. The three of them clearly knew each other already, as they were gathered together chatting and drinking from paper cups and eschewing the ubiquitous plate of cookies from the university's catering service.

Margaret had a special fondness for the peanut butter cookies, so she went over to take one and fix herself a cup of coffee with milk. Just as she finished and was about to approach one of the younger women, she was joined by a Black woman who towered over her by a whole head. She was gorgeous and chic, with her chunky gold hoops and her black turtleneck sweater and brown leather skirt joined by a braided black belt.

"I can't stop eating these flipping cookies," she said as she plucked a chocolate chip one off the plate and took a big bite.

Margaret laughed. "The peanut butter ones are my problem."

"I moved off those last year. Got to keep it interesting, right?" She held out a long-fingered hand with a wide gold cuff bracelet over the sleeve of her sweater. "Phyllis Williams, graduate student working on my dissertation in linguistics. I should finish next year."

Margaret gave Phyllis's hand a firm shake and replied, "Margaret Jones, assistant professor of English. This is my first year on the faculty."

"You think by the time we're them we won't eat the cookies, either? We'll just get tired of them?" Phyllis nodded toward the clutch of older women.

"I don't know. I feel like women of our parents' generation learned to just ignore certain foods to stay slim. I bet they ignored them when they were our age, too."

"So we're doomed. I'll never be able to ignore these." Phyllis took an enthusiastic bite of cookie.

"Pretty much." Margaret smiled and tapped her cup to Phyllis's, who tapped hers back. *Cheers.* "So, linguistics, eh? I'm one of those English professors who's intimidated by people who can actually dissect a sentence or speak more than one language."

"And I couldn't get through a Dickens novel if someone offered me a free week in London in exchange. We all have our talents."

"I don't like Dickens, either," Margaret whispered.

They laughed, then talked more about how long each of them had been at the university, and who else they might know in common—no one, it turned out. But it was the easiest, most fun in-person conversation Margaret had had with anyone other than Gabe in ages. They were just exchanging phone numbers when one of the older women went to the head of the long table, rang a little bell, and, in a voice wrecked by years of smoking, said to the group, "Please, have a seat, everyone."

The women—thirteen of them now, Margaret saw with a quick count—sat around the table with their refreshed cups of coffee and napkins dotted with cookie crumbs.

"Good afternoon, everyone. I'm Harriet Glick of the art history department. I'm what's known as a dinosaur." The glee on her face and in her voice was irrepressible. "I've been here for forty years, and I'll have to become extinct before they cart me away. I began my career here as a graduate student, married to an economics professor. I was hired as an assistant professor as a favor to my husband, but I am happy to report that three children, seven grandchildren, and a near divorce later, my work has twenty percent more citations than does his."

There was an enthusiastic round of applause from the women at the table. As Margaret clapped politely, she snuck a glance at Phyllis, whose expression was inscrutable. She knew she ought to feel more solidarity and pride in Harriet's success, but Margaret sensed that Harriet's spirit of competition, with her own husband of all people, was somehow antithetical to a collective of women helping each other get further in their careers.

As Harriet went on to talk about "changing the culture at the university . . . hiring more women as faculty and *men* into staff positions . . . and cultivating relationships with our female students," Margaret's mind wandered to shameful, shallow things, like how any professor, even a tenured one, could afford the Chanel suit and large sapphire cocktail ring Harriet was wearing. Then Margaret reprimanded herself for thinking such thoughts in a room full of career women. She should be figuring out how to go get what she wanted *herself*, right? And that started with meetings like this one, with women digging in and helping each other. Because they certainly couldn't rely on the likes of Leo Robinson, the head of the English department, who, she'd already learned, assigned the female faculty and staff to bring homemade cookies to department parties and the males to bring whiskey.

After what seemed like an interminable amount of time, Harriet asked the group, "Do you have any questions? I'll put out a sign-up sheet for subcommittees, and you can add your name to whatever group suits your interests."

One of the young women asked, "Will this count as service to the university on our tenure reviews?"

Harriet bared her teeth in a frosty smile and answered, "Of course, dear."

Well. Margaret was glad she wasn't in the art history department! There was nothing worse than a woman who had it out for another woman.

Then again, it hadn't been a wise question. A girl had to find a way to ferret out that kind of information without sounding like she was trying to get away with something. Moments later, after signing up for the Mentor Students subcommittee because it was the only thing she felt qualified for as a junior faculty member, and being pleased that Phyllis put her name on the same piece of paper, Margaret and her new friend stood bundled up in scarves and coats at the edge of the quad, which looked positively majestic under its thin, frozen sheet of early snow.

Phyllis said, "Someone should tell her that you don't ask the lion where she keeps her stash of sheep."

"I suspect she knows now. Still . . . it's too bad it has to be that way. The whole meeting was supposed to be about women helping each other. And wasn't it called a collective? It felt pretty hierarchical to me."

Phyllis shrugged in a *c'est la vie* way. "I only went for the cookies." Margaret laughed.

"I wish I didn't see committee work as so pointless," Phyllis went on. "I may be a graduate student, but I teach and I write same as anyone else. I'll need recommendations as much as you'll need letters of support for your tenure reviews."

Margaret groaned. "I know I should be thinking of that, but I just got this job. I'd like to enjoy it first."

"Good luck with that."

"I'm clearly going to need it. Hey, it was really nice meeting you, Phyllis. Any chance you'd like to meet for lunch tomorrow?"

"Can't tomorrow. How about Thursday? Faculty lounge? Let's keep an eye on these battle-axes."

"It's a date." The unexpected connection with Phyllis sent a rush of relief and possibility through Margaret.

Campus was silent and stunning as she walked back to her office to gather a few things to take home, and again she couldn't believe her luck in landing a job here. *Luck's got nothing to do with it*, she heard her father tell her in her mind. *You worked hard for this.* He'd always been so proud of her. He was the only one in her family to be overjoyed when she'd gotten into a PhD program all the way across the country, which had seemed to her mother like earning a ticket to the moon. Mom had sulked for a week, continually asking, "Why California? Why not a master's degree closer to home? I'm sure you could get into Harvard, if name brand is so important to you. And then you could teach at Abbot Academy or Rosemary Hall." Her mother didn't seem to grasp or care about the difference between being a professor at a major university and being a teacher at the sister school to a small, if prestigious, all-male boarding school. It was so ironic, considering it had been her mother who instilled in her a desire to spread her wings through reading.

And I've actually done it, she thought as she walked past the Gothic buildings through the leafy quad. Other hallmarks of the Chicago skyline—the Wrigley, the Carbide and Carbon, the Tribune—were miles to the north, invisible from the gargoyle-and-ivy-covered splendor of the academic institution. It was as if the architects had tried to protect learning from the world. Not that true intellectual isolation was possible any longer, what with college campuses everywhere erupting in violence.

She remembered the scene that had unfolded on Sproul Plaza during her very first months at Berkeley, when the Free Speech movement had begun. A graduate student protester was manning a table for the Congress of Racial Equality and was arrested for not having a valid driver's license, which was really just an excuse to get rid of him and his radical pamphlets; things like that had been happening a lot on campus. He was put into a police car on Sproul Plaza—a campus quad not unlike the one she was walking through this very afternoon— and hundreds of students had peacefully surrounded the police car and sat down, so that it couldn't leave. And then lanky, wiry Mario Savio had climbed on top of the police car and spoken to the gathered students about freedom of speech and why they should oppose the restrictions on protest imposed on them by the regents of the university.

Margaret hadn't been on campus that day, but she'd watched and listened from the steps of Wheeler Hall two months later when Savio gave an impassioned speech to *five thousand* people gathered on Sproul and in the paved arteries connected to it: *There is a time when the operation of the machine becomes so odious, makes you so sick at heart, that you can't take part! You can't even passively take part! And you've got to put your bodies upon the gears and upon the wheels.*

Yes! She'd cheered with other students, her heart beating in time with the applause.

Her mother had called her that night hysterically crying after she'd watched the news, begging Margaret to come home. "Mom, don't worry. The campus is huge. I'm in the library all day, and I'm safe," she'd reassured her over and over.

"Promise me you won't take part? You won't use your body to stop the engine, or whatever he said? I just couldn't bear to lose you to such . . . madness."

"I promise," she'd said.

And she'd done her best to keep her head down. When asked, she'd voice a muted solidarity with the protesting students. *They have excellent points*, or *I think the regents should listen*. Even though a part of her cried out to participate, she kept her distance.

She didn't regret that choice. Not exactly. But now that her life felt more settled, she thought she'd like to take a stronger stand, make a little noise, for a cause she believed in. She had hoped the Women's Faculty Collective could be that. But after today's meeting, it was clear she needed a stiffer drink than what Harriet was offering.

Inside Walker Hall, a few other professors' offices glowed yellow, though doors were pointedly shut. Flipping on her own light and closing the door, Margaret looked around at all her books in satisfying alphabetical order by author, on one of the two walls of shelves. There was plenty of room for more as her knowledge and career grew. On those empty shelves, she'd arranged a smattering of pictures of family and friends; mugs and other knickknacks that reminded her of special occasions from the last decade of her life, including pennants from Cornell and Berkeley; and a small poster she'd purchased at an MLA conference that said in black script on a white page,

I will be calm. I will be mistress of myself.
—Jane Austen, Sense and Sensibility

Words to aspire to.

Just as Margaret finished filling her bag with papers to grade before bed that night, the phone rang.

She picked up and said, "Hello? This is Margaret Jones."

"I thought I might find you there."

Gabe.

Her heart galloped out of her chest.

"I was just about to head home," she said. "What are you up to?"

"How about you head over here instead?" His voice was so low and inviting. She had papers to grade, but . . . she could do those in the morning. She checked her watch. It was already five. She absolutely had to shower first.

"Give me an hour?"

He growled, and she felt the sound crackle down her body. "If I must."

"You must."

"I'll order us something for dinner. Have you had Italian beef sandwiches yet?"

"Once. They were delicious."

"You haven't had these ones, I bet, from the best place in the city."

"Yum."

"Hurry over."

She hung up the phone with her heart pounding in anticipation of being with him, though a little voice inside reprimanded her for not grading the papers first.

Stop it, she told herself. *I've earned a little time off, a little romance.*
With that, she hurried out the door.

6

VERONICA

A red stream flowed over her hands and faded to clear as water from the bathroom faucet chased blood down the drain. The water felt cool on her skin, and the rushing from the tap was soothing—a familiar, clean sound. Even once the curette was shiny and silver once again, Veronica stood at the sink watching and feeling the water and the surgical instrument, light and firm between her fingers.

She breathed deeply, trying to steady her stomach. The pregnancy had recently added nausea to her usual list of Service shift maladies, though she'd be damned if she let any of the brave women coming to her know that every single one of their vaginas made her feel like she was on a boat pitching furiously on an angry sea. This was never easy work, and her back and shoulders regularly twinged with exhausted pain from the tense hours of leaning forward and—as gently as she could—using forceps and flashlights and speculums to complete the day's roster of D&Cs.

Normally, she didn't mind the physical costs; normally, it felt like sitting down to an adventure. What secrets would this woman, this remarkable body, reveal to her? There was such astonishing variation—

browns and pinks and ruffles and serrations, soft spots and cysts, striations and smoothness, moles and warts and tears and lesions; hair of every brown and red and black hue. In the early months, it had been a trick to remain poker-faced when she was presented with an outbreak of some sort, lice or yeast or blood, and the range of largely maritime smells that went with those problems, but she'd mastered even that.

She soaped and rinsed a speculum, and continued to breathe. If the women coming to her could fight through the turmoil in their minds and bodies, so could she in her own. After all, she was the provider; she had the advantages of a safe home and a (usually) supportive husband and a healthy child and enough money in the bank to afford to have a second child growing inside her.

This was no time for self-indulgence. She'd done eleven so far today, and she had eight more to go.

Veronica shut off the faucet; dropped the last curette into the stainless steel lobster pot, where it clanked against a dozen others; hugged the pot to her; and opened the bathroom door. The hallway was quiet, but the living room it opened into was a hive of activity as always, every church sale sofa and chair in the carpeted room sprawled upon by women talking, reading, knitting, or darning as they either waited to get their abortion or recovered before being taken back to the Front. *Another World*, the second soap opera of the day, played quietly on the television in the corner.

She was proud of this apartment, which the Service had rented just six months ago to be a permanent Place where the abortions could happen; it was a spacious three-bedroom unit at the rear of a large, clean apartment building where there was plenty of coming and going: families with small children, young single professionals with roommates, and, she was pretty sure, two women working as prostitutes on the second floor. The building housed Black and white equally, which was essential because so many of the women Jane served were Black.

Veronica's favorite item in the Place was a beautiful framed water-color that Siobhan had painted of the female reproductive system based on the diagrams in *Our Bodies, Ourselves,* a radical women's health pamphlet published last year by a collective in Boston, com-plete with names for each and every part—vulva, clitoris, urethra, ovary, cervix. Powerful words. Like the Latin words priests of the Middle Ages didn't want commoners to know.

Next to it hung a poster Trudy had found at a garage sale, with the words **TODAY IS THE FIRST DAY OF THE REST OF MY LIFE** from the John Denver song blocked out in rainbow print. *Yes.* To her, that summed up everything the Service stood for. In some ways, Veronica was prouder of this Place than she was of her own tidy house, in which she packed healthy, colorful lunches for Kate and made sure everyone had clean clothes for work and school. *This* room was a vault of female secrets and sovereignty, with none of the shame or apologies that came from asking for what they wanted the moment they stepped outside.

She only wished they could unite the Place with the ever-changing Fronts they had to use as waiting rooms around Chicago, houses and apartments belonging to Service members where the people supporting the woman getting the abortion would await their return. But they had to protect themselves—and the women—and putting some distance between the crime and the bystanders had always seemed prudent.

No blindfolds, though. As soon as she and Siobhan had realized they could do the D&Cs themselves, that they could make the Ser-vice an entirely female organization, they had burned every scrap of fabric they'd ever used to take women to see male abortionists. In-stead, drivers between Fronts and the Place took a circuitous route and turned onto the apartment block from the corner where the street sign was hidden in a tangle of oak branches.

Veronica took the lobster pot of surgical tools into the kitchen, where she found Trudy making more coffee. The Service consumed *a lot* of coffee between Fronts and the Place; since they asked women not to eat before their abortions, it was the only thing with flavor they could consume for hours; afterward, women were always served a treat like a Danish or sandwiches or stew, depending on the time of day. When no-nonsense Trudy with her trusty black notebook and calculator took over the ordering of basic supplies, she quickly saw they went through two cans of Folgers every day, pretty consistently. Plus twelve extra-large boxes of Kotex, eleven boxes of Kleenex, nine cartons of plastic gloves, a gallon of bleach, and a partridge in a pear tree.

"How's it going?" Trudy asked Veronica as she turned up the heat on the other lobster pot, which was full of water on the stove.

"More vaginas than Mick Jagger sees on tour. And the same number with the clap."

Trudy snorted a laugh. "Ours are healthier overall, I bet."

"You don't think all that LSD makes for healthy pussies?"

"Don't you mean honky tonk pussies?" Holding an invisible mic to her mouth, Trudy sang, "Hooo-o-o-o-o-o-onky tonk pussies . . . Gimme, gimme, gimme . . . the . . . honky ton—"

The two of them laughed too hard for her to keep singing.

"That's as good as 'Blue Suede Balls.'" Veronica practically hiccuped her words, recalling Trudy's pee-in-your-pants-funny rendition of the Elvis classic from last year's holiday party.

When they recovered, Veronica wiped a tear from her eye and asked, "How are you, anyway? Still studying for the CPA exam?"

"I took it and passed," Trudy said with a proud smile.

"Congratulations! So what's next?" *And please don't tell me you have to quit the Service; you're the best, and we're short-staffed as it is.*

While she waited for the water to boil, Veronica listened to Trudy describe interviews at accounting firms and whether she might also want to study international tax law, and was immensely relieved when she concluded, "And don't worry, I'm going to stay at the Service. A new job just might mean I have to work nights and weekends instead of weekdays, though."

"Anything you want," Veronica said, meaning it. Trudy had come such a long way since her own abortion a year ago, one of the very first Veronica had performed with her own hands; then, Trudy had been ready to drop out of college and was high half the time, but the scare of the pregnancy and release of the abortion had woken her up to the life she wanted to live. A month later, she'd come back to Veronica and said she was going to stay in college and give up the weed and wanted nothing more than to work with the kindest women she'd ever known. And thank God, because no one could keep books like Trudy.

Veronica went to the cupboard and got out the Oreos. She unscrewed the top of one and licked out the creamy middle. The baby inside her just could not get enough junk food. Lately, she craved things she never would have eaten normally: every kind of grocery store cookie, flavored potato chips, and strawberry ice cream. Strawberry! Usually she hated strawberry; in fact, when faced with a carton of Neapolitan, she always scooped out the chocolate and vanilla and left the pretty but ultimately unappealing strip of pink untouched.

Danielle wandered in looking freshly showered, her wet hair pulled back in a ponytail, her jeans hanging off the blades of her narrow hips. Veronica inhaled deeply to see if she could detect the smell of pot, but thankfully all that hit her nose was the fruity scent of Danielle's shampoo; her eyes seemed to track pretty normally, too. What a relief. She'd shown up high to a shift about a month ago, and Veronica had sent her home, whispering furiously, *Never come here on any kind of drug again.* Way too much was at stake to risk it all on a sloppy D&C. Danielle had never come in smelling of anything worse than nicotine since then.

That day, Danielle was Veronica's partner in the OR for the afternoon, since Siobhan, who'd been her morning partner, had to leave to meet Kate and Charlie. Fingering her long braid with fingers denuded of their usual rings, since it was Service policy to pull back their hair and wear no jewelry when in the OR, Veronica admired the sliver of impossibly small, supple midriff that showed between Danielle's belt and shirt hem. Oh, to be twenty-three again. How was it possible thirty-one could feel so old?

"That guy is chain-smoking again on the corner," Danielle informed Veronica and Trudy as she poured herself a cup of coffee.

"The one in the Cubs cap?" Trudy asked.

"Yep." Danielle slurped her coffee, unperturbed. "You think maybe he's competition? Or, like, a Peeping Tom?"

"Nothing to peep here," Veronica said, enjoying the irony—what there was to see here would make most people, especially men, quake in their Cubs caps.

"Peep!" Trudy chirped, and the other two laughed.

"How many times have we seen him now?" Veronica asked. "Three? In as many weeks? Is he always here on the same day? Wednesday?"

"I think last time, Melanie saw him on a weekend," offered Danielle.

"Good thing we have friendlies at the precinct," said Trudy, looking to Veronica for verification.

"Yep, there're plenty of officers looking out for us." Every pore on her body erupted in goose bumps, however, as she thought about Officer Sam Wilder, who'd been champing at the bit to raid Jane for ages. They were safe because Wilder's boss, Chief Robert Sullivan, had sent his daughter to the Service, then recommended it to several other officers in the city, who sent their own wives and daughters and nieces and girlfriends to Jane and made them the safest open secret in Chicago. Doug's connections at the police station said those guys kept Wilder in line. Still, she worried about him occasionally. If she let herself think about him too often, she started to feel sick, so she'd walled him off in a part of her mind.

"How many D&Cs this afternoon?" Danielle asked, changing the subject as she opened the fridge and took out the sandwich supplies.

"Eight," Veronica replied.

"Ten," Trudy corrected her.

"What?"

"I had to add two more," she said apologetically.

This is why we need to hire more people. Veronica sighed.

"Tomorrow is full, too. I already added three to that schedule. You can go home, if you need to, and I'll do them," Trudy offered.

"I can stay late," said Danielle.

"I can't," Veronica said, filling with dread at the thought of the long afternoon ahead of her. "I need to meet a new prospective member tonight." Much as she hated to admit it to herself, she was starting to realize that she couldn't book her days quite so solid. The pregnancy just made her too tired, and she regretted her agreement to meet with this mysterious Phyllis, who'd insisted on meeting Veronica in person. But in order to maximize her time with Kate all the days she wasn't at the Service, she had to fill her workdays to the brim.

"That's fine, I can fill in tonight when you have to go," Trudy insisted.

"Thank you." Veronica sighed. "And I'm sorry."

"You've worked late a thousand times." Trudy shrugged, and even though it was true, Veronica felt guilty.

"Still. Thank you," she said again.

The pot of water had come to a rolling boil, so she began dropping the curettes and speculums from the other pot into the water for sterilization. Veronica liked these mundane tasks, when she felt like she was being productive but her mind could also wander, and she didn't have to be as fully present as she did every other minute of her life, when there were so many—*so many*—other demands on her time.

———

Valois was Veronica's favorite place to meet in the neighborhood. No matter the time of day, it smelled like cake and meat loaf, and on a cold day like this, the windows were steamy from the reassuringly moist heat inside. Her fingers were frozen because she'd walked the six blocks from the Place without gloves, her hands stuffed into the pockets of her peacoat, which had been a mistake, since November was already starting to feel like winter. Scanning the patrons at the square Formica tables, she looked for a woman wearing a red coat, as she'd been instructed to do on the phone. For the same reason, she'd tied a red scarf around the handles of her purse.

They recognized each other at the same time, their eyes meeting over three tables. So. Phyllis was Black, which was probably why she'd insisted on meeting in person instead of just coming to one of the open orientation meetings at the Union. *Thank God. We've needed someone who isn't white like us for ages.* Veronica thought of the woman at the fundraiser the other night with a surge of relief.

Veronica waved and headed over to where this woman was sitting with a cup of coffee and plate of apple pie à la mode. When she reached the chair on the other side of the table, she thrust out her hand and said, "Veronica Stillwell, Jane."

The woman in the red coat stood up and shook her hand. She was so tall. And all arms and legs. Gorgeous, too. "Phyllis Williams."

"That looks delicious." Veronica pointed at Phyllis's plate. "Let me just get something, too."

Phyllis nodded and sat back down.

"How's the pie?" Veronica asked.

"Not as good as my sister's, but it's alright."

The sight and smell of it was so sweet and promising, Veronica thought she could put away two or three dishes of it. With a cheese-burger. And fries. She was ravenous.

She made her way to the counter, glancing around as she went, not that anyone would be able to hear her conversation with Phyllis, as the diner was always so noisy with dishes and chatter, which was one of the reasons she invariably picked it for public meetings of the Service. She didn't want anyone from the Lab School, progressive as it was, to hear the wrong words escape her lips.

No one she knew was in sight, however, and so she relaxed as she went ahead and ordered two slices of pie and a large chocolate milk, *for the baby*. Back at the table, Veronica smiled as she set down her food and slid into a chair. "Nice to meet you, Phyllis. So tell me . . . how did you find out about Jane?" Veronica took a big bite of warm pie and cold ice cream and washed it down with the sweet milk. Heaven.

"So the fact that I'm Black isn't a problem?"

"Definitely not. In fact, I'm *glad* you're Black. We've wanted Black members, especially since New York made abortion legal last year, and more than half the women who come to us now are Black." And pretty much everyone was flat broke, or too proud or scared to ask family for money, since any girl with access to funds would fly herself to New York for a hospital abortion and the good drugs that went along with it. The Service had thought about going back to being a referral organization at that point, and figuring out how to bus women to New York, but all twenty-one women at the meeting where they'd discussed it felt that the need in Chicago, their hometown, was too great and too immediate. The Service needed to help local women.

Phyllis narrowed her eyes suspiciously, and Veronica took another bite as the other woman's ice cream melted and formed a puddle on the thick, chipped plate.

"So . . ." Veronica waved her fork in a circle between them, trying to lighten the mood. "Why Jane?"

"Well, a friend of mine went to you for an abortion about a month ago, and she observed that all of you are white but most of the women in your waiting room were Black. I bet that most of them would like to see someone like them, *Black* like them, on your side of the transaction."

"Exactly." Veronica liked Phyllis. She wasn't afraid to use the words. *Abortion. Black. White.* "And exactly why I'm glad you're here. Jane has only grown as like-minded women have drifted toward us, often as a result of their own abortions. Recruiting is difficult, as you might imagine. We have to rely on word of mouth."

"I've heard you don't always make people pay. Is that right?"

"We ask for a hundred dollars per abortion to cover costs. If a woman can pay more, we ask for a donation on top of that so we can run a scholarship fund. That means that anyone who can only afford twenty bucks pays just the twenty. We're all in this together, so we ask everyone to contribute what they can."

"That makes sense."

"I used to work in education, and I joined the Union, of course, and I was really inspired by the work they did around equality in education, so I've applied some of that thinking to Jane."

"You taught? Did you know Keith Johnson?"

"I did. The assistant superintendent? He was a rock star, especially after Freedom Day. How do you know him?"

Phyllis looked slightly embarrassed. "He's my boyfriend."

"Seriously? Well, I doubt he'd remember me, but tell him Veronica Stillwell said hi."

"I will. Did you do the boycott on Freedom Day?"

"I wish I had. But I was stuck at home with a newborn. A lot of my colleagues did it, though. The Chicago schools could be the absolute best in the nation if the higher-ups would listen to educators like Keith, who have such great ideas." *And if Keith loves you, you're hired,* she wanted to say, but that sounded too personal and unprofessional. "What a small world. Anyway. So. Tell me more about yourself. Do you have any special qualifications?"

"Depends on what you mean by qualifications. I don't have any medical training, but I hear you all are the first to admit you don't, either. And that you learned to do it because all the doctors were men and unreliable."

"That's partly true. Abortion is the only medical procedure any of us know how to perform. But as we like to say, it takes a vagina to know a vagina."

Phyllis laughed. Veronica went on, "And, true, the doctors were men and their fees were too high, and they made demands for a certain number of clients per week, and sometimes they took vacations without telling us. But the real reason we do it ourselves is because we are women. The people who come to us are women. And as you said, women want to be surrounded by others like them at a crucial moment like this in their lives. We don't ask them to tell the fathers. We say, *We're in this with you; we're doing this together.* So when we decided to take control of the process, we convinced one of our doctors, our very best, to teach me and one other Jane before he moved to California."

It didn't matter how often she said this, Veronica felt her heart fill with pride at these words. She *believed* in the Service. She wanted Kate—and this new life inside her, for that matter, girl or boy—to grow up surrounded by Janes. How she wished she herself had grown up that way; all she'd had was Aunt Martha, who was halfway around the world much of the time. Her own mother had spent her precious time on bridge and Scrabble and cocktails, supporting her husband with dinner parties and the community with charity events—which, Veronica was discovering as Kate's mother and Doug's wife, was only half a life. She often wished Patty's mother, whom she'd admired from afar all through their teenage years, had survived—not just for Patty's and Eliza's sakes but for her own as well. She'd have liked to see what Mrs. Callahan might have done with the second half of her life once both her girls were out of the house; she was the only mother in her childhood orbit who'd so much as attempted to work outside the home, starting as a librarian when Patty was in fifth grade.

Phyllis leaned back in her chair and studied Veronica for a few seconds before replying with a sly smile, "It takes a vagina to know a vagina."

"Exactly."

They each chewed a bite of pie, then Veronica said, "All joking aside, what do you do for a living? Tell me more about yourself."

"Well, I'm getting a PhD in linguistics at the university, and I've read Betty Friedan, though I don't think she or NOW goes far enough. I think it was a crime that Marlene Dixon was fired from the sociology department for being a socialist, and I prefer Audre Lorde to Maya Angelou. And I've repaired every broken car and dishwasher I've ever encountered, so I'd say I'm also good with my hands."

"Those do sound like solid qualifications." Veronica made a mental note to ask about Audre Lorde at the Seminary Co-op Bookstore. "I agree about Marlene. I sat in with the students when they protested." It was the last protest she'd gone to, in fact. The whole thing, being surrounded by nineteen- and twenty-year-olds unencumbered by husbands and children, so many exciting possibilities for summers and jobs and classes being bandied between them as they sat and sat and sat in Walker Hall, had made her feel old. "And linguistics? Like, the study of sentences?"

"More like the study of languages across cultures. I got interested when I did some traveling after college. I was a model for a few years."

"Wow."

"Everyone always says that."

"It just seems so . . . glamorous."

"It's not, I promise."

Veronica hoped she'd get close enough to Phyllis one of these days to find out more about this intriguing past—for now, she seemed like a locked box.

"Tell me more about the linguistics department."

Phyllis shrugged. "I'm one of three women in the whole place, and the only Black person. They like to think they're enlightened, but I have to be careful."

Veronica nodded. "I'm sure."

"With all due respect, there is no way you understand."

"Are you always this direct?"

"Yep. As often as I can be."

Veronica liked Phyllis more and more. She could see why Keith was with her. He called everything like he saw it, too, which had made him a lot of friends and even more enemies. In Veronica's opinion, everything he wanted for the Chicago schools was right on target.

"And," Phyllis went on, quieter now, "I had one myself. A long time ago. I was just a kid. But if I'd had that baby, I wouldn't be where I'm sitting today."

"You're like the Jane poster child, then."

Setting her fork down purposefully and lowering her voice, Phyllis said, "Let's get one thing clear from the start. I'm done modeling. I will never pose for other people's purposes again."

Veronica raised her hands between them, palms out. "Hey, I don't want you to do any posing or fronting for us. All I meant was that you took advantage of the freedom the abortion gave you, and you did something with your life. That's it. And it's one of the core values of Jane."

"Alright, then."

Sheesh, the woman could be a porcupine. But everyone at the Service had an edge of some kind; they needed one, to do the work.

"Okay," said Veronica, "so Jane requires fifteen hours a week, minimum. More if you can give it. If you want to learn to give the abortions, and I have the very strong impression that you do, then there is one two-hour meeting every Tuesday morning, one morning or afternoon weekday shift, and one long, grueling weekend shift. A few extra training sessions will get you started."

"I have that to spare. I'm done taking classes. I teach one class per semester and I'm working on my dissertation, so my time is mostly my own."

Offering her hand over their empty plates, Veronica said, "Welcome to the Service," just as she felt a stab of pain where her uterus met her cervix. No, she thought, *no no no no no*. This was a different sensation from the miscarriage cramps last time, but no less harrowing.

This cannot happen again.

Phyllis reached across and shook Veronica's hand as the pain dissolved, and the stack of bangles on her arm rang like a hundred tiny bells.

7

PATTY

"An illegal abortion ring? Here? In our neighborhood?" Patty whispered urgently, holding her coffee cup in one hand and a plate of Christmas cookies in the other. It was the day of the annual St. Thomas Women's League cookie exchange, and her house was decked out with two twinkling trees, fragrant boughs above the doorways, wreaths and holly and big plaid bows everywhere, and her beloved crèche from her honeymoon in France on the mantel in the living room.

"Not Kenwood. No, no. *Hyde Park*," clarified Jan Wilder, as if that explained everything, as if the church they were raising money for today wasn't *in* Hyde Park. But this was a common oversight, Patty had come to realize. As Hyde Park became more integrated, many families were disentangling from the neighborhood—very often moving out of it entirely—even as they clung to the church, which a lot of them had attended since childhood. But the geographical lines were blurrier than any of the talk made them sound.

The northern edge of Hyde Park was only three blocks away from her own house in coveted Kenwood, where many of her league guests that day lived, and while the two neighborhoods rivaled each other for graciousness and architectural interest, Kenwood's streets were lined with more uniformly large houses and yards that required gardeners. As comforting as she found the stalwart, stately homes around her, they did sometimes remind her of the stifling sameness of Park Forest. She'd thought that living in the bustling, dynamic city, to which she and Veronica would so often sneak on Saturdays in high school when they told their parents they were just going to a double feature, would make Patty feel more alive than she had in the suburbs. She couldn't escape the sense that the place she'd landed *in* the city was more like where she'd grown up than she'd expected. It was near the hospital, though, which was a necessary evil for Matt, who so often had patient rounds there. And really, who was she to complain about this beautiful home, with a bedroom for each child and an enormous kitchen with plenty of space for every gadget?

Outdated blond bob bouncing around her pearl earrings, Jan went on, "Sam's made it his mission to shut it down, but there are other officers protecting the organization, so he has to bide his time and look for the right opportunity."

Becky Cousins laid her right hand on her red sweater beside a crystal-encrusted Christmas tree pin. "God in heaven, I hope he prevails."

"Thank goodness Nixon's appointed this William Rehnquist to the Supreme Court," said Lilian, the oldest of the group of them, a former lawyer who'd quit to raise her third child, who had arrived eleven years after her second. *I don't want to miss it all again*, she'd told Patty a few years before, reminding her of her own mother, who'd just started back to work as a librarian when she'd gotten pregnant with Eliza, then quit to stay home with the new baby. "You know, the court will be hearing an abortion case that's sure to decide things one way or another in the coming year."

Patty watched as Jan's and Becky's eyes glazed over. Lilian had that effect on people sometimes, when she steered conversation to the law.

It must be hard for her, being a decade older than Patty and two decades older than the youngest mothers in the school. She'd had a whole career, a different kind of life. It had to be a challenge to fit in.

"Maybe Sam will succeed before the Supreme Court," said Becky.

"Goodness, I hope so." Patty shook her head. "The world seems to be coming apart at the seams." The holiday cheer around her suddenly looked like a farce. Cookies? *Abortion.* There was so much death everywhere. Vietnam. College campuses. Protests in the streets of her own city. At least soldiers and protesters knew what they were getting into. But babies . . . Patty couldn't even think about it. Especially when she knew of at least three couples at St. Thomas desperate to adopt a healthy child.

As Jan and Becky and Lilian nattered on, she wondered what Veronica would say if she was standing here. Nothing welcome to these ears, that's for sure. Veronica had been a member of the church's league back when Kate and Junie were small, but she kept trying to get the group to be louder about protesting the war in Vietnam and supporting women's lib causes like equal pay and universal child care.

"Vee, we want to stay home with our kids and raise money for schools and hungry children in Africa. It's like you're insulting us, but you're one of us," Patty had finally told her friend after a particularly contentious morning meeting where Veronica had made an impassioned speech about the need for women to stand up and fight for feminist causes in Chicago.

She half expected Vee to storm out at this honesty, but her friend had only said, "You know what? You're right." Then she'd quit the church group and joined the Women's Liberation Union. Not coincidentally, that was also when Veronica had started spending more time with Siobhan Johnson.

In the blur of green-and-red-clad people and glimmering lights around her, Patty felt bereft. Oh, she was surrounded by friends, but they were dinner party friends, not true confidants; none of them knew what Vee knew. Patty ached for the early days of their mother-hoods, when life had seemed *lighter,* full of the promise of brand-new strollers and uncracked books on how to keep your home and mar-riage humming once baby arrived. It was amazing what eighty thou-sand loads of laundry could do to a person.

I'll call Vee when the party's over. The thought was comforting, just enough to help her get through the afternoon, though it was a slog. Toward the end of the party, she found herself on the couch with Crissy and Becky, who were gossiping about Gabe and his new girl-friend, mostly traversing territory she'd already covered with Crissy on the playground a few weeks ago, which sullied the memory of her moment with the other mother. She'd thought the two of them had shared a confidence, not idle gossip.

"How do we find out more about her?" Crissy wondered.

"Someone should invite her to something," Patty mused.

Becky snapped her fingers and said, "I live around the corner from Gabe, so I can just happen to bump into her while I'm walking Cup-cake one morning. I already do, anyway. She always leaves around eight thirty, right after the kids have gone to school."

"But invite her to what?" asked Crissy. "A couples thing with Gabe? I always liked him. Siobhan is so . . ."

"Detached?" Becky offered.

So I'm not the only one who thinks so.

"Exactly," Crissy said.

"Let me feel her out and get back to you," Becky said, looking positively Machiavellian.

While the prospect of meeting Siobhan's ex's new girlfriend was certainly appealing, and it propelled Patty through the end of the party, she practically shoved the hangers-on out the door with a "See you tomorrow!" Once she was alone with the three college students she'd hired to help serve and clean, she put her favorite holiday album, *White Christmas,* on the turntable and hurried to finish the cleanup.

After bidding the helpers goodbye with hefty tips, she called Veronica. She just needed to hear her friend's reassuring voice, to reminisce for a few minutes about happier past holiday seasons. The past seemed so much safer than the present.

Ring.

Ring.

Ring.

Ring.

Ring.

Ring.

Ring.

At last she placed the receiver back on the hook. Veronica never seemed to be around lately. Shouldn't she be home *more* with a baby on the way?

Perplexed, Patty was about to set the needle on Bing and Peggy one more time, when Tad and Junie came charging into the kitchen.

"Is it time for *Rudolph* yet?"

Oh, God. How could she have forgotten?

She checked her watch. It was six o'clock already.

Was Matt even home? Where had he gone to get out of the way of the party? She couldn't remember.

"*Rudolph* starts in an hour," she said to the children.

"Can we have some cookies, then?" June begged.

"Cookies with the show, fish sticks and carrots first."

Banging around the kitchen for what felt like the thousandth time that day, Patty wondered again where Veronica and Matt, friend and husband, were at six on this Saturday night. Maybe Vee and Doug had left Kate with a sitter and gone to a movie. Maybe the three of them were all out to dinner together. Patty couldn't remember the last time she and Matt had done either of those things.

Once the kids were at the table inhaling their dinner, Patty went in search of Matt. He wasn't in the bedroom. Nor in the rec room downstairs watching a game. The door to his office was closed, and she saw a light from inside cast its glow under the door and into the hall. She knocked gently and said, "Matt?"

Her hand went automatically to the doorknob, which was locked. She jiggled it.

"Matt?"

She heard some shuffling inside and Matt's voice saying, "Be right there."

He took long enough to open the door that by the time he did, her heart was racing and her voice was strangled. *What has he been doing?*

She peered into his office, and it didn't seem any different. Her eyes landed on the phone, and a horrible thought occurred to her: *Was he on the phone with someone? Another woman? What was the shuffling about?*

"Everything okay?" she asked as calmly as she could, even as she realized that the idea of Matt having an affair seemed to answer all her other questions about why he'd been so distant, so disinterested in sex, so *gone* so much of the time.

"Everything's fine," he assured her, hastily turning out the light and giving her a quick kiss on the cheek. "How was the party?" Then he shut the door firmly behind him.

"Fine." She nodded. "Good." *But nothing is good! I want to throw up.*

"Fish sticks?" he asked, sniffing the air.

"For the kids," she replied, realizing that she hadn't thought about what to serve the two of them. Mentally, she checked the contents of the fridge. Oh, right, yes, she'd gotten steaks yesterday. Yesterday: when the world still made a modicum of sense. "I'll make us something while they watch *Rudolph*."

"*Rudolph*." He smiled. "I love that one." With another kiss on

Patty's cheek, he set off to join their children, whistling the tune about the misfit reindeer with the red nose.

After about three steps he stopped, turned around, and said, "Let's all watch it together. We can order something for us to eat, and you can rest. I know how that party takes it out of you."

"Okay," she said, her stomach churning and her mind ablaze with questions and fears.

"Chow mein?" he asked.

"Sure."

"I'll call it in. Pour yourself a glass of wine and put your feet up."

She nodded. What on earth had put him in the best mood she'd seen him in for weeks?

8

VERONICA

White flakes swooped in the wind as Kate bounded out of the school building, backpack bouncing on her shoulders. "Mom!" She flung her arms around Veronica's hips, her cheek pressing into her mother's stomach. Her heart felt as tender as a bruise when it came to these little moments with her daughter.

She bent over and kissed Kate's head.

"I thought Charlie's mom was picking me up today," Kate said, slipping her hand into Veronica's.

"I missed my girl," she said, steering them both toward home. "Charlie and her mom are meeting us at the house in about an hour, which gives us just enough time to make some brownies, if you feel like it?"

Kate's eyes widened. "Yummy, brownies," she said.

Veronica's spirits lifted with her daughter's. The truth was, she'd needed a break. Though today was only a counseling shift, she'd complained about some back pain, prompting Melanie—the one trained nurse among them—to tell her she should go home and rest. Even that she'd cover the rest of Veronica's shift if necessary.

Walking down the street with her daughter, feeling perfectly fine now, Veronica felt silly. She should be at work. *Okay, now* that *is silly,* she corrected herself. *Enjoy Kate.*

When they got home, she put on Elton John's brand-new album, *Madman Across the Water,* which all three of them had become obsessed with. Kate squealed and clapped when she heard the notes of the first song, "Tiny Dancer," and immediately started twirling around the kitchen.

"Daddy's teaching me how to play this song," Kate said as Veronica got out the brownie mix, eggs, oil, bowls, and measuring cups.

"Oh, fun. Want to show me?"

Kate shrugged. "No, I want to make brownies with you." Then, stepping up on the little stool they kept at the counter so she'd be taller, Kate nuzzled her head against Veronica's shoulder. *How can I leave her in an hour?* She felt so divided. As often as she felt she wasn't giving enough to the Service, she was equally jealous of the time Doug and Kate spent together when she worked weekends, when the two of them would have all kinds of fun, from a university basketball game to his mini piano lessons on the baby grand they'd inherited from his parents when they downsized to a condo.

It was easy to forget now, but Doug had been a piano "prodigy," to use his mother's term; he swore he was just "mildly talented," but he'd competed all over the country when he was a boy. By the time he was sixteen, he'd decided he'd had enough, and didn't play for almost a decade. "I hated it by then. I couldn't even hear the beauty in the notes anymore," he'd told Veronica in their dating days. For years, he refused to play so much as "Happy Birthday" on his parents' beautiful Steinway—which, they always told their son and daughter-in-law, they kept in perfect tune, just in case he changed his mind.

Then, during the horrible Christmas of 1963, when everyone was arguing about everything from John F. Kennedy's assassination and LBJ's policies on Vietnam to the "best" kind of gravy (with or without giblets?), Doug had sat down at the piano he hadn't touched in a decade and played "Greensleeves." Then "White Christmas" and "Little Drummer Boy" and even "Here Comes Santa Claus." What a gift. Veronica had been in awe of his gentle fingers gliding over the keys, the gorgeous sound he coaxed out of the gleaming instrument. Everyone had stopped arguing to listen, then applaud. He'd changed the whole mood of the night. She liked to joke that his playing saved Christmas.

After that, he'd play on special occasions. At Easter a few years ago, when toddler Kate plopped down on the piano bench in her grandparents' former home, Doug sat next to her and said, "Want to see?" and he'd played a Chopin nocturne that was so moving, Veronica had to excuse herself to wipe away tears in the bathroom. These days he played almost entirely with Kate, but once in a while, if Veronica requested something, he'd play it for her. "What's it like to play now?" she asked him once. "I'm still trying to figure that out," he replied. This musical past intensified her attraction to him, and she loved that he'd been playing more lately, by himself as well as with their daughter. He'd started spending an hour most evenings puzzling out radio songs at the piano.

As Elton John serenaded them, Kate and Veronica got the brownie batter together and into the oven. Siobhan and Charlie arrived just as the scent was permeating the air, and even though it was barely three thirty, it was dark as night outside and Veronica felt exhausted.

"It feels like we're going to get a foot of snow," said Siobhan as she hung up her coat and Charlie's on the hat rack in the front entry of the house, a classic Hyde Park greystone with the front bay window and wood paneling throughout the narrow downstairs.

"Hey, Kate, give me a hug before you head upstairs, okay?" said Veronica.

Kate obeyed, giving her mother a tight but perfunctory hug, then charging up to her room with Charlie.

"When do you think they'll ask what it is we do when we go to work?" Veronica asked Siobhan.

"Charlie's already asked me, though I suspect the question actually came from Gabe."

"What did you tell her?"

"I lied and told her I was teaching a painting class to women."

Jane was a thread they could not afford to have Gabe pull, not only because of what he might do with the information that his ex-wife—with whom he was still furious for leaving him—was involved in an illegal activity, but also because it could lead him back to the very origin of the Service. *I just can't have another baby with him,* Siobhan had whispered to Veronica, her tone strangled by grief and fear and anguished secrecy as the girls role-played princess and dragon up-stairs.

"Well, at least the women part is true."

"That's why I say it."

Veronica glanced at her watch. *Shit, I'm late.* "I have to get going. I'll probably be a little after seven tonight."

"No problem."

"There's a chicken and potatoes and carrots, and . . ." It was their long-standing arrangement for whichever of them was home with the girls to get dinner started. Thankfully, Doug never complained and only joked about Siobhan being his second wife.

"I'll figure it out. Go."

"Save me a brownie."

"If you're lucky." Siobhan winked.

Veronica smiled, shrugged into her coat, and hurried out. It was still hard to believe sometimes that the daily tasks of family life could coexist with the illegal work of the Service.

But that was exactly the point, wasn't it?

They *had* to coexist. *Children and independence. Brownies and*

*curettes. Babies and abortions. Quitting piano and playing piano. New
friends and old friends. Life and death. Holidays and every days. Snow
and sun,* she added to her mental list of not-actually-opposites as she
pulled her hat down over her ears and stuffed her hands into the pockets of her coat, and kicked the white flakes on her way to her shift.
What would any one of them be without the other?

A long, black-and-white police car marred the genteel block on which
Marion Gilbert's home was located. It was just sitting at the corner,
three houses down from Marion's, where the counseling sessions were
taking place that snowy day. Usually this was Veronica's favorite location to work, with its magazine-worthy interior and former servants'
quarters of three little rooms and a separate side entrance, which
Marion gave over to Jane for counseling sessions once a month.

Marion Gilbert was Jane's least likely member, as she was in her
late forties with two children already in college, one of whom had
needed Jane's services about a year before. Her daughter had had such
a good experience with Siobhan and Trudy, Marion had volunteered
to help the organization however she could, which included consider-
able donations to the scholarship fund as well as offering her home
when her husband was out of town—which was frequently. Her one
stipulation was that no actual abortions take place on the premises,
which Veronica respected. Jane was composed of concentric circles of
women, and while some moved from the outer circles to the inner,
many of those in the outer circles had no desire to get anywhere near
the actual service Jane provided.

The police car had not been there earlier when she'd left to get
Kate.

She had to pass it on her way to the servants' entrance, and her
heart started beating faster as she neared. Out of the sides of her eyes,

she tried to glimpse who was inside. The officer in the passenger seat was a kid she didn't recognize, but in the driver's seat was the unmistakable eraser head of Sam Wilder. She felt his eyes on her, but she kept walking with purpose. Instead of going to the side entrance, she went right to Marion's front door and rang the bell.

Surprised, Marion opened the door and said cheerfully, as if nothing was out of order, "Come in, come in."

"Thanks."

As soon as the door shut behind her, Melanie and Phyllis came out from the kitchen into the grand foyer and gave Veronica nervous looks.

Veronica looked at the perfectly coiffed Marion, whose hair couldn't possibly still be that shade of brown naturally but who managed to wear it as effortlessly as her black wool slacks, claret-hued sweater, and pearls. "Do you have a couple of coffee mugs you don't mind donating?"

"I'm sure I can find some," she said, heading into her kitchen, where she rummaged around in a lower cabinet and produced two white McDonald's mugs that said *You deserve a break today* on them. One of them was chipped at the lip.

"Perfect," said Veronica. Then she filled them with coffee and headed back out onto the street, aware that the women inside were watching her discreetly from a window.

She marched right up to the police car and stopped at the driver's side window, where Sam sat in his pristine blue uniform and crew cut, which had the effect of making him look younger than he was; he was probably ten years older than Veronica, with his oldest kid a teenager by now, barely younger than the kid sitting in the passenger seat. Back when she occasioned St. Thomas with Patty, she'd see Sam Wilder and his large family taking up most of a pew.

He rolled down the window when he saw her, and she handed him one mug of coffee, while reaching a little into the car to give the second to the boy, who seemed frozen in place, terrified. "I thought you could use something hot to drink while you sit out here in the cold," she said.

If Wilder was surprised by her brazen move, he didn't show it; he casually took both mugs and said, "How thoughtful of you."

"I can bring you some milk if you like," she said, leaning over so she could smile at the boy on the passenger side. She wondered if being in the police force was what had saved him from having to go to Vietnam like most kids his age. Or maybe he'd already done a tour. She doubted it, though. He didn't look at her, and swallowed nervously as he kept his eyes glued to the windshield. "Make sure he lets you take a break," she said to him, smiling sweetly.

"I will, ma'am," the boy said, still not looking at her.

Fixing her eyes on Wilder again, she said, "What are you looking for on this lovely street? Is there anything we women should be concerned about?"

"We'll let you know if there is, Mrs. Stillwell."

She nodded. "I certainly hope so."

The two of them stared at each other for a few seconds. The boy swallowed once more, his Adam's apple bobbing above his blue collar.

"Enjoy the coffee." Then she rapped her knuckles lightly on the car door and went back into the house, her heart thudding to beat the band.

Back in the foyer, she was greeted by Marion and Phyllis and Melanie, and as soon as they made eye contact with Veronica, all of them burst out laughing.

"That was brilliant," said Melanie.

"A worthy purpose for those hunks of ceramic," agreed Marion.

When they'd gotten ahold of themselves, Veronica said, "Okay, we proceed as normal today. We aren't doing anything except talking.

Wilder's just trying to rattle us, and now he knows we're not rattled, so maybe he'll slither on home. But, Marion, I'd understand if you didn't want us to use your house again after this. I'm sorry."

"What? And miss all the fun?"

God, I love the women of the Service.

"The girls who come to us today might need some extra reassuring," said Phyllis, "especially if they're south siders."

"Good thing you're here to help with that," Veronica said.

Just then the dull buzzer at the servants' entrance sounded, and she and Phyllis and Melanie hurried to answer it.

Time flew by. Wilder left after about an hour. Veronica's last woman of the day called herself Holly Brown, and she came into the room wearing a long black coat, a ski hat, a scarf wound up to her nose, and sunglasses, despite the fact that it was evening. Disguises, like aliases, were not unusual. She'd seen it all: wide-brimmed hats, oversized sunglasses, wigs, construction coveralls, vampire capes with high collars. And most women ditched them after the counseling session, when so many of their fears were put to rest.

Holly Brown hurried inside, and Veronica closed the door gently behind her.

"Please, have a seat." Veronica gestured to the love seat opposite the armchair she'd been sitting in all day.

Once they were both facing each other, Veronica said, "Holly, I'm afraid I have to ask you to take off at least the sunglasses, scarf, and hat. We understand the desire for anonymity in getting here, but it's impossible to maintain in these rooms. We show you our faces, when most abortionists do not. In fact, we started out as a referral service, sending women to doctors who required anonymity, and we came to feel that was antithetical to the process. We must trust each other. We are all women here, and I hope you'll leave here today feeling you don't have a single thing to hide or be ashamed of. We certainly don't think you do."

A few seconds ticked by before Holly began to slowly unwind her scarf, pull off her hat, then pluck off her sunglasses.

Her face was familiar, but it took Veronica a second to place her.

Senator Smith's daughter. Not Holly, but Heidi. Heidi Smith. Her father had paraded her around on every campaign for the state senate, along with his beautiful blond wife and quiet, round-cheeked son. As everyone knew, Smith's daughter was a sophomore at the University of Illinois at Chicago Circle—*not* the University of Chicago or Yale, where she'd also been accepted, as her father was fond of pointing out whenever he was asked about the state of public education in Illinois. Keith had hated this guy; he said Smith was all talk and no action about public education.

Heidi wasn't the first famous or important person to come to the Service. Since they officially started calling themselves Jane, they had helped three actresses, the daughters of two judges, a union boss's mistress, the wife of a powerful Presbyterian minister, and a mobster's girlfriend. Veronica's rule about such women had always been the same: treat them exactly like anyone else.

"Thank you," said Veronica, as Heidi began shrugging out of her coat, revealing a Yale sweatshirt a size or two too big, which was often a sign a pregnancy had progressed into the second trimester, but Heidi still looked slim beneath the baggy top; there was no telltale bulge. With a shaky sigh, the girl sat back on the love seat and shoved her hands between her blue-jeaned thighs.

She does not want to be here.

"It's okay, we're only talking today," Veronica said, using the tone she'd want someone to use with Kate.

Tears rushed immediately to Heidi's eyes, the rims glowing red. She swallowed loudly and nodded.

"You've taken an enormous step in coming here today, and you should be proud."

No nod this time, just a glassy stare fixed on the richly colored

Persian rug covering the hardwood floors. Veronica wondered why Heidi hadn't gone to New York, but then quickly answered the question for herself: word would then get out that the senator's daughter was pregnant. She'd come here for discretion.

"Jane does ask that you tell us a bit about your circumstances, so that you can have the best possible experience. You don't have to use any real names. And I have some information for you as well. Where would you prefer to start? With my information or yours?"

"Yours." The syllable was sopping wet with pain and sadness.

"First, there is no reason to feel shame or regret. No matter how you got here, it's okay." While there was some possibility that Heidi— or any of the women who came to the Service—was the victim of rape or incest, the overwhelming likelihood was that this was an accidental pregnancy, the result of the appalling difficulty in procuring birth control. It was hard to know exact ratios because the Service didn't— couldn't—keep records, but anecdotally, sexual violence accounted for a far smaller number of pregnancies than did those made in relationships where there was consent, and even love, but other circumstances made having a baby unimaginable. In some ways, the women Veronica admired most were the wives who came to the Service because they knew they could not have one more child; it was wrenching to say no to a child conceived in love if money, health, a career possibility, or ten thousand other reasons made keeping it impossible, but it was also so amazingly, affirmingly liberating, in the true sense of "women's lib." Every woman who said no to a system that kept women barefoot and pregnant, every woman who instead embraced her own independent future, in which she made her own choices *thank you very much*, was one woman closer to equality.

Heidi still wouldn't look at her, and in fact Veronica's words only seemed to make her shake and swallow back more sobs, which wasn't a surprise. The counseling rooms of the Service were very often the first place in their lives where these women heard their choices validated. Their default emotions, Veronica had learned, were guilt, shame, and devaluation. So it was a lot to take in, this notion that there was nothing wrong with them, that their feelings mattered.

Gently, Veronica went on, taking one of the Service's birth control pamphlets off the stack on the table beside her and handing it to Heidi. "One of Jane's most important goals is to help women take control of their lives by helping them control their bodies, so that *you* can decide when you want to have children. An essential way to do this is to prevent an unwanted pregnancy in the future. Have you heard of these methods of birth control?"

The girl took the pamphlet from Veronica and didn't even look at it. "Our condom broke."

Veronica nodded. "That happens. Which is why there's information there on how to get on the birth control pill even if you're not married."

Heidi laughed bitterly. "Yeah, right. And risk having the doctor call my father?"

"The doctors on our list will not violate your privacy that way. There's one in particular you could go to, whom I could call first, to make sure."

"You'd do that?" Heidi raised those bloodshot eyes, suddenly full of surprise and hope.

"Of course I would."

Whatever flimsy emotional container the senator's daughter had built inside herself busted open, and she broke down in heaving sobs. "I'm so sorry."

Veronica moved from the chair to the love seat and put an arm around Heidi while she cried.

One minute ticked by.

Two.

Three.

Four.

Finally, Heidi evened out her breathing, blew her nose one more time, and looked at Veronica. "I wish I didn't have to do this."

"Of course you do. Would it help to talk about why you are doing it?"

"I don't want to embarrass my father."

"I can understand that, but this is a decision you have to make for *you*."

"It doesn't matter what I want. If it were up to me, I'd keep it. My boyfriend and I . . . we love each other."

Veronica suspected the girl's boyfriend went to Yale, hence the security blanket of a sweatshirt.

"You could keep it, you know. I'm here to help you make the right choice for you."

"Daddy's got an election coming up. I can't do that to him."

"You're not doing anything to him." Veronica couldn't quite believe she was trying to talk the girl into keeping the child. But what if the right thing for this girl's future as a liberated woman was to defy her father and keep the child? That was possible. It was hard to tell.

"You don't understand." Heidi shook her head.

"This is *your* decision. No one else's."

Senator Smith's daughter made full eye contact for the first time, and for a second, Veronica saw it: the nascent strength, the power, the ability to make the hardest choice of her life so far and live with the consequences.

But it was fleeting.

Her face crumpled once again, though there were no more tears.

"Listen, how about this? Take another day to think. If you want the baby, you *can* keep it. There are resources available to help you, and we can help you find those. Call me at this number." She scribbled her home number on an index card, which she *never* did. After a year of answering a second phone line that rang off the hook, she'd given the role of "Hello, this is Jane," to Danielle and Siobhan, who not only answered calls but also delegated the duty to other Janes on a rotating basis.

Heidi nodded vacantly.

"Do you have a good friend you can talk to today?"

Another nod.

"Talk to her. Think it through. Then call me tomorrow."

Veronica helped the girl back into her coat, scarf, hat, and sunglasses, and then she told herself sternly not to give her a fierce hug and tell her everything would be okay. She was this girl's counselor, not her mother.

"Tomorrow," she said again, but got no reply.

"I hope she calls," she said to Doug as she finished relaying the eventful afternoon to him while they lay in bed after making love, the lamp on his side of the bed filling the room with a warm, dim light. They'd had such a nice evening after she got home from her shift. She'd returned just in time to enjoy Siobhan's delicious chicken soup and homemade bread slathered with butter and honey, plus a brownie, with Doug, Kate, Siobhan, and Charlie.

In an expansive Friday night mood, Doug and Kate had pounded out a few Christmas carols at the piano while everyone sang along, then Doug had surprised everyone with a positively cinematic version of "I'm a Believer" that had Kate and Charlie squealing with laughter and dragging their mothers into the center of the living room to do the twist. Then, he'd given her a sidelong glance as he twiddled a few bars of "I Want to Hold Your Hand," and Veronica felt his desire tug her close. Once Siobhan had finally extracted an oversugared and overtired Charlie to head home, Veronica and Doug rushed Kate to bed so they could savor the best part of the evening, just the two of them.

Her head was on his chest now, and her right arm was wrapped around his warm form. When she'd started telling him about her day, he'd been playing with her hair as he often did in these moments, but she noticed now that he had stopped, and in fact, his hand was resting inertly on her shoulder.

He didn't reply.

"Hey, did I bore you to sleep?"

"No."

He sounded angry. But why? She'd been so careful to tell the story about Sam Wilder as a comedy, and a win. Her stomach began to churn, and she felt her exposed arm get cold.

"Talk to me?"

He sighed and kissed the top of her head. "I really want to be able to laugh at Wilder with you. I know we used to do that, and I loved it. God help me, I *still* love that you're ballsy like that. I remember when we met, you were sitting in the dean's office refusing to leave unless they got you a seat on the Freedom Bus. You were ferocious and brilliant. I loved you right away."

"But you're worried about the baby," she said, rolling off of him and lying shoulder to shoulder with him. She was getting tired of this *protectiveness* of his. She didn't need protecting.

"It's not just that, Vee, although I feel like that should be enough," he said, and she could hear the impatience in his voice, too, now. "What if Wilder actually nabs you? What if we wind up in court? We could lose this house. We could lose the life we've built together."

"Wait. You're not just suggesting I take time off for the baby? You're suggesting I quit?"

"I'd like to at least talk through our options."

"I'm not quitting, Doug. Jane is *mine*."

He didn't reply. So. That was what he really wanted, for her to stop being Jane.

"I thought you didn't want me to be Carol Brady. Or Patty."

"I don't! There is a world of difference between Carol Brady and a woman who can't see her kids because she's in jail. I want you to have a career. Work in politics, if you want to make a difference. I'd hold your hand on every stage and cheer you on."

"Why is this all of a sudden getting to you? We've talked about the risks of Jane at every step of the way, and you've been supportive."

"Things moved slowly. For a long time, I thought everything would be okay. I have tried to talk myself out of being worried, believe me. But our situation has changed. We're going to have a second child. Sam Wilder is out for blood. Abortion is getting more attention because of the case the Supreme Court is hearing."

"But we're as protected as we ever were. It's not like dozens of important people haven't known about us for two years. Cops and priests and rabbis and city councilmen."

"That actually makes me more nervous than it did before, because it means that the target on your back is brighter red."

"Don't be melodramatic, Doug."

"Vee, I do this for a living, remember? I'm a criminal attorney. I see how this shit works. You are in danger. We are in danger."

"Do you think Coretta said all of this to Martin? Or Eleanor to FDR?"

"I certainly hope they did."

Veronica folded her arms over her chest. He could be so annoyingly fair-minded.

"Anyway, King and Roosevelt were trying to change the system, not commit a crime within it."

"Doug, that's low. You know as well as I do that what we do empowers women, and more empowered women mean better voters, better citizens, and better mothers. A *better system*." Still, his comment stuck in her craw. The Service *was* protest work, as surely as marching on Washington or writing letters to senators. Ironically, though, the work was so overwhelming, it didn't leave any time or energy to perform those other system-changing tasks. She wrestled with the guilt of that sometimes.

He rolled onto his side so he could look at her face, though she stayed on her back, eyes fixed on the ceiling. "I do know," he said in a softer tone. "I love your passion. I don't mind coming home to Siobhan instead of you some nights, as long as I know you'll get home eventually."

She wanted more than anything for this conversation to end, so she said the only thing she could think of to end it. "I'll think about it."

"Alright," he said, and though both of them tossed and turned all night, neither of them said another word to the other, and Veronica couldn't shake the sense that she'd just lost her best friend and closest ally. Was this the true cost of liberation?

9

MARGARET

"Hello?"

"Hello, sweetheart. I've missed you! This new job of yours is keeping you awfully busy."

Shoot. She almost regretted picking up the phone. It had been way too long since she'd talked to her mother, but she was in a rush to get ready for a date with Gabe.

"Hi, Mom. I've missed you, too. How's Dad?"

"Oh, he's fine. Working almost as much as you and on a flight to Vancouver as we speak, so tonight I'm babysitting for Clark and Wanda so they can have a nice meal out. I can't wait because little Terri is getting ready to crawl! She's so cute when she gets up on her hands and knees and rocks back and forth, like she's getting ready to go, go, go!"

"Sounds adorable." And it did. Margaret just wished she didn't hear the underlying message: *If you don't hurry up, you'll miss out on all of this!*

And lucky Clark, her brother who ran a ski school at the mountain near where they'd all grown up. The fact that she'd never liked skiing—and she was the only one in the family who didn't—should have been her first clue that she didn't belong in Maine. She wished she had; maybe then her life would be easier, like her brother's.

"Anyway, your father and I celebrated our anniversary weekend with some antiquing in Portland, and fish and chips at your dad's favorite place. Something for him, and something for me. I got a lovely little Queen Anne console."

"Oh, gosh, Mom, I'm sorry I forgot. Happy anniversary!" *Shit.* She hadn't been good recently about checking her agenda with all the important dates in it—birthdays, anniversaries, and whatnot. On a little pad by the phone, she dashed off a note to herself in dark black pen: *CARD FOR MOM AND DAD.* Margaret sat in her own faux Shaker kitchen chairs and looked at the deco clock on the wall beside the oven that her mother had bought for her at one of those antiques stores in Portland. Apparently, it had been made by a famous clockmaker sixty years ago.

"It's alright, Margaret." Her tone said the opposite, though.

I have to throw her a bone. "There's actually another reason I've been so busy lately. I . . . I've been seeing someone."

"Oh?"

Oh, God, I'm really doing this: opening the door to a thousand questions and future interrogations. "His name is Gabe Johnson and he's a history professor here. I actually met him a few years ago when he was a visiting professor at Berkeley. He's great. We have a lot in common." *And he's divorced and has a seven-year-old daughter.*

"Well, I admit I did hope this was the reason you'd been so hard to reach lately. But you get rather absorbed in your work, so I didn't dare . . . Anyway! Tell me more. Where is he from?"

"Michigan."

"How old is he?"

"Thirty-eight."

"A decade older than you! Goodness, has he been married before?"

Yes indeed, we are doing this. "He has, and he has one daughter."

"Well, I suppose at your age you can't hold out for a nice unmarried man. And the widowers are too old to have more children. Does he want to get married again?"

Geez, Mom, this is why I don't tell you anything. "I don't know. We've only been going out a few weeks."

"Well, I hope you talk about that soon so you don't waste your precious time."

"I'm sure we will. Hey, Mom, I'm actually supposed to meet him soon, and I still need to put on my face." *You'll approve of that, no doubt.*

"Why don't you wear that lovely blue sweater from last Christmas? It brings out the color of your eyes."

"I wore it on our first date."

"I knew it was perfect when I picked it out at Filene's." Despite it all, Margaret felt a pang of nostalgia for their mother-daughter fall and spring trips down to Boston, when they would stay one night in a hotel near the Common, visit the Museum of Fine Arts, and carefully paw through every rack and bin at Filene's Basement; they would each leave with at least two bags full of new clothes, thriftily purchased. She still wore a few pieces she'd found there years ago—a classic belted trench coat, an A-line black dress—and got compliments every time she put them on.

"It is perfect," she agreed.

"Have you worn the corduroy dress yet?"

Got rid of that three years ago, since it made me look like an undergrad. "Good idea. I'll look for it."

"Have a *wonderful* time," gushed her mother.

"Thanks, Mom. Have fun at Clark's."

"Have you heard from Harriet since the meeting?" Phyllis asked as she and Margaret walked from Medici, where they'd just met for egg sandwiches and coffee before their first classes of the day. The sky was stone gray, and flakes drifted unenthusiastically from the clouds.

"Yeah, she sent me five or six female students to advise on preparing for graduate school."

Phyllis laughed and shook her head. "Figures. She never called me."

"Because . . ." *You're Black?*

"I'm Black."

"That's what I thought."

"You can say it, you know."

"I'll work on that."

"Anyway, there aren't many Black undergrads to advise."

"She could send you anyone, though."

"*Could.*"

"This is ridiculous. Can we do something?"

"About Harriet? Nah, there's not much point. Her day's coming soon. She can ride off into the sunset with her citations and grandchildren. By the time she retires, the high school kids I'm tutoring downtown will be filling the seats in her old classrooms. Plus, I have some other irons in the fire."

"Is there anything I can do? I've got a little free time."

"Your hot new man isn't keeping you busy enough?"

"He is . . ." Margaret flashed to Aaron and how hard it had been to get over him, and to the way she'd felt on the steps of Wheeler Hall. "I want to prioritize more than just my relationship, you know? But since you brought him up, I was wondering if you'd want to get together for a double date? You and Keith?"

"I think we could manage that. How about this weekend?"

"I wish we could, but we were invited to some shindig with the parents of some friends of his kid. We're going to Jenny's."

Phyllis whistled. "Parent friends and prime rib. Now *that* sounds hot."

Margaret laughed. "I know, I know."

"Don't get old before your time, friend."

"You know I'm twenty-eight, right?"

"I'm twenty-nine! It's all up here, anyway." Phyllis tapped her temple.

"Fair enough. How about next Thursday?"

"A school night. Now you're talking. Might have to be in our neighborhood, though."

"Fine by me."

"We'll see if this Reconstruction professor of yours can put his feet where his brain is. You never know with these guys. They talk a good lefty game, and then . . ." Phyllis wiggled her fingers as if dissipating smoke, implying that Gabe might not be willing to put his ideals into action.

"I feel certain he'll be fine. And you're being evasive about those other irons in the fire."

Phyllis stopped walking, so Margaret did, too, and her friend studied her closely for a minute. "You heard of Jane?"

"Sure. The phone number's all over the bathroom stalls. *Need help? Call Jane.* I assumed it's . . ." She lowered her voice and leaned closer to Phyllis. "It's an abortion service, right?"

"Right. And they need all kinds of help. Lots of ways to get involved that aren't even illegal."

Phyllis was challenging her, same as she had when she asked to do their double date in her neck of the woods. *Be cool. This is why you're here, not in Siberian Maine.*

"I'll call them," said Margaret.

"You can also go to the Union office and ask. That's probably more direct, actually."

The Chicago Women's Liberation Union. She'd seen flyers for them on most student bulletin boards. "Guess it's time to check them out."

"Guess so."

They had reached the ivy-covered archway of campus with the gargoyles menacing down at them.

"Ask Keith about getting together."

With two fingers to her forehead, Phyllis saluted her, then turned on the high heels of her shiny boots and went the other way.

The afternoon seemed to conspire to keep her from going to the Union, however, with a stack of essays she absolutely had to finish grading and students who stopped by out of the blue. Finally, at four minutes to five, with the papers graded and piled into a satisfying stack, waiting to be handed back the following morning, Margaret rose from her chair and stretched. Then she picked up the phone and dialed Gabe's number.

"Hey there," she said. "I'm running a little behind today, so I'll be over later than we'd originally planned, maybe closer to seven."

He was quiet just a little longer than she expected, and an irritation rose inside her.

"Alright," he finally said.

"I'll see you soon," she reassured him.

"I'll be waiting."

He was annoyed. *Fine*, she thought. *He'll get over it.*

It took another fifteen minutes of organizing, but she finally hoisted her messenger bag on her shoulder, turned out the lights in her office, and buttoned her coat against the December cold for her walk to the Union.

As soon as she walked in, her cheeks flushed with the warmth and her ears filled with the sound of phones ringing, women busily talking and laughing, papers riffling, and people milling about, even though it was dark outside. It smelled of coffee and stale cigarette smoke and the faintest notes of a musky perfume. There was an enormous bulletin board completely covered with flyers and photographs that hung off the edges, fastened with cheerfully colored tacks. There were fishbowls full of pins, at least one on every surface, and the rest of the available wall space was papered over with posters, framed magazine covers, and billowy banners that must have been used in marches. **WOMEN UNITE**, said one painted with hands in every shade of black, white, and brown. **DON'T IRON WHILE THE STRIKE IS HOT**, read one banner with a line drawing of an iron; she recalled seeing this very slogan on the television and in the newspapers during the 1970 Strike for Equality that NOW had organized—it was thrilling to see it here, now, in the flesh so to speak. And handwritten with black marker on a stark white board: **ABORTION WITHOUT APOLOGY**.

Now this is more like it, she thought, recalling the cookies and stagnation of Harriet's meeting.

She approached the large desk that served as a counter of sorts, and tried to catch someone's eye. It wasn't long before a young girl, with a mane of tightly coiled hair wrangled into a tie at the nape of her neck, came over to say, "Hello there, I'm Crystal," with as confident a smile as Margaret had seen on tenured professors.

"Hi, Crystal, I'm Margaret, and I'd like to volunteer. I've heard you do quite a lot of work here, and I'm . . . I'm particularly interested in one of your subgroups. Jane, I think it's called?"

If Crystal was surprised by this request, she didn't show it. She just nodded. "Jane has information sessions every Wednesday at seven o'clock here at the Union. If you're interested in other ways of getting involved, I recommend you also come to our weekly information sessions on Monday nights at eight."

Margaret nodded. It was Thursday, so she'd have to wait a while for either of those, which felt disappointing. Now that she was here, she was itching to get busy.

"And," Crystal went on, "you can check out our community board for other opportunities."

"I'll do that. Thanks for the information," said Margaret, then she headed over to the board with its many flyers. Some were geared toward younger women like her students, and others toward women with children, but a few were all-purpose, like a self-defense class and several consciousness-raising groups. Although nothing spoke to her like Jane did, she jotted down the phone numbers, addresses, and times of a few other groups, then circled Monday and Wednesday nights in her calendar. She was pleased that the Wednesday one at least was at the same time Gabe was always with Charlie, so she wouldn't have to explain where she was. She'd tell him eventually, of course, but right now, this group felt private, like it was just for her.

Peering into one of the fishbowls, she glanced over the many pins, then stuck her hand in to stir them up and reveal others. Finally, she plucked one out.

Don't Call Me GIRL.

Wasn't that what Dr. Metzler had called her? *Whenever a girl like you comes to see me . . .*

Recalling his patronizing tone and surprise at her advanced degree, she thought, *I'll be damned if I ever let something like that stand again.*

10

VERONICA

"What do Vietnam and vaginas have in common?" Phyllis asked Veronica.

"What?"

"Dishonorable discharge."

Veronica laughed. "I haven't heard that one yet."

"I just made it up."

"Then you're definitely ready for this shift." Once a Jane had the humor down, Veronica knew she'd be able to put that necessary distance between herself and the work. And she'd be able to use that humor to pick herself and the other Janes up when they got down.

In the kitchen, Phyllis was settling in well during her first shift at the Place, making the coffee and setting up the electric kettle, stacking boxes of doughnuts and Danishes beside paper plates and napkins. Veronica popped a pink box open, took out a chocolate-glazed doughnut, and sank her teeth into it. *Heaven.*

Not all Service members made it to the Place, and many of them never wanted to. A month before, Phyllis had been part of a monthly group training for new members, and only about four of the ten women at that session continued to the next step, which was about the norm. Likely only one or two of those would stick with it; there was attrition at every stage, as words like—let alone jokes about—*vagina* and *labia* and *cervix* gave most women the heebie-jeebies. Very often, that was as far as a Jane was willing to go, and that was fine—the Service needed plenty of women willing to work Fronts and Places. Only the most dedicated, the most passionate, were prepared to do the intimate work of dilation and curettage.

No one liked working Fronts. They were stews of husbands, sisters, grandmothers, and children waiting for their wife/sister/granddaughter/mother to return from the Place after her abortion. The locations were always changing to keep everyone, especially people like Sam Wilder, guessing. The space was often cramped, and lacked enough places to sit. To make it harder, emotions ran high in the Fronts.

Front shifts prepared Janes well for working the kitchen and common room of the Place, though; those shifts were a kind of baptism by fire of greeting people, calming nerves, answering last-minute questions about pregnancy and other matters of a woman's reproductive cycle, birth control, and Jane protocol. The question they answered most frequently was *How much is it going to hurt?*

"I need to set up," said Veronica. "I'll see you in a few hours. Good luck."

Phyllis nodded, and Veronica chewed on her last bite of doughnut as she made her way down the hall to the last room, her favorite, the one with the pink bedspread and one of Siobhan's O'Keeffe-like watercolors of a peony on the wall. She switched on the radio and sang along to "Me and Bobby McGee," trying to make her voice sound as husky as Janis Joplin's as she got out the waterproof covering for the bed, the boxes of Kleenex, the speculums, curettes, and other supplies from the closet. "Freedom's just another word for nothing left to lose . . ."

No kidding, sister.

About midway through the next song, "Ain't No Sunshine," there was a quick knock on the door, then Trudy stepped in holding a cup of coffee. "Morning," she said.

"Morning," Veronica replied, then the two of them worked together as they hummed along to the music and finished prepping the room. When they were ready, Veronica switched off the radio and said, "Listen, the first girl today is Senator Smith's daughter. I just didn't want you to be surprised."

Trudy smiled. "You know I love the famous ones."

Veronica laughed, recalling how starstruck Trudy had been when one of the comediennes from Second City had needed the Service: *I don't think I can actually look at her cervix, Vee. It would be like staring at the sun too long or something. Can I just do the hand-holding?*

"Do you mind if I do the first set today, then we switch?"

"No problem," Trudy replied. "How are you feeling, anyway?"

"I'm finally starting to feel pregnant, not just fat."

"Well, you look beautiful. You have that glow thing everyone always talks about."

"Thanks." The compliment made her feel weirdly shy, though. "I feel far from glowing. I feel hungry and tired pretty much all the time."

"Are you . . . Are you going to keep doing the D&Cs when you're really showing?"

"Absolutely," she said.

Trudy nodded but didn't say anything.

"Listen, I know it might seem strange, but I think it's important for women to see that both things are possible. That pregnancy and abortion are all part of the same cycle in a woman's life, and with a good abortion, women can still have children when they want to."

"Right." Trudy fussed with a stack of towels.

Oh, for the love of God, we let pregnant Janes do counseling all the time, she thought. But she didn't want to get into anything too heavy with a partner going into a shift.

There was a knock on the door at that moment and the two women looked at each other. "You think her ears were burning?" Trudy whispered.

"Four-alarm fire," Veronica whispered back, then opened the door to see Phyllis with Heidi Smith, who wore her full disguise again.

"Come on in," Veronica said, gesturing like a hostess for Heidi to come into the room as she gave Phyllis a little wave and shut the door.

"Good morning," she said as brightly as she could. "This is Trudy, and she'll be helping me this morning. Trudy had an abortion with us almost a year ago, so she can answer any of your questions with authority."

Heidi nodded.

"Why don't you get out of your coat and set your shoes and things on that chair in the corner. You can leave your top on, but we need you bare from the waist down."

Trudy handed her an old, soft sheet. "You can wrap this around your waist, loosely, though, then lie on the bed, okay?"

Heidi nodded again. Her stress and also her resolve were palpable, almost as if the air around her was hot and thick; she just gave off an aura like that. Veronica had almost delegated her to someone else, because she had very mixed feelings of her own about this abortion. The girl obviously wanted to keep the baby, even though when she'd called Veronica the day after her counseling session at Marion's, she'd said firmly, "This is the only choice for me. I need to come in as soon as possible." But no matter her own feelings, Veronica felt a personal responsibility to follow through with this girl.

Veronica and Trudy gave her a little privacy in the corner of the room with the armchair that functioned as a clothes rack. Even though most women in their care were about to show them parts of their bodies they'd mostly never seen themselves, and sometimes hadn't even truly shown the men who'd gotten them pregnant, Veronica understood the need for privacy in such a moment. It was the same with sex. It was one thing to take off your clothes and roll around with your man in bed, and another, much harder thing to walk straight to him, naked, from across the room. It had even taken her a few months of sleeping with Doug before she felt ready to walk around naked in front of him. Veronica was always impressed by the women who came to Jane and didn't even bother with the sheet until they were lying on the bed, striding with pride from the chair. They were few and far between, but they did exist.

Heidi was not one of those girls.

Heidi wrapped the sheet around her lower half—loosely, as instructed—holding a fistful of it at her right hip as she waddled to the bed. She was wearing the baggy Yale sweatshirt again.

As she lay down on the bed, the white waterproof sheet they laid over the bedspread let out its familiar soft crinkle.

"So, we need your bum as close to the edge of the bed as possible. We don't have stirrups like the doctor's office, but you can put your feet on each of these two chairs," Veronica said, waving each hand over the simple wooden chairs on her left and right. "Bend your knees and scoot yourself down to the edge."

Heidi did as she was told, and Veronica noticed that her toenails had flecks of red polish on them. "If your feet are cold, we can put something on them."

"They're fine," Heidi said, a little more forcefully than necessary.

Veronica exchanged a glance with Trudy, who was standing near Heidi's head. *Time to get this thing done. She doesn't want to be here, so let's get her out as fast as possible.* Trudy nodded.

"Would you like to hold my hand?" Trudy asked, hovering her hand over Heidi's chest.

She took it with a silent nod, then shut her eyes tight.

"How much does it hurt?"

"Not as much as you think," said Veronica, giving the well-used and often-verified answer. "And not more than you can handle. It will feel like period cramps, the kind that come in waves, and I'll tell you when you might expect a twinge of something more. You are strong. I promise it's going to be okay," Veronica said, as much to Heidi as to herself. She was sweaty and her hands had started shaking—imperceptible to anyone but herself, but shaking nonetheless.

This had never happened before. Usually this was the moment when the world fell away, when she picked up the speculum and gently slipped it inside the woman on the bed, ready for whatever awaited her once the walls of the vagina were parted.

It's going to be okay, it's going to be okay . . .

She knelt on the two pillows she'd set down to cushion her knees, and felt the baby inside her own belly poke her navel from the inside. She gasped. *Well, hello in there.*

"Is everything okay?" Heidi asked, and Trudy raised an eyebrow.

"Oh, yes, everything looks great. Sorry, my knee just cracked, that's all."

Her hands stopped shaking at the healthy movement in her uterus. The cramps of a few weeks ago had disappeared.

Everything's okay. It has to be okay. For Heidi and for me.

11

PATTY

"What do you mean you have to work late? We have dinner plans."
The round plastic receiver clicked against the emerald stud Matt had
given her three Christmases ago.

His harried sigh on the other end of the line was so loud, she practically felt it blow into her ear. "I'm sorry, sweetheart, but Nick has the
flu and I have to cover his patients at the hospital."

"I got a sitter and everything." She sounded petulant. Like Junie.
But she'd been looking forward to this for days. Dressing up under her
mother's fur coat, which she rarely wore, and dining at Jenny's, not to
mention finally getting to meet Gabe's mystery girlfriend—it had been
a light shining in her week. With four couples, it promised to be a
festive night.

Couples. Four *couples*. She and Matt, Gabe and Margaret, Becky
and Tony, Crissy and Max.

"You should go," he said, his voice softer, apologetic.

Go stag? "I don't know, Matt."

"You have my blessing. Enjoy it. Buy a round of drinks on us and
make my apologies for me. Take a cab."

Though it hadn't happened since the night of the cookie party, she

111

recalled his locked office door and the nervous shuffling after she'd knocked. Everything had been normal enough since then, and she'd begun to think maybe she'd just imagined all that. But now . . . canceling a date night he knew she was looking forward to? She had half a mind to call Nick herself to verify just how crappy he really felt.

"What time will you be home?"

"I wish I knew."

She was silent.

"Maybe eleven," he finally said.

"Fine. Don't wait up for me."

Then, on top of everything, she arrived first.

She soothed herself by placing an order with the maître d' for two bottles of bubbly for their table, courtesy of the overworked doctor. Then everyone else arrived in a flurry of *Isn't this beautiful* and *What fun to be out without the kids* and *How nice to get out on a school night*, and before Patty knew it, coats had been checked, outfits lavishly complimented, and seats taken to exclamations of gratitude and excitement at the two gleaming buckets with Veuve nestled in mountains of ice cubes.

Patty was seated between Margaret and Crissy and across from Gabe.

"To Matt," Max said, and everyone lifted their sparkling flutes and clinked them together amid echoes of the same, above the arrangements of red roses and carnations atop the white linens and heavy silverware.

Her first sips of champagne racing through her, Patty turned to Margaret to strike up a conversation and was momentarily distracted by how . . . mousy she was. She was pretty enough, sure, in a plain way, but she needed to *do* something with her looks. Her brown hair just sort of hung there, framing her face like two sheets. She wore a red velvet blazer over a black dress, which was fine, but it had no flair. So far, she was the opposite of Siobhan in every way—the painter would have been wearing something sultry and alluring, with perfectly placed embroidery or ruffles, and subtly sparkly earrings that would glint suggestively from her waves of copper hair.

"So I hear you're an English professor?" Patty asked her.

"Yes," Margaret replied, "I focus on the nineteenth century. Writers like the Brontë sisters and Louisa May Alcott."

"Oh?" Patty brightened at this and the inkling that Margaret appeared more impressive, and quite self-possessed, when talking about her work. "I wrote my senior thesis on *Wuthering Heights*. And I reread *Pride and Prejudice* this summer." This last bit was a lie, but Patty had read Austen's classic enough times that it hardly mattered which was the last time; she could practically recite the first chapter from memory.

"I love Austen. She's as important to the nineteenth century as Queen Victoria, if you ask me."

"Austen's come up in the world, then. When I went to school, most of my professors thought she was little better than a romance novelist."

"Male professors, I assume?"

"Now that you say it . . . yes. And one real battle-ax who thought the only writer worth anything in the English language was Shakespeare."

Margaret rolled her eyes playfully, and the women laughed; all at once, things felt relaxed and natural between them. Maybe she'd been too hard on Margaret earlier. Who cared if she was a little plain? Patty was *glad* she was nothing like Siobhan.

"And where are you from originally? Chicago has a strong pull for those of us who grew up here."

"Oh, no, I'm from Maine. Completely backwoods. Chicago might as well be Paris to the people I went to high school with."

"It *is* Paris to a certain kind of devoted Midwesterner."

"I can see why. Truly. The campus is gorgeous, and I love being just a short L ride to the Art Institute and the Field Museum. Before this, I lived in Berkeley near San Francisco, but that's such a small city. They had the de Young, of course, but that's nothing compared to what Chicago has."

Patty shivered, recalling Veronica's obsession with the happenings at Berkeley back in '64. While Patty was chasing after Karen, hanging on for dear life as Matt finished med school, her friend would not shut up about what was happening on the West Coast: *And this guy, Mario Savio, got up on his car in the middle of the quad and started talking about how the regents of the university were lying to them all, and trying to silence them, but it was their First Amendment right to speak out.*

"Is Berkeley still so radical?"

Curiously, Margaret didn't answer right away; she seemed to be calculating something behind those brown eyes. "Berkeley's a huge school. There were plenty of places to take refuge from the protests. Isn't the same true here in Chicago? You live near the campus, right? And the university hasn't exactly been quiet."

"That's true," Patty said. "But honestly, I stay away from the campus when there is anything likely to require the police."

Suddenly the waiter was standing between them and Patty was flustered that she hadn't even looked at the menu, so she made a rushed decision to order the wedge salad and the roast chicken with popovers, but then Margaret had gotten sucked into a conversation with Max, who was sitting on her right. Patty took a moment to look across the table at Gabe, who wore a white shirt and red sweater under a brown tweed blazer with corduroy patches on the elbows. She caught him glancing across the table at Margaret at the same moment his girlfriend's eyes flickered to his, and they smiled at each other with an intimacy that made Patty blush and look away.

How long had it been since Matt looked at her like that? Oh, sure, Margaret and Gabe were in the first throes of love, and a decade-long marriage couldn't compare to that kind of chemistry, but . . .

But.

Becky put a hand on Tony's wrist, her fingers disappearing for a second under his sleeve, and he gently squeezed her arm in response.

Patty turned to Crissy to ask about the St. Thomas nativity play.

Conversation wound its way through schools and sports and holiday break plans, all standard fare as they ate their salads, then their mains, draining both bottles of champagne and three bottles of red as they ate. Just as everyone was trying to decide if they had room for dessert—"The apple cobbler is especially good here," Becky informed everyone—Patty heard Max say to Gabe, "How about this thing with the abortions, eh?"

For crying out loud. Patty had forgotten this about Crissy's husband, the way he liked to wade into controversial topics after he'd had a few. Crissy actually rolled her eyes and said, "Darling, let's not get into that tonight."

"Alright, alright," he said good-naturedly enough. "But I should think everyone would want to discuss the fact that there are abortions happening right here in Hyde Park."

"Oh, we wrung that topic dry two weeks ago," said Patty, hoping she could move the conversation along. Abortion and holidays were not a good mix.

"Apparently," Max bulldozed along, "there's a group that hands out flyers at these women's lib meetings. They call themselves Jane. Such an innocent-sounding name, right? And Jane is just women. Like our wives. Not even doctors."

The derisiveness in his tone was unmistakable, and Patty noticed that Crissy flexed her jaw muscles and sipped her water, looking away from her husband. Patty was against abortion, too, but Max's hostility to the words *women's lib* and *just women* could have filled a gun with bullets, and *that* she couldn't abide. She might not agree with everything Veronica and her new friends said, but her skin prickled at the hostility to all women implied by Max's tone.

"How did you come by this information, Max? Are you attending the meetings yourself?" Gabe surprised Patty with this jab, expertly delivered with equal amounts of levity and pushback.

Clearly I should be spending more time with Gabe and Margaret.

"Just as good, Gabe," Max sparred. "Crissy went. My little infiltrator." He kissed his wife sloppily on her temple.

Still holding her water glass aloft, Crissy smiled frostily.

Patty glanced at Margaret beside her. The young professor actually *looked* like she was trying to bite her tongue. Interesting. So she was more liberal than her penchant for century-old novels suggested.

"I told Max that I didn't see anyone I knew," Crissy said almost apologetically, though Patty detected a note of dishonesty. She wondered what the secret was—had she told Max who the woman at the Union meeting was and sworn him to secrecy, or had she (wisely, it would seem) kept the woman's identity to herself?

"But she did see a flyer about this abortion service right here in our backyard," said Max.

"Whatever I might feel about the . . . *procedure* itself, I feel genuinely bad for those poor girls with nowhere else to turn," offered Becky.

"Poor girls?" Max snorted. "I bet less than a tenth of them even tell the fathers."

If you were the father, I wouldn't tell you, either. Almost immediately, Patty was horrified by this knee-jerk thought, which sounded more like Veronica than her own true self. Of course a father should know.

No one took the bait of Max's remark, and Patty saw Margaret give Gabe a wide-eyed pleading look that seemed to say *This is more than I signed up for.*

Me, too, sister. Patty was also worried about Crissy, who appeared to have shrunk into some sort of invisible shell.

"Anyway," Max said in a winding-down tone, "wouldn't it be interesting if we knew someone who's a member of the group? I bet we do."

"Then I hope I never find out," said Becky.

Beautiful little fool. That was a line from a book, right? Patty nearly asked Margaret which one, but Gabe broke it all up by making a show of wiping his mouth on his napkin and setting it to the right of his plate, then saying, "I may not have Charlie to get home to, but I do have an early morning class to teach."

There was grumbling around the table about Monday morning that gave way to the usual throwing down of credit cards and cash and tallying of tips, the getting of coats and kissing of cheeks and congratulating of everyone on the festivity of the evening.

In the cab on the way home, Patty felt anxious from the last conversation, and wished so much Matt had been there so they could dissect it together. The idea of this clandestine abortion service operating within walking distance of their homes, and all the schools and churches and playgrounds and libraries, made her feel hopeless and lost, as if she'd suddenly been transplanted to Oz, but without the security of the damn ruby slippers.

And why hadn't Matt come tonight, anyway? She had a hard time believing it was really work, and the very thought made her dinner feel heavy in her stomach. When she stumbled into the house around midnight, the sitter had already been dismissed and all the lights were out. After kicking off her heels by the door, she tiptoed in stockinged feet to the kitchen, where she took out a glass and filled it with water. Between gulps, she went over to the pad of paper where anyone who answered the phone was instructed to write down messages. Instead of the usual litany of other mothers' names, there was one name written in the babysitter's tidy teenage handwriting: *Eliza.*

That was it?

Just *Eliza?*

No phone number or address or time and place to meet?

She downed another glass of water, then groped her way up the stairs and found Matt asleep in their bed, though he couldn't have gotten home long before, because his hair was damp on the pillow and the bedroom smelled of Irish Spring soap, a familiar and comforting scent trapped in a humid cloud that had rolled in from their bathroom.

Lying down beside him after washing her own face and brushing her teeth, she considered waking him with a kiss, a suggestive hand brushing his hip. Her heart was still hammering in her chest with the adrenaline from that name by the phone. *Eliza.* Sex would be somewhere to put all this pent-up energy. And a way of feeling less alone. Then she remembered the last times she'd tried, and the way he'd said no, and she rolled over with her back to him, closed her eyes, and prayed for sleep to come soon.

12

MARGARET

Back at Gabe's place after Jenny's, he threw his keys on the book-shelf by the door. "I'm not quite ready for bed yet. Want a cup of decaf?"

"Sure," Margaret replied.

On his way to the kitchen, he plugged in the lights of the Christmas tree he and Charlie had decorated the previous weekend, which stood cheerfully in a corner. Though it was late, Margaret was wide-awake and nervy from the dinner. She'd felt like a fish out of water the whole time, as the only woman with no children and a full-time job. Sure, everyone had been nice enough, but it had been exhausting to perform her mother's brand of femininity for them, talking mostly about products and restaurants and clothes and travel, and listening patiently when they talked about their kids. Then there had been the showstopper of Jane.

Gabe had muttered, "What a blowhard," about Max as soon as they were in the cab, and Margaret had leaned on him cozily and agreed, then said as lightly as she could, "Dare I ask what you think about abortion?" She wasn't about to add, *Hey, I'm going to a training session on Wednesday.* He had replied with what she'd come to think of as the standard answer of most Democrat men: "It makes me queasy, and I'm glad I've never had to consider it, but I think women should be able to have them, and I'll vote for their right to have them."

Margaret was tempted to probe the issue further but then heard her mother counsel, *Don't rock the boat.*

Not entirely comfortable with letting herself off the hook like that, but also unable to motivate herself to say more, Margaret examined the homey decorations around the room to try to change the channel in her brain.

So many of the ornaments had obviously been made by Charlie and collected over a long period of time, with paint and glitter fleck-ing off of glass and wood. It was a lovely counterpoint to the otherwise spare decor of his place that she vaguely identified as Swedish, with lots of ninety-degree angles, teak, and well-dusted empty surfaces, a style at odds with the lumbering nineteenth-century architecture over which a Corinthian column at the foot of the stairs regally presided. His many Persian rugs and full bookshelves felt a bit more at home here, and several potted plants also helped warm the place up. She loved her own apartment in a newer building done in slim orange Chicago brick, a U shape around a small grassy courtyard. Every eclectic piece of her furniture was hard-won, procured with leftover grant and fellowship funds, at going-out-of-business or sidewalk sales. Gabe's place felt *adult* in a way hers did not, more organized and well thought out.

"I love that pine cone angel," she said, pointing to one of the orna-ments at the top of the tree. "I assume Charlie made it? I think my parents still have one I made exactly like it."

"That's one of my favorites," he said, handing her a mug of steaming coffee. "Our first Christmas by ourselves, Charlie and I took a little art class together, and at the last session, we all made ornaments. I think it showed her that her mom isn't the only artistic one in the family."

Margaret couldn't help wondering if Siobhan would have taught history to make the same point. Had their relationship always been competitive? He didn't seem competitive in other situations. "Which one did you make?"

He pointed to a pine cone made into a Santa face.

"Nice work, Picasso."

"Oh, you're going to pay for that," he said, as he set his mug, then hers, on the coffee table and started to tickle her.

At first it was fun, and she laughed and squealed, saying, "Stop, stop, stop," and when he didn't, she said more firmly, "Seriously, Gabe, stop."

He stopped, but he looked a little put out. She kissed him on the cheek and said apologetically, "Sorry, I just can't stand being tickled for long."

"How about you make it up to me upstairs," he said, leaning into her neck and kissing it lightly. Usually, she loved it when he did that, but this time, it tickled and made her squirm again.

"I think I might need a short break," she murmured.

He pulled back with a look of hurt and surprise on his face, and said with a flat tone, "Alright. You take a break. I'm going to get ready for bed."

Suddenly alone on the couch, Margaret felt abandoned. The tiny lights on the tree blurred in her peripheral vision.

After a few minutes of wondering what the hell was going on, she told herself, *Don't be ridiculous. You've had a nice night.* So she padded upstairs and found him wiping his mouth after brushing his teeth. She kissed his ear in the way he liked, and he said, "That tickles."

"Are you making fun of me?" She tried to keep it light and flirty, but this new dynamic was starting to turn her off.

"Maybe just a little," he said.

"That's not very nice," she breathed in his ear, still trying to turn this into a game and hold on to her arousal as she slid her hand between his legs, her palm on the fly of his trousers. She felt his body respond to her touch.

Finally, he turned toward her and kissed her, and soon they were in his bed, where she was able to set aside all the questions and discomforts of the evening.

"Welcome, everyone. Thank you for coming to this training session. I'm Siobhan Johnson, and I'm one of the founding members of Jane."
Siobhan Johnson.
Gabe's ex.
Holy shit.
I will be calm.
Except she was anything but calm. As Siobhan smiled and spoke warmly to the group of nine women gathered Wednesday night at the Union—Wednesday, the night this woman's former husband had their daughter for dinner!—Margaret's heart raced and her mouth felt dry. She tried to focus on Siobhan's words, which was hard because she was distracted by the woman's creamy skin and lush reddish hair, the sinewy figure beneath the paint-flecked bell-bottoms and the chunky gray cardigan that hung loosely over the yellow T-shirt with a tropical scene stretched across her breasts. *Well,* Margaret thought bitterly, *at least I'm not some carbon copy of his ex.*
She just wished Siobhan wasn't so *pretty.*
And so nice.
"We all have our own reasons for being here and wanting to volunteer," she went on. "Maybe you had an abortion like I did—"
You did?!
"—or maybe you know someone who's had one. Maybe you just know the law is wrong and you want to do something, to be part of the solution instead of complacently sitting by and watching the law hurt millions of women.
"Whatever brings you here, thank you. Jane needs volunteers of every kind, and I'll describe all of the jobs to you tonight so you can

think about what you might want to do. There are jobs for every comfort level. Only a small handful of our very large pool of volunteers actually perform and assist in the abortions, so if the thought of that makes you nervous, but you still want to help, that's perfectly fine. We still need you."

The warmth of Siobhan's smile was palpable, an incongruent beam of sunlight on this cold winter evening.

"I hate to emphasize this at the risk of scaring anyone off, but it's actually better for you to be scared now than later, and no one will think any less of you. But what we're doing is illegal. You could go to jail for performing abortions. Even if you never touch a single woman who comes to us, if the court is in the right sort of mood, you could be considered an accomplice to a felony.

"And I cannot emphasize enough the need for secrecy. Many police officers and officials in the mayor's office know about us, and have even sent women to us, and they protect us. We are, as they say, an open secret. Which is good, because it's critically important to us that we are not anonymous to each other or to the women who come to us. We do not hide, because we have nothing to hide. Using blindfolds and other methods of subterfuge are forms of emotional violence that validate the patriarchy.

"Jane believes that a woman should feel good about her abortion. That her abortion is a tool of her liberation from the systems in place to keep all of us down. We believe that by helping individual women out of their specific situations, we are by extension helping all women. If there is even the tiniest sliver inside you that doubts this, we ask that you quietly not sign up to help us. Again, no one will think less of you. This is a big request. You need to deeply ask yourself if you can make this kind of commitment to the cause."

The answer burning inside Margaret was *Yes. I can and will make this commitment.*

But do I have to be committing to you? My boyfriend's ex-wife?

Siobhan went on to describe the many jobs that Jane members performed. There were Janes who answered phone lines (which often changed) and took down information, and call-back Janes who returned those calls and provided and recorded more information; there were counselors at changeable sites all over Chicago, and women who offered up their houses and apartments as counseling sites, Fronts, and occasionally alternative Places, to distract from the site of the permanent Place; there were Janes who drove women on circuitous routes between Fronts and Places; Janes who made coffee and talked with friends and family at Fronts, and Janes who did the same at the Place for the women actually getting the abortions; Janes who were assigned to pick up supplies like tissues and coffee at grocery stores and specific medical supply warehouses who didn't ask questions when Janes dropped in for fifty plastic speculums and hundreds of tablets of tetracycline; Janes who washed and folded mountains of sheets and towels. All Janes were required to attend two training sessions, then a monthly meeting thereafter, and if you worked at the Place, you had to attend a weekly Tuesday morning meeting.

At the end of this litany, Siobhan smiled and said with laughter in her tone, "Hey, no one ever said breaking the law was glamorous. Mostly it involves hundreds of mundane tasks. But it all adds up to a remarkable, *liberating* act. Women helping women. It is revolutionary, and we really hope you want to be a part of it."

Siobhan took a long breath in through her nose, and Margaret watched as the woman's chest inflated, making the leaves of the flowers on her T-shirt larger and rounder.

"Alright. I'm going to leave sign-up sheets on the table here behind me for various jobs. All you have to do is leave your first name and daytime phone number. And thank you for even considering this. If you do sign up, plan to come to the next training session the first Saturday of January. We'll be in touch about a location."

With her mind swimming in information and conflicting emotions, Margaret rose from the folding metal chair she'd been sitting in, and went to the four yellow legal pads that were sitting on the table. *LOCATIONS. DRIVERS. COUNSELORS. FRONTS.*

She wondered what Phyllis did, and immediately, intuitively knew she was one of the most inside Janes who worked at the Place. She had the sense that Phyllis didn't do anything by half measures.

And neither did Siobhan, it appeared.

She'd had an abortion.

When?

Had it been Gabe's?

If it had been, there was no way he knew. *I'm glad I've never had to consider it*, he'd said.

Suddenly, everything felt so complicated.

Still, she wanted to be involved—and strangely, she was drawn even more to Jane now. But she'd have to stay only minimally involved, so as not to risk her worlds colliding. At least not yet. Not until she knew more.

Siobhan had said they especially needed apartments and houses during the day for counseling sessions and sometimes also to use as Fronts. Nothing technically illegal happened at those locations, so the risk of trouble was lower. Well, Margaret's own apartment was empty most of the time these days. She preferred working in her campus office, and she spent most evenings with Gabe at his place because it was so much bigger and better equipped.

So she wrote her name and number under the word *LOCATIONS* and told herself that this was a big enough step forward for today.

"Thank you," Margaret said to Siobhan as she shrugged into her coat.

"No, thank *you* for coming."

What happened between you and Gabe?

"I'll see you at the training session in January?" Margaret asked.

"I'm not sure yet who's leading that. But in the meantime, happy holidays."

"You, too." And Margaret was surprised to find that she meant it. In a single hour, Siobhan Johnson had gone from hated ex-wife in her mind to genuine and generous feminist leader, which made her all the more of a conundrum.

Perhaps both things could be true. Perhaps Siobhan could be a good leader and have been a bad wife.

Perhaps nothing was as clear as that.

Pride *and* prejudice.

Sense *and* sensibility.

And. Not *or.*

Margaret had always embraced paradoxes in literature. Clearly, it was time to embrace them in her own life, too.

She'd never been one for New Year's resolutions, but with 1972 about to begin in a matter of days, maybe that was the right note to start on.

13

PATTY

If someone had told her six months ago—no, even two months ago, even when she'd first started having suspicions—that she'd start the first week of 1972 by staking out her husband's medical practice in the freezing cold, she'd have wondered what they were smoking. And yet here she was, parallel parked one car up from the redbrick medical building, sitting in Becky's Chrysler, which Matt had never seen and Patty asked to borrow, telling her friend her own car needed work and the dealer didn't have a loaner. She wore an ugly black hat and coat she'd dug out of her closet, binoculars on the passenger seat, and eyelashes almost sticking together in the frigid air. She'd turned the car on and idled three times already, but it hardly warmed the interior enough.

It was an ill-conceived plan, which she hadn't fully appreciated till she got there. Though she'd lined up friends' houses for all three of her children to go to after school, she would only be free until five, at which point she had to return the car, collect the kids, and get home to make dinner. Matt *never* left work before five. So really she was waiting to see what might happen on his lunch break.

On a single day.

How much information could she really gather this way?

She'd been consumed with a need to do *something*, though, to know *something*, *anything* more than what she knew now, which was only that her husband felt like a different person to her and kept his office door locked on occasion.

It was all so sordid.

And then, too: What if his bit on the side came to *him*, in his office, rather than him leaving the office to go to her? And if he did leave the office, what did that prove? She'd have to follow him to his destination in this boat of a sedan. Would he notice? Or would he be so consumed with lust and anticipation he wouldn't notice a stranger tailing him?

This was obviously a terrible idea.

Oh, and speaking of worrying things that kept her up at night, her sister had called once. Once!

One measly time. Not even on Christmas or New Year's. And then she'd fallen off the planet again.

Nothing about life felt right.

Toward noon, she very nearly threw in the towel, but then an amazingly beautiful young woman parked her sporty little blue MG three spaces down from hers. She emerged wearing a fur-collared leather coat with a belt cinched at the waist, and stiletto-heeled boots that clicked as she walked from her car to the office's entrance, her mane of chestnut-colored hair shimmering down her back.

Now Patty just had to sit there *wondering* if her husband was screwing that woman in his office right now? Or if the woman was actually there for a problem with her heart. Or if she was going to the chiropractor on the floor below Matt's office—*She must need a chiropractor if she wears heels like that all the damn time.*

Patty certainly couldn't make a surprise visit to his office herself to see what might be happening—not with the wardrobe choices she'd made in the hopes of remaining incognito.

No, a career as a PI was not in the cards for her.

Jesus, though, was she really going to have to *hire* a PI if she wanted to know what was going on?

That sounded even more sordid than what she was already doing.

Well, at least she could wait to see how long the woman was in there, and if she looked . . . rumpled, or something, when she came out.

Minutes and minutes and minutes ticked by as Patty tried not to picture Matt bending that long-haired woman over his desk and pulling her hair and . . . No, *stop*.

She should leave.

And go where?

At home she just felt restless, wondering why things couldn't be the way they'd been before.

She could go to church and see if there was anything for her to help with, but she was still smarting from the conversation she'd had a few days before with Father Miller. Once again Matt had been at home while she and the kids were at St. Thomas for Sunday mass and the gathering after, for which she'd been the volunteer to bring cookies, doughnuts, and coffee. All three children were zooming around the room, playing tag, and as Patty packed up the last of the paper cups and sugar and napkins, she'd said, "May I have a word, Father?"

"Of course, Patricia," he said, inclining his graying head toward her in that avuncular way he had. "What's on your mind?"

"Well," she said, lowering her voice and darting her eyes around the room to make sure none of the children were in earshot, "I've heard that there might be"—voice lower still—"an abortion service here in Hyde Park."

Realization dawning on him, he nodded in an exaggerated way. Then, fixing her with a probing look, he asked, "And why does this concern you?"

"Because! Because . . . it's *abortion*. It's a . . . sin, isn't it?"

He nodded slowly, thoughtfully. "I am afraid I know little about this local service other than that it exists."

"Shouldn't the church be helping . . . I don't know, the police? To find out who's part of it?"

Father Miller was quiet longer than she would have liked, looking down on Patty from the foot or so of height he had on her. For the first time, she considered that despite his salt-and-pepper hair, his face was really quite youthful. Unlined. Was it possible they were the same age? Thirty-one? She'd always thought of priests as being older than she was.

Finally, he spoke: "Patricia, I appreciate your fear for the unborn of Chicago. I share your worry, but my primary concern must be first and foremost with members of the flock standing in front of me. And here you are, looking distressed, if I may say so. How can I help *you*?"

Damn him, she broke down in tears at his kindness. So many tears it actually got the attention of her oblivious children. Tad rushed over to hug her legs while Father Miller lightly embraced her shoulders and patted her back, telling her she could come in and speak to him in confidence anytime. And Junie had said in the car, "Are you sad, Mommy?" Karen's resolute silence had felt like a rebuke to her mother's messy public display of emotion.

Just as she'd finished replaying this terrible movie in her mind, the harpy in the leather coat clicked out of the building and walked to her car, not a strand of glossy hair out of place. She didn't so much as tug on her skirt.

Well. That was informative.

For God's sake, I'd like some answers, please, for once.

Patty turned the key in the ignition and headed back to Becky's three hours earlier than she'd planned. What a stupid idea this had been.

Inside her empty, silent home, she took a scalding shower, then put on soft, loose Levi's and a thick cowl-neck sweater in a shade of oat-mealy beige she found comforting. In the kitchen, she made herself a pot of tea and set herself out some cookies. Oreos, since there was no one there to see. She took out five of them, which she pulled apart one by one and licked the filling out of between sips of tea. She and Ve-ronica used to sneak Oreos all the time, because Veronica's mother insisted they eat fruit and Patty's mother said that if they were going to have a treat, it should at least be homemade. *It's never too early to watch your figure*, Vee's mother used to tell them both, splitting the slices of an apple between the girls when they came home from school, ravenous. Patty and Veronica had made what they called an Oreo Oath that neither of them would impose such obnoxious restric-tions on their own kids, and yet here Patty was with her secret Oreos, which she stashed away because she didn't want her kids to develop a taste for their chemical sweetness.

This is ridiculous, she told herself, vowing to serve her kids Oreos with tall, cold glasses of milk, like in the commercials, for dessert to-night.

But no cookie was going to fix the problems she was facing now.

She could call Father Miller. He *had* offered to listen to her trou-bles. There was still plenty of time to see him before she had to get the kids; she could cry some more, and maybe find comfort in his wis-dom. But the priest had no way of knowing whether or not Matt was actually cheating, and he was likely bound by some sort of moral code of the confessional not to tell her even if he did know, so how much use could he be?

What she really needed—and she felt wet and wobbly just admit-ting this to herself—was a hug.

She picked up the phone and called Veronica.

Ring.

Ring.

Ring.

Ring.

Ring.

And.

On.

And.

On.

With her right index finger, she depressed the plastic button on the phone to hang up, then she released it and punched in the digits for Crissy's number.

"Hello?" the other mother said, and Patty could hear one of her children send up a cry in the background.

"I think Matt might be having an affair."

"What? No."

Patty summarized the last few months of her marriage, and her paranoid activities of the morning, and noticed that by the time she'd finished, Crissy had found a quiet place to be.

"I'm so sorry. Even if it's not true, it's terrible to feel like it might be." Crissy paused. "Could you ask him? I mean, is it safe?"

"Safe?"

"You never know."

"I'm not worried he'll hit me or anything, if that's what you're concerned about."

"Good. I had a friend in high school whose dad did that, but no one ever would have been able to tell from the outside."

Patty swallowed. It was more than just a lump in her throat, and more like her pride. "Have you . . . heard anything?"

"About Matt? No. Absolutely not. I would tell you."

"He's too smart to pussyfoot around with the other moms anyway. If he's doing it, it's with someone at work."

"So could you ask him? He might not be honest, but I think you'll be able to tell one way or the other."

Patty didn't reply right away, trying to imagine how such a conversation would actually go, and she couldn't do it. "Maybe."

"Hey, do you want to meet for lunch tomorrow?" Crissy's solicitous tone only made Patty feel worse; then she remembered Crissy's husband, Max, and his aggressive, belittling bluster at their couples dinner before Christmas and wondered again what was going on in *her* house. Patty realized just how different complaining about husbands coming home late or not helping enough with dishes and diapers was compared to actually fessing up to the possibility that there might be something truly wrong. Would Crissy be willing to admit serious problems in her own marriage? Not today, it appeared.

"Sure, lunch would be nice," Patty replied.

"Great," said Crissy brightly. "You know, I do have one more thought. . . ."

"Yes?"

"Well, I have an old college friend whose husband cheated and she got him back by getting pregnant again; he gave her a beautiful diamond necklace as a promise. And another friend who said it was fine if he slept around as long as she could, too."

Patty seriously doubted the first friend's husband would stop cheating just because of a baby. More than likely, the baby and the jewelry had just been distractions, but since she was a friend of Crissy's, Patty didn't want to put her opinion where it wasn't wanted. She did feel she could say, about the second example, "I don't want to sleep with other men."

"I'm just saying, think about what *you* want."

A tit for tat? Ick.

Anyway, what she *wanted* was a fulfilling marriage.

A faithful marriage would be a good start.

Later, while Patty made the rounds of picking up her three kids at their friends' houses, she happened to drive by Veronica's place, and she glimpsed her old friend hugging Siobhan in the front yard as

Charlie and Kate threw snowballs at each other. For hours after, Patty felt a suffocating weight on her chest, all through dinner and bath time and TV and books and putting the children to bed.

Surely Matt had noticed she wasn't herself. But there they were, in bed with their separate magazines at ten thirty that night, and he said nothing.

Could you ask him? Is it safe? Suddenly safety had several more meanings than the obvious. Patty knew that if she said anything vulnerable to Matt now and didn't receive the response she wanted, she risked her heart shattering into a million tiny pieces.

"How was your day?" Her voice was small. "How are things with Nick?"

"Oh, Nick's fine. He's Nick. You know."

"Tell me about your most interesting patient today." He used to come home and regale her with stories of truck drivers with clogged arteries and pack-a-day spinsters with murmurs.

Setting down his magazine, he turned and peered at her over the top of his reading glasses. "You don't have to pretend to be interested in my work."

"I'm not pretending. I like hearing you talk about work." *Just talk to me, please.*

"Then why can't you remember anything I tell you? Especially for the last year or two."

"I can't?" *Truly?* In her mind, he'd simply stopped talking. Was it possible his silence was in response to something she'd done, or not done? She felt her eyes well up, and she whispered, "I'm sorry."

"It's okay," he said softly. "You've been busy. The kids are really happy, and that's great." He reached out and put his hand firmly behind her head, and drew her close to him, kissing her forehead and setting her head on his shoulder. Her heart was beating wildly, and the fact that she could feel his pulse, steady and calm, made her feel even more desperate. She wasn't sure how long she lay like that, a crook forming in her neck as she breathed in the clean scents of his soap and the laundry detergent, swallowing back the tears. *Is this distance between us actually my fault?*

Surely it took two, though . . . right? Two to tango and all that? Weren't there things he should apologize for, too, even if it wasn't infidelity?

"I just want to be like we were," she said.

"That would be nice, wouldn't it?"

She sat up straight and looked at him incredulously. "What does that even mean, Matt?"

"Just that . . . I don't know if we can be those people anymore. Three kids and ten years. It's been . . . a lot."

"I seem to remember part of our marriage vows saying something about good times *and bad.*" Her voice was clearing and her eyes drying as she spoke. Yes. They were in this together. It couldn't be any other way. They *both* had to take some responsibility for making it work between them.

"True." The sound of his voice was so warm and familiar. Maybe there was hope.

"Can we try, please? I'll listen more carefully, I promise. Can you try to . . . be a little less distant?"

He squeezed her hand. "I'll try."

It wasn't makeup sex, or a passionate defense of their marriage against all intruders, but it was a start.

14

MARGARET

"I've always wanted to go to this place," said Gabe in the cab on their way to Izola's to meet Phyllis and Keith. This double date had been postponed too many times since before the holidays, with everyone's busy schedules, and Margaret was glad to finally be doing it.

"Why haven't you?" Margaret asked, nervous that maybe Phyllis's warning about her Reconstruction scholar boyfriend had been on the mark after all.

"Hyde Park is pretty integrated as Chicago neighborhoods go, at least now. But it's still a very segregated city."

"You know, I've never lived in a racially divided place. Maine had no one to segregate, then Berkeley and San Francisco had everyone and everything, and people just seemed to coexist there. Like they do here near the campus. Except that the campus itself is overwhelmingly white. And now that I'm saying all that out loud, I'm realizing how wrong I probably was about the racial divisions at Berkeley. They were there, but I couldn't see them because I was stuck in the ivory tower." She suddenly felt embarrassed that she'd never even heard of Izola's before Phyllis suggested they meet there. There must be hundreds—thousands—of other restaurants and clubs and shops like this one that weren't on the beaten path of Italian beef sandwiches, the Wrigley Building, and gangster ghost tours.

"Hey, there's no shame in aspiring to the ivory tower," Gabe replied. "Anyway, we're going now, and I'm excited to sample the menu. I've heard the chicken and dumplings are not to be missed." He rubbed his stomach in anticipation.

"Sounds delicious," she said, noting as she glanced out the window that it looked like they'd entered another city. Storefronts for hair braiding, soul food, and electronics maintenance punctuated the more familiar grocers and laundromats, and every pedestrian was Black.

Don't act different. Phyllis likes you. She's not asking you to be someone else.

Keith and Phyllis were waiting for them under a big red awning that read **IZOLA'S FAMILY DINING**. Like Margaret herself, who'd chosen cords and her tried-and-true lined galoshes from Maine, Phyllis was much more casually dressed than she was on campus, wearing widely flared bell-bottom jeans and thick brown clogs. It looked like Keith was the same height as Phyllis and very handsome but obviously quite a bit older, with at least half his close-cropped hair gray and deep crinkles at his temples when he smiled in greeting.

"Thanks for meeting us down here," Keith said as he shook Gabe's hand, then Margaret's; his palm and fingers were warm and dry, his fingers long. Margaret gave Phyllis a hug.

"I'm glad you suggested it," Gabe replied.

"I put in our name for a table, so we shouldn't have to wait too long," said Keith. "Let's go inside and warm up, though, right?"

Keith held the door open for all of them, and stepping inside was like entering a movie set. The place was hectic with the clatter and buzz of the busiest restaurant Margaret had ever seen. Huge mirrors lined the walls, and tables edged with metal densely populated the place; if you sat at one of those tables, your back was pretty much touching the back of the person at the next table. *And what am I smelling?* It was some combination of bacon and yeast and cheese and something she couldn't put her finger on, but it made her mouth water.

The four of them shouted some small talk about the weather and the holiday season as they waited for their table, and when they were seated and handed big plastic-coated menus, Margaret opened hers, glanced over all the items, and said to Phyllis and Keith, "I just want to order everything."

Keith laughed. "That's not a bad idea. Everything's good here, but their fried catfish is something special."

"We could also order everything family-style and share so Margaret and Gabe can get the maximum experience," suggested Phyllis.

Keith raised his eyebrows at Gabe. "What do you say?"

Gabe closed his menu and set it down on the table. "When in Rome."

After some conferring, Phyllis and Keith ordered what seemed like half the menu, except for the chicken and dumplings. Once the ordering was complete, Phyllis leaned back in her chair, and Keith draped his arm lazily around her. They looked entirely relaxed together, which made sense, Margaret supposed—they'd been together for two years. For the first time, she wondered why they weren't engaged yet.

"So, Keith, I understand you're an assistant superintendent," said Gabe, with an admiring chuckle. "As someone who chose higher education, I have to say I'm impressed. I don't think anyone could pay me enough to address K–12 headaches."

Keith cracked a winning, confident half smile, and Margaret immediately knew it was one of his most powerful weapons, the one he fired at someone whenever he needed a job done. "The schools are one headache after another, it's true. But I wouldn't want any other job. Elementary school is where I learned to read. Old Miss Drake used to hand me bags of books from the library every Friday morning. I'd finish most of them by Monday. She had me reading Richard

Wright by sixth grade. Then in high school, I learned to be a man. Some of that had nothing to do with school, but the building and the people inside it were like a *container*, if you know what I mean. I knew I was safe there. In some rooms, anyway. Rooms where they understood who I was and what it was like to be me in this city. Nowhere else in my life was like that."

"I had a similar librarian in my school in the sticks of Michigan," said Gabe. "I don't think I ever would have discovered Steinbeck or Frederick Douglass without her."

Keith whistled. "Frederick Douglass?! At a school in the rural Midwest? Man."

"Best I got in Maine was the Transcendentalists," Margaret said, realizing how much of her adult scholarship had been shaped by that early reading. Even though she'd certainly read Douglass and Sojourner Truth and Wright later in her life, it was that childhood reading—*Little Women, Walden, The Scarlet Letter*—that had set her on the path she was on now. As Gabe and Keith talked on, she turned to Phyllis and asked, "What did you read as a kid? Did you have a favorite librarian, too?"

"I went to a more integrated school than Keith," she said. "And the librarian was white, so I read a lot of the same stuff you would have read. I was heartbroken when I realized there was no way a Black girl could have lived the same lives as Meg, Jo, Beth, and Amy. It kind of ruined it for me. It wasn't until college that I started reading people like Maya Angelou and Angela Davis. I really like Audre Lorde."

"I don't know her."

"She's a poet. Emerging. She only has two books, and they're hard to find. Sometimes I see them at the Co-op."

"I'll ask about them."

The whole evening was like that, with conversations shifting between pairs and all four of them, mainly focused on schools and teaching. When Keith found out Charlie was at the Lab School, Margaret was worried this superhero of the public schools might frown, but he admitted, "If I was Midas, I might send my kid to the Lab School, too. They do some pretty amazing work there."

"I get a discount as a professor," replied Gabe, obviously uncomfortable about the Midas comment.

Every mouthful of their meal was delicious, and Keith clearly enjoyed regaling them all with explanations of how certain dishes were prepared regionally, and how his mother and granny did them; at these mini monologues, Phyllis rolled her eyes affectionately and said, "He's not so subtly trying to improve my cooking."

To which he replied, "You're too busy saving academia from itself," and planted a kiss on her cheek, which made Margaret aware of how self-contained she and Gabe each were, keeping their hands and lips to themselves.

Gabe tried to pay the bill, but Keith said, "Next time, in your hood, you can pay."

"Deal," said Gabe.

In the cab ride home, Gabe said, "I'm stuffed."

Margaret laughed. "You weren't disappointed we didn't get the chicken and dumplings?"

Gabe shook his head, closed his eyes with satisfaction, then set his head on the back of the seat. "No way. I'm going to dream about that corn bread forever."

"Maybe we can get Keith's grandma's recipe," she said. She didn't love cooking, but she wouldn't mind putting that look on Gabe's face again.

Between Phyllis and Gabe and Jane, Margaret was the most engaged and alive she'd felt since she started grad school. Jane in particular made her feel engrossed and vital. The two training sessions she attended in January had been run by women named Trudy and Melanie, the latter of whom was surprisingly and reassuringly close to her mother's age and a former ER nurse. She hadn't seen anything more of Siobhan, which suited her fine.

It was initially distracting that one of her students from last semester, Belinda Silva, was also one of the trainees. The girl was smart, and had even written an impressive final paper on the costs of secrecy to women characters in *The Scarlet Letter* and *Jane Eyre*. Until Jane— or the Service, as she was instructed to call it to other members— Margaret had assumed that once she was tenure-track faculty she'd never be at the same level as an undergrad for anything, ever again. So that was her first lesson of Jane: there was no hierarchy, at least not among new recruits. Education and age meant nothing. Hard as she'd worked to get where she was on campus, she found that in this community organization, once the surprise wore off, she didn't mind this leveling approach.

Still, after greeting each other and chatting about their respective holiday breaks over coffee and cake and fruit the first morning, they didn't talk much. Belinda gravitated toward the three other younger women in the trainee group, and Margaret toward the two closer to her age: Mary, who was in school to be a dental hygienist, and Noel, a young mother who lived in the north part of town. Both of them had used the Service in the past year, Mary because she couldn't afford to stay in school and have a baby, and Noel because she'd had so many complications during her last birth that her doctors had warned her not to have another child—and for some terrible reason, the vasectomy her husband had endured to prevent just that had not worked— but she hadn't been able to get a legal therapeutic abortion in a hospital. "I stood in front of a hospital board of five men and one woman, and they all told me that the hospital had made major strides in obstetrics, and I'd be glad I took the risk and had the baby. I mean, fuck them. I can't be glad if I'm dead, can I?"

"I heard a lot of stories like that in California, where it's technically legal if you need it, but *need* is a highly relative term," Margaret commiserated, remembering a few grad school parties where fellow female students would get sloppy and spill the most personal details of their lives.

Until the Jane sessions, Margaret hadn't given a lot of thought to the many reasons why women needed abortions, but there was such a wide range: maternal health, money, rape and incest, shocking cluelessness about how pregnancy even happens, lack of access to birth control, failed birth control, and age, both too young and too old. Margaret was truly appalled—at herself, for her lack of inquiry before Jane, more than at the stories themselves. It had never occurred to her before that a woman who really wanted a child, who might have four children already, might not be able to feed a fifth, or that an unmarried college graduate might not know how to put on a condom correctly.

"We don't ask them why they are coming to us. That's an invasion of privacy and none of our business," said Trudy, making meaningful eye contact with each of the trainees. "Very often they tell us on their own, and very often you'll wish you didn't know. Our job is to make this as easy for them as possible and help them prevent it from happening again."

Trudy and Melanie were born teachers, and Margaret learned as much during the two training sessions as she had during her long hours in Bancroft Library studying for orals. She learned the accurate names of each of her reproductive parts and her cycle, how to locate ovaries in a pelvic exam, the varying shapes of a woman's cervix— there were so many!—and the fact that her clitoris had no anatomical purpose other than sexual pleasure (which she'd intuited but never bothered to confirm). "We encourage all of you to go home and look at your labia in a mirror," said Trudy. "There's no anatomy lesson like the one you can give yourself. When I did this, I fell in love with myself a little. It is just amazing what's hiding down there. And if you're going to work for Jane, you must never be shocked. Not by anything. So start with getting to know yourself. As a bonus, you'll more likely be able to tell your partner what you like."

It had been a little jarring after that to learn how to identify the major sexually transmitted diseases, but also a relief to know she'd never experienced a single symptom. She also learned about how diaphragms and condoms and sponges and the pill all worked, and why the pill was the only really foolproof method for preventing pregnancy but was still useless against the diseases.

"And the so-called rhythm method?" Trudy blew a raspberry. "You know the joke, right? What do you call a couple who uses the rhythm method?"

Trudy waited a perfect, delicious beat, then said, *"Parents."*

Everyone laughed.

"Hey," Belinda said to the group, "what does a mama bear on birth control have in common with the World Series?"

All the women looked at each other in smiling anticipation.

"No Cubs."

More laughter.

"Extra credit for Chicago-based reproductive humor," said Melanie. *Dr. Metzler should do some professional development here.*

Recalling him, Margaret noticed that the word *girl* was notably absent. Everyone was a woman. Even Belinda. Even the teenagers Trudy and Melanie said regularly availed themselves of the Service were referred to as women.

"You're in a great mood," Gabe had commented the Saturday night after the first session, as the two of them played Scrabble and ate pizza and Margaret was on fire with letters and puns and kisses on the cheek.

"I had a really productive day." She almost went on to tell him where she'd been and what she'd done, then she stopped herself. Jane had become an even stickier subject since she'd found out about Siobhan, and she was still sorting out her own feelings about that. Also, Trudy's words rang in her ears: *none of our business*. She and Gabe were doing well, and she hoped more would come of it, but they hadn't used the word *love* yet, nor had he mentioned introducing her to Charlie. There were still parts of their lives that felt private. He didn't need to know where she was every minute of every day.

"Oh? Tell me about it. I called your office a few times and you weren't there."

"I was in the library." The lie sounded smooth enough, but the way he nodded and didn't reply made her wonder if he could tell.

"Next time, can you let me know where you are? I get worried when I can't reach you."

"Is my schedule so boring and predictable?"

"I like that about you. Siobhan used to be so . . . mercurial. I used to wonder if there was someone else."

Maybe *someone else* had been the reason she'd needed the abortion? Margaret kissed his cheek. "You have nothing like that to fear with me."

"Just . . . call, okay?"

"Okay," she said, though she chafed at the promise. She wasn't asking *him* to account for every minute of the day. Then again, she *was* lying to him, wasn't she? Just not about the thing he feared.

At the second session, she'd learned about the ethos behind and specifics of the counseling, the ways that Janes put the women who came to them at ease, reassuring them about their choice, explaining that abortion was a tool of liberation not just for them but for all women. "When one woman is more free, all women are more free," said Trudy.

Margaret loved this way of thinking. She fully embraced the idea that a girl—*woman*—trapped by her life circumstances was more free if her sister or friend got an abortion. Because that other woman had led by the example of her liberation, she had also shown her friend what was possible when a woman took her life into her own hands. Just like the examples of Mary Shelley and Jane Austen and Louisa May Alcott had inspired other women to pick up a pen. *We're all in this together.*

The ideas they discussed at Jane gave Margaret an urge to get more involved, but she just didn't have the time to dedicate to hours of counseling, not with the book she was writing and the three classes per semester she had to teach. And being a girlfriend took a shocking amount of time, she was realizing. Hours when she'd normally have read for pleasure or tried a new hobby or given to a worthy cause like Jane were taken now by getting to know Gabe. *Partnership is a worthy cause, too,* she told herself. *And something I've wanted for so long.* Anyway, if freeing one woman with abortion moved all women closer to freedom, it had to be equally true that one woman balancing a meaningful and fulfilling career with a meaningful and fulfilling relationship also moved other women closer to the same.

Additionally, she told herself, *I have a lot at risk by getting more involved with Jane*—Gabe and the possibility of a life with him and Charlie and maybe one or two children of their own, her job and the career she'd worked her whole life for, a career that she'd alienated her own mother to pursue. And she'd surely lose her mother entirely if she ever found out her daughter was aiding a group of feminist abortionists.

During that second session, though, Margaret's plan to be minimally involved hit a snag. When Trudy discovered that Margaret's apartment was only an eight-hundred-square-foot one-bedroom with no door between the kitchen and living room, she said they couldn't use it as a location for counseling because they needed a space with more doors and private spaces.

"But," Trudy said, eyebrows raised hopefully, "we could use it as a

Front. I know it's a little closer to the action than you planned, but we do need Fronts pretty badly. Here's a refresher on how Fronts work," she explained to the group. "After the women come to us for counseling and we put them on the schedule, we have specific days when we actually do the abortions. Those happen at the Place. For the protection of everyone, including the family and friends who accompany the woman getting the service, we use a different location called a Front as a waiting area. Then we have drivers to ferry the women between the Front and the Place, then back again."

Turning back to Margaret, Trudy said, "If we use your apartment as a Front, we usually need it from eight in the morning to eight at night. We'll have to use your kitchen, bathroom, and everything. You can keep your bedroom closed. We'll bring some supplies, including food and paper plates and some toys for the kids who sometimes come, and I promise we'll leave your home as clean as we find it. Cleaner, usually. And we try not to use any Front more than once, maybe twice, in a month."

The reality of scores—hundreds?—of strangers hanging out in her apartment all day made Margaret feel uneasy. "I don't have many places to sit," Margaret said, embarrassed by her own hedging.

"That's okay. People can sit on the floor. And we won't have more than twelve or so in there at any one time. Do you think you can accommodate that?"

Twelve at a time did sound more manageable.

She nodded; she was committed. *I will be calm.*

Belinda raised her hand and said, "What if we want to do more than counseling or driving? What if we want to learn to do the abortions?"

"Well, the first thing is to let us know you're interested," said Melanie, taking over from Trudy. "And the next thing is to pay attention and be available. Volunteer for the pregnancy test and Pap smear clinics first. As you can imagine, the OR of the Place is the hardest of all the jobs. You need more anatomy lessons and a lot of observation hours and hands-on training. And . . . think about it deeply. It's not easy work, physically or emotionally."

"You know that I know that already," Belinda said meaningfully, and Margaret knew in the moment that the girl—no, not *girl*, the young *woman*, her former student, no less—had gotten an abortion with Jane. And here she was, asking to climb over the table to the other side.

Margaret had no desire to get that close. It was the same character trait that made her an academic, she supposed—a deep desire to learn and immerse herself in the thoughts and lives of others, but at a distance. She tried not to think of this as a deficiency. The people she admired and studied got their hands dirty. They got into the mix and changed things. But the world needed helpers and observers as much as leaders. And she *was* pretty close to the action, as Trudy had said, closer than she'd planned, letting Jane use her apartment as a Front.

When she left, her address was on the schedule for later in February. She couldn't take it back now.

And she was surprised to discover she wasn't even tempted to do so.

15

VERONICA

"I'm so happy to be doing this with you," Patty gushed. "It feels like so long since we've teamed up for anything."

"I'm happy, too," Veronica said, though her mind was elsewhere.

Sitting at her friend's kitchen table, she was up to her elbows in the colors and shapes of love: sheaves of pink, white, and red construction paper, ribbons of heart-shaped stickers, bags of Sweethearts and Red Hots and Hershey's Kisses they were distributing into red paper bags, all in the service of Kate and Junie's annual Valentine's Day party, set to happen that afternoon. She caught sight of her fingernails, which Kate had insisted on varnishing crimson the previous night in preparation for the festivities.

Veronica wanted to relax and enjoy the profusion of red and pink, this simple activity that Patty's natural precision and organization had made even easier, but she kept thinking about the Service. They were hard up for volunteers, and even harder up for locations, and Danielle—never one to pull punches—had told her point-blank yesterday during a shift break that Veronica should take time off once she got closer to her due date, or at least restrict her activities to driving and maybe—*maybe*—counseling. "It's going to scare women away if you're performing the abortions with a baby in your own uterus. It just feels . . . insensitive."

Trudy had stood frozen in the Place's kitchen, obviously waiting to see what she would reply. Veronica chose her words carefully. "I've thought about that," she said slowly. "But there are two other realities that I think need more consideration. The first is practical: we are incredibly short-staffed, and the demand is ever growing. I suspect women are more scared not to get their abortions than they are of having an abortion performed by a pregnant woman. The second is philosophical: one of the pillars of Jane is that abortion is just one part of a woman's reproductive health, like our periods and menopause and, yes, pregnancy. Having a pregnant abortionist, who can honestly say as I can that I've gone through a D&C and still here I am, makes the theoretical tangible."

Danielle had looked to Trudy, seemingly for support, but Trudy said nothing.

"Maybe," Danielle had said with a shrug, but her misgivings had dogged Veronica ever since. When she rehearsed her reasons to herself in her mind, one of the others that lined up like good soldiers was the fact that she didn't *want* to stop and didn't feel that she should have to stop. Society—*even husbands like Doug*—was always telling women to stop working when they were pregnant, since the assumption was that they were only going to quit anyway when the baby arrived. Every time a woman took that advice, it only perpetuated the myth that women were the weaker sex. And Jane was all about showing women their strength.

She wished that she wanted to stay home and repaint the guest room she and Doug had decided to turn into a nursery, to shop for baby clothes and blankies and mobiles and all the ridiculous capitalist trappings of motherhood that she'd flatly and proudly rejected when she was pregnant with Kate, when she'd told everyone that all she wanted was books at her baby shower. In retrospect, she should have seen that impulse as early evidence of the direction she was heading with regard to the *Good Housekeeping* life. Patty had overridden her desire for books—and would again, Veronica had no doubt. Siobhan had told her about Patty's call and the baby shower on the horizon, and Veronica had added it to her mental list of things she didn't want to think about.

More and more, it seemed, the contrast between her two lives was becoming sharper. As Jane grew and she became more invested in its mission, the appeal of her domestic life waned. She loved Kate and Doug, and she still took pleasure in the little rituals of her homelife, like snuggling with her daughter before bed and handing her husband his first cup of coffee in the morning, milked and sugared exactly how he liked it. But she had the sense that the duties of mothering and wifing had become more precious as they also became more rare. Gone was the Veronica who made an elaborate dinner every night from scratch, who did all the laundry before every last sock was dirty—who even darned the socks when she found holes in the toes; now she just ran to the store for a new pack of six. She didn't have the time for that kind of attention to family details anymore.

Did that make her a bad mother? A bad wife? She refused to believe it did, and she wanted both of her children to grow up with a mother who was self-actualized as well as a mother who paid attention to her children in the important ways, unlike her own mother, who had essentially checked out once Veronica was old enough to pack her own lunch and make her own after-school plans.

If only she could get better sleep, to shore up more energy for the double life she had to lead. The baby had become a gymnast in there, performing what seemed like entire Olympic floor routines just as she was trying to fall back to sleep at five most mornings, after her fourth pee of the night.

And Sam Wilder, or one of his supporters, had started parking menacingly outside of at least one Service shift per week—another nagging worry to put out of her mind, along with the progress of her pregnancy, Jane's wait list, and the fact that Doug had avoided any conversation about Jane since the fight they'd had before Christmas.

Veronica tried to emulate Patty and focus on cutting more hearts.

"Vee?" Patty asked her, snapping her out of her thoughts. "Vee, where'd you go?"

"Oh, gosh, I'm sorry," Veronica said. "I get distracted all the time lately."

"That happened to me when I was pregnant with Tad, but . . . I have to tell you it seems like more than baby brain with you. What's got you so preoccupied?"

"I took on some more responsibility with the Union," Veronica said, which felt at least partly true because the Service was primarily advertised through the Women's Liberation Union.

Patty frowned. "Please, Vee, be careful with them. I heard they were handing out flyers for . . . *abortions* at their meetings."

Any temptation Veronica might have felt to tell Patty about Jane was instantly erased by this dramatic show of concern. "I'll be careful," she assured Patty.

Patty shook her head. "Abortion is wrong. Not just for the child but for the mother. It can make her sterile if it doesn't kill her. How is *that* liberating women?"

Veronica felt her ears flush hot at her friend's misinformation, courtesy no doubt of the head of St. Thomas before Father Miller, and whatever nincompoops she was friends with in the Junior League.

"You know," Veronica ventured, "an abortion isn't that different from the D&Cs women like me have after a miscarriage. We aren't sterile." She rubbed her protruding belly for emphasis.

"Get real, Veronica. You can't possibly be comparing a procedure done in a nice clean hospital, by a doctor, with some travesty in a back alley with a knitting needle."

It's not all crochet hooks and wire hangers, Patty! Geez.

The baby inside Veronica punched her right under her belly button, which she took to be an instruction to keep her mouth shut. "I'll be careful, I promise," she repeated, feeling exhausted by the effort of having to pretend around Patty, as she pretended around pretty much everyone who wasn't in the Service. *I'm a mother who also runs what amounts to a thriving business!* How many people actually knew that? How many people knew what it cost her, at both ends of the candle?

"On a happier subject, how are you feeling?" Patty asked, keeping her eyes on her scissors and the red paper.

"A lot better. I haven't had any weird cramps in ages, and incredibly, I'm moving into the third trimester this week."

"That is hard to believe," Patty said. "You're carrying so small!"

"Fuck." Veronica exhaled sharply, just after her scissors went into the pad of her left middle finger, which bloomed red with blood immediately. She went straight to Patty's sink and ran her finger under water so cold it stung painfully, then numbed her fingertip.

Patty came to her side. "Ouch. Here, press this paper towel to it and hold the finger above your head." Patty held out two large squares of paper towels as she peered down at her friend's finger.

Veronica did as her friend instructed, and felt ridiculous with both hands over her head. Glancing over at the table, she saw that she'd dripped blood on several of the Valentines. *Perfect.*

Patty noticed what Veronica was looking at, and said, "Don't worry about any of that. You sit on the couch and I'll finish up."

"No, I want to help."

"While you bleed all over everything? No, thank you."

Patty showed her over to the couch and asked if she wanted anything. Veronica felt frustratingly helpless. "Just rest a few minutes," Patty said.

She listened resentfully to Patty bustle around the kitchen, cutting paper and filling bags and opening and closing containers. Against her will, she began to feel drowsy as the sounds slowed her pulse. It felt like being a kid, being home on a sick day with her mother preparing toast with applesauce and ginger ale.

Veronica's eyes started to droop.

The next thing she knew, Patty was gently shaking her awake, saying, "I have to go."

"Go? What? Why?"

Patty handed her a plate with two heart-shaped cookies, frosted in white with red sprinkles. "Eliza is in Madison. As in, Wisconsin. She needs me to pick her up. She sounded really bad. She was crying and begging me to come right away. I have to go."

This news was like cold water waking her up. *Eliza. The prodigal sister.* She'd been gone for three years, and all of a sudden she called her sister begging to be picked up. Veronica could understand why Patty was rushing out the door. "Yes, alright, of course. Go."

"You'll be okay with the girls?"

"I sliced my finger. I didn't have a lobotomy. Just go. Have you told Matt?"

Patty shook her head. "Help me think the logistics through first."

Veronica checked her watch. "Do you want to just hang tight until Junie gets here in, like, twenty minutes, and let her know where you're going?"

"That's a good idea. Except . . . you really think I should tell Junie before I know what's up with Eliza? I mean, she was doing drugs before she even left. Who knows what kind of shape she'll be in when I get her."

"Does Junie remember Eliza?"

"Barely."

"Just tell her your sister needs you, and you have to help her. I bet Junie will be so excited about the party, she won't mind."

"You're probably right, though I'm not sure what that says about her relationship with me. Won't she miss me?"

Veronica rolled her eyes. "No. It should tell you nothing more than that you've raised an independent girl."

"Alright." Patty seemed distracted enough not to be able to give that more thought. "Okay, so Madison is about three hours away in the car, and I'll leave a little after three, so I should get to Eliza by six thirty, maybe seven if traffic is heavy."

Veronica nodded.

"Then three hours home, so I should be back by . . ."

Her friend seemed distressed enough not to be able to do the calculation, so Veronica supplied the answer: "You'll be home between nine thirty and ten."

Patty nodded. "Depending on the shape she's in, I might purposely take a little longer, stop and get something to eat and stuff, to make sure the kids are in bed when I get home. The last thing she probably needs is some big reunion the moment she walks in the door."

"Sounds like a plan."

"I'll call Matt."

While Patty went to Matt's office to make her call, Veronica heaved herself off the couch and packed a little care package for her friend and Eliza: tissues, bottles of Coke and a thermos of water, cookies, and a full bag of Valentine's candy.

No sooner had Patty reemerged than two carloads of second grade girls burst into the living room exclaiming over the decorations and the treats. Mercifully, Siobhan had been one of the drivers and she came in to help, as originally planned. While Patty took Junie aside, Veronica quickly whispered Patty's news to Siobhan, then took the reins of the party, clapping her hands to get the girls' attention so she could explain the agenda: cookies and chocolate milk first, then make-your-own Valentines, a card exchange, then pin the heart on the snowman, Heart-Hug-Kiss (a variation on tic-tac-toe that Patty had invented), and last but never least, musical chairs. Then everyone would collapse for a special treat: *Lady and the Tramp* on television.

The girls cheered wildly at this agenda, including Junie, who had rejoined the group. Veronica waved at Patty over the heads of the girls, and her friend waved back. *Good luck*, Veronica mouthed, and Patty silently replied *Thank you*, then stole out the door.

Veronica had to reapply Band-Aids to her finger three times throughout the afternoon, and she kept finding spots of blood on her own sleeves, but otherwise the party was a success, and she found herself enjoying the buoyant energy of the girls, as they shared candy and paper and scissors and giggled about a boy in class who'd given one of them a special Valentine with a box of chocolates at school.

Miraculously, there weren't even any signs of unrest during the sugar-fueled blur that concluded with the exhausted girls draped on every last couch and chair in Patty's family room, anesthetized by the flickering cartoon dogs on the large TV. It was amazing, Veronica mused, what this electronic box brought into their houses every day. Spaghetti-soft Disney romance, like now, as well as murders and marches, footage of American boys killing Vietnamese boys halfway around the globe, and the National Guard shooting college kids just hours away in Ohio. The contrast was dizzying. What kind of person would Kate—and this new little human incubating inside her—grow up to be in a world of such profound incongruity, all right there for the viewing?

While the girls watched, Siobhan and Veronica cleaned up the kitchen and talked quietly.

"I hope Patty's doing okay," Siobhan said.

"Patty will be fine. She's stronger than she thinks she is. It's her sister, Eliza, I'm worried about. She barely graduated high school, and the guy she left with, this bass player in a band, was bad news."

"Was she in the band, too?"

"No. Honestly, I think I could have gotten behind her leaving, and helped Patty understand it better, if she was in the band, if she was pursuing some kind of dream. But she was only trying to escape. She was a kid, like fourteen, when their mother died, and Patty had just had Junie. The death was awful, so unexpected. It was like she was diagnosed with cancer one day and gone the next. Everyone was in shock, and their dad, who's a really sweet man, just retreated into himself. So when Eliza started hanging out with a rough crowd in high school, he barely noticed. She started cutting school and getting drunk a lot, doing drugs, and . . . You know how the song goes.

"Patty and Matt took her in for a little while, in the hopes of providing some structure, but it didn't work out." Veronica remembered the many nights her friend would call, frantically wondering where her teen sister was at midnight. Inevitably, Eliza would stumble in, drunk or high, around one or two. Patty had been so anxious for almost a year like that, until she finally told her sister she had to go back to their dad's place. "They all hoped, when their father remarried, that things would improve, but they only got worse. Eliza viciously hated Linda."

"That's terrible. I had no idea," said Siobhan. "Is there anything I can do?"

"I wish there was."

The two women were quiet for a minute while Lady and her friends yapped on the screen.

"I almost hate to mention this, after learning all of that," Siobhan said hesitantly, "but . . . I have an exciting piece of news, and I do need to tell you because it will affect the Service."

"Ooooh, tell me. I need some good news."

"I was offered a gallery show in New York this summer."

"Oh my God! That's wonderful!" Excited happiness rose like a helium balloon inside Veronica. She hugged her friend. "Congratulations!"

"It's great," Siobhan agreed, hugging her back, then releasing her. "But I'll have to go to New York later this spring to set things up, and then again for the opening. So I have to be away for two separate weeks, and I have to put in a lot of extra studio time to finish the paintings."

"Of course you do! Oh, man, I'd love to come with you."

"That would be so fun. . . . But . . . listen, I think this is the kick in the pants we need to train more Janes. Only four of us know how to do the . . ." Siobhan glanced back at the girls in the adjacent room and lowered her voice even more to say, "Only four of us know how to do the procedure itself, and you and I are half that. It's not enough to meet the rising demand, even without me leaving for two weeks, and you with . . ."

Veronica sighed. Siobhan was right. Even if she worked till the day this baby was born, she'd have to take *some* time off once it arrived. And if her partner was also limiting her hours, they needed quite a lot more help. "Well, Phyllis is already on her way. How many more do you think we need?"

"At least two, but probably more like four. Six to eight total."

"Double. Wow. You're right, though. I know you're right." And yet where would these qualified abortionists come from? Even as demand grew, volunteer numbers stayed the same. They were all so *young*. Could an undergraduate learn to do a D&C? She and Siobhan had been dodging that question, but a few of them might have to—the women from the university were the most into Jane's mission, the most dedicated. Maybe dedication and a steady hand were all they needed. That was all she and Siobhan had had when they'd started. Fortunately, the younger ones had time, too, which the older members had far less of.

"We'll get it done," said Siobhan. "The latest group of trainees is excellent. Some of them will want to do it. We'll double down on posters at the university and the other colleges around. I've already told the Union to send more volunteers to us."

"And then . . ." Veronica had been about to say *Then we'll sip champagne together at your fabulous gallery opening*, but then she realized, "Then I'll have a newborn and you'll be famous."

She didn't think of herself as a jealous person, but something about that statement made her feel heartsick. A *gallery show in New York. Wow. Good. Good for Siobhan. She deserves it.* Veronica remembered the shambles of her friend's life three years ago, when the two of them, both blindfolded, had held hands in a stranger's car, heading into the great unknown.

Siobhan's strength, and her ability to say no to all the expectations and rules laid down for her life, had filled Veronica with a hope and excitement she hadn't felt . . . ever. She wanted to feel that way again. And she had, every time another woman called her saying she needed help "like your friend." The Service had long been her missing piece.

But now . . .

She was pregnant. With a child she wanted, a child she'd chosen to have, as much as the women who came to the Service chose the opposite. And yet she felt like her life was closing in on her—her options were closing in—just as doors and windows everywhere were opening for Siobhan.

Doug had made it clear he wasn't comfortable with her continuing to work with Jane, and even though he hadn't forced the issue yet, Veronica knew it was only a matter of time. He checked for bugs in their phones every damn day, which was so passive-aggressive she wanted to scream—but she didn't dare, because then she'd have to talk to him about all of this. Once she was home with a newborn, up to her neck in diapers and laundry and bottles, how was she going to look at him and say she was going back to her illegal volunteer work? It had seemed possible when she'd gotten pregnant, before the demand for the Service had exploded, before Sam Wilder had started breathing down their necks, when Siobhan was able to help with Kate and Doug was entirely supportive of her. But with his change of heart, and her friend's real career taking off, and universal child care defeated, what the hell was she supposed to do? Hire a nanny with money she wasn't making?

She was furious with herself for not thinking all of this through in more detail, for not considering contingencies, for allowing motherhood to make her a fool.

Get ahold of yourself. You still have three months to figure this out.

She had no choice.

16

MARGARET

"Thanks for suggesting I get involved with Jane," Margaret told Phyllis on Valentine's morning. Her friend had arrived with paper cups of coffee and doughnuts in exchange for using Margaret's office to grade papers in peace instead of in the mayhem of the grad lounge. The last time they'd done this, Margaret had told her that it wasn't necessary to barter anything for a little bit of peace on campus, but Phyllis had insisted and added, tapping a stack of student essays, "Honestly, I need a sugary incentive to get through these."

As Phyllis nestled into the comfy, oversized armchair Margaret had found at a church jumble sale, she said, "I'm glad."

After a moment's hesitation, Margaret said, "Did you put together that Siobhan Johnson is Gabe's ex?"

Phyllis stopped her rustling around and looked at Margaret in surprise. "Seriously?"

Margaret shrugged. "I know. It's weird."

"Did you tell her who you are?"

"No, and I don't want to. Are you okay with that?"

"Fine by me. It's your call. Have you told him?"

"No. I'm still wrestling with that one. I haven't even told him I'm involved with Jane. Does Keith know, about you and Jane?"

"Yeah, he does. He's okay with it. Actually, he thinks it's great. He'd already sent a couple of colleagues to Jane. But he's unique. I can see why most women might want to keep it a secret. But if you get involved enough, you'll have to tell Gabe, because it takes up a lot of time."

"At the moment, I'm just volunteering my apartment."

"That's good. We need locations."

Margaret nodded. She'd been waiting and hoping for Phyllis to say something about Gabe since their double date, but she hadn't, even when Margaret had gushed about Keith and what a great time they'd had at Izola's. All Phyllis had said was, "We had fun, too."

"Are you and Keith going out later, for Valentine's?"

Phyllis rolled her eyes. "God, no."

Margaret laughed. "Too sappy for you?"

"For me, but not him. We'll do something. Maybe go bowling. I'm trying to . . . avoid something with him."

"Oh?"

Phyllis sighed. "He wants to get married. And I'm . . ."

Margaret raised her eyebrows expectantly, hoping Phyllis would go on.

"I can't believe I'm telling you this, but my shrink thinks maybe opening up to some people will help me, so here goes. I'm afraid I can't have kids. My sister and I are both prone to miscarriages. I've had one, and she's had three. What if I have the same kinds of problems she does? You hear about that stuff all the time, problems with pregnancies running in families. I'm worried that if Keith knows I might not be able to have kids, he'll want to move on with someone else."

"But he's obviously crazy about you," Margaret said. "I can't imagine he'd be able to ignore his feelings even with this news."

"People tend to lose all perspective when it comes to kids."

Margaret laughed. "That's true. All my mom wants is a horde of grandkids. But she's a different generation."

Phyllis went back to her bag and papers. The conversation was clearly over; she'd done what her shrink told her, and she wasn't comfortable going any further. Margaret, on the other hand, was dying to indulge in deeper girl talk—*Shit, do I have to think "woman talk" instead?*

"Anytime you want to talk more, you know where to find me," said Margaret.

"Thanks," Phyllis said with a nod.

Margaret caught a glimpse of the Jane Austen quote and thought, *Five minutes ago, I'd have said that of all the women I know, Phyllis is the most mistress of herself.*

You just never knew what people were pushing below the surface.

"Sooooo . . . what about you? Any romantic plans for tonight?"

"Gabe and I are going to a place called Lawry's. They're known for their steak and oysters."

"Oysters? In the Midwest? I had no idea."

"You can get oysters everywhere, Mom."

"Not minutes off the boat, like you can here."

Margaret rolled her eyes, for no one's benefit but her own. "That's true. But they are still yummy, and flying all that shellfish around keeps pilots like Dad in demand."

"You know he flies people, dear, not shellfish."

"I know, I know. It's the principle of the thing." *Forest for the trees, Mom.* She wondered how Phyllis was doing with Keith—would they really go bowling, or would he get her to talk by forcing the issue with a ring?

"Well, I hope you and Gabe have a good time. Valentine's can be a special night. Do you think anything might . . . happen?"

"Like a proposal? No. We've only been going out a few months."

"I suppose that's true." Disappointment was evident in her mother's deflated tone. "You children wait so long to decide these days."

"You and Dad dated for almost two years before you got married!"

"There was a war. Times were different."

The war made a lot of people get married faster!

"Hey, Mom, can I call you tomorrow? I need to get ready for my date."

"Of course! Have a wonderful time tonight."

"Thanks." She knew her mother wanted the best for her; she just wished "best" didn't mean a life that looked more like her brother's.

In the little velvet box lay a pair of elegant gold hoop earrings.

Jewelry. For Valentine's Day. It felt significant.

"These are beautiful," she said, slipping her usual pearl studs from her earlobes—a sweet sixteen gift from her parents—and setting them in the box so she could put the hoops in. "How do they look?" She turned her head from side to side, showing them off.

He smiled, obviously pleased. "See for yourself. Take a minute in the bathroom. We have time before our appetizers arrive."

She hurried to the ladies' room and was thrilled with what she saw in the mirror—the gold glinted subtly against her hair but didn't get lost. They were sophisticated and classic without being boring. She loved them. She loved the man who'd given them to her, the man who'd gone to the jewelry store and made this perfect, beautiful selection. And, she couldn't help thinking, her mother would love them, too—not just the style but everything they suggested.

When she returned to their table, their oysters Rockefeller had arrived and looked absolutely delicious, and she couldn't stop smiling.

"I love them, thank you." Before sitting, she bent over and kissed him on the lips.

"Happy Valentine's Day," he said.

"I have something for you, too, though it hardly compares," she said, pulling the wrapped package and card out of her bag.

"It's not a contest," he said, accepting the gift across the table, then pulling the wrapping paper off.

"Jeff at Powell's said this book is favored to win the Pulitzer or National Book Award. Maybe both. And it's about a historian."

Gabe grinned widely at *Angle of Repose* by Wallace Stegner. "I read about this in the *Tribune* when it came out. It's perfect, thank you." Then he opened the card and her heart beat nervously in her ears as she recalled what she'd written:

> *Happy Valentine's Day, Gabe. I hope it is the first of many happy ones together.*
>
> *Love, Margaret*

He slid his hand across the white tablecloth, palm up, and she reciprocated by putting her hand in his. "I love you," he said.

"I love you, too."

Her cheeks burned.

She'd been looking forward to this meal ever since they made the reservation, because she'd been hearing for months how terrific Lawry's was, but now all she wanted to do was leave and make love to Gabe.

"Let's eat quickly," he said quietly.

"You read my mind," she said.

Hours later, sleepy and satisfied in his bed, with her head resting on his shoulder and his arm under and around her, he said, "How would you feel about meeting Charlie?"

"I would like nothing more." She'd been wondering when this might happen, and now, after four months of dating, it felt right. They were in *love*, after all, she thought smugly to herself. Using the word for the first time, and wallowing in the lust that accompanied it, made her feel positively incandescent, like there was a lantern burning behind her sternum.

"She's going to love you," he said, bringing her hand to his lips for a kiss on her fingertips.

There was that word again.

"How about you come over for dinner with us this Wednesday night? That should be a low-key first meeting."

The day Jane was using her place as a Front. But that shouldn't matter, should it? She'd already told them she would be in and out all day. She had planned on being there all evening, though, and if she was at Gabe's, she wouldn't be able to help out as she wanted to.

But the man she loved had just told her he wanted her to meet his daughter. She couldn't let this opportunity go by.

"I can't wait," she said. *I can pull this off. I have no choice.*

17

PATTY

Though she'd returned with Eliza at midnight, after making several stops to get gas and food, and let her sister pee a remarkable number of times, Patty still woke up at six thirty, as she did every morning to get the kids ready for school. Matt was in their bathroom shaving when she stumbled in, bleary-eyed, and he gave her a surprised and concerned look. "Why don't you go back to sleep? I'll get the kids off to school."

"I have to make their lunches and everything."

"I think I can handle three peanut butter and jelly sandwiches."

Patty knew he meant well, but she didn't have the heart to tell him that Karen would faint from starvation rather than eat a PBJ; she was obsessed with cheese and apples these days. "It's okay," she said. "I'm awake."

He looked at her dubiously, and clearly—like her—thought better of wading into dicey territory. Instead, he said, "Tell me about Eliza."

"Well, she got in the car and just stared out the window. I asked a few questions and got one-word answers. She reeked of pot, which was actually preferable to the BO. She's such a mess. She practically sleep-walked into the house and collapsed on the bed. Oh, and she ate like seven orders of french fries. No burger, because of course she's a vegetarian."

Matt raised his eyebrows. "Wow."

"I know. I'm really worried about her."

Patty squeezed toothpaste on her brush and scrubbed her teeth and gums then tongue with gusto, as if cleaning her own mouth would somehow make sense of everything.

Matt also brushed his teeth, and when they were both finished, he gently held her shoulders in his hands as they faced each other. "I have a light day at work. I'll let Gilda know she can interrupt me anytime if you need me."

"Thanks." Her husband, the doctor. She remembered how safe she'd felt going into labor for the first time, knowing that even though he was a cardiologist, he'd still had to deliver a few babies as a resident. He knew the human body inside and out, and he exuded confidence when he spoke of it. When Karen had broken her arm falling out of a tree, and when their neighbor Jonathan had needed a tracheotomy during a summer block party, Matt had known exactly what to do. Even when she'd needed someone other than the oncologist to explain what was happening to her mother, Matt had been able to do that, always calm, always steady.

She leaned forward and rested her head on his chest. Would their marriage, which already felt precarious, survive having Eliza in the house again? Maybe this change in circumstances would actually bring them together. Because even though they'd had the one promising conversation weeks ago, nothing had really improved between them. They needed *something* to jump-start—resuscitate? rekindle?—their marriage. It was hard to imagine it would be Eliza, but . . . well, stranger things had happened, hadn't they?

For now, she calmed herself by breathing in the scent of his soap and shaving cream and mouthwash.

Kerri Maher

———

Eliza was still asleep when everyone left the house. It was ten a.m. on a Tuesday, and snow was falling outside. Patty held her breath and cracked open the door to the guest room, and there was her sister, sound asleep and silent.

What made her so tired? And so dirty?

And when's she going to wake up?

The phone rang as she was pondering those questions, startling her half to death.

"Patty?" *Veronica. Thank God.* "How are you? What happened with Eliza?"

"I'm okay, I guess. Eliza's asleep. She inhaled every french fry between here and Madison, then got in bed when we arrived, and that's the whole story at this point."

"How does she look?"

"Terrible."

"I'm not surprised. She obviously called you for a reason, and it had to be to get out of whatever she was in. Does she look . . . thin?"

"Not especially. What would it mean if she was?"

"It *might* mean drugs. But not necessarily. It's probably a good sign she's sleeping so soundly. If she was in some kind of withdrawal, I don't think she'd be able to do that."

"That's comforting, I guess." *And how do you even know that?*

"How are *you*?"

"Honestly, Vee, I have no idea." *I want to crawl out of my own skin.*

"Listen, I have to get to a few appointments today, but I'll be home tonight, so call if you need anything, okay?"

"I will."

"Maybe take a nap? Some extra rest would probably help you, too."

"Shouldn't I be giving that advice to you, my pregnant friend?"

"Okay, let's make a pact that we'll both be in bed by nine tonight."

"Deal."

They hung up, and Patty suddenly felt full of energy, as if her sister's appearance had lit the fuse on something inside of her that needed to blow.

The next thing she knew, she was in Matt's office, opening drawers.

The contents were an onslaught of boring: Bic pens, pencils, one fountain pen, paper clips, envelopes, rubber bands, staples, bills, family photos, old postcards, an inkwell, stamps, baggies with screws and nails, a small hammer, lightbulbs, erasers.

She moved on to the cabinets below the bookshelves.

Aha, jackpot. Boxes.

One was full of old medical school files.

One was full of pictures, which she sifted through, and though she didn't find anything surprising, she did get a little weepy at the snapshots of their children as babies, their big heads and round bums and Cupid's bow smiles.

Another box was full of stuff from their wedding and engagement, which she was touched by his keeping so close to him. The invitation. The menu. The card she'd given him for his birthday that year, the letters she'd written when he was doing his residency in another part of the city and it had felt like another state. Candids of them dancing, feeding each other cake, slipping rings on each other's fingers. Holding hands. Who'd taken these? Why didn't she remember ever seeing them?

The questions didn't feel important enough to keep her from moving on to the fourth and final box.

The contents of it flared up at her, an inferno of skin and lace and tongues. So many tongues! There was *Playboy*, of course, that one at least she'd heard of, and she took comfort in the covers that mentioned stories by writers of repute. But there was also *Candid, Twilight*, and one called *Blast*, whose tagline was "rugged men and willing women."

And a sticky, half-empty bottle of K-Y Jelly.

Was this what he'd been doing during her cookie party? When she was at church with the children?

Well. It was better than screwing an actual, live woman.

But oh, God. What if he's doing both?

Flipping through *Blast*, she felt more and more lost, Gretel in the forest with no breadcrumbs, as she looked at a picture of a woman cradling her enormous breasts in one arm and fondling herself with something that looked like a fuchsia-colored plastic penis with the other hand. The worst part, the absolute worst and most unexpected part, was that these images turned her on. The unexpected frankness of them, the pleasure on the women's faces, and her own mind's-eye image of Matt standing where she stood, looking at this picture and getting off to it, bloomed hot and wet at her own core, an arousal so intense it nearly hurt. She was about to slip her hand down her jeans— it would only take a minute to relieve this unbearable tension—when she smelled it.

The rot of her younger sister wafting down the hall, accompanied by the light sound of bare feet padding on the carpet.

Quickly, Patty put everything back in the box and closed the lid just as Eliza appeared in the doorway and said, "Hey, thanks for letting me sleep so long. And for coming to get me. Any chance I could . . . eat something? I'm starving."

Patty plastered on a smile and said, "I'm glad you got some rest. How about I make us something to eat while you take a shower?"

Eliza blushed. "I guess I need one of those, too."

"I just got some really nice soap and things for the guest bath." *Get sudsy at least three times*, she was tempted to say, as if to one of her children, but she bit her tongue.

"I need some clothes, too."

In the strangeness of last night, Patty had barely clocked the fact that her sister had gotten in the car without a suitcase. She had a backpack, and that was it.

"No problem," she said, struggling not to breathe through her nose as she led Eliza to the coral pink guest bathroom and checked to make sure it was fully supplied with shampoo and towels and everything— check, check, check. "I'll find something comfy for you to wear and leave it by the sink while you're in the shower."

"Thanks," Eliza said.

"Just put what you're wearing on the floor and I'll wash it." *Or burn it.* Did she really want those ripped black jeans and holey socks, or the ragged gray sweatshirt over the plaid shirt? And would those tangles ever come out of her fine blond hair?

When the bathroom door shut between them and she heard the water running, Patty sprinted around the house, cracking open windows and letting in the frigid, snowy air, cranking up the heat to warm everything and keep the fresh air circulating, then she stuffed all the bedding Eliza had rumpled into the wash before she grabbed a Fair Isle sweater and turtleneck and well-washed brown cords, plus underwear and a soft bra, and set the clothes next to the sink in the bathroom, which was full of floral-scented steam, thank the good Lord.

As the air in the house cleared and her sister's shower went on longer than she'd dared hope, Patty made cheese and cucumber sandwiches and even had a chance to shut all the windows before Eliza emerged in the kitchen with wet, miraculously combed hair and pink cheeks, looking nothing like the girl from twenty minutes ago or like the sullen teenager from three years ago, whom Patty remembered wearing nothing but black.

In that moment, what Eliza resembled most was their mother. Patty had a photograph of her from when she was little older than Eliza was now, twenty-one, and they might as well have been twins.

Except Eliza had puffy purple circles under her eyes, and a slouch that their mother never would have tolerated.

"Hey, you look great," Patty said, because it was mostly true.

"I feel like shit," Eliza said.

"Let's see how you feel after some lunch."

They sat down at the kitchen table, where Patty set out a plate with the sandwiches, another with two sliced apples, a bag of potato chips, and a dish of the cookies from the previous day's party. And a bottle of Coke each.

"There's so much." The marvel in Eliza's voice broke Patty's heart.

"Help yourself."

Eliza filled her plate. Patty wasn't hungry but made herself eat so her sister wouldn't feel like a zoo animal.

"Do you want to tell me how you are?" Patty asked.

"Not yet, okay?"

"Alright. Well. I'm glad you called."

"There wasn't anyone else."

Don't take offense. She's here now and that's what's important. Anyway, what can you expect from someone who's run off with wolves?

"Are you planning to stay? The kids will be thrilled to see you, and they'll want to know."

Eliza used the sharp edge of a potato chip to poke at the soft white bread on her sandwich. "I'm not sure."

Patty couldn't bring herself to say, *You can stay as long as you like,* because what if it was like last time? And now, Karen and maybe even Junie would pick up on their aunt's nocturnal activities. That couldn't possibly be good for two growing girls.

"I hope you stay." That, at least, was true.

Eliza nodded, ate what was on her plate, and then ate two more helpings.

Recalling what Veronica had said, she took comfort in her sister's appetite.

When Eliza was finished eating, she pushed the empty plate away and said, "Thanks. Listen . . . can we . . . not tell Dad yet that I'm here?"

"Sure, for a little while. Why?"

"I just . . . want to figure some things out first, that's all."

Patty just barely swallowed down the words *Alright, but we have to figure out what you are going to do, and soon.* "That makes sense. I only see him about once a month now anyway because of Linda."

Eliza sighed and shook her head. "She's such a bitch."

Patty winced at the harsh language. "Is she? I just thought she was kind of clueless."

"You weren't there with her."

"Did she . . . do anything to you?"

"I don't want to talk about it." And Eliza stood up from the table, brought her plate to the sink, and went straight to the family room, where she turned on the TV, found a soap opera, then lay sideways on the couch to watch it.

As the string music swelled around a dramatic scene before the ad break, Patty cleared the rest of the table and wondered what on earth she was going to do, about Eliza, about Matt, about the porn, her marriage, and this overwhelming, engulfing loneliness she felt, even with her sister home. She had to do something. It was her responsibility, as the wife and mother and older sister, to fix all of this.

There was no choice.

18

VERONICA

In Father Miller's tiny office, Veronica kept glancing at the clock on the wall. This was not a great day for him to be late for their monthly meeting, with the seven-month midwife check-in she'd squeezed in before Kate got home from school. Every single damn day felt like it was bursting at the seams.

"I'm sorry I'm late," he said as he hurried in and shut the door, sitting on the other side of his desk and setting his folded hands on the surface in front of him, which was covered by a green blotter.

"It's okay." It was hard to stay mad at this priest, who was part of the Clergy Referral Service that had sent countless women to Jane, along with a handful of other like-minded rabbis, pastors, and even one imam. "I'm so sorry about this, but I do have to run by ten thirty. I have less time than I'd like today."

"Can you give me a quick update on your family? We miss seeing you at church."

"I know, I wish we could come more often," she said, meaning that she wished they could see him more often; the rest of church and its rules could go straight to hell. "But I've been so busy and preoccupied." She laid a hand on her belly, which was, as Patty had said, still

174

small for the start of the third trimester, though the little one inside was about the size of a head of lettuce.

He smiled with recognition and a shadow of concern, for he knew about the miscarriage. "How are you coming along?"

"I'm doing alright," she replied. "Things seem to be progressing fine. I'm just getting into the seventh month."

"Goodness, that *is* excellent news," he said with a beatific smile. "Well. I'll be brief. I've been hearing some concerning talk after masses and at various other church functions."

"Sam Wilder?"

Father Miller nodded. "He is openly speaking about what he calls 'the back-alley abortion ring' everywhere he can, asking questions and drumming up support for his cause. He is turning members of our community against each other by encouraging a kind of spying I cannot let go unnoticed. I spoke to him sharply after mass on Sunday."

"What did you say?"

"That these subjects have no place in a house of God, nor do attitudes that separate our community."

"And what did he say?"

"That he was surprised at my cavalier attitude toward thousands of unborn souls." Remarkably, the priest looked both grave and amused at once.

"What about the thousands of *living* souls we *are* helping?" she snapped, and felt immediately bad about it, since Father Miller was just the messenger. She was always at the end of her tether these days. "Sorry, I didn't mean to get upset. I know we need to be on high alert, Father. But all of it . . . it's . . ."

"Stressful?"

"To say the least." The Janes were complaining more about the police surveillance. "It's not a joke anymore," Danielle had said. "Yeah," Phyllis had agreed, "and most of our patients are at higher risk of arrest just because they're Black." But no one had any idea what to do about it. They had to rely on the sympathetic men in the precinct to protect them. "I hate depending on men," grumbled Danielle. "I'd feel a whole lot better if there was something we could do." Veronica always invited their ideas, but no one had come up with anything other than constant vigilance: checking for bugs, looking over their shoulders, regularly changing the Jane phone number. They'd even stopped handing out flyers and instead started asking women to copy down any information they needed from a master flyer they kept at the Fronts and the Place. They'd also taken their name, and the Union's, off of the birth control pamphlet.

"I hate to add to it, but I do feel I should counsel you to be wary of all forms of surveillance. Anybody following you, for instance. Trust your instincts. Make sure your real name and address aren't on a single scrap of paper."

Veronica nodded, wishing Father Miller could offer some bright new ideas. "We're doing much of that already. I'm worried about getting too paranoid, though. We're supposed to be a safe place for women, and too much worry will make everyone feel unsafe." *The paranoia's already taking its toll on all of us; we're trying so hard not to pass it on to the women who come to us.*

"I understand the culture of kindness and openness you have so carefully cultivated, and I admire it. But for the greater good, please be careful. What is the better path: continuing the Service with some modifications, or having to close down because you're in . . . trouble?"

"I hear you, Father."

He nodded. "That's all I needed to know. I know you're a wise and thoughtful woman. A mother. A leader. You'll do what's best for your flock."

"Just call me Mary." Then, seeing the momentary look of confusion on his face, she added, "As in 'had a little lamb.' Not the virgin. Or the whore."

His laugh in reply felt reassuring, and she joined him, though she didn't feel lighthearted in the slightest.

Wearing only her bra under a soft sheet draped over her, Veronica lay on the daybed that her midwife, Amy, used for her patients and tried to relax as the plump, gray-haired woman laid her cool hands on her rounded stomach, rolling up from the base of her palms to the tips of her fingers in long moments of silence, as if listening with her hands. Then she applied some light pressure everywhere, but especially at the base of her uterus.

"Tell me if anything feels tender," she told Veronica, but nothing did. Then Amy got out her fetoscope, a stethoscope-like tool that always made Veronica laugh a little because it looked so improbable. She put the buds in her ears and the little cone at the end of the tube on Veronica's belly, then listened. "Strong heartbeat," she observed.

"Well, that's a relief," said Veronica.

"Let's take your blood pressure next."

"You're not going to take a peek inside?" Veronica seemed to recall the doctors during her pregnancy with Kate doing a cervical exam at every visit.

"I don't like to look unless there's a reason. Why take the risk of infection or disturbing the peace? I only do it if you or the baby gives me a reason."

Veronica rolled up to sitting and let Amy take her blood pressure.

"Excellent," Amy said, taking the soft cuff off with a flourish.

As Veronica reclined against the pillows of the daybed, cozy beneath the sheet, Amy pulled a red velvet armchair closer and said, "I wish I had seen your previous pregnancies, but everything looks good to me. If you hadn't miscarried once, and you hadn't had those cramps early on, I wouldn't have a single concern."

"But we've gotten all the way through the sixth month, and I can feel her—or him—moving, and the cramps are gone. So . . ."

"You know as much about the female body and pregnancy as I do. Do *you* notice anything different at this point?"

"It's actually hard for me to even remember my pregnancy with Kate anymore. It was so long ago, and I was so young. I knew nothing. The whole experience just felt wild. Then the other one kind of . . . erased that experience somehow."

Amy nodded and frowned, folding her arms over her chest. "I think you're very likely in the clear. If you were going to have a miscarriage due to a chromosomal abnormality, or another problem like that, it would have happened by now. But this is still what I would call a high-risk pregnancy."

Veronica rolled her eyes.

"I know you hate labels, but I would be remiss if I didn't take everything into account. Women who miscarry have a higher incidence of preeclampsia and other delivery problems even once the baby seems to be on track."

"But why?"

"We don't know."

"If men were the ones getting pregnant, I bet we'd know." Wasn't it Patty who'd said something like this recently? "Doesn't the patriarchal bullshit surrounding pregnancy ever piss you off, in your line of work especially?"

"Every single day," said Amy. "But if I let that get in the way of my care, I'd be doing you a disservice. *You* are the person in front of me, and you need specific advice and compassion. You're right, though: pregnancy hasn't been studied enough. But that fact doesn't impact the more immediate truth that right now, you are at higher risk of problems than other pregnant women."

Veronica folded her arms between her heftier breasts and rounded belly. "So what do you recommend I do?"

"Drink much more water than you think is necessary. It's possible that those early cramps were due to dehydration. And with the work you do, I imagine it's easy to forget to hydrate. And in these later months, hydration is more important than ever. Try and drink a glass of water every hour. Otherwise, keep doing what I believe you're already doing. Tune in to your body and call me if anything seems out of the ordinary. And promise me, but more importantly promise *yourself*, that if you feel anything amiss—anything at all—you'll slow way down. Take time off work, take more naps, eat plenty of nutritious food, and again, drink as much water as you can stomach."

"Alright," she agreed, trying to sound like a dutiful patient, even though she felt panic surge inside her like heartburn. Her due date was getting closer, and even though Phyllis and a girl named Belinda, along with two others, were in training to learn D&Cs, she felt woefully behind.

Amy put her hand on Veronica's arm and said, "I know it's hard. But you're almost there, and you're doing great."

This kindness made everything in Veronica gum up with emotion. *I am not doing great.* "Thanks," she rasped, and as if on cue, the baby stretched an arm or leg so long it made a cherry-on-top bump above her belly button.

Amy laughed. "Apart from anything else, you'll need to be careful of that one. I think you have an eavesdropper on your hands."

"Just what I need," Veronica joked back, doing her best impression of a new mother who was receiving Amy's humor the way it was intended, to lighten the mood, and wishing mightily that a precocious child was her biggest worry.

"Mom, can I ask you something?" Kate said squeakily that night after bath time, one of Veronica's favorite hours of the day, when her daughter smelled of shampoo and mint, and she was cuddly in those black pajamas that had faded to gray and would need to be replaced soon because they were capri length at this point.

"Of course, sweetie, anything." Veronica picked Kate's favorite books off the floor—*Goodnight Moon* and *Rumpelstiltskin*—then sat on the bed next to her daughter, wondering what was weighing on her, because Kate looked quite nervous about something.

"What do you do when two of your friends don't like each other?"

Veronica put her arm around Kate and nestled them into the pillows. "That's a tough one, even for an adult. Can you tell me who the friends are?"

"Junie and Charlie."

"They don't like each other?" *How did I miss this?*

"It's more like Charlie doesn't like it when I'm friends with Junie."

"That's strange. Why?"

"I don't know. She just says that she wants me to be her best friend and that means I can't be friends with Junie."

"And how do you feel about that?"

"Bad. I like Junie."

Veronica put a hand on her daughter's knee. "You're a good friend, Kate. Don't stop being friends with Junie. She needs you as much as Charlie does."

"But what if Charlie gets mad?"

"Hm, that is a good question. . . . What if you say to Charlie that she'll never stop being your friend *and* you'd like to include Junie, too?"

Her daughter actually rolled her eyes at her. *Already?* It was such a mature gesture, it startled Veronica. "I've already tried that, Mom."

"I'm proud of you for trying. Sometimes people need to hear a thing more than once before they accept it, though. Keep telling Charlie she'll always be your friend and that Junie is your friend, too."

"Okay," she said dubiously. "I'll try."

"And I'll do my part and talk to Charlie's mom, okay? I think Charlie needs Junie, too. We girls have to stick together."

"Thanks, Mom." Kate put her head in Veronica's lap, and she stroked her daughter's damp hair. *Incredible.* Veronica recalled a conversation when Siobhan had revealed to her that Gabe didn't like it when she made plans with friends. "I used to think it was because he loved me so much that he wanted to spend all that time with me," she'd said. "Now I feel like he doesn't want me to have my own life."

Now here's his daughter making my kid feel the same way.

After saying good night to Kate, Veronica put her own head in Doug's lap where he sat on the couch watching *The Carol Burnett Show* on a low volume. He stroked her hair as she'd done Kate's, and the sensation was so soothing.

I saw Amy today, she wanted to say, but she didn't want to get into what the midwife had told her. If she did, Doug would surely pounce and say he agreed, that it would be better for her to take it easy. She wanted to stay as long as possible in the détente at which they'd arrived, where if she didn't mention any problems, he didn't push her to stop working. The problem with that arrangement was that she felt pent-up most of the time, a bottle of champagne half-uncorked.

"Want me to play something?" he asked softly as the audience on the television roared with laughter at Carol making a guppy face.

Veronica nodded, and he gently got up and switched off the TV, then sat at the piano bench and played an embellished version of "Love and Marriage," which made her laugh in spite of herself. God, she loved him for playing that instead of, say, "The Way You Look Tonight"—which might have been funny also, but in an ironic way, and its more overtly romantic tone would have absolutely undone her.

Sitting down on the bench beside him, she said, "Thanks for that."

He kissed her tenderly on the lips, and her body immediately responded with heat and tension. She leaned in and trailed her fingers down his back. He turned toward her and pulled her close, and their kisses deepened until they started pulling off each other's shirts, then laughed that they should really go upstairs instead of putting on a show for the neighborhood at the piano in their bay window. It had been a long time since they'd come together like this, in a lust born of longing and a wordless physical need, and it was, like his song, exactly what her soul needed to help it rest.

19

MARGARET

The day that Jane used Margaret's apartment as a Front felt confusing and messy from the moment Trudy arrived in the morning with arm-loads of coffee canisters and paper plates and cups and napkins and boxes and boxes of Girl Scout cookies. "My niece is in a troupe, so I thought I'd support her. Plus, I'm addicted to the Chocolate Mints. . . . Oh, thank goodness you have a full-size coffee maker. I forgot to ask about that."

Margaret pitched in to help Trudy set everything up, then Belinda arrived to be the third Jane on the first shift. Having her former stu-dent in her home, then having her home fill up with strangers, mostly women of varying ages but also a few men and quite a number of children, was distressing. There were definitely more than the prom-ised twelve at once, and at one point Margaret counted eighteen. Also, there was so much coming and going. Trudy would spot the station wagon as it approached the end of the block, then she'd call three names, and there would be a commotion of standing and hugging and reassuring. As the day progressed, there were regular swaps of people—one batch of women leaving as another arrived—every hour or so.

She hoped no one else in the building would stop these women and ask questions. She hoped no one in the building would ask *her* questions tomorrow. She was only a renter. Suddenly her decision to loan the apartment felt ill-advised.

Then she felt distressed that she was distressed. These people were here illegally! *They* were the ones in need of comfort and understanding. Mothers and sisters and grandparents were crying. In her living room.

Oh my God, this is how my mother would react. Her mother also never let anyone into her kitchen, even at the holidays; at Thanksgiving, she did *all* the cooking. Margaret was only allowed to snip the ends off the green beans, and Clark's wife was only allowed to bring pumpkin pie, because, as her mother always said, she, Margaret, hadn't gotten the pie gene but thank heavens Clark's "darling wife" had.

Margaret willed herself to not feel shaky and anxious, but it did nothing to assuage the intense desire she felt to ask everyone to be quiet and sit down. Trudy and Belinda seemed entirely at ease in the chaos, which just made her feel all the more restless. She tried to throw herself into it by walking around with the pot of coffee and a box of cookies, asking if anyone wanted a refill or a snack. And she attempted to practice the skills she'd learned in the training sessions by asking a few people if they had any questions. It helped steady her, to a point.

One girl—*woman, woman, woman,* Margaret instructed herself, which was counterintuitive because this person was clearly a teenager—looked into Margaret's eyes as she accepted a cup of coffee, and said, "I'm scared." Margaret could see the fear in the bright whites of her eyes, the rapid back-and-forth movement of her irises, and in a flash Margaret felt the teen's fear in her own chest.

"That's entirely natural, but I promise you that you're in excellent hands. And remember, this is the day you claim your life as yours and no one else's." Margaret added that last sentence, recalling that throughout her training it was drilled into her that Jane's mission was not abortion but liberation, and that it was imperative that the women who came to them left the experience feeling more in control of their bodies and lives than when they arrived. The heading of the birth control flyer they handed out read "Birth Control Saves Lives."

"Have you had one?" the young woman asked.

"No, but . . ."

At these two syllables, the teen visibly deflated and looked away.

"Both of the women in the kitchen have had one, if you want to talk to them," Margaret offered, telling herself it was absurd for her to be the one with hurt feelings here.

The young woman picked her eyes back up at this information and leaned a little to peer into the kitchen. "Alright, thanks," she said, though Margaret noted that she never rose from her chair to ask anything.

Margaret watched another pair of women with interest. One was at least five years older than Margaret herself, and had come with a baby and a female companion Margaret guessed was her sister, given the resemblance between them. With an adoring smile, the woman with the baby sat on the ground picking up various blocks and other small toys and waving them over her baby, a sweet little boy who kicked his legs and waved his arms excitedly at every object. Her sister had an Afro and looked around the place with an eyebrow cocked and her lips pursed. If Margaret had to guess, she'd say this woman was as dismayed by the circus around them as she was herself, and by the fact that all except seven of the people currently in the apartment were Black, and three of those worked for Jane. Margaret, too, felt unbalanced by that stark reality. Though she'd read some Audre Lorde since Izola's, Margaret felt ill-equipped to look this incongruity in the eyes and wished Phyllis was there. Regretfully, though, her friend wasn't due to arrive until four thirty. She also wished the racial disparity had been discussed in training.

She took several breaks to escape, always outside because the one time she tried going into her bedroom to work with the door closed, hearing everything on the other side and picturing it in her mind just made her more anxious. When she returned from a late lunch—a Chicago-style hot dog from a place she loved around the corner, eaten on a street bench and washed down with a Fanta because she wanted to care for herself in a comforting childhood way—there was a police car parked just down the block from her building, and her heart practically stopped.

Two men in uniform were sitting in the car, drinking coffee out of paper cups.

She'd never seen police around here before. This couldn't be a coincidence.

She hurried into her apartment and saw Phyllis in the kitchen. Early!

Phyllis smiled at Margaret and said, "Nice digs."

"Thanks," Margaret said. Then, in a low, quiet tone, she said, "There's a police car on the block."

To her surprise, Phyllis only rolled her eyes and sighed in an exasperated way. "Again? Don't those pigs have anything better to do?"

"I think I need some context."

"There's a cop in the local precinct that has a bee in his bonnet about the Service, and he likes to shadow us to scare us."

"If he knows that much about us, why doesn't he do anything?" *Us.* The word was simultaneously thrilling and terrifying.

"His boss, whose daughter used the Service, has him on a tight leash. We have more friends than enemies in Chicago, and our friends keep our enemies in check."

"And that doesn't worry you?"

"All the time, when I let it, so I try not to let it," Phyllis said. "There's not much we can do about it. Anyway, remember, nothing happening here is illegal. You're just having some friends over."

"What if they follow one of our cars to the Place?"

"They've done it before." Phyllis drew in a deep breath. "Listen, Margaret, this is something you're going to have to learn to ignore. If it makes you feel better, I've heard there's also a mob boss on our side, paying off some of the hotter-headed officers to stay cool."

"That does not make me feel better. But having you here does." *The Mafia? What have I gotten myself into?*

Phyllis nodded, her expression serious and compassionate. "Hey, I get why you feel tense. After my first few shifts, I went home and slept hard for like twelve straight hours."

"I'm supposed to meet Gabe's daughter tonight."

Phyllis whistled. "Oh, man, I'm sorry. You can take off for a few hours if you need to. Go hide in your office or the Regenstein for a little while."

"I feel bad about leaving so early."

"No one wants you to burn out on your first shift. Go."

Phyllis's words made her feel lighter, a relief immediately followed by a crashing wave of guilt. "How do you do it?"

"We *have* to do it. This is how change happens."

Phyllis's words gave Margaret a burst of confidence, and a reminder of why she'd volunteered in the first place.

"You'll get there," Phyllis went on. "I know you want to. Anyway, I happen to know you've got a lot on your mind today of all days. It's not a small thing meeting your boyfriend's kid for the first time."

"It's not," Margaret agreed.

"So go. Rest up and get this meeting out of the way so next time you can last longer."

"*Thank you.*"

In her bedroom, she changed into clean cords and the first-date blue sweater. Back in the kitchen on her way out, Margaret opened her fridge and plucked two bright green apples out of the crisper, then tossed one to Phyllis. "Thanks again."

Phyllis took a big, crunchy bite. "Anytime."

Outside on the sidewalk, Margaret turned her back on the police car and walked the other way.

"It's so nice to meet you," Margaret said to Charlie, who was surprisingly tall for a seven-year-old. Leaning against her dad, Charlie gave Margaret a wide, ready smile, showing off a mouthful of mismatched big and little teeth with a few gaps.

Margaret hadn't predicted just how off-balance it would make *her* feel to see Charlie standing in the house where she and Gabe had spent so many cozy nights eating and reading and watching TV and making love. And now here was Charlie, an intruder. Which was ridiculous, because of course she, Margaret, was the intruder. To Charlie.

"Nice to meet you, too," Charlie said dutifully. Then, twisting around and looking up at her dad, she said, "You didn't let her in my room, did you?"

He laughed, then said, "Squirrel, we talked about that already. Of course not. Don't be rude to Margaret."

"I completely understand," Margaret said with exaggerated deference. "I don't like strangers in my room, either." *And boy oh boy did today show that to me!* "But I'd love to see it when you're ready to show me."

Charlie looked up at Gabe for a cue of some sort, and he said, "It's up to you, Squirrel."

Squirrel. What a cute and funny nickname—and a second nickname at that, since Charlie was already short for Charlotte. There must be a history to it, which he hadn't explained—and the way it unified the two of them made Margaret feel even more like an outsider.

Charlie shrugged. "Alright," she said noncommittally. "If you want to see."

So. She wasn't going to be easy to win over. Margaret wished Gabe had let her bring a gift, even just a book, but he'd said no. "I don't want Charlie to think you're always going to spoil her," he'd said.

Gabe's daughter turned and led the small parade of them up the stairs and down the hall to her room—which Margaret had indeed never been in before and had always been curious about. The girl swung open the door with a creak and jumped over the threshold like it was the final stop in a game of hopscotch. "Ta-da!" She flung her arms open and smiled wide.

Margaret could see why. It was a very large room at the corner of the house, filled with light from two large windows on each of the perpendicular walls, and it was full to bursting with toys and activities. She had bright red bunk beds, and the floor was littered with stuffed animals, including several squirrels. Flanking the doors to her closet were two waist-high bookshelves with so many books, there was hardly space for more. Up against another wall was a card table that had a small sewing machine and piles of fabrics in a riot of colors and patterns, and a small desk next to it on which was a variety of papers and crayons and watercolors and scissors and glue. Margaret could see part of a drawing of a girl and a cat on one of the pages, and it was quite good. *Well, her mother is an artist, after all.*

"What an amazing room!" Margaret exclaimed. "You appear to be quite the artist, and"—she quickly tried to talk over this inadvertent reference to Siobhan—"I see you have a fondness for squirrels?"

"Dad's always called me Squirrel, so I collect them."

Margaret flicked her eyes to Gabe's, hoping for an explanation.

He smiled and shrugged. "She was always squirreling things away, even when she was tiny. Her mother and I would think we'd lost things, like a fork or a cup or a new roll of stamps, until we discovered this one's hiding place."

"I'll be sure not to leave my earrings around."

"Da-ad, I don't do it anymore, tell her!"

Gabe looked dotingly at Charlie and said, "Of course you don't, Squirrel."

Margaret wondered if Charlie liked the nickname or not. "I was only kidding about the earrings," said Margaret. "I can see you have much better things to do than put trinkets away like nuts for winter. Look at that sewing machine! When did you learn? I used to sew all sorts of things when I was a little older than you."

"Like what?"

"Clothes for my dolls"—which was when she realized there were no dolls in Charlie's room—"and little purses and pillows, and later I even made myself skirts and wore them to school."

"Cool! Will you show me?" Charlie's face brightened in a way that made Margaret feel nearly as excited inside. A connection between them. So soon. And it was also a connection to her own mother, who'd taught her to sew. Unexpectedly, she missed her mom. She had many fond memories of rainy spring afternoons spent at the sewing machine together.

"I'd love to show you, unless your dad has other plans? I know we don't have a lot of time together tonight."

"Far be it from me to stand between two girls and their crafts," he said. "I'll be in my office going through some paperwork."

Two girls and their crafts? Seriously? Want me to tell you what I was doing earlier today?

Girls.

The *craft* part was a link to Charlie, though, so she said nothing to Gabe. It wasn't the way she'd envisioned the evening going—she'd assumed the three of them would be spending time together—but Margaret was glad of an opportunity to get to know Gabe's daughter. Sewing had always been a relaxing hobby for her, and what she needed most after the day she'd had was to relax.

Charlie was adept with her hands and already knew how to thread the needle on the machine and sew a straight line. She also liked pairing seemingly disparate colors and patterns that nonetheless complemented each other—like a pillow with a pink and yellow polka-dot front and a yellow, pink, and green striped back. She proudly placed this pillow on her unmade bed. "Now let's make one for Dad," she said.

"Let's," Margaret agreed. "What fabric shall we use for him?"

Charlie dug through the brighter colors until she found a piece of navy velvet.

"For the front or the back?" Margaret asked, utterly swept up in their little project and impressed by Charlie's focus and careful hands.

"Both," Charlie replied.

How well she knew her father.

No sooner had the last stitch closed off the stuffing inside than Charlie ran down the hall and stairs, saying, "Daddy, Daddy, look!" Margaret caught up with her just as she presented the square pillow to Gabe, her arms poker straight and her smile so wide it practically split her face.

"Wow," he said, taking the pillow from his daughter. "This is beautiful. You and Margaret make an amazing team."

"Much better than me and Mommy, right?"

What a strange thing to say.

If Gabe thought it was strange, too, he didn't let on. Instead, he pulled Charlie onto his lap and kissed her on her bright red, happy cheek. "I think this hard work deserves a reward. How about . . . pie?"

Charlie's eyes went wide and round. "For dinner?!"

Gabe laughed. "Why not? It has fruit in it, doesn't it? I got a cherry one for dessert, but there's plenty to make a meal. But you have to drink a big glass of milk with it."

Margaret's heart expanded at this endearing moment and at this charmingly indulgent side of Gabe.

Charlie leapt to her feet and punched her fist in the air. "Yes!"

As she took off down the hall, Gabe looked at Margaret with a bright, proud smile and said, "Pie is her favorite, year-round. Sometimes I think it's the only way to get her to eat fruit."

She kissed him on the lips. "It's very sweet. Pun intended."

Gabe kissed her again.

Later, after he put Charlie to sleep, he slouched next to Margaret on the couch and said, "I love her, but she is exhausting."

Yeah, and you weren't even the one sewing with her after having scores of women tromping through your apartment. But it wasn't Gabe's fault that her own day had been so grueling.

"She's adorable," Margaret said.

"She said you were 'super fun.' I loved watching you two together."

"The girls and their crafts?" She meant for her sarcasm to be light, but feared maybe she'd overdone it.

"You're not going to get all Betty Friedan on me, are you?"

"Betty Friedan is a worthy role model."

"Please. She doesn't even have a PhD to give her work credence."

"I think she found it impossible to balance family life with higher learning. And by the way, despite her lack of degree, the research in *The Feminine Mystique* is top-notch. Have you read it?"

"I'm not into pop psychology. Maybe if her work lasts as long as Freud . . ."

"You'll be too dead to know. And it's not psychology. It's more like sociology. It's serious work, Gabe." Margaret folded her arms over her chest.

Gabe smirked and kissed her on the cheek. "I like this feisty side. I didn't know you were such a feminist."

"Is that a problem?"

"Of course not. And by the way, *you* don't seem to have any problem balancing family life and higher learning."

She appreciated the compliment but sensed it was just a way out of the conversation, and she didn't know how to reply without sounding ungrateful.

Gabe laughed. "Hey, we're not going to let Betty Friedan ruin our evening, are we? It was so great to see you and Charlie together. She doesn't respond to everyone like that."

He bent over and kissed her with intention, and his lips and his words about Charlie tugged at her heart.

"With Charlie home?"

"She's a sound sleeper."

She needed an indulgence after the day she'd had. And sex with Gabe never disappointed. But at eleven, when she rolled out of bed, saying, "I shouldn't be here when Charlie wakes up tomorrow. Not the first time," she regretted her decision to stay later with every fiber of her exhausted being.

"You're the best," he said sleepily, as he made himself comfortable in his bed. He'd be dreaming before she even reached the front door. *Lucky you*, she thought resentfully.

Hey, you're the one sneaking around, she told herself. Somehow, she knew that wasn't the point, but she was too tired and grouchy to think through the real point.

On her hurried, frigid walk to her own apartment, she braced herself for a mess. But true to the Service's word, the place was in better shape than it had been before Trudy had arrived, every scrap of paper and cookie crumb gone. Someone had even fluffed the pillows on the couch and vacuumed the rug. A little note was propped up on the clean coffee maker.

Thank you.

The recognition, which she hardly felt she'd earned, brought tears to her eyes. So this was what it felt like to be part of something truly essential.

20

VERONICA

After a terrible night's sleep, tossing and turning while even her dreams filled with the many tasks she had to accomplish, Veronica finally admitted defeat around five and carefully got out of bed so as not to wake Doug, then slipped downstairs to make coffee and a double batch of muffins for her family and the Service meeting later that morning.

The baby inside her greeted the day with some slippery calisthenics, and Veronica couldn't help but laugh a little. "You better not be an early riser on the other side, kiddo," she said quietly while rubbing her stomach. It had felt like a major victory to get Kate to sleep past six on the weekends, then go watch cartoons until she and Doug emerged closer to eight.

With the radio on very low in the background, she tried not to make too much noise with bowls and whisks and measuring cups, but Doug still appeared in the kitchen puffy-eyed and barefoot, tying his gray robe around his waist as she was putting the trays into the oven. "What's got you up so early?" he asked, taking a mug out of the cupboard and filling it with coffee. "I thought you said last night you were exhausted."

"I was," she said. "I am. I just . . . couldn't sleep."

"Want me to finish in here so you can try and get some more rest?"

"That's a sweet offer," she said, kissing him on the cheek. "But I'm into my second cup of coffee, so I don't think I could sleep now if I tried."

"Can you take a nap later, once Kate gets to school?"

"It's Tuesday, hon. I have a meeting."

He nodded. "Right, right. I forgot."

They stood in silence for a few uncomfortable seconds. Veronica knew what he was thinking: *You're choosing Jane over the baby. Again. You need to rest.* But he didn't say it, which was something. It helped that the pregnancy was progressing nicely, but she was acutely aware that every conversation, every interaction between them, contained a choice. Lately they had both been choosing peace. Though often it was strained, it was better than the alternative.

"I made your favorite apple muffins," she said.

He half smiled, and she could sense the tug-of-war inside him regarding what to say next. She started getting a little nervous when he took a moment to sip his coffee instead of replying. The last thing she wanted was to start this day on hardly any sleep and a fight with Doug.

"You know I'll do anything you ask to make your life a little easier, right?" he said, and she was startled by the question. She *didn't* know that. Which was ridiculous, because he already did a lot, more than any other husband she knew, taking care of Kate alone half of every weekend, and putting up with her late weeknights, for no monetary compensation.

She stepped closer to him and covered his bare toes with her socked feet, then looked up and kissed him. "Thank you," she said.

He put his hand on her rounded belly, and the baby kicked right in the middle of his palm. "She's happy this morning," Veronica said.

"That makes two of us," Doug said.

"Three," agreed Veronica, putting her hand on Doug's. Neither of them was being entirely honest, but still she took comfort in this stolen moment of togetherness and the bit of truth it contained.

Veronica managed to stay ahead of schedule all morning, arriving early at the Place to set up for the Service meeting. She was all finished making coffee and putting out the cooled muffins when Siobhan arrived to help.

"You're done already?"

"I couldn't sleep, so I got up early," Veronica replied. Then, not wanting to talk about herself, she asked, "Are you excited about New York?"

"I can't wait," her friend replied, and Veronica could hear her buoyant anticipation. "I don't even mind leaving Charlie with Gabe, even though I know she'll be a pill when I get back."

"His girlfriend hasn't softened him?"

"Well, Charlie certainly seems to like her. They sew together, which seems sweet and harmless enough. But Gabe is definitely introducing her as a fixture in his life. She's always there when Charlie's there now, at least during the day."

"Just as you predicted, I seem to remember." Siobhan had always guessed that Gabe would get involved with someone without kids of her own so she could look after Charlie when he had his time with her.

"Unfortunately, yes."

"Unfortunately for whom?"

"For Charlie, mostly. She wants to be with her father, such as he is. But he's never been able to handle her for long periods of time on his own, so he has to have help. And he's too cheap to hire anyone."

Veronica recalled how trapped Siobhan had felt when Gabe had refused to hire anyone to care for Charlie so she could paint, saying that spending time with their daughter was her job and painting was a hobby. He wouldn't even agree to getting a second car to make it easier for her to do the parenting job, for crying out loud. Siobhan used to call Veronica crying after increasingly nasty rounds of arguments: *I know we can afford it. He's just saying no to keep me from painting more.* "You must get such satisfaction from knowing that your painting is really paying you now."

"That and the teaching," she said. "I have to admit that my mean side also enjoyed telling him I was going to have a show in New York. I could practically hear him eating his hat on the other end of the line. That moment reminded me of why I live in a tiny place and don't take any support from him. So that he won't have power over me anymore. Everything I gave up felt totally worth it. I can do what I want, when I want."

"Amen, sister," Veronica said. She pictured the look on Siobhan's face when she'd shaken the keys to her clunker of a used car, the first thing she'd purchased when her divorce was rubber-stamped by the court.

"Annnnnd . . ." Siobhan smiled slyly. "There might be an old flame from art school I'm having a drink with in New York."

"No!" Veronica smiled hard.

Siobhan raised an eyebrow and smiled broadly herself. "He saw the gallery notice about my show, looked me up, and *called* me. He's also divorced, but no kids."

"Is he a painter, too?"

"Graphic artist. He does amazing work; it's all over the magazines."

"Sounds very promising!"

"So far, so good." Siobhan held up her right hand with index finger crossed over middle.

Slowly, then all at once, the women of the Service populated the

Kerri Maher

Place, chatting and laughing and slurping and munching. Even though her own exhaustion was finally starting to tug on her again, distracting her with thoughts of a nap before Kate got home, Veronica loved these meetings, the fresh morning hopefulness of them, all caffeine and sugar and can-do determination.

The meeting began with the usual agenda of mundane items: reports from the call-back Janes; reports on income and who was receiving financial aid and how much money was in the coffer; reports on new recruits and counseling shifts; volunteers for picking up more speculums and toilet paper; who would attend the Northwestern women's lib conference. Veronica found the daily grind soothing, the idea that their feminist protest could be plotted out in shopping lists and ledger entries; it made the Service feel less illegal.

Once the necessities were addressed, Veronica moved to the next agenda item, which was recruiting new members and training existing members to do D&Cs. "I'm pleased to report that Phyllis here is an absolute magician." She beamed. "I think she'll be ready to lead her own shifts in a week or two. Who else do you think is ready?"

A few names were bandied about, and the group of twelve Janes present that morning agreed that Belinda, Sue, and Roxanne were all ready.

"So in a few weeks, we'll have Phyllis and Trudy and Melanie and Danielle, plus Belinda, Sue, and Roxanne all ready to go. That's seven Janes who can do the D&Cs, without me and Siobhan."

There was a subdued round of applause, and Veronica felt some relief, though she was worried that any one of the three new women might still bail.

"What about recruiting more Black women into our ranks," said Danielle. "Can you help us with that, Phyllis?"

Phyllis inhaled deeply through her nose and flicked her eyes down, then back up at Danielle. "Listen. Good, clean, respectful abortions are our best recruiting tools, which is all well and good if you're a white college student or housewife with time on her hands. From what I've seen, a majority of the Black women who come to us are in service jobs, and those women are so busy making ends meet by cleaning your houses, or teaching your children, or waiting on your tables, scraping together enough money to come to us at all, or send their daughters or granddaughters or nieces to us, that they don't have any time left over to *help* us."

The truth of Phyllis's words stung. Veronica's cheeks burned with surprised shame, even though the words *I pay Shirley fairly* rose all the way to her mouth, but she kept her lips closed, the phrase caged.

"I do have friends with white-collar jobs and college degrees who'd be predisposed to help, but most of them are running around after their own kids when they get home from work. And they're already volunteering their time at church or for other causes that feel closer to their needs. The Black college students I know . . . I don't feel right about asking them to volunteer for something illegal. I mean, you're not exactly *asking* white undergrads to work for us, either. They find us on their own."

"Speaking of the illegality," ventured Trudy, "part of our problem with recruitment and retention in general is the cops on our asses all the time."

Nods and murmurs of assent reunited the room.

"True," said Phyllis. "We *definitely* won't get more Black women to work with us if we can't shake that problem, since they'll face at least twice the punishment of white Janes."

"Look, I know the police presence has increased recently," said Siobhan, "but we already take as many precautions as we know how to, and anyway, there is a very delicate balance in place here, where the law that's on our side keeps the law that hates us in check."

"Do we pay the ones who hate us?" Phyllis asked. "Because I've heard rumors, but I don't know for sure."

Shit, this is turning into quite the meeting. Veronica and Siobhan exchanged a look, and Veronica said, "Money does exchange hands, but we don't do it ourselves. We made a friend a long time ago, at the very beginning, who . . . helps protect us."

Luigi Galleani, he called himself, after the anarchist blamed for inspiring the bombing on Wall Street in 1920. "He sent his mistress to us, and he was so grateful to us for treating her well, and making a house call so she'd be comfortable, that he promised to make sure no one touched us." Veronica hadn't thought about that night in a long time, another memorable few hours spent blindfolded in Siobhan's company. It had been the most opulent house she'd ever seen, once they arrived and the blindfolds came off. In a weird reversal of her friend's abortion that had started it all, Galleani had arranged for a limo to pick the two of them up at the Drake, and once they were inside the luxurious vehicle, they'd been instructed by handwritten note to put on the black silk blindfolds until they reached their destination, which had been about an hour outside the city.

"How can we be sure he's still doing it?" Phyllis asked.

"I don't think he's the kind of guy to forget his debts," said Veronica, "but honestly, I think the problem isn't the ones he's paying. It's the holier-than-thou ones who won't take the money, like Sam Wilder. He knows he'll get fired if he does anything to us, though."

"Can't we get him to stop terrorizing us?" Danielle asked.

"Could we get your gangster friend to make some threats?" Phyllis asked.

Veronica's eyes widened. "I don't even know how we'd contact him."

"Didn't he leave a number?"

"Whoever called us did it from a pay phone."

"I'm sure we could figure it out."

"How? With a Bat signal?" Veronica was getting tired of this conversation. Police watched them. People disapproved of them. Those facts were part of the damn job.

"We should all ask around," said Danielle. "And if any of you buys drugs, even just some clean weed now and again, ask your dealer. All these guys are connected."

No one nodded, but Trudy drank in Danielle's words like Kool-Aid, and Veronica felt torn between relief that those two didn't get high before shifts and the certainty that they were still using in their spare time. Drawing in a deep breath, she felt the baby strike up another floor routine.

The meeting wound down with the usual review of women who'd called and needed to be scheduled. As per usual these days, everyone had to add an extra hour or even two to their already long shifts to cover the demand. God, she hoped the three new Janes pulled through. The uncertainty weighed on her as she distractedly helped clean up after the meeting, loading the dishwasher and wiping up the crumbs.

"Are you okay?" Melanie asked quietly. Their one resident nurse. Of course she'd check in with her.

"I'm great." Veronica smiled for emphasis.

"You know . . . if you need some time off, I can work a little more. We all could. No one wants you to—"

"I'm fine," Veronica interrupted. It had been sweet and unexpected when Doug had offered to take something off her plate, but this second offer was starting to make her feel inept. Jane might be overwhelmed, but it was still running, wasn't it? And her pregnancy was fine. She wasn't a china doll.

"Alright," Melanie replied. "You'll let us know if that ever changes, won't you?"

"Of course," Veronica said.

Melanie nodded.

"Hey, are you really asking all this because you don't think I should be working while I'm obviously pregnant?"

"No," Melanie replied firmly. "As long as you feel okay, how long you work is your choice."

Melanie's conviction surprised Veronica, and she was relieved by her answer. Well, she supposed, Melanie had three kids herself, and she'd worked in a hospital during all those pregnancies. Of anyone, she understood this particular issue best.

Buoyed by the support, Veronica nodded. "Thanks."

Had it not been for the police car she passed on her own block as she headed home for what she deemed a well-earned nap, she'd have said this amounted to a damn fine morning. But there was always something, wasn't there? A blight, a worry, a stain. Would life ever feel simple and safe again?

Come to think of it, had it *ever*?

21

PATTY

During the midmorning lull at Medici on Friday, Patty and Veronica took their coffees and muffins to a table in the corner of the room.

"It's such a relief to get out of the house, but I'm also so nervous about leaving Eliza alone."

"Has she done anything to make you worry?"

"Other than being herself?"

Veronica laughed a little. "She did call you, and she's been with you a few weeks now, right? Has she done anything recently?" Veronica popped a bite of blueberry muffin into her mouth.

"Not like she used to. She hasn't snuck out or done any drugs as far as I can tell. But she's also not *doing* anything. She sleeps and eats and watches TV." Patty sipped her coffee.

"I'm sure she's exhausted from whatever she asked you to get her out of."

"Sure, but . . . how long do you think I should give her?" Patty asked. "Before I . . . I don't even know. Tell her she needs to get a job or go back to school? *Something*."

"I'm sure this is driving you crazy, and I'd probably be impatient, too, but she was gone for three years and she's only been back a few weeks. More time seems like a good idea. The best ideas for her future will be ones she thinks of herself, not anything you make her do."

"She also doesn't want me to tell our dad. I went to lunch with him the other day and lied. Not that he ever asks about Eliza. But it was a sin of omission nonetheless."

Veronica nodded and blew on her steaming coffee.

"So . . . in other news, I found a big box of porn in Matt's office."

Veronica's eyebrows shot up. "What? What kind?"

"What do you mean, *what kind? Porn*. Women with no shirts, licking their lips, using . . . *things* on themselves."

"Was there anything violent?"

"Nooooo. Does that exist?"

"Everything exists."

"Should I worry if it was violent? What if he's found a better hiding place for that stuff?"

"That seems unlikely."

Veronica seemed remarkably unperturbed by all of this. "Aren't you . . . surprised?"

"I don't love the way a lot of porn treats women, but I also don't think it's bad for men, or women for that matter, to have a fantasy life. I once gave Doug an issue of *Playboy* because I wanted to see the pictures of Honor Blackman."

"*You did?*"

"I did. And it was . . . fun."

Recalling the strange stew of arousal she'd felt looking at Matt's magazines, Patty thought she might be able to see why. She also wondered if she could ever be as bold as Veronica. But something more pressing nagged at her. "Since we are *not* currently doing this together, is what he's doing *cheating?*"

"Absolutely not. Pictures are not cheating."

"Then why does it feel that way? He satisfies himself with the pictures instead of with me."

"A picture can't blow you."

"Jesus, Vee. You're not helping."

"I'm trying, I promise. But I can't tell you I think it's cheating because I don't."

"I just don't get it. I mean, I wear sexy lingerie. The sex we have . . . had . . . wasn't boring." She stopped short of admitting out loud that she *liked* blowing him.

"Talk to him."

"Talk to him about the other women he's imagining . . . *screwing?*"

"*Masturbating* to. It's not the same as actually having sex with someone else. Also . . . maybe he's not even imagining himself in the scene. Just looking at the pictures might be enough for him. And it's entirely possible he's thinking of you when he looks at the pictures."

Patty rolled her eyes. "Come on, Vee."

"Sometimes, when I'm with Doug, I think about Robert Redford."

Patty giggled in spite of herself. She loved this about Veronica, how she often knew the exact, funny, confessional thing to say to ease the hurt, if only for a moment. "From *Butch Cassidy and the Sundance Kid* or *Barefoot in the Park?*"

"Butch Cassidy all the way."

"Of course. Rebel."

Veronica shrugged and smiled as if to say, *Guilty as charged*. "So. Come clean. What about you?"

Patty rolled her eyes. Was she really about to admit this? Yes, yes, she was. "Warren Beatty."

"Still? *Splendor in the Grass?*"

"I'll admit to finding him sexy in *Bonnie and Clyde*. So, you really think that's the same thing? Thinking about an unattainable movie star to . . . warm up, versus *you know* to a magazine?"

"Not exactly the same. But very similar. It's all imagination, but within the bounds of the relationship."

Patty sipped her coffee. *Imagination.* What an appealing word. The last time she'd used hers was . . . for Junie's Valentine's Day party?

She used to use her imagination all the time—wasn't it her who'd devised plans to take the L into Chicago when she and Veronica were teenagers? Hadn't she been the one to mastermind all the group Halloween costumes in her sorority? Her harem costume had won a prize.

Maybe it was time to use her imagination more often. And for different ends.

"Eliza?"

"Eliiiiiiza!"

"Eliza? Are you home?"

Patty searched everywhere in the silent house, but her sister was nowhere to be found.

I knew I shouldn't have left her alone.

She went back into the guest room, where Eliza had been sleeping, and snooped, feeling both fearful and expectant about what she'd find after her escapade in Matt's office. She looked under the bed and in the closet and in the medicine cabinet in the bathroom, and then she opened the drawer in the nightstand. Curiously, there was a whole stack of paper with writing on it, a combination of what looked like musical notes and poetry.

Is Eliza writing music? She wanted so much to know. She wanted to know her sister better, to know more than the hard protective shell she was encased in.

On one ripped scrap of paper was a phone number written in her sister's handwriting.

She felt an impulse to pick up the phone and dial it. Was it a clue to where her sister was?

Wait, she told herself, putting the paper back in the drawer.

Hours ticked excruciatingly by as she tried to busy herself with laundry and mundane but necessary tasks, and after lunch it occurred to Patty that her sister's backpack was gone. She looked everywhere for it, re-treading her steps from a few hours before. But it was gone.

She started to feel panicky.

Surely she'd leave a note if she ran away again, right? She did the last time.

She was jittery with questions that *needed* answers, and her eyes fell again on the side table with the piece of paper and the phone number.

I can't lose her again. We lost Mom. We can't lose each other, not now, not after she came back.

With shaky hands, Patty opened the drawer and took out the paper, then headed into her own bedroom, where there was a phone on her nightstand. She sat on the edge of her bed and dialed.

"Hello, this is Jane," the woman said in a tone that was friendly, warm, even solicitous.

Jane. The abortionists.

And: she knew that voice; she just couldn't quite place it.

Patty opened her mouth to reply, then hung up.

Hello, this is Jane.

Jane who?

But that was a ridiculous question. Patty knew "Jane" wasn't a person; it was the name of the organization. A name that presumably made it easy to pick up the phone, to leave messages, to ask for people.

But who was it that had answered the phone? That voice was so familiar.

Hello, this is Jane became like a line from a song she couldn't stop humming in her head: *The wheels on the bus go round and round . . . ABC, easy as one, two, three . . . Doe, a deer, a female deer.*

Hello, this is Jane.

Who *was* that?

And was Eliza with her?

She wished she could turn her damn imagination off at times like this.

Patty dialed the number again.

"Hello, this is Jane."

"Hi. This is Patty Buford, and I'm looking for my sister. She's about five foot six with blond hair, her name is Eliza, and . . ."

"I'm sorry, I can't give out that information."

Who are you? "She's my *sister.*"

"Then I suggest you speak to her."

That infuriating tone . . .

Oh, I know who you are. "Is this Siobhan Johnson?"

The silence was short, but it was also just long enough for Patty to know she'd guessed right.

"This is Jane," Siobhan said.

Patty burst out laughing, but it had no mirth to it. "Okay, fine." Everything was spinning and swirling, and she felt as though she might actually faint. "Go ahead and keep your secrets, but send my sister *home.*"

She slammed the phone down, her breath and heartbeat racing each other.

Siobhan Johnson was part of Jane.

And I'll just bet Veronica's in on it, too.

22

VERONICA

"What? Patty called?" Veronica clutched the phone's receiver.

"Yes, she was looking for her sister, Eliza," Siobhan replied.

It seemed impossible. She'd *just* had coffee with her friend, and Eliza hadn't been missing then. But then Veronica recalled all the sleeping and eating Patty had reported her sister doing. Of course. Of course Eliza was pregnant. How stupid of her not to have thought of it before. She wondered if this was the real reason Eliza had come home. The Service got a lot of women from Madison. Then again, she might not have known for sure if she was pregnant yet when she called Patty. "Have you seen her? Eliza, I mean."

"Not that I know of, but I wouldn't recognize her."

"She looks like a blond Patty."

They were silent for a moment.

"Fuck," said Veronica.

"Yeah."

"Well, probably the thing to do is to ask anyone if they've seen her and to alert me if they do. I'm sure I have a picture of her somewhere. It'll be a few years old, but . . ."

"Vee?"

"Yeah?"

"Isn't that an invasion of privacy for Eliza?"

"This is different."

"Is it?"

"Come on, Siobhan. This is Patty's little sister."

"Exactly. If Patty meddles, Eliza might not get her abortion."

"Patty's going to come to me about this no matter what. Because I guarantee that if she knew it was you on the phone, she knows I'm involved, too. She's been asking me for months why I'm so busy all the time, and this is the missing piece she's been looking for."

"If you leave this alone," Siobhan said, "you can at least plead authentic ignorance to Patty. When she asks what you know about Eliza, you can tell her the truth. You don't know anything."

"Patty's probably going to lock her in a tower the minute she gets home, anyway."

"You really think she'd do that?"

"I honestly don't know. A long time ago, Patty was the risk-taker of the two of us. And once she got married and had Karen, then Junie, and her mother died . . . I don't know, she just became less herself. It was like she tried to become her mother, or a version of her mother that she idealized but didn't actually exist. You know, before she had Eliza, Patty's mom was the only mother in our whole neighborhood to work. At the local library. But she quit when Eliza arrived, and it's almost like Patty's erased that chapter from her memory."

"That's too bad. The fact that my mom worked gave me a role model of what it could be like, even though I know she was exhausted all the time."

"I totally get that. I am bone weary." Veronica paused, then said, "Do you ever feel torn? Like you're leading a double life? Never a good enough mother, never a good enough Jane?"

"All the time."

The two women were quiet, the truth buzzing through the phone line that connected them, then Siobhan said, "I didn't realize you felt that way, too, even with Doug."

"I never feel like a good enough wife, either."

"You know that's bonkers, right?"

"Is it? Doug thought he was marrying a schoolteacher who liked to write letters to Congress. The future lawyer didn't know he'd be marrying a future felon."

"You're more than that, and you know it. So's he."

"Sometimes it's hard to see beyond the irrefutable facts."

"When I do get down on myself, I try to remember that I'm showing Charlie another way of being in the world. If I didn't show it to her, she'd never know."

"You absolutely are. I just wish this other way didn't wear us down like this."

"I hope it won't in Kate and Charlie's generation. Isn't that what we're working for?"

"I used to think it was for us, too. Maybe I'll rest better if I can think of myself as the bridge to something better for our daughters."

Thinking of the girls reminded Veronica of her conversation with Kate. "Speaking of Charlie . . . I know this is a terrible time to bring this up, but Kate mentioned to me that sometimes Charlie makes Junie feel left out."

Siobhan sighed. "I know."

"I figured you did."

"I'm trying to convince her that many girlfriends are better than just one. But she's an only child, and her dad has convinced her that it's him and her against the world. Or against me. So this feels like a pretty natural result of that kind of thinking."

"I'm sorry, Siobhan."

"No, I'm sorry. I'm sorry it's putting your kid in a hard position. I'll talk to Charlie again. And you need to cut yourself a break. You're doing a lot. Kate adores you, and everyone at the Service admires you. We're training new women. It's okay to take care of yourself."

"Thanks," she whispered, then cleared her throat. "Okay, so . . . let me think some more about this Patty situation. I hear what you're saying, and I know you're right about letting Eliza have her privacy."

Veronica's doorbell rang, and she glanced out her front window to see Patty pacing her front porch. "Speak of the devil," she said to Siobhan. "Patty's here, waiting for me to get the door."

"Breathe. You can do this," said Siobhan.

"I guess I have to. Thanks. I'll catch up with you later."

She hung up the phone and took a deep breath as her friend had instructed. The doorbell rang again. The impatience told her exactly how outraged Patty must be.

Veronica tried to walk to her front door calmly and with purpose, but her racing heart was telling her to panic; she felt so torn about what to do. This was her oldest friend's little sister they were talking about. Veronica had lived through the hell of losing their mother with them. Maybe it was worth breaking a Service rule for them. Except the Service rule was meant to protect Eliza—all the Elizas.

She opened the door, and before Veronica could even say hello, Patty stormed inside, planted herself in the middle of the living room with hands on her hips, and demanded, "When were you planning to tell me?"

Veronica shut the door. "You mean about Jane?" She paused. "Because I just found out about Eliza." She only meant to clarify, but it came out more defensively than she wanted it to sound.

"Oh, of course Siobhan got to you before I could. That's just great. I've always known you two were up to something. I just never dreamed it would be *this*. I mean, *abortion*, Vee. You're a mother! How could you?"

Veronica shook her head, trying to sift through Patty's words.

"Wait. Are you upset about me being friends with Siobhan or the fact that we provide abortions?"

"Or the fact that *my own sister needs you more than she needs me?* I'd say I'm upset about all of it, Vee."

Veronica noted that Patty hadn't mentioned Matt in all of this. It seemed that she didn't yet know about his involvement with Jane.

"Listen, Patty, let's try and calm down here. You have a lot going on. We just talked this morning about your marriage, and now there's Eliza, and . . ."

"Don't tell me what I have going on. Maybe if you were around a little more to help your friends, you'd have a better handle on everything I have going on!"

You're not the only one with stuff going on, Veronica was desperate to say; the words practically rushed out before she could stop them, and yet even so, Patty's words struck a harsh chord inside her, another source of her guilt. *Never a good enough mother, wife—or friend.* Instead, she said, with conviction, "You know I'm always there for you, Patty. That's never changed."

Patty shouted a bitter laugh, paced Veronica's living room a few lengths, then stopped. "So. Tell me. How can you do this? I mean, do you actually *do* it? With your own hands?"

"Yes."

"But you're not a doctor! Matt went to school for *years.*"

"It's a simple procedure. We've helped thousands of women, and only a very small number have had complications. The vast majority go on to have healthy reproductive lives."

At this, Patty's chin trembled and her eyes filled with tears. "So . . ." Her voice was hoarse. "Eliza could still . . ."

"Have children later. Yes. Anytime she chooses. When the time is right for her."

Veronica watched this news sink in as her oldest friend nodded and swallowed and tried not to cry. *Damn the system that willfully feeds women false information!* Her friend was suffering in part because she just plain didn't know the facts. Veronica held out her hand in a gesture she hoped conveyed her willingness to hug Patty, and said, "It's okay to be upset. This is a lot to digest. It's also okay to be relieved that Eliza would be okay."

Patty took a step back from Veronica's hand and said in a low, steely voice, "Don't tell me how to feel."

"I'm not."

"Come on, Veronica. You've been telling me how to feel all day. Telling me it's okay that Matt likes porn and that I should be relieved that my little sister can have an abortion, and then telling me that I can still be upset."

"I don't think I said anything quite that way." Veronica's own anxiety rose inside her to meet Patty's. "Listen, I'm happy to talk to you about abortion and how safe it is, and how really and truly, it would—*could*—be the best thing for Eliza. It's amazingly empowering for a woman to take charge of her own body like that. We have women like Eliza come to us all the time, and very often it's getting the abortion from women who understand the predicament they are in that helps them turn their lives around." She'd been about to say *Some of them even work for us now* but thought better of it.

"Don't give me that women's lib bullshit, Vee. These are babies we're talking about."

"No matter what you want to call it," Veronica said, steering clear of words like *cells* and *fetus* that might further inflame Patty, "it resides inside a fully grown woman with a life to lead. Jane helps those women lead better lives."

Patty, her expression now distant and stony, didn't appear to have heard any of what Veronica had just said. "Just tell me where she is, Vee."

"I don't know," Veronica replied, relieved that this was—for now—the actual truth.

"I don't believe you."

"I really don't know."

"Would you tell me if you did?"

Veronica didn't answer.

"Time to choose, Vee. Eliza or Jane."

"Eliza *is* Jane, Patty."

Patty looked at Veronica with the same pity and disgust with which a person might regard a dead tarantula, then stalked out of the house, slamming the door behind her.

Veronica went straight to her phone and dialed Matt's office number, told his secretary who she was, then waited a few minutes for him to pick up the line.

"Hi, Veronica," he said. "How can I help?"

"Well, I'm calling with a red flag. You're going to get an earful about all of this from Patty tonight, I'm sure, but she knows about the Service because Eliza made an appointment. I haven't seen her, and neither has Siobhan, so we don't know where she is in the process yet. Somehow, Patty called our number and recognized Siobhan's voice when she answered the phone, then she put two and two together, and she just came over here to confront me. She doesn't know about you, though, as far as I can tell."

Veronica heard Matt expel a long, thin sigh, like air being slowly let out of a balloon.

"Thanks for the warning," he finally said, his tone resigned. "I had a feeling about Eliza, too."

"Patty is really pissed, Matt. I've never seen her like this."

"I don't blame her, to be honest."

"Neither do I. So . . . are you going to tell her?"

"I think I have to at this point, right?"

"Yeah. I'd do it," Veronica agreed. There was no way she could tell Matt that the deck was already stacked against him because of the damn porn, though.

"Okay, well, thanks."

"I'm really sorry, Matt."

"Why? This isn't your fault."

"I dragged you into this."

"I've been happy to help."

"And you know how much we appreciate it," Veronica said, unsure how to end the conversation, then realizing a question she should ask. "Can we keep sending people to you?"

"Of course."

"Thanks. You're one of the good ones."

"Tell that to Patty."

"Believe me, I've tried."

"I'm grateful for that."

"Bye, Matt. Good luck tonight."

"I'm gonna need it, that's for sure."

Veronica hung up the phone and was surprised to discover that part of what she felt was relief. One small piece from each side of her divided life had joined together: her oldest friend now knew about the Service. It was one fewer person she had to hide from.

If she didn't lose her first.

23

MARGARET

Daffodils began poking their intrepid heads out of the frozen, filthy earth, and they made Margaret smile from the window of her office, where she'd been hiding all day because the Service had needed her apartment as a last-minute counseling location that day. Even though they had to use her bedroom, it was a far less nerve-wracking experience than when they'd used it as a Front, mainly because she'd handed Trudy her keys and left.

Margaret had just finished grading a stack of papers when there was a knock on her closed door.

"Come in!"

The heavy oak and glass door swung open on its creaky hinges and in walked Leo Robinson, renowned Chaucer scholar and chair of the English department. He must have been at least fifty, and he still had a full head of thick, curly hair cut close to his skull and a dark, trim beard to go with it; he always wore a button-down shirt, sweater-vest, and bow tie.

"Leo!" Margaret said with a wide smile. "What a nice surprise." *And also, what on earth are you doing here?* She worried this was a little like getting sent to the principal's office, though Leo appeared relaxed and congenial.

"May I sit?"

"Of course," she said, gesturing to the hefty wooden chair across from her desk.

"I'm sorry I haven't checked in before this," he said, leaning back in the chair and lacing his fingers together over today's pale gray sweater-vest. "How are you doing? Is there anything you need?"

"Everything's been excellent so far," said Margaret. "The students are eager and engaged, the faculty has been nothing but friendly"—*if a little detached*—"and I'm starting to get involved in a few committees."

"Ah, yes, I heard you joined Harriet's little committee."

"It's a little committee with big aims," she said, mirroring Leo by sitting back in her own chair.

"Harriet and I have always enjoyed a friendly rivalry, and I admire her gumption. Her scholarship is impeccable, if a tad safe. I've always said she could take bigger risks in her arguments, but . . ." He shook his head and smiled at Margaret. "That's not the reason I'm here. *I'm* here to invite you to join a committee of mine."

"Oh? Tell me more." *Not that there's any possible way for me to refuse as a junior faculty member.*

"It's for a scholarship we give out every year to an undergraduate of great promise, a student who is a junior this year. His—or her—senior year becomes essentially free."

"That's quite a deal."

"And an honor. We have a one hundred percent success rate of placing these students into the graduate school of their choice. Last year, Ralph went to Yale Law, and the year before that Marcus went to my alma mater, Princeton, for a PhD in history. In previous years, we've sent them to Columbia Medical, Oxford, and even Berkeley English, *your* alma mater."

"Who was that? Any chance I might have known him? Or her?"

"Chip Arnoult."

"I did know him, though not well. He was a medievalist, right?" Margaret feigned puzzlement, because she wasn't about to let on that one of Leo's pets, who happened to be in her class at Berkeley, which meant she knew him pretty well, had gone so far off the deep end on acid that he'd dropped out after orals and moved with a group of other former grad students to a commune near Mendocino. Last she heard, he was part of a Gregorian chant troupe that was working on a record.

"Yes," replied Leo. "He wrote a brilliant thesis on the Paston Letters."

"I'm honored you're asking me to join," said Margaret. "When do we meet?"

"Wonderful!" He clapped his hands and rubbed them together. "The first step is that all faculty who want to participate—as we're nothing if not democratic—submit two names from among the juniors they've taught or advised, then I make a short list of five from among those names, and we ask each of those students to write an essay on their postgraduation plans, and how they will apply what they have learned here in the hallowed halls of Walker to their future pursuits. Then our committee convenes to drink Scotch and pick a winner." Leo recited this process with such glee, Margaret thought he might actually burst out with a "Ho, ho, ho, Merry Christmas."

"How do you come up with the list of five? Who else is on the committee?"

"The five are never hard to agree on. Usually, faculty submit the same names, so there is a great deal of overlap. Some years, the short list has only had four names. And the committee is composed of you, me, Pamela, Francis, and Stephen."

Margaret nodded and wondered whose place she was taking. She'd have to ask Pam, though she was hard to snag, as she had three children under the age of six and was already at work on her second book about Enlightenment poetry. "Sounds like important work. Count me in," she said.

With another loud clap of his hands, Leo pronounced, "Excellent. The call for names will be in this week's faculty newsletter and due by next Friday. I should have the application essays to you by the end of April, and we'll meet the first week of May."

"I'm looking forward to it."

"It's a very fine way to bolster that Service section of your tenure portfolio," he said, rising from his chair. "Do let me know if there are any other ways I can help you with that."

"Thanks, Leo." *But something tells me I'm better off asking Pam and Harriet.* She already knew whose two names she would submit for this scholarship: Belinda Silva and Marcie Green. Not only were they the strongest female students she'd had, they were head and shoulders more advanced than the best male student, Henry Lloyd. And she happened to know, though she'd never let on, that Belinda had been through an awful lot; she deserved this award for many reasons.

As he was opening the door to let himself out, Leo stopped and said, "Forgive me for being personal, but have I heard correctly that you and Gabriel Johnson are an item?"

"We are," Margaret said.

Leo nodded. "Congratulations. He's a good man. Many of us were . . . *saddened* when he lost everything in that wretched divorce. It's so good to see him with a spring in his step again."

Margaret knew that Leo meant well, but his comments made her skin crawl. *What am I supposed to say—"I'm glad I make him happy"?* She laughed it off, trying to put on a more masculine chuckle than a girlish giggle, and replied, "We're doing well."

"Bravo. Well. I'll be in touch with those essays before you know it, and be sure to submit your nominees."

"Oh, I will." *Smile.*
And with a wave, he left.

A glowing early spring sun was setting in a fuchsia sky when she arrived at Gabe's house, and she found Charlie zooming around with a little friend, flying some sort of homemade kite.

Gabe gave Margaret a happy but defeated smile, kissed her on the cheek, and explained, "They begged and begged, so I finally had a beer and said yes."

"Good plan," she said, her heart bouncing with the boisterous footsteps and laughter in the hall, the yeasty taste of hops and barley on Gabe's lips. "Can I get one, too?"

"Help yourself," he said. "And pizza is on the way."

"Even better," she said, cracking open a bottle of German lager she didn't recognize, not that she was any connoisseur of beer. It was cold and crackly going down her throat, and it tasted good and strong. This was what Friday night was supposed to be all about, she thought brightly—after a long, productive week, easy food and drink and family. Her heart felt full. Maybe she'd even tell Gabe tonight about the Service. But after Charlie was in bed. They'd decided tonight would be the first night she stayed over and woke up with them in the morning. Though cooking was not her favorite way to spend Saturday morning, she promised to make chocolate chip pancakes to ensure a good impression on Gabe's sweets-loving daughter.

"Junie's staying for dinner and for a sleepover," Gabe said, almost apologetically.

"Junie? Isn't that Patty's daughter?"

"The very one. She's a good kid. For some reason, Charlie didn't initially want to play with her. She wanted to see Kate instead, but I insisted. I feel like she spends too much time with Kate, and I know Veronica's never liked me. I don't want that rubbing off on Charlie."

"Not possible. Charlie thinks the sun revolves around you."

"I don't know about that, but as you can see, I was right. The girls are getting along famously."

Veronica, Margaret had gathered, was the founder of Jane and a close friend of Siobhan's. She hadn't met her yet, but all the other women talked about her like she was some sort of goddess. She supposed it was understandable that Gabe would be wary of her, since she was close to his ex-wife.

"Anyway, originally, Junie was only supposed to stay until dinnertime, but then Patty called me and sounded really weird, and asked if I could keep her tonight. No one ever asks the dad to help, so I kind of wanted to take the opportunity to be the good guy."

"You *are* the good guy." Margaret kissed him on the cheek for emphasis. "But," she said, fighting her own disappointment, "I guess this means I should go home tonight."

"No," he said firmly. "You're staying. I told Patty that you would be here tonight, and all she said was 'How nice you'll have help with the girls.'"

"Really?"

"Honestly, I'm not sure she was thinking it through. She sounded pretty distracted, but I'll take it. So you'll stay?"

"I'll stay."

"Good. I have some things to talk to you about later, once the girls are in bed."

"Can you give me a hint?"

Gabe lowered his voice and said, "Siobhan made a request I want to talk over with you."

Margaret nodded, understanding why they couldn't discuss it now and even feeling a little excited at being let further into Gabe's world. They were hosting a sleepover and discussing something important. Together.

She took another long swig of beer and put Van Morrison on the turntable and set to work making a salad to go with the pizza. This was definitely *not* the night to bring up Jane, and letting herself off the hook like that made her feel that much freer and happier.

The next hour was a whirlwind of pizza and juice and more beer, with two seven-year-old girls bouncing up and down in their seats with overexcitement at being together, racing through answers to questions like "What's your favorite part of school?" *Recess!* "What do you like to do at recess?" *Four square!* "Tell me something funny about your teacher." *She wears ten-inch heels and big bracelets!*

As they tucked into strawberry pie à la mode, Gabe said, "I'm afraid I have to warn you that bedtime will be at nine p.m. sharp, and that's already an hour past Charlie's usual bedtime."

A chorus of high-pitched *aaawws* went up around the table.

"Can we all play Clue?" Charlie asked.

Gabe looked at Margaret, who nodded her approval.

"Sounds like a plan."

"Yaaaaay!" went the next chorus.

Charlie turned to Junie and said, "He's the best dad in the whole world. I want you to come *only* here from now on, not to my mom's house. It's so much more *fun* here." Charlie scowled at the word *mom*, then looked at her father in an obvious bid for approval.

"Thanks, Squirrel," he replied.

Margaret understood why he'd enjoy the compliment, but it didn't sit right with her. Especially not when she noticed a few comments like this every time she saw Charlie. It was one thing for Gabe to be hard on Siobhan in adult conversation, but for him to allow Charlie to criticize her as well? She might understand better if Charlie wanted to get something from her dad, like a toy or even an extra scoop of ice cream, but all she seemed to want was to impress him. Last week, on arriving at Gabe's place, Charlie had gotten out of her mother's dinged-up old Saab and theatrically stuck her tongue out at Siobhan as she slammed the car door and ran into Gabe's arms. He'd tousled her hair and said, "Good girl! Your dad misses you so much when you're away." Margaret had watched all of this from the upstairs window and had mostly been trying to forget it ever since. She wished it hadn't been called back to mind now, on this otherwise lovely Friday evening.

Clue to the rescue, though; the game was loud, laughing fun, and Junie even won though it was her first time playing. Then, while Gabe got the girls through toothbrushing and bedtime, Margaret put the stereo on low and shimmied and sang along to "Brown Eyed Girl" while she did the dishes and had another beer and banished all unpleasant thoughts. *Channeling Mom by focusing on the positive*, she thought. *Maybe she's onto something. . . .*

By the time the girls were asleep, she and Gabe were exhausted and lay fully clothed on his bed.

She was about to roll over and snuggle next to him suggestively when he propped himself on his elbows and said, "So, I got some news from Siobhan earlier today."

"Oh, right." Gosh, she'd almost forgotten.

"Yeah, she needs me to watch Charlie for a couple of full weeks in the spring and summer, *and* some extra days in the next few weeks while she puts in more hours at her studio."

"Isn't that nice for you two, getting to spend more time together?"

"Sure, sure. But Siobhan is just using me as a babysitter. She's got a big show in New York, and she needs child care. I'm free."

"You're also her father. I'm sure she wants you two to spend time together."

"It's only when it *suits* her that I get to see Charlie more."

Margaret felt an urge to protest—how could that possibly be? Surely Siobhan wanted Charlie to be close to him, whatever her feelings might be about Gabe. Also, should time with his own child ever be called babysitting, no matter why the time came his way? And yet there was that other thing that nagged at her: Siobhan's abortion was part of Jane lore. No one had said whose baby it was, but Margaret had done the math and it was clear that she'd gotten it right around the time of the divorce. It was possible the child belonged to someone else, but since Gabe had never complained about infidelity, Margaret assumed it had been his. Though she was ashamed of herself for thinking it, she was relieved that Siobhan had made the choice she had, however terrible it must have been for her, because a second child—especially one that would still be very young now, not even in school yet—would have tethered the two of them together even more. "I'm sorry, Gabe." *You have no idea for how much.*

"I have half a mind to charge her for the babysitter I'll have to hire to take care of Charlie when she's not in school and I'm working."

"Does she do that, too? Hire a babysitter, I mean? So she can work?"

"Not that I know of."

And yet she's painted enough to get a show at a New York gallery while working at Jane.

"But I'm sure she'll start getting babysitters now that she's *so impor-tant,*" he added. "Even though her work is hardly full-time."

"Let's think of ways to make the time with Charlie fun," Margaret said cheerfully, attempting to steer the conversation in another direc-tion. "Maybe between the two of us, you won't have to hire anyone."

Gabe looked at her with a forlorn but hopeful expression. "You'd do that?"

"Of course. Charlie's great, and I love you."

"I love you, too." He leaned toward her and slid his hand over her waist, then kissed her gently on the lips. "Thank you."

She wanted to feel good about this conversation, but she couldn't banish the thought that she was keeping a rapidly growing secret from him, just like Siobhan had.

Soon, she told herself. *Telling him tonight would have been too much.*

Soon.

24

PATTY

After her fight with Veronica, Patty felt hopeless and torn between wanting to explode and wanting to crawl under the covers and never come out. She felt completely unable to face her kids in either case, so she managed to farm out both Karen and Junie for the night by the time Eliza wandered in around six. Her sister just appeared at the kitchen sink as if nothing special was happening, and washed her hands while Patty drank a second glass of wine and contemplated what kind of takeout to order for dinner. Tad, dear little easy-to-please Tad, was happily watching TV in the living room.

Don't yell at her, Patty told herself. Though, good God, she wanted to. Angry words were practically dancing on her tongue. "Did you have a nice afternoon?"

With a shrug, Eliza replied, "It was fine."

"It was such a sunny day, did you take a walk?" *Did you already have the abortion?*

"No."

Patty set the nearly empty glass down on the counter with a clink. "Eliza, please don't just disappear like that. I was worried about you."

"Why?"

"You're my sister!" Her tongue felt surprisingly heavy in her mouth. Maybe that second glass of Chablis hadn't been such a good idea.

"You didn't come and look for me these last few years."

"You didn't leave an address."

"Would that have mattered?"

"Absolutely! As soon as you called and told me where to find you, I came, didn't I?"

Eliza shrugged again. "That was different. I was in trouble."

"Oh, yes. Trouble. Are you finally going to tell me what kind of trouble you're in?"

"I need a hundred dollars."

Patty took a deep breath, slightly relieved that her sister's need for money implied she hadn't gotten the abortion yet. "Eliza. I can't just give you money unless I know what it's for." *Even though I know exactly what it's for.*

"Why not? No one asks you what you spend money on."

"That's not true. Matt and I make a budget and account for every cent." *Well, almost.* She'd been known to inflate the grocery number so that she could splurge on indulgences here and there—a new scarf or fur-lined gloves, a Halston dress instead of a store brand, a new set of throw pillows for the couch.

As if reading her mind, Eliza said, "You mean Matt knows about all the shoes in your closet? Even the ones you put behind the sweaters?"

"When you're married, you can talk to me about those shoes. Right now, we're talking about you and the trouble you're in."

I just want you to tell me. Please tell me so I don't have to call you out.

"Tell you? Like you'd understand. I mean, look at all this!" Eliza moved her head and arms in a big circle as if *this* was every single thing in her line of sight—the kitchen appliances, the food, the cloth napkins. "We have nothing in common. There is no way you'd understand what's going on with me."

"Try me." The wine made it hard for Patty to know how she sounded, but she didn't care. Her sister was still in this conversation with her. They seemed to be making progress.

Eliza folded her arms over her chest in a defensive posture but appeared to be considering Patty's offer.

"I need an abortion. How's that?"

Thank God. Finally, someone willing to come clean of their own accord. Feeling hope burble in her chest for the first time that day, she replied, "Can you tell me more?"

"I don't know, Patty, what do you want to hear? I can't have a fucking kid. I don't have a doctor husband and a big house and shoes so expensive I hide them."

"What about adoption?"

"And ruin my life for the next year? It's not like I'd be able to get a job while I'm pregnant or while I'm recovering. Plus . . ." Eliza swallowed, and her next words sounded much softer, much sadder. "I don't think I'd be able to give it up if I . . ."

"So you still love him? The father? Could you . . . call him? Make it work?"

Eliza's tone and expression iced over. "Not after he slept with the person I thought was my best friend. Fuck him."

Fuck him, indeed. If Patty found out Matt was sleeping with Veronica, *fuck him* would barely cover it. What bridge to trust could there be after a betrayal like that? "Okay," Patty said. "I understand. You shouldn't call him. But what about . . . having the baby here? With us?"

"I don't want any reminders of him or that life and those mistakes," Eliza said. "I need a clean slate."

Patty and Eliza stared at each other for another few seconds as

Patty wracked her brain for something to say, but she'd lost track of her goal here. Her sister's plight was more complicated than she'd imagined. *Had* she truly imagined it?

Before either of them could say more, Tad trotted into the kitchen on his stick horse and said, "Howdy, Eliza."

"Howdy, pardner," Eliza said, looking down at her nephew with sudden and genuine affection.

"Come back to the ranch and play Trouble with me?"

"You think your horse is big enough for both of us?"

Tad turned his back to Eliza, as if inviting her onto the back of his horse. She played along, pretending to swing her leg over the end of the stick.

"Giddyap," said Tad, and the two of them trotted out of the kitchen.

Oh, Eliza, you'd make such a good mother.

It's okay to be upset, Veronica had said to her, just a few hours ago. *This is a lot to digest. It's also okay to be relieved that Eliza would be okay.*

God damn it. Veronica, why do you always have to be right?

When Matt walked through the door with a giant bag of Chinese food, she almost wept with relief. She'd had enough of today. All she wanted was to feed the troops, thinned out as they were, and get to bed. She even let everyone eat in front of the television, which she never did because it was impossible to agree on what to watch, but miraculously everyone was okay with watching *The Love Bug*, which happened to be showing. Or maybe it was because Matt and Eliza knew she was in a mood, and no one wanted to have to make polite dinner table conversation. She didn't care.

At ten, though, when she and Matt lay in their usual platonic positions on the king-size bed, she found she couldn't resist saying something. Apart from the porn and that whole category of horrible, sticky questions, Matt was her husband and partner. A doctor who was good in a crisis. "Eliza is pregnant and wants an abortion," she said. "From that group Max mentioned at the Christmas dinner. Jane." *Oh, right, you weren't at the dinner,* she thought resentfully. She'd told him about it the next day, though, so he should know what she was talking about. "And if that wasn't bad enough, I also found out today that Veronica *works for Jane.* She actually *performs* the abortions."

Matt didn't reply right away. He'd gone eerily still.

What now?

"Matt?"

"I have a confession to make."

Here it comes. Bad things always come in threes, and this will be the magic number of no-good terrible very bad things to happen today. You're having an affair. I've known for months, you know. She kept her eyes on the ceiling, bracing herself.

"I've known about Veronica and Jane for close to two years."

Fast as a jack-in-the-box, Patty sat up in bed and stared at Matt. Infidelity she'd been prepared for, but participating in the same lie as her best friend?

In a voice that was little more than a whisper, he went on, "I have never been involved in the abortions. I prescribe the birth control pill for women they send to me. Women who can't get it any other way."

His desperate, hot-chocolate-brown eyes told her he was telling the truth.

"I'm sorry, Patty. I should have told you ages ago. At first, it was just one prescription here and there, and then it became a few a week, and now . . . I don't know, it all just snuck up on me. And I was afraid of what you'd say."

"Honestly, I'm surprised my opinion is that important to you."

He looked surprised. "Of course it is. You're my wife."

"Maybe you should have thought of that before *lying to me.*"

"You're right. You're absolutely right, and I'm sorry."

He wasn't even going to disagree with her?

Patty recalled the woman in the leather trench with tall boots the morning of her stint as a PI and wondered if she'd gone to Matt because of Jane.

Eliza is Jane, Patty, Veronica had said.

No!

This can't be happening.

Adrenaline coursing through her again, which was all the more uncomfortable for the wine that had made her head tight, Patty said, "While we're getting everything out in the open, I found your little box."

There, I've said it. Now no one is hiding anything.

She watched as recognition dawned on him, and a blotchy red flush—*of anger? embarrassment?*—rose from his neck into his cheeks.

"How long have you known about that?" he asked. "And what were you doing snooping in my office?"

"I've known for a few weeks," she said, "and I've been trying to bring it up but haven't known how."

"So you waited till I was already in a compromised position to throw it at me?"

"No. How could you say that? I thought we were clearing the air."

Matt got off the bed and stood glowering at Patty. "This doesn't feel like clearing the air."

"Matt, I'm sorry for looking in your office, but I thought . . . I thought you might be cheating on me! You'd been distant for so long, and skipping events we used to go to together, and—"

"I've been skipping things because I've been unhappy. Work has felt really unfulfilling lately, which is part of the reason I wanted to help Veronica."

"At least you *have* work. All I have is this marriage. This family. Which is falling apart." This thought had not occurred to Patty until she said it out loud, and the truth of it rang in her ears.

"I'm sorry if we are *all* you have," Matt snapped. Then he snatched his pillow and bundled the comforter in the other arm.

"Where are you going? Eliza is in the guest room."

"My office. The den of iniquity. I can't keep talking about this now. We both need to cool off."

The adrenaline curdled into panic in her stomach. "I'm sorry, Matt. Can't we talk about this?"

"Later. I can't right now."

And then he was gone.

Her own combination of anger and abject terror made her sweat and shake. *What time is it?*

Only ten past ten. I could call V—

No, I can't.

Veronica's betrayal was deep and double: not only was she doing something unforgivable, she had been lying to Patty for years. Years! *With her husband.*

And that thought turned up the volume on her shame and fury so loud, she actually heard it ringing in her ears.

I can't believe I didn't see it before. Didn't see something before.

Was this the same kind of betrayal as cheating on her with her best friend? The unforgivable sin she'd just hours before thought to herself that she could never recover from?

No, came an automatic answer from somewhere inside her.

God, she found herself saying, though she hadn't spoken directly to Him like this in prayer since she was a little girl, *why are the people I love most becoming strangers I no longer recognize?*

The responding silence was so vast and so complete, she had the sense of being swallowed by it whole.

To her surprise, Matt met her at the coffee maker the following morn-ing wearing sweatpants and his ratty old Northwestern hoodie that she used to wear herself early in their relationship when she'd tiptoe out of bed to make coffee in his freezing kitchen, then bring back two cups for them to sip together in their warm bed.

"I'm sorry about last night," he said quietly.

"So am I." At least she was sorry about throwing the porn in his face like she had. And after the lonely night she'd spent without him, hoping he'd come back into their room, all she wanted was to reopen the lines of communication between them.

Matt glanced down as he sighed and ran his fingers through his hair. "I don't think there *is* a right and wrong about what Veronica's doing, at least not in any clear-cut way. The legal and moral complications of what she's doing are huge, but I see my role as preventing more women from having to use her service. When women are on the pill, they don't need abortions." He paused to sigh and run his fingers through his hair again, then went on. "I said last night that work had felt unfulfilling, seeing the same kinds of patients day in and day out. I started to wonder if I should try a different line of work. Around the same time, Veronica asked if I could do this for her, and I thought, at least it's different. I wanted to feel like I was actually helping people again. That's why I wanted to become a doctor in the first place. And I needed to shake myself out of the rut I was in."

"Did it work?"

"In a way. But the satisfaction I felt in helping those women was tainted by the dishonesty with you. And again, I'm really sorry about that."

Relief at Matt's soft, loving tone washed over her. "And I'm sorry for bringing up the magazines like I did. It wasn't fair."

Matt fixed her with a deadly serious stare and said, "I want you to know that I have always been one hundred percent faithful to you. Yes, I have been less than honest about a couple of things recently, but never about that. The magazines were a . . . they were a distraction, and I can see why they bother you. I want to talk that through, but right now, can we please just focus on getting Eliza through this? Then we can talk about the rest of it."

One thing at a time. Yes. A kind of answer, a hacked path through the brush toward some sort of clearing.

Hungover and scratchy-throated from yesterday's yelling, Patty nodded silently and leaned on her husband. She didn't want to lose him. She *couldn't* lose him, not when she was already losing her best friend.

Enveloped in his arms, she listened to his steady heart and felt her tears come.

Tad skidded into the kitchen and said, "Mommy! Where's Aunt Eliza? She promised to play horses with me this morning."

"Did you check her room, cowboy?" Matt asked, gently loosening his arms around Patty.

"Duh, Dad. I went straight there after I got up."

"Let's go check," Matt said, offering his son his hand, which the little boy took, in a simple gesture that split Patty's heart in two.

She followed them up the stairs and across the threshold of the guest room, where the bed was made, seemingly untouched. Leaning against the pillows there was a creamy envelope from Patty's own stationery, the stack she kept in the little secretary desk in the hall by the kitchen. The letter *P* was written in Eliza's hand on the front.

"Well, Ah'll be." Matt whistled, laying the cowboy accent on thick to distract their son. "You're right, Sheriff. Where's that horse of yours? Can I take a look at 'im?"

Confused but placated, Tad took off with his father to get his horse as Patty plucked the envelope off the bed.

> *Patty—*
>
> *I don't want to cause any more trouble than I already have. I took the cash you keep at the bottom of the drawer where I found this paper. It's enough so you won't have to*

*deal with me again. I'm really sorry I brought my shit to
you this time.*

—Eliza

She didn't cry.

She didn't pick up the heavy glass bird that sat on the guest room side table, the result of decorating advice from some magazine, and hurl it against the wall in protest.

Even though she really, really wanted to.

When Matt returned with Tad and the horse, she handed him the letter, and once he'd read it, he wrapped his arms around her and kissed her temple. "We'll find her," he whispered in her ear. "We'll figure all this out. It's going to be okay."

She wanted so much to believe him, but staring down the barrel of a full weekend with the kids—the girls would be home from their sleepovers very soon—she had no earthly idea how that was possible. She'd never missed her mother as much as she did in that moment. More than anything, she could use the counsel, the love, the *help* her mother would have given her. It was all up to her now, and that prospect had never felt so terrifying.

25

VERONICA

Midway through her Saturday morning shift, Veronica started to see spots, little exploding dots that were black at the center and flaming red around the edges, and they were making it impossible to find the already hard-to-find cervixes. Normally she could search out even the most tilted or hidden openings; it was a point of pride with her, and even a joke among the other Janes. Today it was taking her twice as long. Worse, she had to contort her shoulders and neck around her bowling ball middle to see. Even when she was able to straighten up a bit, to arch her back and give herself some relief, her legs throbbed with the blood that suddenly rushed into them. Melanie's and Phyllis's chatter with the women about Easter plans made her want to scream for silence.

By the eighth D&C, the spots had increased and begun to cloud her vision, and the talk in the room started to sound like it was coming from the other side of a long tunnel. Her breaths became shorter and shorter, until she was gasping for air, and her hands shook, and she realized that if she didn't get out of this room *right now*, she was going to throw up on the floor between the legs of this poor woman.

"I'm sorry," she rasped. "Melanie, can you finish?" Then, leaving the curette inside the woman, Veronica stood up from the chair where she'd been sitting, and staggered out of the room.

In the kitchen of the Place, which was mercifully empty, Veronica washed her hands, then opened a window and leaned out, feeling the chilly, wet air on her face. Though it was midday, the clouds and rain conspired to make it feel close to night. She kept breathing, but she couldn't get more than a sip of air at a time, and her pulse refused to slow. The stench of blood and isopropyl alcohol was like an infection in her nose all the way down her windpipe, making her gag. When that graduated to a dry heave, she hurried to the bathroom, where she threw up the toast and eggs she'd eaten a few hours ago.

Vomiting didn't make her feel any better. When she washed her shaky hands, it was like her fingers weren't part of her; she hardly felt the water hit her skin.

There was a quiet knock on the door, and then Melanie's voice. "Veronica? Can I come in?"

Oh thank God, a nurse, she thought as she opened the door.

When they were both cloistered in the little bathroom, Melanie put a hand on Veronica's arm and said, "Tell me what's happening to you."

"I can't . . . catch . . . my breath. My heart's beating so fast, and I threw up, but . . ." Veronica started to cry. Melanie hugged her.

"You're going to be okay," she said.

"No, I'm not," Veronica wailed.

"Come with me," Melanie said, sliding an arm around Veronica's back and under her arms, holding her up.

"Just lean on me, that's it," she cooed, as she led Veronica out of the bathroom and into the second bedroom, which happened to be free that day. *Because the new Janes aren't trained yet, and we are so far behind,* thought Veronica. Melanie sat her on the love seat they sometimes used for counseling, cracked open a window, then came and sat beside Veronica, held her hands, and said soothingly, "You are okay. I promise. Try and breathe with me, okay?"

Veronica fought to focus on Melanie's face and breathe normally. *Why is this so fucking hard?*

"Breathe in through your nose and out through your mouth. That's it. Iiiiiinnnnnn, ooooooouuut."

Slowly.

Slowly.

Her breaths began to even out, and she started to come back into the room. She felt Melanie's warm hand on her back, a link, a cord, connecting her to another human.

"That's it. See if you can time your breaths. Count of five in, count of five out."

One.

Two.

Three.

Four.

Five.

One.

Two.

Three.

Four.

Five.

Again.

And again.

Until she could lift her head and look at Melanie and see her face right in front of her, like normal. Like she'd never been on the other side of a tunnel.

"What happened?" Veronica asked.

"You had a panic attack."

"Oh, God." *How embarrassing.* "Please don't tell anyone."

"It's okay, Vee. You're under a tremendous amount of stress. It's nothing to be ashamed of. It happens. But it is your body and mind's way of getting your attention and telling you to slow down and rest," Melanie said.

For once, she agreed with this assessment. The thought of going back into that room and doing another D&C made her hands shake again. "But who will finish today?"

"I will."

"I'm so sorry."

Melanie put her hand on Veronica's, and she was astonished at how warm and soft and comforting it was. "You only have to be sorry if you harm yourself further. Go home. And . . . I hesitate to say this because I know how you feel about it, but I do think you should consider taking off the rest of your pregnancy."

Veronica opened her mouth to protest, and Melanie held up her hand, putting her palm a few inches from Veronica's face to stop her.

"Veronica, given your history of miscarriage, and what just happened to you, you are putting this baby in danger by continuing to work. You're putting *yourself* and the women who come to us in a kind of danger, too."

Oh, God, Melanie's right. And she didn't even know about all her stress, about the trouble with Patty and Eliza, or the precarious peace in her marriage.

In a horrified rush of embarrassment, Veronica remembered getting on Danielle's case for showing up high, recalled all the times she'd entreated the women of Jane to model the kind of self-possession they wanted the women who came to them to feel. Right now, she was the opposite of self-possessed. She was a puddle of fear and anxiety.

But. "Siobhan is in New York so soon, and the new ones haven't even been trained yet. How will we cover everyone?"

"We'll manage."

Veronica looked down at her belly, then back up at Melanie.

"Is it because I'm not strong enough? Have I been beaten by the patriarchy?"

"The patriarchy only wins when women stop listening to themselves. Listen to yourself, Veronica. If you can trust us to get everything done at the Service, do you *want* to go back in that room for ten more D&Cs today?"

Slowly she shook her head.

"Alright then, there's your answer. Did you walk or drive here?" Melanie asked.

"I walked."

"Good," said Melanie. "Whenever you feel up to it, you can go home."

Veronica wished so much there was another way out of the Place than through the little waiting room, and she wished she had a disguise like Heidi Smith as she swiftly walked out, making eye contact with no one.

Veronica was thankful she didn't have to get in a car; she didn't think she was safe to drive. Her knees were wobbly, and she had to hold up an umbrella with arms that felt like Play-Doh, but she made it to her house.

When she walked inside, she was greeted by haltingly played notes to the *Sesame Street* theme song.

"Mommy!" Kate leapt up from the piano bench, where she'd been sitting with Doug, who looked at her with a curiously raised eyebrow.

Veronica and Kate hugged, and she said, "I missed you both." She smiled at Doug, then added, "I think I need to lie down."

Kate bounced back to the piano, and Veronica made her way to the bedroom. No sooner had she made herself comfortable on the bed and could feel sleep coming for her than Doug entered the room and quietly closed the door.

"I let Kate watch some old Shirley Temple movie that's on television." He lay down next to her, then asked, "What happened?"

"Melanie said I had a panic attack, then sent me home."

"I know you're disappointed, and I'm sorry."

"I just wish . . ."

"What? What do you wish?"

He really did seem to want to know.

Here goes nothing.

"I wish you could understand what it's like to have to stop doing something you love, something *important*, just because your body is made to carry children. No one else can do this for me, and no one can help. Today my body forced me to finally choose."

Doug didn't answer. He didn't say *I'd do it for you if I could*, because they both knew that wasn't true. No matter how much a pregnancy was wanted, there were still costs.

They were quiet a little while, and the opening bars of "On the *Good Ship Lollipop*" drifted into their room from downstairs.

"You're right," he said. "I can't understand. But I am glad you have people in your life who do."

This admission was so tender, and so unexpected, that when he reached over to run his hand from the crown of her head down her hair to her shoulder, she loosened her hold on the tumult inside her and cried. Doug moved himself closer and cradled her in his arms while she cried and cried, until finally the sobs gave way to the kind of deep sleep she used to enjoy as a much younger person, before the demands of womanhood had made her into someone who dreamed of *better*.

26

PATTY

Matt went with her to church Sunday morning for the first time in—
how long?—around eight or nine months. In the pew he held her
hand, and he was the one to tap Tad on the knee when he started
getting restless, and generally kept an eye on the kids, which he'd
been doing a lot since Eliza went missing the day before.

During the gathering in the hall after mass, she thanked Father
Miller for the service and then found herself saying, "My sister, Eliza,
is missing," the words out before she could think better of them. But
maybe he could help?

"I see." His tone was solemn. After a beat, he said, "Would you like
to speak in private?"

Patty nodded.

She flashed the fingers of her right hand to Matt and mouthed *Five
minutes* to him before following Father Miller into his office.

"Have a seat," said the priest. "Can I get you a cup of coffee?"

"No, thank you." She sat in the wooden chair on the visitor's side
of his desk, and he took his place across from her. She almost wished
they were in the private dark of the confessional instead.

"How can I help you?" he asked.

"Could you ask God to send Eliza home?"

"I can do that." He smiled, then said, "And I will. But how will that help *you?*"

"I just feel so lost, Father. Matt and I have been having problems, and Veronica and I had a big fight, and my sister . . . who I thought had come home, is . . . in trouble. And she ran away again. She doesn't even want my help. I think I scared her off."

The priest leaned forward and said, "You are not a scary woman. I know you to be kind and generous and thoughtful. If your sister is scared, it's for her own reasons, her own internal turmoil. Do you have a sense of what might be going on for her?"

I don't want to get my sister in trouble with God.

Then she remembered that Father Miller had taken a rather liberal view of Jane when they'd last spoken of it.

"She . . ." *How do I put this?* "She wanted to go to Jane, and I tried to convince her otherwise."

Father Miller sat back in his chair and made a steeple of his fingers in front of his face, patiently waiting for her to go on, presumably to say more about Jane.

She hesitated.

"If it makes a difference," he said, "let's just say that Jane is a friend of mine."

"What do you mean?"

"You might be surprised to discover how many men and women of God are friends with Jane, and others like her, all over the country."

"So you don't think it's wrong?"

"I don't think it's up to me to judge. It's up to me to help the people who come to me with their life crises."

For reasons she didn't understand, this sentiment made Patty well up again. "I miss my mother. Our mother, Eliza's and mine."

"I know you do. Of course you do. But . . . if I may . . . you are yourself a wise mother."

"I don't feel wise. I feel completely inept. I tried to help Eliza twice, and she left both times. She needs a mother, but . . ." Her throat gummed up at the loss that welled up in her.

"I wonder," said the priest, "if perhaps what Eliza needs is not a mother so much as a friend. A sister. Someone who will stand beside her, not someone who wants to protect her."

Like Veronica has always been for me, she realized with a stab of guilt.

Also, the idea that she wasn't Eliza's mother, and didn't even need to be, loosened some of the tightness in her chest. What a freeing thought.

She had one more question for this man of God, though. "So . . . you don't have a problem with what Jane is doing? Or the women who go to them? It's not . . . a sin?"

"Is a life defined by one act? I'm inclined to think it isn't. In moments like this, I pray to the God who defended Mary Magdalene against those that called her a sinner. Whenever I do, I am not inclined to cast stones."

Patty nodded. His words felt like a flashlight in the dark tunnel she was in.

"Could Veronica help you find Eliza?"

With that one question, Patty knew that Father Miller understood her old friend's connection to Jane.

"I hope so," she said.

"I believe in her, as I believe in you. Let me know how it turns out."

"Thank you," she said.

Father Miller smiled.

There was no time for prayer. She knew what she had to do.

Matt promised to hold down the fort until she returned. Then she set off to knock on Veronica's door unexpectedly for the second time in two days.

It was Doug who answered, and he looked surprised to see her, but not in a guarded way. "Come in, come in," he said. "Let me see if Veronica's up. She was taking a nap."

A *nap before noon?* That wasn't like her.

A minute or two later, Doug came down the stairs. "She said to just go to our room. You okay to talk there?"

"Anything's fine," Patty said. "Thanks."

She hurried up the stairs and stepped into Veronica and Doug's bedroom, where her friend had propped herself up on some pillows, still wearing a flannel nightgown. "Are you okay?"

"Yeah," said Veronica. "I've just needed to rest a lot this weekend."

"The baby . . . ?"

"It's fine." She rested a hand on her rounded belly for emphasis. "I'm glad you came back. I've been feeling bad about our fight."

"I know. Me, too."

"Want to come and sit on the bed?"

Patty half sat, half leaned on the end of the bed, below Veronica's feet, and turned to look her friend in the eyes. "I'm sorry for storming out on Friday," she said.

"I understand why you did."

"I know about Matt now, too."

"I am sorry about that, Patty. Really. I never should have asked him . . ."

Patty held up her hand. "Don't. He and I have talked. I'm not over it, but I do kind of get it. I'm starting to, anyway. A lot of things . . . well, I don't want to be the one throwing stones, you know?"

Veronica slowly nodded her head.

"I've realized that what's really important to me here is that Eliza comes back, and we have a chance to start over. After you and I fought on Friday, she came home and actually told me she wanted an abortion, but of course I tried to convince her to do something else. Call

the father; adoption. Anyway, true to form, because of our disagree-
ment she was gone by the time we woke up. She took enough money
to get the abortion and get out of town, which is basically what the
note she left said she'd do."

Patty paused to take a breath. "Has she come to Jane?"

"I don't know."

"Can you please, please, in the name of twenty years of friendship,
help me find her?"

Veronica didn't answer right away. She had that look she got when
she was concentrating really hard, evaluating something. Finally, she
said, "If I do, will you promise to let her get the abortion, if that's what
she wants?"

Is a life defined by one act?

"I'll support her in whatever decision she makes," said Patty. Her
heart thudded in her chest. She felt afraid, but not of whether she was
making the right choice. She just wanted to make sure she got to Eliza
before Eliza got to a Greyhound. "I want to help her, and to finally get
to know her. The real her. Not the person I thought I knew before
Mom died, or the person I wanted her to be. Eliza."

Veronica leaned over and took Patty's hand. "Let's go find her."

Then, after reaching across the bed to put the salmon-colored
phone on the pillow next to her, Veronica picked up the receiver and
punched a number into the keypad.

"Hi, Melanie. I have an unorthodox request."

She had to trust that Veronica would find Eliza. Her best and oldest
friend had given her word.

Also, she really had no choice. The police were out of the question.
She couldn't risk getting Eliza in hot water with someone like Sam
Wilder who had it out for Jane, especially not since she'd remembered
Eliza had spent a night in jail once before, her senior year of high

school, for possession of marijuana at a football game. She'd gotten off with some community service, but Patty had a feeling the punishment wouldn't be so lenient this time if she was caught getting an abortion.

While she waited, Patty threw herself into the usual mothering tasks, and found herself wondering how Veronica managed to do all of this for Kate—lunches, laundry, making and keeping doctor's appointments, having friends over, buying clothes and groceries, scheduling activities—and run Jane at the same time. Suddenly she understood what that child care bill President Nixon had vetoed was really all about; when it was making its way through the House and then the Senate and the news was full of chatter about it, she'd hardly paid attention; it hadn't seemed to apply to her. Damn him for vetoing it. It could have helped girls like Eliza, too.

She and Matt tiptoed around each other. He complimented her dinners and dresses and never set foot in his office; she made his favorite meals and asked how his day went and never set foot in his office. They came to bed exhausted and immediately turned out the lights.

Finally, when she climbed into bed the fourth night Eliza was missing, he set down his *National Geographic* and glasses, and said, "Do you want to talk about the magazines?"

"I thought we were going to wait until Eliza came back."

"We can do that."

His willingness to wait—his help with the kids lately, his reassurances, his apology at the coffee maker after their fight—was melting her, reminding her of the reasons she loved him. "No," she said. "Let's talk. If I were you, I'd want to talk, too."

He cleared his throat, in that way that suggested he'd rehearsed what he was about to say. "So. Listen. I'm sorry the pictures became a substitute for being with you. I never intended for that to be the case. In fact, when I started buying them, I used them as a way to . . . get ready to be with you."

Patty's eyebrows arched involuntarily. "You're not attracted to me anymore?"

"No! No, no, no, no, no. I'm sorry, I didn't mean it to sound like that. It's more that *I* don't feel attractive anymore. My hair is thinning, and I have this paunch I can't lose, and work takes it out of me every single day. Sometimes it all just makes me feel like a hamster on a wheel. But I *want* to be with you. Ironically, this is all because I wanted to keep our physical connection alive, but I needed . . . help." Matt reached over and held Patty's hand under the covers, his sense of shame evident in the way his eyes rested on their feet, not her face.

"You talked about feeling dissatisfied with work before," she observed, squeezing his hand. "Do you want to stop being a doctor?"

"No," he said, and his tone was reassuringly emphatic as he lifted his eyes to hers. "Actually, working with Jane reminded me of why I love being a doctor. I think I do need to make a change, though. I want to go where my skills make a difference, not where I check a lot of boxes for people who are just going to continue to smoke and eat what they want."

"What would you do?"

"I'm not sure yet. I've put in phone calls with veterans' hospitals, though. There are a lot of guys coming back from Vietnam who need care. And I'm looking into a few pro bono opportunities, too."

Patty smiled. "That all sounds exciting."

"You know, if you wanted to get a job, I'd support that," he said. "You sounded . . . kind of jealous of me working the other night."

"Oh, that," said Patty. "Maybe. I have been wondering what might come next for me once all three kids are in school more."

He gave her hand a warm pulse. "You are an extremely talented woman and I love you, and I am still attracted to you. To get back to the pictures . . . I just . . . needed a little help getting started. So I used the magazines, and they worked, for a while, to get me in the right mindset. But then they became something else. A release I didn't know I needed. Something . . . different."

He paused, then went on. "Anyway, I threw them all out. I don't want to use them as a crutch anymore."

This was the outcome she'd wanted, but instead of being happy about it, she felt remorse and loss. Curling in a ball at his side and resting a hand on his chest, she said, "I'm sorry you've felt so worn-out. And I understand feeling like maybe your spouse doesn't want you anymore."

Matt covered her shoulder with his hand and said, "I never meant for you to feel that way."

"Neither did I."

"Veronica will find her," he said quietly.

Patty nodded, and tried to focus on the soft, soothing sensation of Matt's body beside hers.

In good times and bad. No one ever told you that the kicker, though, the thing that made you want to cry with gratitude and frustration both, was when they existed side by side, as if the good wasn't even possible without the bad.

27

VERONICA

Diving into her own organization to look for Eliza was like following the White Rabbit into the alien upside-down world of the Cheshire Cat. She herself had infused the Service with so many layers of protection and obfuscation, and with hundreds of women calling, and eleven women doing counseling in three different locations that week, it was nearly impossible to locate one twenty-one-year-old girl who didn't use her real name.

Still, Veronica dropped into the Place and the Front and the counseling locations every day with a picture of Eliza and asked everyone to keep an eye out for this woman who was her oldest friend's flight-risk younger sister. It was hard going to the Place and seeing the activity happening without her, especially because everything looked exactly the same, almost as if her presence was not necessary.

All the Janes asked how she was doing. None of them asked when she would return. The message was clear: Stay home. We've got this.

Amy echoed the sentiment at a brief checkup Monday morning: "A panic attack isn't always a reason to take it easy, but in your case, why take any chances?"

On Monday afternoon, just as she finished putting away a third load of laundry and was contemplating what to make for dinner, and felt like she might scream from the boredom, the doorbell rang.

It's almost five. It must be a salesman, she thought with annoyance as she went to her front door.

But there on her front stoop was Phyllis, holding a small paper grocery bag.

"Well, this is a surprise," Veronica said. "Come on in."

"Thanks," Phyllis said as she stepped inside and handed Veronica the bag. "These are for you."

Veronica opened it and saw two boxes of Oreos and a carton of milk. "How well you know me," she laughed. "Would you like some?"

"Nah, I'm good. I won't be long."

She led Phyllis into the kitchen and set the bag down on the counter. "Was everything okay today at the Service?"

"Oh, yeah, yeah. It was fine. I'm just worried about you, that's all. I wanted to see if you needed anything."

"That's sweet, Phyllis, but I think what I mainly need is rest."

"Is that what you're going to do? Rest?"

I never pegged you for a mother hen. "I'm doing my best. It's not in my nature, though, as I'm sure you know."

"Yeah, I get that. And that's why I'm here." Phyllis drew in a deep breath, looking like she was steeling herself against something. "So, I really hope I'm not overstepping, but I'm going to risk it. I just want you to know that the Service will be okay without you for a while. It's good to take time off for yourself and the baby. I . . . well, you already know about my abortion, but I never told you about a very short marriage I had years ago, when I had a miscarriage and my doctor told me I might not be able to have children because of the abortion."

"But you know . . ."

Phyllis held up a hand. "I know. The doctor was wrong, and just trying to shame me. I had a good, clean abortion, so there shouldn't be any problem. The irony is, really, I'm also prone to miscarriages, so

I might have miscarried that baby, too. Maybe I wouldn't have needed the abortion. I'll never know. My sister's had miscarriages, too, so it's always made me wonder if it runs in the family. But that's not my point. My point is, I know how much it hurts to lose a baby you're carrying. One you want."

A lump rose in Veronica's throat, and her nose itched inside, as she recalled her own miscarriage, and the months of depression afterward when Patty and Siobhan had stepped in to run her life until she felt able to do it herself. She'd walled that pain off in her mind, told herself to forget it, but now she wondered if some of that pent-up sadness had been what caused her panic attack the other day.

"In one way," Phyllis went on, "the miscarriage was a gift. It ended that marriage, which turned out to be a good thing, even though at the time it felt like the end of the world. That ignorant fool called me damaged goods. Said he needed a wife who was going to help him make healthy, strong Black children." Phyllis laughed bitterly and shook her head. "I didn't know anything back then. But I do now, and I wanted to tell you it's okay to take care of yourself."

Veronica was tempted to hug Phyllis and sob on her shoulder, but instead she ground her teeth together to keep from undamming this fresh wave of emotion.

"And because I'm sure you're curious, no, I didn't tell Keith for a long time. I wasted a lot of precious time with him because I worried maybe I *was* damaged goods. You know what he said when I finally told him last week?"

"What?"

"He said that if we—*we*—couldn't have kids of our own, there would be plenty of other causes worth fighting for together. He gets that work can give a life meaning same as kids. And if we wanted to adopt, he was open to that, too."

Veronica cleared her throat. "That sounds like Keith. Does he know about Jane?"

Phyllis nodded. "He's a fan."

Veronica coughed this time to do a better job of dislodging the gunk in her throat, then said, "I was just about to get dinner started. Would you stay and eat with us?"

"Only if you give me a job."

"I'm sure I can do some delegating."

"I'm sure you can."

Veronica felt something set down its sword inside her.

Maybe it finally was time to rest.

Alone in the house once again on Friday morning, she almost jumped in surprise when the phone rang as she was cleaning up the breakfast dishes.

"Hello?"

"Veronica?" It was Danielle. "I think I found Eliza. She's here at the Place. She used the name Patricia."

"When's she scheduled?"

"Technically, she's next, but there are three others, so I can delay her."

Veronica's heart pounded, then the baby did a somersault. "Do that. I'll be there in just a few minutes."

Though it was only a few blocks and a gorgeous blue-sky day perfect for walking, Veronica drove because it was slightly faster.

She forced herself to walk slowly up the stairs of the apartment building, and to open the door as calmly and steadily as she could, almost like she was trying to balance a teacup on her head. As soon as she stepped over the threshold, she saw Eliza, sprawled out on the cracked leather armchair, reading a *Ms.* magazine and wearing Patty's clothes. *Wow, she really does look exactly like their mother.*

Standing before her, Veronica cleared her throat demurely, then said, "Patricia?"

Eliza looked up into the face of her sister's oldest friend and muttered, "Fuck." Which made sense; she probably thought Veronica was there to bring her back to Patty.

"Can you come with me for a second?"

"I guess." Eliza stood.

There were four other women in the room, and all eight of their eyes followed Veronica and Eliza into the kitchen, where Veronica shut the door. "Hey, can you give us a few minutes?" she said to Danielle, who had been leaning against the counter reading a book as a fresh pot of coffee brewed behind her.

"Sure," she said.

Once she stepped out, Veronica said, "Hi, Eliza."

"Hi, Veronica. Patty sent you, didn't she?"

"She did." Veronica nodded. "But what you probably don't know is that I started Jane."

Eliza's eyes widened. "You did? Does Patty know?"

"Yes, and she's . . . working on digesting it. Anyway, I believe one hundred percent in your right to have this abortion, no matter what anyone else thinks. But. I love Patty, and we've been through a lot together. And she loves you. I'd like to help you two figure things out."

Veronica could see Eliza's mind working behind her eyes, which betrayed nothing; the woman would be a great poker player. Was she trying to solve this conundrum of her square older sister being friends with an abortionist?

"Also," Veronica added, "I promise you that Patty can be the older sister you need."

Eliza finally showed some emotion with a snort of disbelief. "Do you really believe that? All she does is chase after her own kids all day."

"Chasing after three kids is way more than a full-time job, and I refuse to hear anyone disparage it. Women marched on Washington two years ago to get paid for that kind of work. We *should* get paid for it. Or we should get free child care to help us get jobs that pay us."

Eliza looked stunned. Veronica felt momentarily annoyed; younger women rarely understood this issue because they hadn't had children of their own yet. *Well, at least she knows she can't handle a baby on her own. That's the first step.*

"How about this? I promise you'll get your abortion today, no matter what Patty says. But will you talk to Patty first? I know it's not ideal, but I think she'll be more . . . *flexible* if you haven't had the abortion yet."

Eliza folded her arms over her chest, thinking. Then she said, "Will you stay while we talk?"

"If you want."

She nodded.

"Then let's get this over with."

28

MARGARET

"Daddy, pleeeease!" Poor Charlie looked like she was on the verge of collapse, her eyes full of tears, her shoulders sagging down.

"Do you really need *that* set of paints and paper? We can go to a store and get you new ones later today."

"No, I *need* those. Mommy sa—" She took a breath. "I just want those. Please? She told me she's working at home today! Can't you take me back so I can get them?"

Gabe stood looking down at his daughter, arms folded over his chest.

Margaret couldn't stand watching Charlie in such distress, and when a simple solution dinged into her head, she offered it: "How about I take her to get the supplies? I know you have a lot to do." He hated going to Siobhan's place, and frankly, she was curious to see it; constantly missing her at the Service had only increased the woman's mystique.

You'd have thought she'd handed Charlie a whole pie to eat by herself. "Thank you, Margaret!" She clasped her hands under her chin and begged her father one more time. "Pllllleeeease."

"Fine," he said, but he seemed even more angry now.

"Let's go!" Charlie grabbed Margaret's hand and pulled her toward the door.

"Do you know how to get there from here?" Gabe asked his daughter.

"Yes!"

Buckled into Gabe's pristine Volvo, Charlie gave Margaret simple directions to a street not far away, though it was a little closer to campus and obviously a student street, with a few random tables left out for people to take if they wanted, and fewer pots of flowers and other homey accoutrements on the stoops of the houses, which looked as though they'd been subdivided into shared homes. Paint peeled in curls off of many doors.

"This is it!" Charlie sang out when they reached a redbrick apartment building, the only place on the block with a lovely pot of pansies and a door that looked like it had a coat of fresh glossy black paint. The stoop was nicely swept.

Charlie unbuckled herself and leapt out of the car as Margaret idled, watching as the girl rang a doorbell, then jumped off the stoop and leaned back so she could see into one of the higher windows. Siobhan appeared in a third-story window, and Charlie waved, then Siobhan held up a finger and disappeared. Charlie raced back up the stoop and bounced on her toes as she waited to be let in.

Siobhan opened the door to the building, and she and her daughter hugged tightly. Then she said something to Charlie, who pointed at the car, then dragged her mother inside the building as Siobhan put up her other hand and waved at Margaret with a sweet smile.

A genuinely *sweet* smile.

This was a terrible idea. The last thing she needed was to be doing this favor for Gabe's daughter, and wind up feeling inadequate compared to his ex-wife—the beautiful painter who'd also brought a pretty amazing group of women together in the Service. Siobhan didn't

Kerri Maher

seem to recognize her from that months-ago meeting, but the possibility made Margaret nervous. *I should have thought of that before.*

Then something else occurred to her: this was a very modest home. It looked like there were several apartments in the building, which wasn't all that much larger than the entire town house Gabe had all to himself. Siobhan's living circumstances were much reduced from those of her married life. Then, in the side mirror of Gabe's far nicer Volvo, Margaret caught sight of the beat-up Saab Siobhan drove whenever she dropped Charlie off. An unbidden resentment rose up in Margaret, a sense of the unfairness that Charlie should have to live with her mother in a place half the size of her father's, even though she was with her mother most of the time.

Before she could think much more about it, she glimpsed Charlie and her mother hugging in the big window of Siobhan's apartment. Then, suddenly, Charlie was bounding out the front door and down the steps with a canvas bag in her hand. She flung herself into the back seat of the car and said, "Phew, glad that's over. Let's go to Dad's."

Phew?

"It must have been nice to get to see your mom, right?" Margaret eyed Charlie in the rearview mirror.

The girl shrugged, staring out the window. "I guess."

None of this made sense to Margaret. A few minutes ago, Charlie had been desperate to get those paints, and had seemed so happy to see her mom, but now she was acting like she was glad to get away. And she'd entirely withdrawn into her own world. What was the girl thinking? Did she wish she could stay with Siobhan? Despite the "phew," she didn't exactly seem *happy* to be going back to Gabe's with Margaret.

Margaret turned on the radio, but it was all talk, not a single song playing on any of her favorite stations, so she turned it off. "I'm excited for our pottery class tomorrow," she said solicitously. She really was looking forward to the class and the other activities she and Gabe had planned for their extra time with Charlie, starting with a Bulls game tonight.

"Me, too," Charlie said listlessly, studying the passing scenery as if it knew the answer to a question she'd been asking herself as long as she could remember.

Charlie went straight to her room when they returned, saying she wanted to use her paints, then the house went dead silent. Margaret padded around, looking for Gabe. She found him with wet hair in the bedroom, pulling a gray sweater on over a long-sleeved T-shirt atop blue jeans.

"Hi," she said. She felt nervous, like she was about to get in trouble, though she didn't feel she'd done anything wrong.

"I wish you hadn't done that," he said.

"Why?"

"Because I'd already said no."

"I thought I was offering a simple solution. I know you don't like going over there, and I don't mind, so . . ."

"But I said no. Now Charlie thinks that when she wants something she can just go to you."

This sounded so preposterous, Margaret laughed. "I doubt that, Gabe. She knows I'm just your girlfriend."

"And I wish my girlfriend would have stopped to think about *my* feelings."

"I thought I was rescuing you from an errand you didn't want to run!"

"I didn't want to run it because I didn't want Charlie to see Siobhan again. She's with that woman too much as it is. When she's with me, that's it. Period."

"Listen, I'm sorry. I didn't think . . . You know what, it doesn't matter what I thought. I won't do it again."

Her apology didn't alter his scowl.

"So," she said brightly, though her stomach felt leaden with dread, "Bulls game tonight, right? What do you want to do between now and then? Shall we plan to have dinner at the stadium?"

He shrugged. "It's a waste of money, but Charlie'll want to do it, so . . ."

"Hey," she said softly, putting her arms around his waist and kissing his cheek. "How can I make this better?"

He looked at her, despondent, and said, "Just leave me alone for a little while."

The house stayed quiet for hours, with Charlie in her room painting and Gabe in his office . . . writing? Margaret wasn't sure, and she didn't want to bug him, so she settled down on the couch with some back issues of the *PMLA* she'd been meaning to get to. The silence was so distracting, though, she kept reading the same page over and over before getting up to see if Charlie wanted to try any of their new patterns.

"Not right now," the girl said, surrounded by sheets of paper on which she'd painted pansies just like the ones on her mother's front step.

"These are really good," Margaret said, marveling at the saturated blues and purples and yellows the girl was coaxing out of simple watercolor trays.

"Thanks," Charlie said. "My mom showed me how."

"I heard she's a great painter. Maybe you take after her."

"Don't say that to my dad." The girl whispered this with a furtive glance in the direction of his office.

Was this another reason he hadn't wanted Charlie to get the paints? They'd remind the girl—and him—of her connection to Siobhan?

What a mess. An increasingly loud voice in her head was telling her that the situation with Gabe and Charlie and Siobhan was not right. She couldn't put her finger on how or why, exactly, and it was so easy to argue with the voice: Of course he's mad at Siobhan; she left him. Of course he wants to protect the time he spends with Charlie. He's doing the best he can. He's so sweet with his daughter—most of the time.

At the basketball game, Gabe plastered on a big smile and bought Charlie everything she so much as glanced at, including a Bulls hat, cotton candy, and an ice cream sundae. Margaret was starving, but he only ordered them a hot dog each and a single beer to share, and the whole time she had the sense of being on the outside. This wasn't like their other outings, where the three of them palled around, playing I Spy and twenty questions. This was a father-daughter event where she was made to feel like a third wheel, purposefully excluded as Gabe explained the game to Charlie, pointing out specific players and the ways they dribbled the ball and made jump shots. When the Bulls made a basket that put them ahead right as the halftime bell rang, all three of them jumped to their feet and cheered, but it was only Charlie's cheek Gabe kissed in jubilation, without so much as glancing in Margaret's direction.

For the first time, Margaret wondered, *Is this why Siobhan left?*

Hungry and frustrated, she excused herself to go to the bathroom, and got a beer and another loaded Chicago dog, both of which she devoured quickly while standing in the mezzanine. Tipsy and sated, she was less bothered by the father-daughter dynamic for the final quarter.

The next day, things returned to their regular equilibrium. Both Gabe and Charlie effused over Margaret's waffles and sausage, and Gabe seemed genuinely impressed by the Polaroids they showed him of the hand-thrown bowls they made in the pottery class, which they'd be able to bring home glazed and finished in a few days. Gabe and Margaret snuggled on the couch with books after Charlie went to sleep, and made love Saturday night and Sunday morning while Charlie watched cartoons.

In fact, the rest of Charlie's extra weekend with them was so relaxed and fun, especially with the weather turning toward the sunny embrace of spring, Margaret told herself again that Gabe's earlier mood was perfectly understandable, and not even as bad as it had seemed at the time. *And,* she reminded herself, *you're still keeping a whopper of a secret from Gabe.*

No one's perfect.

The first time that idea had really landed in her was when her father came to visit her in California. After long, shin-pounding walks through the hills of San Francisco, touring the Presidio, Golden Gate Park, and Coit Tower, Margaret had asked her father, "Can you convince Mom to try and fly out here? I miss her."

"She misses you, too, Maggie. But neither of us wants to repeat the experience we had when we tried to go to the Grand Canyon."

"But you love to fly and travel. How do you stand it?"

"No one's perfect, sweetheart. Least of all your old man. And your mother's a blessing in so many ways. I try to see the balance."

She'd always felt those were words to live by. *No one's perfect. Try to see the balance.*

Gabe would make a wonderful husband in many ways—he was attentive, thoughtful, intellectually curious, and steady in his work. More and more, though, Margaret had been trying to convince herself that he was the right man for her, that certain behaviors she didn't agree with were okay on *balance.*

Could she love Gabe's imperfections, like her father loved her mother's?

29

PATTY

When the doorbell rang on Friday, Patty was in the middle of vacu-uming the family room—which she did almost daily to suck up all the crumbs from the snacks the kids were not supposed to be eating in there to begin with—so she almost didn't hear it.

She switched off the machine and hurried to the door as she fixed her ponytail. Her heart nearly stopped when she saw Veronica and Eliza standing there on her front step.

"Thank God," she said, as she pulled Eliza into a huge hug—which, miraculously, Eliza returned. Lightly. But her arms did encir-cle Patty, and it was enough. For a start.

"Come in, come in," she said to both of them, trying to transmit *Thank you thank you thank you* into Veronica's eyes. She thought she succeeded, because Vee's eyes seemed to reply, *You're welcome.*

She led everyone into the kitchen and nervously asked if they wanted anything to eat or drink. Eliza looked at Veronica for a cue. Patty looked at her, too.

"Can we just talk?" Veronica suggested.

"Of course," Patty said. "Eliza, I'm so glad you're here." Patty felt flooded with gratitude and love. *Don't mess this up.*

The three women sat at the kitchen table, and Patty needed something to occupy her hands, so she reached for a random nickel one of the kids had left along with some other detritus at breakfast, and started to rotate it between her fingers as she searched for the right words.

"So," ventured Veronica. "Eliza has not yet terminated her pregnancy, and she wants to talk with you first. But not about whether or not she's going to have it. She says she's willing to talk to you about what happens after."

"Thanks, Vee. And you, too, Eliza." Patty fixed her eyes on her sister, even though her sister looked at her own fingers sweeping crumbs into a little pile and shifting them around. "Thanks for talking to me. I . . . well, I've done a lot of thinking since we talked, and I want you to know I support whatever decision you make. If this is what you want, then I'll pay for it and make you comfortable when you come home. I just . . . I'd really like you to think of this as your home."

Eliza raised her eyes to Patty. "If all that's true, why did I have to come and talk to you first?"

"You're right, that wasn't a great method. I just didn't want you to run immediately after. I wanted to have a chance to tell you I'm sorry, and I want to be a real sister to you. Which means not expecting that we're always going to agree." Patty glanced at Veronica as she said this, hoping her friend would understand she meant "sister" in the broadest possible sense.

Eliza kept moving the crumbs around.

"Please come back here once you're done with Jane today?" Patty didn't care that she sounded desperate. She *was* desperate. "Stay a few more weeks. Think about what you want to do next. Let me help if I can."

Eliza quit playing with the crumbs, looked at her sister, and asked, "Do I have a choice?"

"Yes," Patty replied immediately. "The choice is yours. If you want to leave right after, I won't try and stop you. I'll even give you another thousand dollars to help you get wherever you need to go."

Eliza's expression didn't change, but she said, "Okay. I'll think about it."

Patty didn't like staying in limbo any longer, but also saw there was nothing she could say or do in this moment to change the situation. Pushing Eliza more would surely result in her sister leaving. "Thanks for considering it," she said.

Eliza turned to Veronica. "Will you do it? The abortion?"

"Yes," said Veronica. Then, turning to Patty, she said, "As long as you're comfortable with that."

Comfortable with it? I'm relieved. "I am." Patty set down the nickel and said to Veronica, "Can you do it here?"

"I need some supplies, but I think I have everything at my place. We can do it there. Eliza, are you ready? It should only take fifteen minutes."

Eliza nodded.

An hour and a half later, without any further discussion, Patty tucked her sister under a blanket on the couch in front of the TV in her living room, after retrieving her sister's backpack from a tiny hotel room near the college, where she marveled again at her sister's lack of worldly goods. She brought her everything that sounded good to eat, starting with sandwiches thick with cheese and pickled vegetables that they ate together while watching *Days of Our Lives*, then later Fluffernutters, which all the kids wanted as well when they got home from school. The relief she felt at having her sister in her home, safe, on the other side of this crisis, made Patty feel almost drunk with joy.

While she was making dinner, Eliza appeared at the counter by her side and said, "Can I help?"

"Absolutely not. Go lie back down."

"My back is actually bothering me from too much sitting. I feel like I need to do something."

"Alright, well, you can peel some carrots, but if you start feeling bad at all, go lie down upstairs, okay?"

"Can I put on some music?"

"Sure."

Eliza fiddled with the countertop radio and found a station playing jazz music, then she started peeling long ribbons of skin off the carrots into the sink.

"I didn't know you liked jazz."

"Christopher played an upright bass before he started with an electric. He was really good." Her voice was full of loss. She stared down at the carrots for a few seconds, then shook her head. "Anyway, he taught me some things about music, and I noodled around on the band's guitars."

"What can you play?"

"I can play a lot of what's on the radio. Joni Mitchell's my favorite. Joan Baez is good, too. And the Mamas and the Papas."

Finally, an opening. "You know," Patty said as casually as she could despite her mounting excitement, "Veronica's husband is an amazing piano player. Maybe you two could play together sometime."

Eliza shrugged. "Maybe."

It's a start. Don't push.

When the carrots were finished, Eliza moved on to the potatoes, then chopped tomatoes for the salad.

"You sure you're still okay with all this standing?"

"I'm really okay. It just feels like period cramps."

"Amazing."

That night at dinner, Patty kept marveling at the fact that her children all behaved, no mashed potatoes were flung across the table, Matt was cheerful, and Eliza was there as if she always had been, eating and smiling and talking to everyone about the various nothings in their days—spelling tests, math homework, dodgeball politics, and the bubble-haired widow who came to Matt nearly every week convinced she was having a heart attack. How was it possible that just a few hours ago, her little sister and best friend had been engaged in an illegal medical procedure together, and that it had only taken a quarter of an hour?

And why should it be such a surprise? Hours after her mother died, she'd had to get Karen to preschool and nurse Junie. And those mundane activities had been incredibly soothing, just as this meal, this day, this very minute, was soothing—both a balm and a promise that life did, in fact, go on.

30

MARGARET

The gallery in Old Town had an unassuming black facade, large windows, and a brightly lit white-walled interior, much like the other galleries on the block. Margaret stepped inside, hoisting her purse higher on her shoulder, and began scanning the little plaques next to each painting, searching for the name Siobhan Johnson. *Or maybe she uses her maiden name.* So she just looked for *Siobhan*.

In the second room, Margaret found her. Or rather, two paintings by her, hung less than an inch apart. They were enormous. On each unframed canvas was a woman's naked body outlined in black paint with a wash of pale blues and greens behind them. Both women were far larger than life-size, and while the black outline itself was almost wispy, the bodies were thick and earthy, like a middle finger to the skinny nonsense in magazines these days. One of the women was standing at a stove holding the handle of a pan, her broad back to the viewer, her shoulders sagging like the uneven moons of her rear end. The other woman was reclined on a barely sketched chaise, one arm thrown over her eyes while the other hand appeared to travel down her navel toward her vagina, as if she was about to touch herself.

Woman: At work and play.
By Siobhan Doyle

So, her maiden name.

"Amazing, isn't it?"

Margaret was startled by the tall, slim man who said these words to her. At least Margaret guessed this was a man, but on closer inspection, she was less sure. He—she?—had short hair slicked back, and wore black pants and shoes in the style of the Beatles nearly a decade ago, a white shirt, and a purple velvet vest. But there was a softness to the face, and not even a hint of shadow on the jaw.

"Amazing," she agreed.

Margaret and the gallery worker both looked at the pair of paintings. "This artist is on the rise," said the stranger. "She's shown here for years as she developed her talents, and now she is going to have a dedicated show in New York, with a complete series of these paintings. I've been to her studio, and they are exquisite. So exciting. They say so much about the plight of women today."

Margaret nodded. She wasn't an art historian, but she'd read just enough art criticism, and gone to enough museums, to be able to see that Siobhan was playing with the diptych format, a medieval religious form she was subverting with her sexualized subject. And the size wasn't intimate like the original diptychs; no, these women were on the scale of a nineteenth-century history painting. The fact that she'd chosen such a private subject for large canvases was yet another subversion—though the Impressionists had made this move a hundred years ago; around 1860 or so, Manet had painted a prostitute on a grand scale and scandalized all of Paris. Siobhan appeared to be harkening back to that moment, as well as older, holier paintings, thus suggesting both Madonna and whore in the very shape of her canvases.

The gallery show in New York indicated that there was an appetite for Siobhan's iconoclasms, and Margaret could see why. This two-canvas work was *pretty* at the same time it was challenging. Margaret could imagine a wealthy art collector hanging it prominently in a Manhattan penthouse because the color and texture looked like decor; one had to look closely to see that the subject matter was hardly pretty. Here was woman as domestic servant, and woman as self-eroticizing; as subservient to the implied male gaze, and as liberated from it.

She liked these paintings. A lot.

It wasn't until she found herself fighting against this admiration that Margaret realized she'd come here today hoping to hate Siobhan's work.

"I agree," she said to the gallery worker. Curator? Assistant? Clerk? "The paintings say a great deal."

Back in her office, Margaret called Phyllis on the shared linguistics department graduate line, and her friend picked up.

"Wow," said Margaret, "I was expecting to leave a message and try you at home before actually reaching you."

"I'm just finishing some things here. What's up?"

"Do you have time for a drink?"

"Your timing couldn't be better. Meet you at the gate in ten?"

"Perfect."

Beneath the gazes of the gargoyles, under the pointed arch that was covered in ivy, Margaret and Phyllis met, then walked briskly to the Woodlawn Tap, where they ordered sidecars and slid into a table in the corner.

"Any department gossip?" Margaret asked, avoiding the real reason she'd asked to see her friend.

"I wouldn't know, since I haven't been around much except to teach. I'm way behind on my dissertation, and my sister is pregnant again, so it's hard not to be worried about that. She's, like, ten weeks, though, so . . ." Phyllis held up both hands with middle fingers crossed over index fingers.

Margaret held up her crossed fingers in solidarity, then asked, "How's Keith?"

"We're good." Phyllis smiled like she was remembering something particularly juicy.

"Do tell."

"We talked about my sister, and I finally told him my fears about myself. And he said . . ." Phyllis's voice thickened with emotion here. "He said he didn't care if we could have kids or not."

"I'm so happy for you. That's great." *Maybe I'll find that someday.* She was starting to realize she didn't have "that" with Gabe: openness, trust, optimism.

"What about you, friend?" Phyllis said, swirling the ice in her glass with the tiny brown plastic straw.

"I went and looked at Siobhan's paintings today at a gallery in Old Town."

Phyllis whistled. "Why on earth would you do that?"

"Some things about Gabe have been eating at me. I wanted to know if seeing her paintings would illuminate anything."

"And?"

"They're great paintings. I can see how a woman who painted them would have helped start Jane."

Phyllis was quiet for an uncomfortably long time. Then she finally asked, "You want to know what happened in their marriage?"

Margaret's skin prickled all over; she felt hot and cold at the same time. "Do you know?"

"She's told me a few things. And I've seen a lot of women live their own versions of it."

Do I really want to know this? It felt like a betrayal to find out like this.

"I think you don't actually need me to tell you, though," Phyllis went on. "I think there's a little voice inside your head telling you something's not quite right. You've got to listen, Margaret. Trust yourself."

It's more than the stuff with Siobhan and Charlie, she admitted to herself. It was the little guilt trips. The excluding. The way he never went over to her place and brought her entirely over to his.

"You're only in the first year of the relationship. It's only going to get worse. Slowly but surely. You know the metaphor of the frog in the boiling water?"

Margaret shook her head.

"You put a frog in a pot of boiling water, and it jumps out. But if you put a frog in a pot of cold water and slowly turn up the heat, it dies."

Margaret laughed, but nervously. "That seems a bit dramatic."

"Trust me. Siobhan just barely jumped out in time."

"What are you implying?"

"Let's just say there are plenty of ways to make someone feel like they're going to drown."

"I hardly feel like I'm in that much danger."

"Good. Don't let it get to that point. Monitor the heat. When you're ready to jump, you know where to find me."

"Thanks." Margaret took a sip of her own drink, noting that Phyllis had said *when*, not *if*, and she knew deep down that *when* was the truth.

31

VERONICA

She felt practically homicidal with boredom in the interminable days following Eliza's abortion. She needed to *do* something instead of moping around at home, cooking and cleaning, serving as a call-back Jane, and typing letter after letter to state congressmen—so many bloody *men*—encouraging them to hurry up and ratify the Equal Rights Amendment. *Since President Nixon vetoed the Comprehensive Child Development Act, it's more important than ever that Congress act now and take a stand for women*, she typed again and again. It had been nearly two weeks since Eliza's abortion, one of the simplest, most straightforward D&Cs she'd ever done. She hadn't realized until now what a hands-on kind of person she was, how much she craved physical work, and variety, not being stuck in one place all the time.

Then, like a lightning bolt from above, Aunt Martha arrived unexpectedly one day with a huge hug and gifts from India—a stunning handmade blanket for the couch and a shawl with golden thread woven in for Veronica, a brightly colored set of puppets wearing traditional Indian clothing for Kate, and a decorative sitar for Doug. She looked tan and resplendent in an intricately embroidered fuchsia tunic, clearly purchased in India, which she wore over blue jeans, her gray hair flowing long over her shoulders.

It was close to noon. "I'm so glad you're here, but you know Kate won't be home for a few hours and Doug will be even later."

"Oh, I'll see both of them eventually. Maybe I'll hang around till Kate gets home. Anyway, I came to see *you*. But first, tea. I learned to make the most amazing kind in Delhi." Using a saucepan, she combined water and milk and Lipton tea and half of Veronica's baking spices, and brought it all to a boil, then served it in two mugs. It was sweet and spicy and unlike anything Veronica had ever tasted before.

"Can you write down what you did before you leave?"

"I can try, though it's less of a recipe than a feeling. Now let's sit, and you can tell me everything I've missed. Start with Jane."

Veronica sipped the tea and talked, recounting the events of the last few months, ending with the crisis of Eliza.

"That poor girl," said Aunt Martha, shaking her head. "But thank goodness she had *you* in her hour of need."

Veronica shrugged. "It felt good at the time. But now I feel completely useless here at home."

"What do you mean, useless? You're growing a human being in there."

"I just feel like such a *failure*. This is what women's lib is all about, what I'm trying to help other women achieve! But it feels like I've failed. I couldn't manage it all. I was so bad at being a working mother, I had a panic attack."

"Has it occurred to you that the nature of the work at Jane is part of what's taking a toll on you? It's *hard*, what you're doing, even when you set aside the illegality."

"You worked every day without a problem. And don't try and tell me that teaching isn't grueling."

"Sure, teaching seven classrooms full of hormonal semi-adults without fully developed brains can be grueling. It was also incredibly rewarding."

"So is Jane. We're setting women *free.*"

"But then you come home, where you are not free. Let's not fool ourselves. The only way for a woman to have maximum freedom in her life is never to get married. Doug is wonderful, and Kate is a dear, but they are *responsibilities.* You are required by society to care for them, and there are no support structures in place to allow women to do what you're doing at Jane. Not to mention, men are still paid more, and there's no such thing as affordable child care."

"Amen." She glanced at the stack of letters pleading with the government to recognize women as equal to men.

"I could have gotten married. I had opportunities. But . . ." Aunt Martha shrugged.

"I've always wanted to know why you didn't get married."

"I never found anyone worth giving up my freedom for. But I'll tell you something: if I had found him, I would have stipulated no children."

Veronica nodded. She understood, and she envied her aunt that kind of clarity. The problem was, she *did* want children.

And she wanted Jane.

"I don't want to turn into my mother," Veronica said quietly.

Martha pressed her lips together and studied Veronica just long enough to make her uncomfortable.

"Your mother would kill me if she knew I was about to tell you this, but I can't stand the idea of you feeling so unforgiving of her."

After letting another few seconds tick by, Martha said, "She was married before your father. To a lovely man named Nathaniel Taylor. He was so handsome and kind, and oh, did he worship your mother. They had grand plans to travel together, and . . ." Martha chuckled. "I remember they went to San Francisco for their honeymoon and your mother never wanted to come back. She wanted to stay there and open an antiques shop. Anyway. They did come back, and the plan was for them to work on him finding a job out west, which I have no doubt he would have done. He was an engineer, and highly skilled. But just as things were coming together for them, he was killed in a horrible accident in his lab."

Antiques shop? San Francisco? First husband?

"A part of her just died with him," her aunt went on. "Nothing was the same for her after that. She was so sad she wasn't pregnant, that she had nothing of him to take with her into the rest of her life. She spent a year in bed, and met your father at the first party she went to when she emerged. He also worshipped her. And they were happy, for a while. She was utterly devoted to you. But it wasn't enough, or it wasn't what she'd imagined. When I asked her about opening an antiques shop here in Chicago, she'd just shrug. *That's an old dream,* she'd say."

"That's terrible."

"She made a series of choices. We all do. I just don't want you to think there was no reason for the choices she made. She did the best she could, and she got stuck."

Images of her mother flashed through Veronica's mind: fierce and determined when she told off a little boy on the playground after he pushed Veronica from the top of a slide; happy and relaxed as she held Veronica's hand ice-skating before Christmas; elated and nostalgic when Veronica put on the perfect prom dress in the dressing room of Marshall Field's; proud but barely coherent during the toasts at her wedding; puzzlingly detached when she held baby Kate in her arms for the first time.

Veronica sipped the last of her cooled tea and felt immensely sad. "Why didn't she ever say anything to me?" she said, awash with sudden compassion for her mother.

"Because she didn't want anyone's pity."

"She and I have that much in common, then," Veronica mused, thinking of the strange, sideways similarity between herself and her mother: both of them were putting on a good show, while hiding something big and true about themselves.

They sat in silence for a minute or two, then Martha asked, "Have you considered medical school?"

Veronica laughed. "Because that's so much easier than what I'm doing?"

"Not easier, but *legal*. I think that's the part all of us who love you are most worried about."

This gave Veronica pause. She hadn't thought of that before. Maybe . . . obstetrics and gynecology? And Martha was right—Doug, at least, would be over the moon that her work would be legal.

But what would she do with Jane? She couldn't just leave it.

"It sounds counterintuitive," said Martha. "But sometimes the best thing to do is stop trying to figure it all out. Rest. Let the answers come to you."

"I'll try," she said, her mind already whirring. Even as she told herself that she couldn't possibly abandon Jane, as soon as Martha left, Veronica called Information to get the numbers of the Northwestern and Chicago medical schools, which she then phoned and asked to send her information on applying.

The enormous packets of information that arrived in the mail the following days were overwhelming. It would take a year or two of pre-medical classes, then another four years of med school, *then* some years of residency. She'd be forty by the time she was done—or older, since she'd have to do it part-time, as a mother, which put her in much the same bind she was in with Jane.

Except Aunt Martha was right about med school being legal.

And she couldn't ignore the flutter of excitement she felt when she thought about graduating as Dr. Veronica Stillwell.

She could see why her mother had given up on her antiques shop dream: it was so easy to default to what was in front of you instead of pursuing what you had to invent. Even the Service wasn't something she'd sat down and decided to create, like she was—maybe—deciding to apply to medical school; in fact, if she'd been asked five years ago to describe an underground women's abortion clinic, she wouldn't have been able to do it. And yet here she was, running one.

She felt conflicted enough about the idea of medical school that she didn't tell Doug, and she kept all the envelopes full of material hidden in the back of her closet.

Siobhan was the first person she told. Her friend had just gotten back from New York, and the two of them were having coffee in the same little backyard where they'd sat three years before, watching Kate and Charlie make mud pies after Siobhan's abortion. It was still weedy and underplanted, a product of the mistress of the house having other priorities. She wondered if this ever bothered Doug. If it did, he never said anything, for which she was suddenly very grateful. Then again, she thought to herself, if he did care, he could become the gardener in the family. Clearly, greenery was not a priority for either of them.

"I am thinking of applying to medical school, but it's like ten years of work."

Siobhan's face lit up with excitement. "You'd be an amazing doctor, Vee. You should do it."

"What would I be doing it for, though, you know? What I really want is to get back to the Service."

"Because you like your medical work gritty and illegal?"

"Yes." Her friend had just articulated an aspect of the Service that *did* get her heart going in a way that all those classes did not. It was protest work. She was her own boss and an outlaw. When she thought about what she was getting away with, she felt powerful.

But she also liked the idea of having her own practice focusing on women's health.

"What about becoming a nurse practitioner? That must be less school, right?"

Veronica nodded. "There's also midwife training. But I haven't looked into that yet."

"You should. I'm excited for you."

"Did you always know you wanted to be an artist?"

Siobhan nodded. "Other than the Service, drawing and painting are the only things I've both loved doing and been good at."

"It's funny, but before Jane, I never thought of myself as being particularly good at anything. I was only an okay teacher."

"Sometimes we have to do things to realize we're good. You're an amazing leader and organizer. And you give stellar abortions."

"Not exactly a résumé line, though, is it?"

Siobhan laughed. "True. You're good with your hands, though, and that is a very translatable skill."

Veronica and Siobhan sat in silence for a few minutes, and Veronica heard the birds chirping wildly outside. "I wish it didn't have to be like this."

"Like what?"

"All these choices between what feel like opposites. Illegal or legal. Protest or follow the rules. Mother or doctor."

"I don't see it that way," said Siobhan. "I see it more as a slow process of integration. Mother *becomes* doctor. Protest to *change* the rules."

"That's admirably optimistic."

"I'm in a sunny frame of mind. But it took me a while to get here."

"Must be all your recent success. . . . Speaking of which, tell me everything about New York. I should have asked you first thing!"

"New York was amazing," Siobhan said. "The show is going to be gorgeous. We'll see if I actually sell any paintings, though."

"I'm sure you will! How can you not?"

"The art world is fickle and unpredictable." Siobhan shrugged.

"And what about your old flame?"

"I'm getting to that. . . ."

"Look at you, you're beet red!"

"I've never . . . well, let's just say I'd forgotten sex and talking could be like that."

"It's great, right?"

"I hadn't had sex since that last time with Gabe, the time that . . . sent me to Jonathan. And it hadn't even been good sex. At some point, Gabe had entirely lost interest in making it fun for me. It's hard to remember if he ever did, to be honest, or if I was just so horny at twenty-two, it didn't matter. Derek, on the other hand . . . Derek knows what he's doing."

"I'm so glad for you. He'll come to your opening, then?"

"Oh, yes."

"And he doesn't have kids, right?"

"Nope."

"He sounds blissfully free to be with you."

"Not quite. He lives in New York, which is complicated."

"Pish. A two-hour-long flight."

"Three. And I can't move, so he has to come here."

"Maybe Gabe will get an offer from Columbia or NYU."

"I think it's more likely Derek could get work in Chicago. He's already done ads for a few companies here."

"That would be amazing." They smiled at each other for a minute, then Veronica asked, "Do you think you'd ever have another kid? With him or another new partner?"

"Definitely." Siobhan nodded. "But, you know, that's a ways away."

"Take your time. Enjoy what's happening now." There was a pause, and Veronica couldn't help asking, "And . . . what's going on with the Service?" She'd been consciously avoiding this topic, for fear it would tempt her to return.

Siobhan hesitated, then said, "Well . . . one girl did have to go to the hospital earlier this week for bleeding. Trudy and Phyllis followed protocol and had Melanie escort her to the ER."

Veronica's heart sped up. Nothing like that had happened in months. "Was one of our friendly doctors there? Do you know why there was so much blood?"

"Melanie followed up and said the woman had a clotting disorder she didn't know about. She's fine, but Phyllis said it was pretty gruesome. Blood everywhere. And thankfully, yes, Dr. Randall was on duty and put her down as a miscarriage."

"But that's not the worrying thing," Siobhan said, the reluctance clear in her voice. "Listen, I promised not to tell you this, because no one wants to upset you, but I think you have a right to know. Sam Wilder or one of his cronies is now parked outside the Place every day."

"Fuck. We have to stop using that location."

Siobhan nodded. "We did. But as you know, we're always short on locations, and convincing someone to let us use their house for the illegal work is tough. Marion's letting us use her house, and so is Melanie, and a few others. But it's become a huge juggling act."

"Let me help with that," Veronica said, excitement bubbling inside. "I have nothing better to do than make phone calls and map out every week's locations."

"That's not a bad idea."

"Just tell them I'm going to do it."

"I feel like I need to run it by them, but honestly, everyone's so overstretched, I'm sure they'll overlook the fact that I told you. And you're right, this is something you can do from home."

"Tell them I need to do this for my own health and well-being."

Siobhan smiled. "Just promise me you won't show up, or overdo it."

Veronica crossed her heart with her middle and index fingers, then kissed them and held them up like a Scout.

"I'll confirm with you soon."

———

"Shouldn't we start thinking about names?" Doug asked Sunday morning after bringing her a cup of coffee in bed. Kate was watching cartoons on television.

"If it's a girl," he said, settling down beside her, "how about the name Nora? After my great-aunt."

"The suffragist?"

"The very one."

"I like that." Veronica recalled that Nora Blanchard had even spent time in jail for civil disobedience in 1916. She'd always thought the two of them would have been friends.

Doug smirked up at her. "I thought you might."

Nora.

"Any requests if it's a boy?" she asked.

"It's a girl."

"You're sure?"

"I don't think you are capable of growing anything other than gorgeous, brilliant, headstrong girls."

"Hey! I can grow a sensitive, upstanding man if I want."

"Prove it," he growled, then kissed her neck right where it met her shoulder. It tickled deliciously.

She kissed him back. "The die is cast for this one, I'm afraid."

"Nora."

"Nora."

32

MARGARET

Margaret knocked on Leo Robinson's office door, her other hand hot and trembling around the manila folder with the five essays. She was hardly mistress of herself in that moment, and she knew it, and she didn't care.

Leo swung his door open and greeted her with a smile and a broad "What a fine surprise!" with a sweeping gesture indicating she should come in.

He closed the door behind her, and she noticed how *decorated* his office was, complete with two Persian rugs, a coffee maker, and a carafe of amber liquor and four matching cut-crystal glasses. Every inch of the wall-to-wall and floor-to-ceiling bookshelves was bursting with books, and from the dividers of a few shelves hung gallery-framed abstract paintings. On his desk was a small marble replica of an unfinished Rodin sculpture depicting a couple kissing, entwined, the woman's breasts and smooth, hairless mons pubis facing the viewer.

This prominently featured sculpture on the desk of a male English professor made her feel uncomfortable, and she wondered what it did to his female students who sat here for office hours.

"Scotch? It's five o'clock in New York."

"Oh, no, thank you."

"Suit yourself." He poured himself two generous fingers full and sat at his desk. She sat across from him. His benignly smiling form was flanked by his degrees from Northwestern and Princeton, which were framed and hanging from the shelves behind him. Between them were multiple copies of his three seminal books on medieval poetry. His book on Chaucer was required in every undergraduate class on *The Canterbury Tales* she'd ever seen the syllabus for; even she had read it years ago. Leo Robinson was one of the titans of her discipline, which made it all the harder to believe she was sitting here now, fuming at him for being not a titan but an all-too-human male of the species.

"I wanted to thank you for putting the five essays in my box this morning," she began, "but I noticed that neither of the two students I nominated are among them."

Leo shrugged and took a sip before replying. "That would be because no one else nominated them."

"No one else nominated Belinda Silva? I find that hard to believe. She's a star."

Leo smiled and set down his glass with a rich, resonant thud on his desk—fine, heavy glass hitting fine, heavy wood.

"This is your first time on the committee, so I'll let you in on a secret for next time, should you join us again. If there is someone you favor, it's best to rally some support. Many of our esteemed colleagues don't even bother to submit a nomination. If you could convince them to submit names—names you yourself would like to support—this sort of thing wouldn't happen."

Which isn't at all how you described this process when you asked me to join. Margaret ground her molars. "I also find it strange that in a department where more than half of the majors are female, only one of the five nominees is a woman." Not even Marcie, the other woman she'd nominated, was on the list—and she was a cliché of the perfect student, down to the calligraphic handwriting.

"I sympathize with your frustration. So many of these girls are simply here looking for a husband, despite all this women's lib business. Do you know how many engagement rings I see after Christmas in my senior classes? It's a pity, so many minds going to waste."

"Maybe if they saw more opportunities for themselves in the department, more rewards than diamond rings, they would strive for more."

Leo clapped his hands together. "I see fire burning in that mind of yours. Excellent! I'd love to see you do something about it."

In other words: have at it, Sisyphus.

"I welcome the challenge," she replied, standing to leave. "Thanks for your time."

"Hey, hey, that chicken is already dead," Gabe said to Margaret as she bludgeoned chicken fillets with a rolling pin to make her mother's recipe for chicken piccata, which Gabe and Charlie had loved so much the first time she made it, it had become a weekly request. She wasn't sure how this had happened. This was a simple enough recipe, but she didn't even like cooking. And now she was making most of the meals for her boyfriend and his daughter.

She turned to him and realized she was breathing heavily, like she'd run a long distance, fast.

"Where's Charlie?"

"Upstairs, why?"

"Because I don't want her to hear me swearing like a sailor about Leo Fucking Robinson."

"Uh-oh. What happened?"

"You know that scholarship committee he asked me to be on? He didn't even put the names of either of the female students I nominated on the short list."

"Did he say why?"

"He claimed I was supposed to lobby for them, and get other faculty to nominate them, too. But that is *not* what he told me before. Only one of the four boys on the list is a top-notch student, and the only girl—*woman*—is fine, but she's prettier than she is intellectually curious. She's exactly the kind of student who will be engaged by the end of next year, which apparently he has a problem with, so why not put forward Belinda or Marcie, who might actually *do* something with their degrees?"

Gabe whistled. "Boy, you *are* fired up. I've never seen you like this."

"I'm furious."

"I can see that."

"Wouldn't you be?"

"Sure. It's hard not to get what you want."

"This isn't just *what I want*, Gabe, it's sexism, plain and simple. It's men like Leo Robinson making it so that women think they don't have any other option but to get married and have kids."

"What's wrong with getting married and having kids?"

Oh, for God's sake! "Nothing if it's a choice, and not a default."

"Hey, I'm happy you have a career. But you know that if you ever wanted to quit or take time off, that would be okay."

She had a feeling he was hinting at starting a family together, but this was so much the worst possible time, she wanted to scream.

"Well, I don't," she said, then went back to hitting the chicken.

It was the most tender piccata she'd ever made, and Charlie gobbled up seconds. During dinner, Gabe asked his daughter a few questions about school and otherwise ignored Margaret. Not wanting to make forced conversation any longer than necessary, Margaret offered to do the dishes, then told Gabe she wasn't feeling well and wanted to go home. He didn't even try to convince her to stay the night, and she was relieved.

The way she felt that night, if the heat got turned up one more notch, she was going to have to jump.

Still fuming the next day, she marched herself to Harriet Glick's office and knocked on the door. "Come in," said the older woman from inside.

Margaret let herself in and plastered on a smile. "Hi, Harriet. I'm so glad you're here."

Plucking the red-framed glasses off her face and setting them on her messy desk, Harriet gave Margaret a tired smile. "Happy to have the interruption. What can I do for you?" In contrast to Leo's office, Harriet's was a profusion of unartfully arranged books and papers, with her own diplomas perched on a shelf in the corner. Half-empty cups of tea and coffee dotted every surface, and on the windowsill was a picture of her shaking John F. Kennedy's hand next to a family portrait of what appeared to be a large family of children and grandchildren.

Margaret sat in the very comfortable leather armchair across from Harriet. "I was wondering if our committee could do something about Leo Robinson's English department scholarship."

"Not if it truly belongs to Leo Robinson."

Margaret explained what had happened to her two nominees, and the way Leo had rigged it so his pick would always get the scholarship.

"None of this surprises me, Margaret, and believe me, I'm on your side. But I think you've learned an important lesson here about how to survive in Leo's department."

Harriet's matter-of-fact tone made Margaret itchy. "So there's no recourse here?"

"What can we do? What's done is done this semester. Now. If you have an idea for another initiative, to promote women of promise within your department, *that* I'd like to hear."

"Will Leo allow anything like that to happen?"

Harriet grinned wolfishly. "If he doesn't, he'll risk looking like an old man who can't change with the times. And if there's one thing Leo Robinson can't stand, it's a less-than-flattering image. He doesn't care that he's a snake, or that people know he's a snake. But if you call him an ugly snake, he will listen."

"He won't try to bite in self-defense?"

"Not in my experience."

Margaret studied Harriet. This woman was not someone she wanted to look up to, but she was someone who could help her. *I'll play the game, but only so I can change it.*

"Alright," she said, standing up. "I'll give that some thought. I appreciate your candor."

"I appreciate your nerve."

33

PATTY

Patty and Eliza fell into a habit of eating lunch every day in front of *Another World*, discussing the characters and storylines in detail. Eliza had been watching for years and was encyclopedic on the travails of the Matthews and Frame families. She was amazingly adept at predicting storylines and character transgressions, and Patty never saw her as animated as she was when they were watching the show.

At the end of one particularly tense episode where it became clear that infidelity was going to destroy a long-standing marriage, Patty switched off the television and sat back on the couch next to Eliza. "Have you ever considered writing for this show?"

Eliza looked at her like she'd suddenly sprouted horns. "Are you kidding? Me?"

"Why not? You're great at predicting things, and sometimes I think your predictions are better than what actually happens."

Eliza shrugged. "I bet you have to go to school for that."

"Maybe. But wouldn't studying plots and characters be fun?"

"It never was before."

"College classes are way better than high school. You get to choose what you want to take. It's not all required. You don't have to read nineteenth-century poetry if you don't want to."

Eliza wrinkled her nose.

"Just think about it, okay? You have options. Life doesn't have to be drudgery. The people who make this show are gainfully employed. I bet it's a pretty fun job."

"I hadn't really thought about it before." Eliza paused and took a deep breath, like she was gearing up for something, then said, "Actually, I've started a job. I'm going to work for Jane. I've already done the training."

So that's where you've been disappearing to. Patty was torn between relief that her sister wanted to *do* something and worry about what could happen to her in Veronica's organization, especially with Veronica herself taking time off.

"Are you sure that's a good idea? I mean, I am glad you want to work, but what about your prior arrest? If you were to get into trouble there, it would be a second offense."

"I just feel like this is something I have to do. It's the first thing I've *wanted* to do for a long time."

"Just be careful, okay?"

It occurred to Patty that being a sister—a mother, a wife—was a series of choices between holding tight and letting go. She'd held on so tightly for so long, but lately loosening her grip on the reins had been feeling much better. Certainly, it had brought Eliza back. And since she'd decided in the privacy of her own mind to stop dwelling on the magazines that Matt had thrown out anyway—after making a quick check of the box just to make sure, of course—she and Matt were starting to steal suggestive glances at each other again.

"I'll be careful," Eliza promised.

Patty was seized by an idea—what she thought might be a great idea—and almost spoke it out loud, but stopped herself in the nick of time. It would be better to surprise Eliza with this one. "Well, give the television writing some thought. There are lots of jobs that people are excited to go to every day. And not all of them involve college."

She picked herself up from the couch and said, "I need to run a quick errand. I should be back before the kids get home, but I'd feel better if I knew you were here in case I'm late."

"I'll be here," Eliza said.

Patty bent over to pick up their lunch plates from the coffee table, and Eliza waved her off. "I'll do them."

"Thanks. Back soon."

Patty managed to return with Tad and her gift fifteen minutes before Junie and Karen got off the bus. When Tad saw the big black guitar case in the car, he practically exploded with excitement. "Whoa! A guitar? Mr. Small plays one every Friday, and we all sing along. It's the best part of the week! Can I play it?"

"Well, it's for Eliza. You can help me give it to her, and tell her you'd like to sing with her, okay?"

"Yes!" He pumped his little fist in the air, superhero-style.

As soon as she unlocked the front door of the house, Tad charged in, yelling "Eeeeellllllliiiiiiiizzza!!!" at the top of his lungs.

Eliza stepped out from the kitchen, laughing at her nephew's enthusiasm. "I'm here, I'm here!"

Sliding to Eliza's feet like she was home base, Tad said, "Look what Mom has for you!"

Eliza raised her eyes to Patty, who was making her way to the kitchen more slowly, carrying the heavy case with the instrument inside. Her sister's eyes widened and her smile broadened. "A Gibson?"

"I must admit it's a rental because I didn't know what you'd really want. I had no idea there were so many different kinds of guitars! But the guy in the shop said it's a beautiful instrument. We can talk about buying you one soon, if you're up for that, but I thought you should have something to get started on."

Eliza took the case and set it reverently on the kitchen table, then unlatched it as Tad looked on in utter amazement, practically drooling from his open mouth. Gingerly, she lifted the gleaming rosewood guitar from its red velvet lining, then held it expertly, as if she'd been doing it all her life, and strummed a few chords.

Tad applauded, and Eliza focused her eyes on the neck of the guitar, positioned her fingers deliberately, then played the first few notes of a song Patty recognized right away. "Both Sides Now," by Joni Mitchell.

Right when it felt like she should sing the opening lines, Eliza stopped and Patty saw that her sister's eyes had become red and watery. She cleared her throat and set the instrument back in its case. "I'll play something else later." Then she practically ran to her room.

Confused, Tad looked at his mother and said, with his palms up, "What happened?"

"Sometimes being very happy can actually make you sad," said Patty. Her heart had followed her sister into her room, where she knew the girl was crying. About everything.

"Yeah," he said solemnly. "It's kind of like the day after Christmas. Or finally riding a bike without training wheels."

Patty put her arm around her son and said, "It's exactly like that, kiddo. How'd you get so smart?"

"Aunt Eliza."

"She's taught me a lot, too."

The next day, as she was prepping lunch so they could eat and watch the soap, Eliza came downstairs with wet hair, dressed in brown cords and a blazer. "I'm sorry I didn't tell you before," she said, looking at the meal. "I have a shift at Jane today."

"Oh," Patty said, disappointed. "Well, let me pack this up for you so you can eat on a break."

"Thanks," her sister replied. "And thanks again for the guitar. I'm sorry I got so emotional last night. I want to play, I really do, but I have to figure out what to play that won't remind me of him. You know?"

Patty nodded as she wrapped the sandwich in wax paper. "That makes a lot of sense. I'm sorry I didn't consider that possibility."

"It's really okay. And I *do* want to play. There were plenty of bands I liked that he didn't, so I'm going to work on those tunes. And there are a few songs of my own I have in mind."

"I'd love to hear those sometime."

"I'm not ready for an audience."

"You know where to find me when you are. Hey . . . any chance you might be ready to have lunch with Dad in a week?"

"Yeah, I think I can handle that."

Patty smiled and handed her sister the brown paper bag with her lunch in it. "Have fun."

When her sister left, Patty stood in the kitchen and thought, *Now what?*

Her sister seemed to be starting a new chapter of her life. Matt was also making changes in his career.

Could there be something new in store for her, too?

34

VERONICA

"Chief Sullivan is in the hospital following a stroke last night," Doug said on the other end of the line. "And Wilder got a warrant for arrest from a judge this morning. The judge didn't want to give it to him, but he had to because Wilder had sworn testimony from someone's sister, so he has probable cause. One of the clerks leaked it all to me."

"So this is happening *now*? Wilder's going to raid the Service?" Veronica clutched the receiver tightly.

"Call all of your locations and tell everyone to leave immediately. And if the cops get there, tell them to say nothing. *Nothing*. Until a lawyer gets there to help them."

No one picked up at the Place, which wasn't unusual on a busy day. And anyway, nine out of ten calls were people selling stuff. She did get ahold of Melanie at the Front and told her to evacuate immediately.

It was still morning, and Veronica was in her soft house clothes and feeling filthy, but she didn't have time to fix any of that.

She picked up the phone and called Patty next.

"Hey, can you take Kate and Charlie this afternoon? Something's happening with Jane and I have to get there right away, and I'm not sure how long I'll be."

"Jane? What's going on? Eliza's working there today."

"Shit. Did she say what kind of shift she was doing?" Veronica didn't think there was any way she was qualified for a Place shift yet, but she was so out of the loop, she had no idea. She was *probably* with Melanie getting out of the Front, but she couldn't be sure.

"No, I don't know. Veronica. What's going on?"

"There's going to be a raid. Sam Wilder."

"What?" Veronica could picture her friend blowing her top in the kitchen.

"Patty, this is not the time to panic. I'll get Eliza out." *I don't know how, but I will.*

"Not with that baby you're carrying."

"We don't have time to argue. If you want to come with me, fine, but someone has to watch the kids."

"I'll call Crissy, then I'll be at your house in five minutes."

35

MARGARET

"We have to get everyone out! Now!" Melanie shouted from the kitchen of Margaret's apartment, that day's Front. She clapped her hands as she stepped into the living room. "Police are coming! No time to lose. We'll call you to reschedule."

The sudden commotion was loud and frightening. Women and children stood and cried and shouted every expletive. "What will happen to my sister?" asked one woman holding the hand of a toddler, whose sister was already at the Place.

"They're evacuating, too," said Melanie.

A siren wailed down the block, and the woman picked up the toddler, who was sobbing now, and hurried out.

"Out!" Melanie said as people streamed out in a rushed panic. "If anyone questions you, *say nothing*. Nothing! You've done nothing wrong!"

Margaret was frozen in place. This was her apartment. Could she just leave? Wouldn't that look worse to the police? Melanie told the new volunteer, a young woman named Eliza who'd asked if she could stay, to get out while she could.

Margaret went to her front window and watched a stream of women run out of the building and down the sidewalk as three police cars slammed on their brakes and officers in uniform jumped out, guns raised, and chased the women down the street.

Her apartment was empty.

Melanie shut the door and came to stand next to Margaret at the window, watching as the police officers chased after the Black women, grabbing them by elbows or getting in front of them with the barrels of their guns, then perp-walking them into their police cars. Margaret focused on the woman with the toddler on her hip whose sister was at the Place, because it looked like she might just escape.

She ran, the toddler crying and bouncing, and Margaret's heart raced with her, rooting for her, just as she rounded the corner and out of sight with Eliza, two other white women, and one white child. No officers followed them.

Margaret had trouble catching her breath.

"There is no way for them to know it was your apartment," Melanie said.

"Unless someone in the building tells."

"Let's clean up, just in case."

The purposeful, brisk movement of throwing out paper plates and cups and washing the coffee maker was good for her nerves. She could not have stayed sane and sat still as she listened to police cars yowling away with some of the women who'd been in her apartment moments before, while other officers pounded on neighbors' doors, demanding, "Open up!"

When they got to her door, her apartment looked entirely normal.

"Stay calm," whispered Melanie.

Margaret thought her heart might actually jump out of her throat along with the contents of her lunch as she opened the door.

Two tall men in uniform walked right over the threshold, and with little more than a glance at Margaret and Melanie, they began searching the rooms of the apartment. "You ladies know where all those other girls were staying?" the taller of the two officers asked. He reeked of cigarette smoke and stale coffee.

"Gosh, no, what's going on?" Margaret marveled at Melanie's smooth tone. She sounded genuinely surprised.

The other police officer stopped poking around while the tall one went into her bedroom and opened the closets. "You two live together?" he asked.

Melanie stepped closer to Margaret and slid her arm around her waist suggestively. "Is that important?"

The police officer curled his lip and turned his attention away from Margaret and Melanie. "You find anything?" he shouted to his partner, who came out of the bathroom and said, "Nothing."

The men left without another word.

Melanie and Margaret listened while the pair of men investigated the remaining apartments. Fortunately, since it was the middle of the day, a bunch of people weren't even home.

Time crawled by.

It was torture. Every nerve and muscle in Margaret's body felt like it was on fire.

Finally, miraculously, the police left the building.

As their car drove away, Margaret said, "What do we do now?"

"We pray the other women got out of the Place in time."

36

PATTY

"Crissy, thank God you're home. Can you pick up Kate and Charlie and Junie, plus Tad and Karen, this afternoon and keep them with you?"

"Is this about the raid?"

"How do you know about that?"

"Max and Sam are friends. I think it's horrible. I'd like to help, but I can't have the kids at my place. It'll show Max too much."

"You could bring them all to mine. Please, Crissy. There is something I have to do, for my sister. I'll be home before dinner."

After a beat of hesitation, Crissy said, "Sure. Leave your key under the welcome mat."

When she pulled up in front of Veronica's place, Patty's brakes actually squealed like they did in the movies. Her pregnant friend was waiting on the sidewalk and got in with a wince. "Go straight and I'll tell you where to turn," she said.

Patty's hands were sweating so much, she almost lost her grip on the steering wheel. "Are you okay?" she asked.

"I'm fine," Veronica said through gritted teeth.

What did I expect? Her friend's organization was about to go up in flames.

"Crissy's going to take the kids to my place." Patty tried to sound reassuring, but really, there was no small talk to be made here. She focused on the road even as she worried about Crissy having all the kids at her place, and Max realizing what that meant, thus implicating all of them, but there wasn't time for that kind of worrying now. *I'll get home with Eliza before anyone's the wiser,* she kept saying to herself as she sweated through her blouse and followed Veronica's curt instructions.

"Park here."

Patty found a spot on a leafy street like a hundred other leafy streets in Hyde Park.

"That one. One ten." Veronica pointed to an unassuming orange brick apartment building exactly like the one next to it.

"You stay here," said Patty. Veronica was in no condition to hurry, especially not up and down any stairs.

"No way," Veronica replied in that tone that told Patty not to argue.

Biting her tongue, Patty rushed around to the passenger side to help Veronica out. As they made their way into the building, her friend breathed loudly and purposefully, in through her nose and out through her mouth, leaning heavily on Patty.

"It's apartment 3B."

"Is there an elevator?"

Veronica shook her head.

Great.

Her friend picked up the pace as best she could, but at the end of the first flight, Veronica took hold of the banister and said, "You go ahead."

Patty bolted up the stairs, and didn't even bother knocking on 3B. Bursting in and casting her eyes about desperately for her sister—whom she didn't see anywhere, to her rising panic—she declared to everyone in the room, "The police are coming. Everyone needs to leave."

A young woman with very long brown hair holding a pot of coffee emerged from what must have been a kitchen, and said, "Who are you?"

"I'm Veronica's friend Patty. Is my sister, Eliza, here? The police are coming."

"No one named Eliza is here," the woman replied, putting the pot down on a side table and running down the hallway.

As the women in the living room left, Veronica made it into the apartment, clutching her stomach. "I think I'm in labor," she said.

"What? You're not due yet, are you?"

"Three weeks shy." Veronica's face contracted in pain. "Something feels wrong."

"Sit down," said Patty, helping her friend get to a couch. Was that a painting of a vagina on the wall?

Was that a siren she heard in the distance?

Yes, and it was getting closer.

And yes, it was a vagina. Done in Siobhan's unmistakable style.

Patty had no idea what to do. Eliza wasn't here, but she couldn't just leave Veronica in labor.

The woman with the long brown hair reemerged with two women who were tugging shirts back down over their jeans. "Go see Dr. Cohen or Dr. Warren at the university hospital ER. They'll finish the job. Just tell them that Jane had to quit. They'll understand." And the two women left quickly as the siren blared closer this time. It sounded like it could be on the street. Patty hoped they would make it out.

"Danielle," Veronica said to the brunette. "We need to get out, now. Tell whoever is back there to leave. Forget everything else."

But it was too late. No sooner had Danielle shouted, "Phyllis! Trudy! Everyone! Let's go!" than two police officers, one of whom was Sam Wilder, appeared in the doorway, guns raised.

Then Veronica said, "This baby is coming *right now*."

37

VERONICA

Something was very, very wrong. These were contractions, but they'd come on so harsh and intense.

This cannot be happening.

And yet here were the pains, strong and fast. Too fast for the start of labor. Much faster than with Kate. And the throbbing was prominent in her back, putting hot, heavy pressure on her bowels and making her feel like she might vomit and have the runs at the same time.

And here were the police. Sam Fucking Wilder.

She felt a hot, wet gush run down her legs, another blindingly painful contraction, just as Phyllis and Siobhan—thank God, Siobhan—emerged from the back rooms.

"This baby is coming *right now*," she said again.

"You can wait till we get you to a hospital," said Sam Wilder.

"With all due respect," said Patty, mustering a strength that made her seem taller than Wilder, "over my dead body. You heard her, this baby is coming here and now. In the meantime, you can make yourself useful and call an ambulance." Then Patty turned to Siobhan and said, "I'm guessing you know how to do this?"

There's a first time for everything, Veronica thought. After all the studying they'd done about pregnancy and the uterus and cervix, they all certainly knew in theory how to bring a baby into the world.

Siobhan nodded, and she and Phyllis and Patty helped Veronica up from the couch.

"You're all on house arrest," Sam Wilder said as Veronica let her friends lead her down the hall and into the room where Veronica herself had spent so many hours in communion with women, setting them free.

"You and this baby are going to be okay," said Siobhan.

Veronica nodded, then cried out when another contraction came.

They helped her take off her soaked skirt and underwear, then get on the bed, where she knelt and let them hold her up by her arms, holding her hands, elbows, armpits. She was so inside the pain and fear, she had no idea now who was where, on her left or right or behind her. She only knew she felt safe with them. She wouldn't have wanted to be with anyone else.

Someone swabbed her face with a cool cloth.

Someone else gave her ice to chew.

A set of hands rubbed her shoulders and her back.

They helped her slowly pace the room.

They brought in sterilized instruments to cut the cord. "Turns out we're prepared for this, too," Phyllis remarked.

When Wilder pounded on the door and said, "Ambulance is here!" Veronica told Phyllis to lock the door.

"I'm not going anywhere," she told her friends.

"They'll have to wait!" Patty shouted to the men on the other side.

They held Veronica up so that she didn't have to fight gravity, and all her energy could go toward pushing this baby into the world.

A woman's face was in front of her all the time, on rotation— Siobhan, Patty, Phyllis, Trudy, Danielle, Belinda—coaching her with

x

x

breathing. Trudy, who'd never had a baby, made such a hilarious fish-face imitation of Lamaze breathing that Veronica had to laugh, which hurt so much she started to cry. "Don't," she said weakly.

"So you don't want me to sing 'Honky Tonk Pussy'?" Trudy deadpanned.

Veronica laugh-cried again, and it was the most exquisite kind of pain, that of knowing how much these women she'd assembled over the course of years wanted to help and distract and love her through this.

How much time passed that way?

An eternity was contained in every second.

Siobhan checked her cervix a few times, each time proclaiming, "She's closer."

Then, when it was time, Veronica said, "I have to push now."

She pushed.

And breathed.

And sweated.

She tried to focus on the hands on her, holding her, but *it hurt so much*. She cried.

"You can do this."

"Squeeze my hand as hard as you can."

"That's it."

"Just a few more times, Vee, come on."

"You're doing it!"

"We're doing it!"

"I can't believe this is happening in this room, of all places."

"With the fucking cops outside."

"I do love making a man wait."

"Some men in particular."

"It's going to be okay, Vee. Don't listen to them. *Breathe.* Squeeze Trudy's hand."

"You're so close."

"One more push."

"One . . . more . . ."

She was overtaken by the final waves.

She breathed and pushed, breathed and pushed, looking right at Siobhan and Patty, who'd done this before, whose determined faces told her she could do this.

She.

Could.

Do.

This.

She screamed as she bore down as hard as she could during the last contraction, feeling her perineum rip as the baby slid out with what felt like the entire contents of her body.

And then.

A newborn's cry, that alien shriek to life as air hits lungs for the very first time.

"It's a girl!"

"Of course it's a girl. Could it have been anything else?"

Doug had known, too.

Nora.

Patty handed the slippery, bloody baby to Veronica. She was pink and puffy and perfect. They were still connected by the umbilical cord, and as Nora's womb-warm skin cooled, Veronica felt as though her heart might actually stop beating at the miracle of the moment. With her mother surrounded by friends—*Patty, of all people!*—her daughter had entered the world in this place where countless women had chosen better futures for themselves.

"You knew exactly what you were doing, didn't you, telling Mama that you wanted to come out now," Veronica cooed at the infant, closing one of her hands over a tiny fist.

"Vee," said Siobhan gently, "we have to cut the cord and get the placenta out, okay? Can you give Patty the baby?"

Patty stood with one of the clean sheets they used for D&Cs, open and ready to swaddle Nora.

As Veronica handed Nora into her friend's embrace, she started to feel woozy.

She did as she was told, pushing again, but it made her feel worse. Heat and wetness coated her thighs.

She felt like she was going to faint.

"Blood," she heard.

"Ambulance."

"Cord."

"Tie."

"Clean."

"Stay with us, Veronica, come on," she heard someone say, but everyone was at the other end of a telescope. She was out in space, floating away. At least, she knew, Nora was safe.

38

MARGARET

Margaret could hear the sirens in her ears all afternoon. Paralyzed, she sat by the phone waiting for news.

When her phone finally did ring around five, she almost jumped out of her skin. "Hello?"

"Siobhan's been arrested," said Gabe.

Shit. They got her? Of all people. Who else?

And was it possible he sounded *happy* about it?

She swallowed. *You need to sound surprised.* "What? Why?"

"You know this abortion clinic in Hyde Park? Apparently, she works there, the stupid bitch." Gabe laughed. Laughed! "You know what this means, right? It means we can have Charlie full-time! No judge is going to give her to an abortionist."

"Where is she now? Charlie?" *I hope she's not hearing you call her mother a stupid bitch.* Margaret's heart hardened at his words. Siobhan was a goddamn hero.

"Well, Patty's husband, Matt, just called me, and believe it or not his wife is down at the precinct with Siobhan and the other women. He wouldn't give me more details than that. But Charlie's with a pack of kids at Patty's place, overseen by Crissy. Remember Crissy from that dinner before Christmas? Ditzy blonde. Her husband, Max, is beside himself. I think he might lock her out of the house tonight." *Fuck. Is it possible Gabe sounds happy about this, too? Where is all this hatred coming from?*

Stupid bitch.

Ditzy blonde.

Monitor the heat. When you're ready to jump, you know where to find me, Phyllis had said.

Her friend had known all along.

And if Margaret was being honest with herself, she had known, too. Deep inside, in a locked-away part of her mind, she'd known that Gabe hated Siobhan, and that he wanted Charlie to hate her, too. She hadn't wanted to believe that this hatred could extend to more women than his ex-wife—*he has a daughter, for heaven's sake!* But nowhere in her maelstrom of emotions did she feel surprise.

Sam, Max, Gabe, Leo. They were all the same.

Be cool, she told herself. *Your priority right now is Charlie.* "I can't believe this," she said. "Can I go get Charlie?"

"Sure, that would be great," he said. "Just don't tell her anything, okay? I want to be the one to do it."

If only you weren't so willing to let me do the woman's work. Because I'm going to get to her first.

Amazing. All she felt for Gabe now was anger and hostility. "Okay. What's the address?"

"I'm Matt Buford," a friendly balding man introduced himself after opening the door for Margaret.

"I'm Margaret Jones, Gabe's girlfriend. I'm here for Charlie?"

"Right, right. Come on in. Charlie's in here somewhere."

Patty's house was on fire with activity, with one kid trotting around on a toy horse, a stereo playing upstairs, a television on in the living room, where three girls were zoned out in front of some show, none of them Charlie. There was a stack of pizza boxes in the kitchen, and two women: Crissy, red eyed and blotchy faced, holding an empty wineglass, and the girl from her own apartment today. Eliza.

Margaret and Eliza exchanged looks, and Margaret wasn't sure what to say.

"I'll go see if I can find Charlie," said Matt, then he disappeared out of the kitchen.

"Well, well, well. Small world," Eliza said when Matt was gone, resolving the moment of discomfort. "I'm Patty's sister. I didn't expect to see you again today."

"Small world indeed," said Margaret. "Do you have any more information about what happened today? And for what it's worth, no one outside of Jane knows I volunteer, so I'd appreciate it if we could keep it that way."

"No problem," said Eliza. "Want some pizza?"

"You know what? Yes." *I don't even remember the last time I ate.*

She sank her teeth into a slice of coagulated deep-dish pizza. Even cold it was delicious. After she swallowed, and as Crissy was pouring herself another glass of wine, Margaret said, "Hey, Crissy, remember we met before Christmas?"

"Yeah, and I'll keep your secret from Gabe, too. I'm done with men anyway. Remember my husband, Max? The asshole who couldn't shut up about Jane and my going to that Union meeting? He told me not to come home tonight since I'd decided to 'help the murderers.' Can you believe that? The murderers. I'll show him what murder really is." She appeared to have hit that point of drunkenness when sadness calcifies into righteous fury.

Margaret felt simultaneously sad for Crissy and unified with her in solidarity. She had a feeling she'd be done with men for a while, too.

"So," Margaret said, turning back to Eliza. "Do you have any intel?"

Eliza nodded. "Veronica's husband, Doug, filled us in about an hour ago. Eleven women in total got arrested, and six of them are

Janes." Eliza counted out the names on her fingers: "Veronica, Trudy, Belinda, Phyllis, Danielle, and Siobhan. Of the other five, four were women from the Front, and then there's Patty. My sister! You don't know her very well, Margaret, but believe me when I tell you this is a *shock*. Frankly, I'm impressed. And as if all that wasn't enough, get this—Veronica had her baby at the Place with the police waiting for her to finish so they could haul everyone down to the precinct after. Except Veronica herself, who was taken to the hospital in an ambulance."

"You're kidding. A baby? Are the two of them okay?"

"Doug says that Veronica lost some blood, but she and the baby are going to be fine."

"Wow," said Margaret.

"I know. I wish I was attracted to women," slurred Crissy. "They're so much more impressive."

Eliza ignored this and went on. "Anyway. Veronica's husband is a big-shot lawyer, and he's working on getting everyone out on bail."

"Is there anything we can do?"

"Not right now. I'll let you know when I find out anything. Leave your phone number, okay?"

Margaret was just scribbling her number down when Charlie came into the kitchen, ran straight to Margaret, and hugged her tightly around the waist. "What's going on? Where are all the moms?"

Margaret crouched down and looked Charlie in the eyes. "Your mom, and Kate's and Junie's moms, and Crissy and Eliza here, are all heroes. Like . . . like Joan of Arc. Have you heard of her?"

Charlie shook her head.

"She was a woman a long time ago who took matters into her own hands and fought for what she believed in, even though a lot of men thought she couldn't do it. But she showed them all they were wrong."

Charlie nodded.

"Is Mommy okay?"

"She'll be okay, sweetheart."

They bid farewell to everyone at Patty's house. Then, hand in hand, Margaret and Charlie walked the five blocks to Gabe's place.

"Dad says Mom is a witch."

"A witch?" *Stupid bitch.*

"That's what Dad says."

"Do you think your mom is a witch?"

"I've never seen her do any spells."

"When did he say this?"

Charlie shrugged. "I don't know. He says it a lot."

Margaret tightened her hand around Charlie's. "Remember, your mother is a hero."

"Can witches be heroes?"

Margaret wracked her brain. "Well, there's Glinda the Good Witch in *The Wizard of Oz.*"

Charlie nodded. "Was Jane of Arc a witch?"

Bingo. "No, but she was accused of being a bad witch by people who didn't understand her and hated her for being such a strong woman. And her name was Joan. Though Jane is a great name, too."

Charlie nodded.

Margaret stopped walking and again squatted so she was at eye level with Charlie. "Some people are going to say some bad things about your mom, Charlie, and I just want you to know that none of it is true, okay?"

"Did she do something bad?"

"No. All she did was help other women. There are lots of people who think that is not okay. But it is. What she did was good. Some people think it's bad, but you don't have to agree with any of them, okay?"

Charlie's chin trembled.

"You're strong, too, you know that? Just like your mom."

Charlie hugged Margaret, and Margaret wished she could scoop the girl up, rescue her mother, and get out of here, far away from Gabe.

"Hang on one second," Margaret said, then she rustled around in her messenger bag and got out a piece of paper and a pen. She wrote her phone number, then folded the paper until it was small. "Put this in your pocket, okay? It's my phone number so you can call me any-time."

Charlie nodded, stuffed the paper into the pocket of her jeans, then looked straight ahead.

Gabe was in a great mood when they walked in the door. "Hey, Squirrel!" He picked up his daughter and gave her a big hug.

It was like looking into the face of Snow White's stepmother in the magic mirror, or Rumpelstiltskin when he comes for the firstborn of the miller's daughter.

It was like seeing him for the first time.

"Daddy, what's going on with Mom?"

"Mom got in some trouble today, and now you get to spend more time with me, like we've always talked about. So one bad thing hap-pened, but a good thing happened, too."

Charlie's expression remained serious.

"Is it because she's a witch?"

Gabe poked her in the stomach playfully, obviously hoping to get her to smile like he was. "Exactly, Squirrel."

Charlie turned to Margaret and asked, "Can we sew something?"

The girl's request was like a knife to her heart. "I'll be up soon," she said. "Why don't you get out some of your favorite fabric?"

"It's a little late for sewing tonight," Gabe said. "But you can get out fabric for tomorrow, how's that? Right now it's bath and bedtime."

Charlie turned and trudged up the stairs.

"You are so amazing with her," said Gabe, pulling Margaret in for a kiss. "Which is a good thing, because she's going to need a better female role model now."

In spite of herself, in spite of the anger she was feeling and the man she was seeing with her very own eyes, she looked for a way to let him be a good guy. "But I thought you didn't have a problem with what the S— the organization is doing. I thought you were pro-abortion and women's rights."

He frowned. "I've been thinking more about it, actually. I mean, consider the men, Margaret. The fathers who don't even *know* about these children. I bet Siobhan and her friends allow women—*girls*—to terminate these pregnancies without so much as a word to the very people they blame for getting them into this mess to begin with. As if it doesn't take two to tango."

Don't call me girl. Where was that button? She'd find it as soon as she got home.

"Our lives will be better if Siobhan isn't in the picture. Think of how great it is when it's just the three of us."

Margaret recalled the Bulls game. *Not always so great.* "That's not the point. Charlie needs her mother."

"Her mother is a criminal. And she has you."

"For crying out loud, Gabe, this is more about getting back at Siobhan than it is about the law."

"For once, I'd like the law to be on my side. And I'd like *you* to be on my side."

She wasn't, and they both knew it. *Time's up. I have to be honest. Finally and fully. No more compromising. No more "balancing."*

"Well, I'm not. Not about this. I think what Jane's doing is important work. And honestly, I'm impressed by Siobhan."

"Margaret. Come on. She used me for my job and stability, and to become a mother while she was at it. So she could stay home and play at painting. We could have used a second income, you know. But all she brought home was that tiny adjunct's paycheck from teaching drawing. When she felt like it."

He was seething now. Furthermore, Margaret knew that what he

313

was saying wasn't even true. Siobhan was willing to live in drastically reduced circumstances to *not* be married. And if he'd been this bitter and vindictive when she told him she wanted a divorce, Margaret could also see why she'd wanted to protect Charlie from him, too, by keeping as much custody to herself as possible.

"And now," he raged on, "she's doing *abortions* to make money on the side? I mean, how low can she sink? And she's leaving *my daughter* in someone else's care in order to get rid of other men's children? Think how pissed off she must be at *me* to want to spend her time doing that. All these women's groups are furious at men for keeping them down, but look at the slogans they use at their marches. 'Don't iron while the strike is hot.' 'End human sacrifice—don't get married.' That kind of retributive justice isn't going to make them any friends among men, and they need men to get what they want in government. And it's sure as hell not going to help Siobhan keep her kid."

Margaret wanted to scream. *I'd be pissed at you, too! I am pissed at you!*

Jump.

Get out now.

Only one thing stopped her: *What about Charlie?*

Staying with Gabe, she saw with stunning clarity, would actually send exactly the wrong message to Charlie about the way women should be treated. Siobhan must have come to the same conclusion.

"Gabe," she said, her voice remarkably steady, even to her own ears. "I don't agree with anything you're saying, and it breaks my heart, but I don't think I can convince you otherwise."

"You're not one of them, Margaret. Think about what I'm saying. You're more fair-minded than these angry women."

"I'm no different from them, Gabe. And I *am* angry. At you. I'm angry because *you* are the one who's not being fair-minded. You're rethinking your stance on abortion because you're mad at Siobhan. And I'm angry because you haven't let Siobhan go. Not really. But even worse, you're trying to turn her own daughter against her. And I'm angry at myself for not being willing to admit any of that, even to myself, until now."

Gabe pressed his lips together, and the rims of his eyes were suddenly red. "Please, Margaret, don't do this. I love you." His voice was hoarse.

Her heart tore straight down the middle. Somewhere inside him was the man she'd loved, that Siobhan had loved, the man who loved his daughter deeply and wanted to protect her from the irreparably broken heart he'd suffered. But that Dr. Jekyll was being slowly murdered by Mr. Hyde.

She couldn't let that happen to herself, too. She'd rather live with the pain of loss than the armor of bitterness.

"I'm sorry, Gabe," she said. She picked up her bag. "I'll just go say goodbye to Charlie."

Gabe stepped in front of the stairs and said, "You've just lost all access to my daughter. I'll explain why you've left her just like her mother did."

She glared at Gabe, then went to the door and let herself out.

The lungful of cool-aired relief she inhaled the moment she stepped out of the house told her everything she needed to know about the decision she'd made.

A few yards down the block, Margaret glanced up at Charlie's window, which was brightly lit, probably so she could pick out the fabric she wanted to sew with Margaret. At this thought, Margaret's chest felt tight and her eyes felt hot and wet.

Joan of Arc was not a witch, she tried to telepath into Charlie's room. *Call me.*

And there is no way your mother is going to let your dad win.

39

PATTY

"I just can't thank you enough," Doug said to Patty for the third morning in a row after talking to Kate on the phone for a few minutes before school. She'd been living with them since the arrest. So had Crissy and her three kids for two days until she'd packed everyone into her station wagon and taken them to Ann Arbor to stay with her parents.

"Please. Stop thanking me. Kate and Junie are having a ball, and I'm so relieved Veronica and little Nora are okay."

"So am I," he said. "And we should all be home in a few more days."

"I'm sure you'll need help after that, so let me keep her as long as necessary, okay? It's really not an imposition."

"Alright. If it ever is too much, I can ask Martha."

"Honestly, Doug, it's nice to have Junie occupied with a friend all afternoon. It takes some of the pressure off me." Also, the chaos of having an extra kid around had really coaxed Eliza out of her shell. In the warming afternoons, the kids would beg her to play her guitar, and she obliged—nothing so emotional as Joni Mitchell, but she really got into some Woody Guthrie songs and show tunes that everyone sang along to.

Patty wasn't sure where any of it was going—she wasn't sure Eliza wanted to be a professional singer, or a teacher, or anything else for that matter—but for now, none of that mattered. What mattered was that her sister was in her house every day and starting to look like she felt at home; her best friend was going to survive the uterine infection that might have contributed to her new daughter's early birth—frustratingly, but hardly surprisingly, no one, including the midwife, seemed to understand what had happened inside Veronica's body. *If men were the ones to have babies, there would be no mysteries about childbirth*, Patty thought to herself once again.

Thankfully, Nora was fully baked when she came out; after a week of monitoring, mother and child should be able to return home and proceed as if nothing had happened.

Except for the fact that Veronica had been released on bail and was facing a trial. After thorough questioning by the police once Veronica had been rushed to the hospital, and some backstage hassling by Doug, Patty herself had been released without any charges along with the others arrested at the Front. Doug said that the women of Jane had an amazing lawyer, and that their case might be moot anyway if a big abortion case working its way through the Supreme Court was decided soon.

The case, *Roe v. Wade*, was all over the news, particularly here in Chicago with the arrest of the Jane Six. Editorial pages and the evening news couldn't get enough of the debate over abortion rights, women's lib, and the guilt or innocence of the local women who had taken matters into their own hands, especially after Senator Smith's daughter, Heidi, had spoken on the steps of the precinct where Siobhan, Phyllis, Trudy, Danielle, and Belinda had been held for a few hours. The picture in the paper had shown a crowd of women gathered to pool money to help with the bail. No one had captured Heidi on film, but she was quoted everywhere as having said, "Jane helped me when I needed it, and now I'm here to help Jane."

Tongues wagged at her boldness.

"The afterglow of scandal looks good on you," Matt said to her as she stood at the kitchen sink finishing the dinner dishes.

They kissed, and it felt entirely different than it had in the previous fifteen years of their relationship. There were no longer any barriers between them, and she felt this in the way their lips responded to each other. Their kiss became longer and harder, and his hand lifted her shirt and caressed the bare skin of her lower back. They made love that night for the first time in more months than Patty could remember, and it was a release and a relief.

As they lay in bed, entwined and spent, his fingers trailing down and up her arm, she said, "I've been thinking about maybe finding some kind of work."

"Oh?"

"Yeah. I'm not sure what yet, but with Tad going to kindergarten next year, and with everything that's happened this year, I'm feeling . . . I don't know, itchy to do something new."

"I hear there's an illegal abortion ring that needs people."

"Be serious."

Matt laughed, then kissed the top of her head. "I'll be serious. What are you thinking?"

"I'm not sure. Maybe something with kids. I like kids. I'm good with them." She thought of the playroom she was always cleaning up and restocking, of the parties she'd thrown for all three children over the years, and how much fun they and their friends always had. "But I'd also like to maybe help more girls like Eliza. So I don't know. I'm trying to use my imagination."

"You are a brilliant and talented woman, and you can do anything you set your mind to," said Matt.

"I said be serious."

"I *am* serious. I've always admired your mind *and* your body." He slid a hand down and squeezed her rear end.

"Okay, Casanova."

They made love again, and his words, *brilliant and talented*, warmed her to him like never before. She'd always thought he was the brilliant and talented one, the doctor, the one who saved lives. But that didn't mean it couldn't be true of her as well.

Siobhan surprised Patty by showing up on her doorstep four days after the arrest, shortly after the kids got off to school.

"Come in, come in," Patty said. "Can I get you some coffee?"

"No, thanks," Siobhan said as she followed Patty into the kitchen.

They sat perpendicular to each other at Patty's kitchen table, and Siobhan said, "I have a favor to ask."

"Anything." Another surprise: she meant this. All her anger at Veronica's newer friend was gone, now that there were no more secrets and Patty knew that she and Veronica were square again. And, she blushed to admit, after the birth at Jane, Patty felt like she was kind of an honorary member. She'd even gone all the way to the police station with them.

"Could you help with Charlie after school? I'm trying to get some work done before a big show in New York, which I can't even go to anymore because of the arrest."

"Oh, gosh, I'm sorry about that. What a disappointment. But congratulations on getting the show. That's a big deal."

Siobhan smiled. "Thanks. Also, Gabe and Margaret broke up, so things over there are . . . well, they're not great for Charlie."

Patty could see Siobhan straining to figure out how much to tell

Patty, and she could see that thinking about Gabe and Charlie caused her pain.

"You don't have to explain anything to me. I'm always happy to have Charlie here. And I know that child care is hard to find."

Siobhan exhaled. "Thanks." She paused. "Listen, I know Charlie and Kate and Junie can sometimes have a funny dynamic. Please tell me if she causes any problems."

"I'm sure we'll be able to handle it."

"She's just going through a tough time right now, and . . ."

Siobhan looked close to tears. Patty put her hand on Siobhan's. "Hey, I'll help, it's not a problem. I'm sure I can smooth things over with the girls, and if I can't, then Eliza can. She's amazing with the kids."

Siobhan nodded and swallowed. "I feel like I need to be honest with you here. Gabe might come over here and try to pick Charlie up, but I'm the one who should be picking her up. He's . . . he's trying to take her away from me."

Six months ago, Patty realized, *I'd have been on his side. Times they are a-changin'. . . .*

"I'm sorry, Siobhan. That must be excruciating."

Siobhan cleared her throat. "I have a very good lawyer, though. And public opinion seems to be very much with us."

"It really is. Can I do anything to help?"

"If I ever needed a character witness . . . ?"

"Put my name down."

"Thank you."

"And in the meantime, Charlie can be here as much as you need. We can deal with Gabe if he comes by."

"Thank you. I can't tell you what a relief that is. And I was thinking . . . maybe when things settle down, we can plan that baby shower?"

Patty smiled. "You're on."

After everyone was in bed, Patty took a long shower with her favorite sandalwood soap; the suds were so rich it was almost like slathering whipped cream on her body. She took care to shave the nooks and crannies around her bony ankles, the inconvenient hollows under her arms, and the stray hairs on her upper thighs. In the fragrant steam, she smoothed lotion all over her skin and dabbed perfume on her thighs and wrists, then fluffed her hair so it had a tousled look. *Mascara*. She needed that, too. And maybe a little eyeliner.

With slightly shaky hands, she opened the cabinet under her sink and pulled out the items she'd stashed there after Siobhan had left: a virtually see-through fine mesh black bra and panties, plus a garter belt and stockings with seams up the backs. She'd purchased them almost a year ago and only worn them once. Her heart was thudding so fast and hard, she couldn't calm herself down as she put them on. Then she took out a crumpled shopping bag with the latest *Playboy* in it, which she'd bought a few days before but hadn't had the nerve to look at yet.

She could still reverse course. Take off the black lace and put on the terry-cloth bathrobe hanging on the back of the door.

But no. She wanted to show her husband that this was something she accepted about him, that she—she'd been amazed to realize— wanted to share with him. As she wanted to share all things going forward.

Oops, the shoes!

She'd hidden her black stilettos under the sink as well. Teetering on them, she wished she'd thought to put some vodka under the sink, too.

She heard Matt clear his throat in the bedroom.

Just go out there. You can do this.

With a last look at herself in the mirror and a ruffle of her hair, she picked up the magazine, turned out the bathroom light, and opened the door.

The light in the bedroom was almost blindingly bright. Not the best mood lighting. Initially, Matt didn't even look up from where he was sitting on the bed—T-shirt, reading glasses, *National Geographic*, and all—until she was standing at the foot of it, gently setting the *Playboy* next to his legs.

National Geographic fell out of his hands when he saw her.

She dragged her eyes to his. He was looking at her, and she could feel an invisible cord between them tighten so taut, so fast, it held her immobile. It had been a long time since he'd looked at her like this. With lust, yes, but better—with surprise and curiosity and admiration. *Brilliant and talented.*

She crawled toward him on her hands and knees, feeling his desire and her power rise together. When she straddled his hips with her legs, he put his hands on her hips and dug his fingers into her behind.

"Show me what you like," she whispered, her mouth hovering above his.

"Only if you do the same," he said, his lips feather-touching hers.

She nodded, then met his strength and pleasure with her own.

40

VERONICA

The week in the hospital was a hell of needles and tubes connected to her arm and bladder, pumping antibiotics and water and electrolytes into her deflated form—she couldn't even hold or feed her baby (her own daughter, little Nora!) without getting tangled in the long spaghettilike skeins. When the newborn's little rosebud mouth found her nipple, she felt the fluid rushing from her into the tiny person who was now separate from her, fully inhabiting her own powerful, needy body. It was hot and rashy and red and sticky between them, but this wonderful temporary oneness with her baby was intruded on by those man-made veins all around and between them. Even after they removed the catheter, she couldn't so much as pee without wheeling the whole damn apparatus with her to the toilet.

Nothing so undignified ever happened at the Service.

Would ever happen if she was the OB in charge.

Would never happen *when* she was the OB in charge.

There has to be a better way.

Mercifully, Nora was thriving and healthy at just over six pounds despite arriving three weeks early. She had the sweetest cry. It was hungry and insistent but honeyed, and when she'd glugged her fill from her mother, Veronica would cradle her in her arms. The love she felt for Nora was fierce and feral; she told the nurse to get lost whenever she came to put her in the bassinet so the two of them could sleep. "She's asleep now," Veronica said quietly of the exquisitely mushy little human on her chest.

"But *you* need to sleep," said the nurse.

"I'll sleep."

"Let me just take her for an hour."

"No."

When Doug held Nora, the tableau was like a giant tenderly cooing to a peapod, and Veronica burst into tears.

Kate visited one time and climbed into the hospital bed with her mother and said, "Do you still love me?"

"More than ever," Veronica replied. And it was true. The love in her heart felt thick and hot and endless, a lava that oozed and oozed and oozed. All the constriction she'd felt during her pregnancy had loosened.

Finally, after four or five days—or seven? eight?—she woke up feeling cool and dry. She passed a bowel movement on her own, mother and child were proclaimed healthy, and the hospital let them both go. At home, there was an enormous wicker basket from Patty full of luxurious and adorable blankets and rattles and hand cream and a stuffed rabbit that was softer than anything she'd ever touched in her life.

"Can I have the rabbit, Mom, please?" Kate clasped her hands under her chin and did her best imitation of a choir girl.

Veronica laughed, which hurt everywhere. "Sure, sweetheart."

Kate hugged the stuffed animal to her and kissed her mother on the cheek.

Then Doug was there, too, planting a lingering kiss on Veronica's forehead and rubbing her back gently. "It's good to have you home," he said. He smelled like his shaving cream and their laundry detergent so strongly that she wondered if her sense of smell had somehow sharpened or if he was using too much of both. She loved both scents, though. They were home.

Doug had given her the basics on what had happened with the Service while she was in the hospital. Grace Whitcomb, a young Black lawyer at a Chicago firm specializing in civil rights, had taken Jane's case. She'd gotten all the women who were only "visiting" Jane, including Patty, off without any charges. The remaining arrestees, the Jane Six, she'd gotten released on two thousand dollars bail each, which had been paid by a combination of women who'd pooled resources outside the police station and some last-minute fundraising led by Marion Gilbert. Pride fluttered in Veronica's chest when Doug told her about the hundred or more women outside the police station putting all their money into a paper bag to free them, including Heidi Smith, who had championed them in front of everyone. How she wished she could have seen that.

Grace had also advised the Jane Six to lie low and wait. "She's going to slow-walk the process," Doug explained, "because she has a feeling the case that the Supreme Court will be hearing this year on abortion might actually make it legal. And then the case against you could be dropped."

That was about as much as Veronica remembered from those hazy hospital days. Now that she was home, she wanted to get it straight in her mind.

"So . . . Grace's counsel is paid for by an anonymous donor?" Veronica asked Doug one night as they lay in bed while Nora snoozed in the cradle an arm's reach away. One lamp on Doug's side of the bed was lit, and they each lay on their sides, facing each other. "Do you think it's Marion Gilbert?"

"It's as likely to be her as your friend Luigi Galleani."

"I hadn't thought of him. You really don't know?"

"I have no idea."

"And when is this case, *Roe versus Wade*, going to hit the Supreme Court?"

"The case actually came before the court late last year, but it's going to be argued again in October. Grace and her team have good reason to believe that the court will rule in favor of Roe, which would legalize abortion in all fifty states. If that happens, Grace would move to get the case against you dropped."

"What do you think?"

"I think Grace and everyone at her firm are top-notch, and I trust them."

Veronica took a deep breath. *Now for the hard thing.*

"I'm so sorry I landed us in this trouble. The court case, everything. This is what you were worried about all along, and when I went to the Place, I knew I could get arrested. I'm just so, so sorry, Doug."

He kissed her. "You don't have to apologize. I get it. It took me a while, but I finally really understood. Jane is your passion. You've been happier than you've ever been building the Service. I would never want you to be less than you are."

"Seriously?"

"Seriously. I had this moment after our last fight where I thought to myself, *Would you want Veronica to be any different?* And the answer was no. When I was younger, with the piano, so many people wanted me to play this or that and compete and become famous. No one really asked me what I wanted. You made what you wanted clear, and I really admire you for that. I love you for that."

She kissed him gently on the lips. "Thank you."

"I suggested we name our daughter Nora, right? I meant that as an olive branch."

"I wondered that at the time, but . . ." Veronica shook her head.

"I'm so glad. And we're not going to lose our house, right? Because of the anonymous donor?"

"Because of the anonymous donor who admires *your organization so much.*"

Veronica snuggled close to him, and he put his arms around her. "I'm so relieved."

"I'm sorry for doubting you," he said as he rested his chin on the top of her head and played with the loose strands of her hair at her back. He didn't have to say the rest, because she knew it; she was thinking it, too. *I just hope the Supreme Court makes the right choice; otherwise, we still might lose everything.*

Well, not everything.

Not each other.

The first Tuesday morning in May, Veronica used a beautiful teal-colored sling that Amy had given her to strap Nora to her chest so she could bounce her gently to sleep as she and Siobhan set up for a morning meeting at Veronica's house. So as not to draw too much attention to themselves, they'd decided just to have the six, plus Melanie, in attendance, so there wasn't much to do. Siobhan had arrived with a basket full of soft handmade kimonos for Nora, as well as pastries for the meeting and three boxes of Oreos for Veronica.

"I can't believe I still can't get enough of these," said Veronica, opening the first blue box and taking out a cookie, separating the two halves and licking the cream filling out.

Siobhan laughed, then cooed at Nora, who had conked out on Veronica's breasts, which were already starting to feel full, though she'd just nursed her daughter an hour before. "She is absolutely beautiful," her friend said.

Always embarrassed by compliments on her daughter's beauty,

Veronica quickly changed the subject. "I am so sorry you won't be able to get to New York for your gallery opening."

"I am, too, but you know what? The gallery's phone is ringing off the hook with requests about my paintings. Apparently being arrested for giving abortions in a state where it's still illegal is good for your career in New York City."

Veronica laughed. "Really? That's fabulous."

"The gallery is already raising the prices."

"Even better. And what's happening with Derek?"

"He's going to come out to be with me for a little while, starting this weekend."

Veronica whistled. "You're going to introduce him to Charlie?"

"Yep. She's excited to meet him, actually."

"She must be so happy at your place with her dad seeing red all the time." Siobhan had told Veronica on the phone the other day that Gabe had filed an emergency motion for sole custody because of Siobhan's arrest.

"When's your court date again? What does your lawyer say?"

"Next week, and he's pretty confident that Gabe won't win. He went to law school with my brother and hardly charges me anything, and he thinks we can use the notoriety to our advantage."

Veronica held up her crossed fingers.

"It does mean I can't take any more chances on the Service, though," said Siobhan. "I can't risk losing Charlie."

"Absolutely. I can't, either. And honestly, a part of me is relieved."

"Same." This admission between them felt significant. "It's like the end of an era," said Siobhan.

"Maybe the beginning of a better one."

"But what will we do about all the women who need us now?"

"I'm hoping the others will have some ideas."

As if on cue, the others started arriving, and after making much of Nora and how healthy Veronica looked, and how exciting it was that

Siobhan was now a famous artist, the seven of them settled down in Veronica's living room almost as if no time had passed, as if the world wasn't now a completely different place.

"So," Veronica said with a clap of her hands, "first, I want to say thank you to all of you for getting me through that horrible day."

"No," said Phyllis. "Thank you for helping us get as many women out as we could. And I'm pleased to report that the two women we couldn't finish that day made it to the hospital and got their D&Cs from Dr. Cohen and have recovered nicely."

Everyone clapped, and Veronica felt her heart fill with pride and relief.

"I think you all know we're here today to decide how to move forward," she said. "I'll just speak for myself and say that I have to take time off to be with my family. I wish it could be different, but I just don't feel I can land myself in jail again with a newborn."

There was a murmur of agreement around the room, then Siobhan piped up. "And I'm at risk of losing Charlie forever if I get in any more trouble. My lawyer thinks he can get me a pass this time, but that's it."

More nods around the room.

"You two should absolutely lie low," said Phyllis. "I, on the other hand, have nothing to lose. So I am going to keep doing D&Cs. You'd be surprised how many of the women whose houses we used as Fronts and Places are willing to keep their doors open."

"That's great about the locations, but what do you mean, *nothing to lose?*" asked Veronica.

Phyllis laughed, bitterly this time. "Yeah, I forgot you've been out of commission. The university kicked me out. I lost my scholarship, my classes, everything."

"What? Can they do that?" Anger flared inside Veronica.

"They can do whatever they want," said Belinda. "I got expelled, too."

Belinda and Phyllis exchanged sympathetic looks that made it clear the two of them had become tight. Veronica recalled that Belinda had come to Jane because of her own abortion, and she tried to remember some details but was at a loss. So many students had come to the Service over the years, it was hard to keep track.

"But in better news," said Phyllis, "I've already had offers from other places to finish my degree and teach. I'm talking with Pauli Murray over at Brandeis in Massachusetts."

"Wow," said Veronica. "She's a rock star."

"She seems to think we are, too," said Phyllis.

Veronica smiled, amazed. Pauli Murray knew who they were.

"I've gotten an offer to attend the New School in New York," added Belinda. "I was already planning to live in New York after graduation, so I guess I'll get a jump start. But neither of us can leave Chicago until our case comes to trial or it's dismissed like Grace hopes. So while we're stuck here, Phyllis and I want to keep the Service going."

"You'll have to go deep underground, though, right? I mean, the original Places and Fronts will be watched," said Melanie.

"We have some beefed-up protection," said Phyllis. "Which is one of the things I wanted to tell everyone. If you stay with the Service, we'll be protected. Danielle and I did some checking, and we got in contact with your friend Luigi Galleani. He's going to help us survive. And apparently he said something to Sam Wilder, because I have it on good authority he's moving to Texas."

Even so, are you sure it's safe? Veronica wanted to ask. But mothering Jane wasn't her job anymore.

"I'm up for it," said Trudy.

"Me, too," said Melanie. "My kids are grown. I can risk it."

"Great," said Phyllis. "And we've been inundated with new interest from all over the city. I have two training sessions with sixteen women in each section coming up next week. And three of our volunteers from the past year want to step up their efforts and learn to do the abortions."

"That's great," Veronica said, and she meant it. She was relieved and thankful at her core that someone else was picking up this sword. Exactly the right someone.

Nora woke up with a snuffle and a wail, and Veronica's first thought was, *Thank God.* Her breasts felt like they were going to split open. "Excuse me one sec," she said, then got up to grab the gauzy curtain she threw over herself and the baby while she nursed. While she arranged herself to do just that on the armchair, she listened as the women made plans for weekly meetings, driving and location assignments, and how many D&Cs and miscarriages they could handle each week. Talk wound down just as Nora had drained both of her breasts.

As she buttoned her blouse, Veronica said, "Can we do anything to call attention to what the university's done to the two of you?"

"Grace said to keep quiet for a while. Depending on what the Supreme Court decides, we might be able to sue the university for damages," said Phyllis.

"I would love to see that place pay," said Belinda. "And I'd like to see Leo Robinson join the ranks of stone gargoyles at the gate."

Ah, yes, Leo Robinson—he was the professor who got Belinda pregnant. Now Veronica remembered. *At least he had the decency to pay for the abortion, but the girl was heartbroken when she got to Jane.*

"One thing at a time, Medusa," said Phyllis mischievously.

"Listen, everyone, if you ever need a meeting place, call me."

"Thanks, Veronica," said Danielle. "For everything."

"Now let us hold that baby," said Siobhan, stretching out her arms, and Veronica handed Nora over, relieved that, as uncertain as the future was, she had these women in her life.

There was no better way to raise a girl than this.

Fall 1973

"The place looks amazing," Veronica said, bangles jingling on her right wrist as she bounced Nora on her hip and Kate ran in to find Junie.

In the half hour since the final bells had rung at the local elementary schools, kids had started drifting into the Center, an after-school program in the basement of St. Thomas church that Patty had started. Some were dropped off by mothers who'd taken a few minutes off work to do the shuttle, and others had carpooled with hired help or older siblings.

Veronica wouldn't normally be here at this time, since she had to rush to her biology lab, and Kate would join Junie in walking the two blocks from school to the Center, but today Veronica had arranged to hand Nora off to Eliza so that she could wish Patty well on this first day of her new adventure. Though she'd helped to prepare this big room alongside Patty and Eliza and Matt and Doug, painting walls and assembling chairs and tables, unpacking bags of hand-me-down books, and stocking reams and reams of paper, she marveled at how Patty's colorful and thoughtful touches had really made the room come alive, down to the empty frames awaiting self-portraits and the paper flowers in vases that invited older children to learn the art of origami.

Seeing her friend launch a venture like this made Veronica just a bit nostalgic for Jane. Though her life in premed classes was full and exciting, she sometimes missed the heady energy of the Service. When *Roe* had become law at the start of the year and the charges against the Jane Six had been dropped, just as their aptly named lawyer Grace had predicted, Phyllis had led the final meeting at which fifty-two then-and-now members of Jane had voted, 47–5, to shut the Service down and let legal clinics take its place in the city. Veronica intended to be the head of one of those clinics someday, as soon as her education would allow. She wanted hers to be a place where women felt safe and cared for, where they could come for all their reproductive health needs, from birth control to abortion to basic, loving, and accurate information about their bodies.

Patty watched Veronica's daughter run to greet hers at the rectangular table that had been covered in brown paper, waiting for eager hands to smear paint, buttons, sticks, glue, and other objects of collage over it. She smiled. She had a number of ideas in mind for that table, inspired by the early childhood development classes she'd taken. Patty had joined forces with a woman named Emily, who had long run a small nursery school in the same space in the mornings and was thrilled when Patty came to her with the proposal for the Center—"I've always wanted to expand like that, but with my own kids to take care of . . ." She'd shrugged: *It just wasn't possible.* But Patty's favorite person to work with had been Keith, the husband of Veronica's friend Phyllis. He knew a mind-boggling amount about education and had helped her set up a scholarship program so that half of all the families at the Center could receive financial aid. Too bad he'd had to move to New England so that Phyllis could start her work with Pauli Murray at Brandeis. He'd do great work in Boston, but Chicago—and Patty—would miss him sorely.

Between this project, this surprise *career*, and her rekindled romance with Matt, Patty had never felt so busy and alive, so full of energy and purpose.

Eliza hurried to the entrance at the same time as Siobhan and Charlie. Eliza reached toward Nora with outstretched hands and a goofy smile on her face. "Is that my Nora?"

"How were classes today?" Patty asked her sister as Siobhan's daughter blasted past them on her way to Kate and Junie.

"Fine," said Eliza, scooping up her year-old charge and giving her a raspberry on the cheek, which made her squeal with delight. "I'll be glad when I can stop taking stats and physics for poets and take some actual poetry classes."

"Same," said Veronica, sticking out her tongue in a gagging gesture. "Organic chemistry? Blech. But dissecting frogs and observing surgery? Yes, please."

"Your mommy is bonkers, but she's going to be a great doctor," Eliza cooed at Nora.

"Someday," Veronica said. She was close to finished with her prereqs and still had to take the MCAT, then get *into* medical school. She would, though. Much as she hated chemistry, she loved the rest of it, and miraculously she found she just wanted more.

"And she's going to mop the floor with those little boys in classes with her," added Siobhan with a wink. Then, to Patty, she said, "Wow, this is impressive. And Charlie was so excited to come today."

"I know she likes to paint, and we have some gorgeous new watercolors and brushes," said Patty.

"She'll love that."

"Will you be painting today as well?"

"Actually, I have a class to teach," she said. "Life drawing. One of my favorites."

Patty followed Siobhan's eyes to where they rested on Charlie and Junie and Kate, collaboratively setting up easels and cups of water and paint trays and brushes.

"Doug will relieve you at around six," Veronica said to Eliza, then planted a kiss on her baby daughter's cheek.

Eliza set off toward Veronica's house with Nora, and Veronica and Siobhan walked together toward the university, leaving Patty to take a deep breath and head back inside.

"How's Derek settling into his new job?" Veronica asked Siobhan, who practically glowed with health and contentment. After her wild success in New York, she'd been offered a lectureship at the University of Chicago, and galleries were clamoring for her next series of paintings, on which she was hard at work. It had taken some doing, and almost a year of long distance, but Derek had finally landed a terrific position at a Chicago ad agency, where he led a team of designers. The two of them had moved into a fixer-upper greystone that had studio space for Siobhan.

"He loves it," she replied. "And he and Charlie are getting along famously. It's so cute to watch. She's always trying to get him to take her for ice cream after dinner because of course he always will."

"I'm glad she has another male role model. Do you ever bump into Gabe on campus?"

"Just that one time I told you about after the custody hearing."

Veronica gave her friend a sly grin, recalling the story of Gabe walking out as soon as he saw Siobhan and Margaret in the faculty club a week after the judge had made his decree. Gabe had come after Siobhan for full custody of Charlie, but Siobhan's lawyer had managed to stave off a trial, and when Siobhan became something of a local hero, he'd strong-armed Gabe and his lawyer into dropping his motion in exchange for agreeing to fifty-fifty time with Charlie. Even though she would be with Charlie less than before, the fact was, Siobhan needed more time to work, and Gabe had agreed to let Charlie attend the Center after school.

Remarkably, things were working out better than she ever would have predicted even during the heyday of the Service.

The next hours at the Center were a loud and beautiful chaos. Patty had to negotiate a few toy hostage exchanges, one incident of hitting, and another of tattling, but overall the first day was a huge success. She was paying Karen and a friend of hers a few dollars to help clean up at the end of each day, and the three of them had everything packed up and wiped down in less than an hour.

When they got home a little after seven, the house was rich with the scent of a chicken Eliza was roasting in the oven. *She's good at so many things*, Patty thought, wondering what her younger sister would finally decide to be when she grew up. She was finding her footing. She studied hard and took guitar lessons, and she came to lunch with Patty and their father regularly. She'd even told that cheat of a bass player who'd gotten her pregnant to pound sand when he'd tracked her down in Chicago at Christmastime. Patty didn't think she'd ever been prouder of anyone.

Close to eleven, when Patty collapsed into bed, Matt was waiting for her under the covers and said, "Sounds like today was a smashing success?" The kids had talked about nothing else at dinner.

"It was a great day." She smiled and felt the pride of it in her chest again.

Matt slid his hand over her hip and kissed her neck. "You've never looked so sexy."

Patty raised an amused and dubious eyebrow. "Surely you mean tired?"

"No, you wear the working-mom mantle very well. But if you're too tired, I won't try and take the mantle off."

She kissed him hard on the mouth. "Take it off."

She could hardly believe that this was her life. She loved it.

"This is excellent work," Margaret said to Belinda, the first of the undergraduate research assistants to be hired in the English department, funded by a grant she'd written to employ more female students and mentor them into academic positions.

They were sitting in Margaret's office, in two comfy armchairs that faced each other on the same side of her desk; no more big piece of wood between her and her students. The window was open to the early fall air, and the scent of freshly cut grass wafted in with the birdsong.

"I'm so glad you decided to finish your degree here in Chicago." Belinda's status as a student had been reinstated when the suit against the Jane Six had been dropped, and Margaret had hired her right away, much to the chagrin of Leo Robinson, who—true to Harriet's word—had not stood in the way of the grant. Margaret had also lobbied hard for Belinda to get the department scholarship that year and had prevailed. *That* had pissed him off. On a flat card embossed with his name that he'd left in her faculty box, he'd written:

> *Touché. I see I can't be so lazy around the New Woman on the faculty.*

"Yeah, well, I got so involved with the Union while I was out of classes, and there were things I wanted to finish, so . . . I'm applying to Columbia for grad school next year."

"I'll write a glowing recommendation."

"Thank you. So . . . what about you? What's next?"

"First I have to finish the article you've been helping me research. Then I'm going to meet up with Phyllis in Boston, then my parents in

Maine during the winter break. And I'm toying with a trip to Paris when I'm on sabbatical next semester."

"Oooooh, you should do that. And isn't Phyllis pregnant?"

"Five months." Margaret smiled.

"Tell her I said hi."

"Will do."

Belinda was almost at the door when she turned around and said, "You should really go to Paris."

Margaret laughed. "Why?"

"Weelllll, maybe you'll meet someone there."

Margaret laughed louder. "Belinda! You sound like my mother."

"I doubt I mean it like your mom does. I mean someone to have fun with."

"Point taken. Maybe I will, but that's not the reason I'll go."

Belinda nodded. "I get that," she said. "That's not why I'm going to New York, either."

"Good. You have a bright future in front of you. Focus on that." For the first time in her life, Margaret felt the truth of that in her bones. She, too, was still young, barely thirty. She had time. Surely life had plenty more surprises in store for a woman who was finally mistress of herself.

Author's Note

First, I'd like to issue a warning, especially for readers who have followed me from previous novels (*and thank you, if you have!!*): unlike *The Kennedy Debutante, The Girl in White Gloves,* and *The Paris Bookseller, All You Have to Do Is Call* is not biographical. The Jane of this novel is only loosely based on the real-life feminist group known as Jane, which was a group of women activists who gave safe, inexpensive abortions in Chicago in the early 1970s. I used some of the milestone moments in the history of Jane, like the fact that it started as a referral service and eventually took over the process to become an entirely woman-operated health service for women. The ethos of this novel's Jane—that women's sovereignty over their own bodies is synonymous with liberation, and a cornerstone of the national feminist project—is also very much rooted in historical reality. Though in the novel it's six Janes who are arrested, in reality seven women were arrested in a raid in 1972 and let go when *Roe* became law. Incredibly, it's also true that Jane continued to provide abortions after the arrests.

But Veronica, Margaret, Patty, Siobhan, Phyllis, and the other characters in these pages are entirely fictional. They are women I made up based on my understanding of women's lives at this crucial moment in history. Veronica Stillwell is in no way based on Heather Booth, the actual founder of Jane, who is very much alive today and who's been a lifelong activist for liberal causes. Nor are any of the characters based on Laura Kaplan or Judith Arcana, each of whom wrote a terrific nonfiction book that I read in the course of my research, *The Story of Jane: The Legendary Underground Feminist Abortion Service* and *Hello. This is Jane.*, respectively. If you want to find out more about the true herstory of Jane, including the many women's health services they provided, the details of the arrests, and their radical and remarkable thinking about reproductive justice, I highly recommend both. I also recommend Dolen Perkins-Valdez's novel *Take My Hand*, which taught me much about midcentury reproductive justice from a Black perspective.

I'd like to highlight a few more historical details that I borrowed for this novel, because they were compelling enough to inspire me to write *All You Have to Do Is Call*. Jane was composed entirely of lay practitioners with no medical training; the abortions they provided were remarkably safe with a low incidence of complications, and some estimate that the number of abortions they either referred or performed numbered over ten thousand (but since for safety's sake they could not keep records, there is no way to verify this); Jane also offered free abortions to women who could not pay their modest hundred-dollar fee; and it offered other women's health services, like STD testing, Pap smears, and birth control counseling, much like today's Planned Parenthood. I'd also like to beg your forgiveness for one change to the historical record that I made for the sake of the narrative: I have Veronica reflect on Nixon's veto of the Comprehensive Child Development Act a few weeks before it actually happened on December 9, 1971.

While I tried to capture much of what Jane offered the women of Chicago, the true scope and carefully planned machinations of their far-reaching service were difficult to balance with the needs of plot

Author's Note

and character development. For the sake of narrative economy and suspense, I fictionalized some of the locations and streamlined some of their processes. For instance, the Chicago Women's Liberation Union (CWLU) had an office on the north side of Chicago, with satellite chapters all over the city, but I imagined a version of what an office might have been like in Hyde Park, near the University of Chicago, where my characters live. Kaplan's and Arcana's books will give you a sense of the magnitude of its operation, as will the excellent documentary *She's Beautiful When She's Angry*.

When I first started researching this book in 2018, it was hard to imagine an *illegal* Planned Parenthood, run entirely by women just like me who weren't doctors or nurses, who felt they had to take matters into their own hands. Unfortunately, as I write these words at the start of 2023, illegal reproductive health clinics look increasingly like something we have to imagine again. More than ever, we need to be inspired by heroes like the women of Jane, not only because *Roe* was overturned by *Dobbs* but because, lamentably, the Equal Rights Amendment still languishes, unratified. There is significant work left to be done.

Initially, it was also hard for me to imagine a time and a group of women for whom it was *essential and natural* to see abortion and motherhood in harmonious alignment with each other. Mothers get and give abortions. And yet there is an underlying idea in our culture and in the debates about abortion that have unfolded in the last fifty years that the people who get and give abortions are "other," because abortion is antithetical to family life and motherhood itself. The anti-abortion movement that emerged following *Roe* has carefully and successfully grown this chasm in our minds, even in the minds of pro-abortion liberals, by cultivating the notion that abortion is something to be kept secret and a mark of shame. In fact, though, people who have received or provided abortions are mothers, fathers, sisters, brothers, grandparents, friends, librarians, teachers, and neighbors of every color, and come from every socioeconomic background. It's only "we" here; there is no "other."

By extension, what I found so striking about the women of Jane was that they were "regular" women. We often imbue doctors with magical powers; we see them as able to handle life and death in a superhuman way. But in actual fact, they are human beings who have gone to school and gotten specific training—and I find this incredibly reassuring, as reassuring as knowing that a woman like me with no magical powers can learn to help another person with their reproductive health. What doctors and other health professionals *do* have that sets them apart is a highly developed call to service, which is something we've all borne awed witness to during the COVID-19 pandemic—and something I tried to build into the characters of this novel.

Another inspiration for *All You Have to Do Is Call* has been my own evolving feminism. I'll be forty-eight when this book comes out, and so I'm very much a product of the second-wave feminism portrayed in this novel: they were my mother and friends' mothers, my college professors and writing mentors, my doctors, and cool women I met at conferences and random coffee shops. But as an active consumer of the ongoing work of Glennon Doyle, Brené Brown, Rachel Cargle, Tarana Burke, and many others, I'm learning to embrace the tenets of a far more inclusive/intersectional/allied third-wave feminism.

No social movement is perfect, and feminism is no exception. The Elizabeth Cady Stanton quote that serves as this novel's epigraph is an embodiment of the ways in which feminism has been flawed but still moved society forward every time its leaders spoke boldly. While Stanton was herself a fierce advocate for women's rights and a staunch abolitionist, she opposed the Fifteenth Amendment because it didn't include voting rights for women. In Stanton, patron saint of the suffrage movement, was a tension I wanted to explore: in the fight for women's rights, there have always been disparities along race and class lines, disparities that are still present today. Third-wave feminism, with its long-overdue call to center the lives of women of color, is an inevitable product of the deficiencies in earlier feminist movements.

This tension presented a difficult nut for me to crack. On the one hand, I wanted to celebrate the feminists of Jane who did remarkable, life-changing work that not only improved the situations of the women who came to them but also advanced the feminist and reproductive justice movements on local and national levels. On the other hand, these women were almost exclusively white, and I didn't want to simply extol their virtues without also representing their blind spots. I hope that in our shared experience of this book, writer and readers together can better understand the past to help us move toward a more equitable future.

One final note about Jane and history and storytelling and perspective. As the title of Kaplan's book suggests, the women of Jane have always been "legendary." From the time they did their work, their courage has been told and retold, first by the women to each other— women who spread the word about Jane throughout Chicago—and then beyond, by bards in poetry and essays and eventually books and films, like We, Jane; Ask for Jane; and Call Jane. In fact, one of the best essays I read was an academic article by Kelly O'Donnell of Yale about this storytelling phenomenon, and it was an NPR piece in 2018 that first alerted me to Jane's amazing place in history; the story of ordinary women doing extraordinary work just took hold of me and wouldn't let go. In this way, it seems to me that Jane is like the Knights of the Round Table. Their story became the stuff of myth and retelling the moment the first Jane took up a curette, as surely as the moment Arthur pulled the sword from the stone. I feel humbled and proud to add All You Have to Do Is Call to this body of stories, and look forward to seeing where the legend takes us in our twenty-first-century fight for reproductive justice.

Acknowledgments

This was an all-hands-on-deck kind of book from the moment I was inspired to write it in 2018. It's been through many iterations in my imagination and my computer, and it's thanks to the help of some truly insightful and lovingly honest friends and colleagues that it's sitting in your hands right now. More than any other book I've written, this one required feedback, reimagining, rewriting, and *a lot* of cheerleading. I am deeply grateful to everyone who read drafts, talked for hours, and handed me the Kleenex when I needed it: Aimie Runyan-Vetter, Alix Rickloff, Cheryl Woodson, Danielle Fodor, Diana Renn, Elise Hooper, Janie Chang, Joe Moldover, Kaia Alderson, Kevin Wheeler, Kip Wilson, Lecia Cornwall, Lori Hess, Michelle Flythe, and Renée Rosen. Special thanks to Naomi Lisan and Kelly O'Donnell for our conversations about Jane, to Cory Brown for your legal expertise, to Jesse Olszynko-Gryn for your helpful research on twentieth-century pregnancy testing, and to Angela Rostami for your midwife fact-checking (twice!). Lyonesses, our Friday chats and mutual support are a balm and an inspiration.

Acknowledgments

I am blessed with some truly fabulous friends, scattered across the world and from many decades of my life. The ways in which you support me are amazing. You showed me how to write this book; you are *always* there when I call. Mom, Dad, and Elena—I couldn't ask for more wonderful parents or a more awesome daughter.

Liz von Klemperer: I really don't know what I'd do without you. Your creativity, organization, and perseverance bring me such confidence. Thank you for everything.

Kevan Lyon, you've championed this book from the moment you heard about it, and that has meant everything to me. Kate Seaver, I am so grateful for your persistence in bringing this book into the world, from our first conversations about it to the edits that got it across the finish line. Amanda Maurer, thank you for the comments and the many ways you help me through the publishing process. Claire Zion, thank you for the green light! Our Zoom in the fall of 2020 is one of my career highlights.

Tara O'Connor, Yazmine Hassan, Elisha Katz, Hannah Engler, and Fareeda Bullert—you are truly a writer's PR and marketing dream team. I don't know how you do it, and I am bottomlessly grateful for the magic. Ivan Held, Christine Ball, Craig Burke, and Jeanne-Marie Hudson—I feel lucky and grateful every day that you asked me to be part of the Berkley family. Thank you for the work you do to bring such beautiful books to readers. Speaking of beautiful books—I am in love with this cover design by Vikki Chu. Many thanks to Jamie Thaman, who made sure all the words were nice and shiny. And Michelle Kasper, I'm indebted to your careful overseeing of the book's production.

Since this is my fourth historical novel and I'm still here putting words on paper for publication, I want to give a huge shout-out to all the booksellers, bookstagrammers, reviewers, journalists, podcasters, and other literary influencers who have embraced

Acknowledgments

my work. Every word you write, picture you post, and list you make matters.

Same goes for you, readers. Every purchase, download, and check-out from the library means writers can keep writing. "Thank you" is all I can say, but those two words will never quite cover it.